Praise fo

'One of our favourite women's fiction stars'
Heat

'Hopeful and hopelessly romantic ... A gorgeous, sweep-you-off-your-feet slice of escapism'
Red

'A warm and wonderful read'
Woman's Own

'Cressida's characters are wonderful. A delicious summer treat!'
Sarah Morgan

'Evocative and gorgeous'
Phillipa Ashley

'Uplifting, heartwarming and brimming with romance'
Cathy Bramley

'Gorgeously romantic ... forced me to go to bed early so I could read it'
Sophie Cousens

'I just LOVED this story. All the characters are wonderful'
Isabelle Broom

'Real heart and soul'
Sarra Manning

'The most gorgeously romantic, utterly perfect book'
Rachael Lucas

'A triumph. Breathlessly romantic, it sparkles with wit and genuine warmth'
Miranda Dickinson

'So many perfect romantic moments that made me melt. Just gorgeous'
Jules Wake

'A wonderful ray of reading sunshine'
Heidi Swain

'I fell completely and utterly in love ... it had me glued to the pages'
Holly Martin

'A total hands-down treat. A book you'll want to cancel plans and stay in with'
Pernille Hughes

'Sizzlingly romantic and utterly compelling, I couldn't put it down'
Alex Brown

'Bursting with [Cressida's] trademark warmth and wit'
Kirsty Greenwood

'Funny, sexy and sweep-you-off-your-feet-romantic'
Zara Stoneley

'Perfectly pitched between funny, sexy, tender and downright heartbreaking. I loved it'
Jane Casey

'As hot & steamy as a freshly made hot chocolate, and as sweet & comforting as the whipped cream & sprinkles that go on top'
Helen Fields

'Just brilliant. Sweet, sexy and sizzzzling. It was a pure joy to read'
Lisa Hall

'A little slice of a Cornish cream tea but without the calories'
Bella Osborne

'Perfect escapism, deliciously romantic. I was utterly transported'
Emily Kerr

'Utter perfection ... a total gem'
Katy Colins

'Sexy, sweet, and simmering with sunshine'
Lynsey James

The Happy Hour

Cressy grew up in South-East London surrounded by books and with a cat named after Lawrence of Arabia. She studied English at the University of East Anglia and now lives in Norwich with her husband David. *The Happy Hour* is her fifteenth novel and her books have sold over three quarters of a million copies worldwide. When she isn't writing, Cressy spends her spare time reading, returning to London, or exploring the beautiful Norfolk coastline.

If you'd like to find out more about Cressy, visit her on her social media channels. She'd love to hear from you!

@cressmclaughlin
/CressidaMcLaughlinAuthor
@CressMcLaughlin

Also by Cressida McLaughlin

Cressida McLaughlin

The Happy Hour

HarperCollins *Publishers*

HarperCollins*Publishers* Ltd
1 London Bridge Street,
London SE1 9GF

www.harpercollins.co.uk

HarperCollins*Publishers*
Macken House, 39/40 Mayor Street Upper
Dublin 1, D01 C9W8

First published by HarperCollins*Publishers* 2024
1

A catalogue record for this book is available from the British Library

ISBN: 978-0-00-862374-6 (PB)

Set in Birka Std by HarperCollins*Publishers* India

Printed and bound in the UK using 100% Renewable Electricity at
CPI Group (UK) Ltd

This book contains FSC™ certified paper and other controlled
sources to ensure responsible forest management.

For more information visit: www.harpercollins.co.uk/green

To Mum, Dad and Lee, for all those
Sundays in Greenwich

Prologue

A Tuesday in July

It was the perfect July day and London shone brightly, as if it didn't have a care in the world. Ash Faulkner stood on the deck of the Thames Clipper as the time inched towards twelve o'clock, his hands pushed deep into the pockets of his jeans. It was quiet on a Tuesday morning, only a few passengers on board as the boat chugged through the water away from the city centre.

At the beginning, this journey had filled him with nothing but dread, and he'd always had the desperate urge to get off the moment he'd boarded – to disembark at any stop before he reached Greenwich. But that had changed.

He had met Jess at the market, and she had turned his Sundays into a complicated mix of the best and worst part of his week. She had made him look forward to the journey to Greenwich, had become the good that outweighed the bad. She was the reason he had stopped waking up on those mornings feeling like his chest was full of rocks.

The deck got busier as the boat approached Tower Bridge, and Ash stepped to the side, letting a woman herd her three children to the front, behind the rope barrier that kept travellers well away from the edge. They pointed and gasped at the bridge's blue steelwork, and at the Tower of London, a small boy asking how many people had been locked away in the turret, and Ash thought of how Jess, living and working in the heart of a popular tourist spot, had been nonplussed by the things he'd tried to show her: the Queen's House, the foot tunnel, the view of the city stretching beyond the green expanse of Greenwich Park. She knew it so well, none of it had made her eyes light up.

But other things had – things that Ash had said or that they'd done together: a story about a pigeon that he hadn't expected to tell anyone ever again, and yet he'd been compelled to blurt it out the first time they met; standing on the heath watching a kite soar high above them, her back pressed to his front; a silly hat; when he'd slid one of her ridiculous fluffy cushions underneath her, angling her hips up towards him.

Ash closed his eyes. He couldn't let himself fall too deeply into the memories, even though he was glad to have them, now; to be able to replay them when, for the last few days, his mind had been a fuzzy, impenetrable fog. It wasn't the right time to remind himself that all those stolen moments, those Sunday mornings, hadn't just made *his* eyes light up, but had made his whole existence brighter – his heart most of all.

Today, he wasn't travelling to Greenwich to have another perfect hour with Jess – he couldn't. He had to stop being so self-pitying, stop thinking about what he needed, and do what was best for her.

He waited until the famous London landmarks were out of sight, and the children had gone back inside, then he walked to the other side of the deck.

He wanted to absorb every minute of their approach, to see the *Cutty Sark*'s elaborate masts appear, like a careful ink drawing reaching up into the sky, to watch the busy Thames foreshore come slowly into view, spread out like an open

2

invitation. He wanted to feel the anticipation and the sadness, the fear of what he was about to do, the regret that was already leeching through him like a slow poison.

Mostly, though, he wanted to add this to his catalogue of memories: Greenwich in the sunshine, the place he had found Jess. Because he was fairly certain that this would be the last time he came.

Chapter One

Before: A Sunday in April

Jessica Peacock stood behind the counter in No Vase Like Home, the pastel-coloured gift emporium that was housed in one of the shop spaces along the side of Greenwich Market, wrapping a stone hare in green tissue paper. Beyond the large picture window, the Sunday morning market was a wall of colour and sound, as people pored over the enticing stalls, picked out gifts, ate pizza slices and took photos on their phones. Inside, everything was slower, the quiet punctuated by the chorus of clocks – alarm clocks and carriage clocks, old-fashioned and modern, analogue and digital – that marked time on the shelves. Inside No Vase Like Home, Jess could watch the bustle from her haven of calm. Except, of course, for the hares.

Why were the sinister creatures so popular as mantelpiece ornaments? Was she inadvertently sending witches off into living rooms, under the guise of tall-eared statues? What had compelled Wendy, her boss and the owner of the shop, to introduce them as their latest stock line? Was *she* now under the control of the hares?

Her thoughts were disturbed by a commotion beyond the glass and she looked up, Sellotape stuck to her thumb, and peered past her oblivious customer, only to realise the commotion was actually laughter.

Olga, six foot two and blonde, with wide shoulders that put Jess in mind of Olympic swimmers, sold hats on the stall outside the gift shop, her designs as quirky and eye-catching as she was. Right now her head was tipped back, her laughter cascading out and up, like the bat signal fired into the sky. The cause of her hilarity seemed to be her current customer. He was shorter than Olga by an inch or so, and was wearing a grey jacket, jeans and – at that particular moment – a felt hat. It was a deep red, the colour of crushed rose petals, and had a gold satin band around the crown. It was far too big for him but he was soldiering on, the hat's jaunty angle obscuring most of his head, so Jess could only see the sharp line of his jaw, and what looked like a charismatic, pearly-teethed smile.

The loud buzz of the market made it hard for her to make out anything beyond the sharp splinter of Olga's laugh, but she thought she heard the deep rumble of his voice as he spoke, and then the bat signal sounded again. Jess turned back to her customer, who was tapping away at her phone screen, and to the hare, which was lying on its back and giving her a glassy stare. She was about to shroud it in a final layer of tissue paper when there was a louder sound, a shriek and a '*Stop!*'

Jess raised her head just in time to see figures rush past the window. There was no laughter now, just Olga, staring after the runners and holding the crushed rose hat, her mouth open in alarm.

'What was that?' Wendy appeared in the storeroom doorway, tucking her thick auburn hair behind her ear.

'No idea,' Jess said. 'But it didn't sound good.'

'Go and see, will you?'

Jess bit back a sigh and slipped out from behind the counter as Wendy took her place. The owner of No Vase Like Home treated the market vendors like her flock, and Jess wasn't surprised to be asked to go and investigate. As she pushed open the door she heard Wendy address the customer, who was still lost in her digital world. If that hare really was a witch, then its new owner didn't stand a chance.

'What happened?' Jess asked Olga, but the other woman just pointed and, suspecting time was of the essence, she hurried up the side of the market, dodging tourists who were oblivious to anything except their Sunday morning browsing. She reached the side exit, a wide alleyway that was busy with artists' stalls, a food court that branched out on the right and then, if you kept going straight, led to one of Greenwich's bustling commercial roads.

It was a bright day at the end of April, the sun enticing people out of their homes despite the chilly wind, and Jess's stretchy star-print dress felt too thin without her denim jacket over the top. She slowed down, realising she didn't know who she was looking for, and was about to return to her post and Wendy's unsatisfied curiosity when she saw him: the man who had been making Olga laugh.

He had the jeans and the grey jacket, and without the hat she could see his walnut-coloured hair, short around the back and sides but thick on top, a wavy chunk falling over his forehead. His smile had gone, his jawline was tight, and he was gripping the shoulder of someone who was no more than a navy shadow, slouchy jeans and a hoody with the hood pulled over their face.

Jess stopped and the man turned in her direction. Their gazes snagged, and his eyes widened in an almost comical expression of fear. She felt the hairs prickle on the back of her neck. This situation did not fit into her neat, hassle-free lifestyle. She worked at the market, hung out with her best

6

friend Lola, created motivational prints and sold them in her Etsy shop, and phoned her mum and dad occasionally, to let them know she hadn't fallen off the face of the earth. Predictable, small and safe. This didn't look like it would be any of those things.

'He's got him, the bloody blighter!' The voice, and the accompanying scent of menthol, belonged to Roger Stott, owner of one of the market's antiques stalls. Hat Man was still holding onto the hooded figure, but he was no longer looking at Jess, instead casting his gaze around as if in search of an escape route.

'Was he shoplifting?' Jess asked Roger.

'Technically it's a market stall, not a shop,' Roger said. 'But that is the offence, yes.'

'There's no such thing as stall-lifting, then?' Jess smiled, but Roger didn't return it. He was an ex-policeman, and his stall had a distinctly patriotic feel, selling medals, hip flasks and a range of royal and forces memorabilia. His tan leather jacket and Starsky and Hutch moustache were less regimented, and Jess thought that he fancied himself as a cavalier peacekeeper, when in reality he was as rule-abiding as they came. If Wendy was the market's mum, then Roger was its security guard. It seemed ironic that it was *his* stall the hooded figure had stolen from. 'What's next, then?' she asked.

He gestured towards the shaky standoff. 'I suggest we assist this gentleman, then call my old muckers in the police.'

'Good plan,' she said, just as Hat Man's voice rose above the market chatter.

'Not a chance, buster.' His tone was deep and forceful, and Jess felt as if a mini-earthquake had reverberated through her lower half.

'Right.' Roger stomped forward and Jess followed, though less enthusiastically. Some of the visitors were eyeing them now, clutching burgers or burritos, eating from cartons of chips, as if the scene was part of a street theatre performance and they were entitled to stare.

'It's very commendable, what you've done here,' Roger said, and Hat Man's expression collapsed into pure relief. 'Take your hood down young man,' he added, to the faceless shadow. The reply was an inaudible mumble and a complete failure to comply. Roger widened his stance and crossed his arms, and Hat Man looked as if he was about to let go of the thief, but Roger anticipated it, saying, 'I wouldn't, son. He'll run like the wind, I guarantee it.'

'Right.' There was that deep voice again, and Jess felt her cheeks heat for no good reason.

'Hood down, then I want your name, and then I'm calling the police.' Roger took out his ancient mobile phone, which had a tiny screen and not a single smart feature, and waggled it like a threat.

An arm came up and yanked off the hood, the action sharp with irritation. The man who emerged was young – a boy, really – his blond hair cut close to his head and a spray of freckles over his nose. Jess saw her surprise echoed on Hat Man's face, but not Roger's. He'd clearly seen it all before.

'Braden,' the boy muttered to his chunky trainers.

'Good lad,' Roger said. 'And what did you take from my stall?'

'Nuthin'.'

'Try again.'

Hat Man shot Jess a look over Roger's head that was mostly relieved, slightly amused. His eyes were grey, his cheeks tinged pink. He was put-together and ruffled all at once, like the first, sketched draft of a Disney hero. A bit more polish and he would have been ready to franchise out, alongside a doe-eyed princess in a sparkly dress.

Slowly, Braden reached into his low-slung jeans pocket and pulled out something small and glinting. He held it in his palm like a pebble.

'Ah, the gold-plated Elgin half-hunter,' Roger said. 'You know this was made in New Jersey by the Keystone Watch Case Company? It came to me via a very lovely widow who lives in King's Cross. I paid handsomely for it.'

'Who gives a shit?' Braden said.

Hat Man made a disapproving sound in the back of his throat.

'*I* do, young man,' Roger said. 'It's worth four hundred, at least.'

Braden's eyes became twin saucers.

'You have a keen eye,' Roger told him, and the boy's spine went from slouched to straight. 'You should use your talents for good, not ill.'

'I don't want to be no market trader,' Braden said. 'Much easier nicking things.'

'Not if you end up with a custodial sentence. Then, I promise you, you will wish you were a market trader. Now, am I calling my friend Sergeant Allison to deal with you, or can you and I come to an amicable arrangement?'

Braden twisted his head left then right, his nose scrunching when he realised there was no easy getaway.

Jess decided she wasn't needed. Roger was in his element – using the theft as a teachable moment – and she had enough information to satisfy Wendy's curiosity. She edged backwards, pressing her hand to her stomach when it rumbled from being in close proximity to the fish-and-chip stall, but Braden pointed a finger in her direction.

'What about her?' he said. 'What's she doing here? She just a nosey parker, or . . . I bet she put you up to this!'

Roger glanced at her. 'That's Jess. She's one of the linchpins of the market, and—'

'What's a linchpin?' Braden cut in.

'Someone who's crucial to something,' Hat Man said. 'They hold it – in this case, the market – together. It's a pin that goes through an axle to hold a wheel in place. The wheels would come off without them.'

'Ta very much, Dictionary Corner.' Braden scowled at him.

Hat Man looked exasperated. 'You *literally* just asked what a linchpin was.'

'Yeah, but I didn't—'

'Enough!' Roger raised his hands. 'Braden, do you want me to get on the telephone to my police sergeant friend?'

Braden's trainers were interesting again. 'Nah.'

'Good,' Roger said. 'So let's talk about this sensibly. No running, understood? Because I *will* track you down.'

'Can't be arsed now, anyway,' Braden murmured.

Jess went to turn away, and saw that Hat Man had also decided he wasn't adding anything useful. He edged past Roger, shoving his hands in his pockets as he gave her a tentative smile.

'Nice to meet you, Jess the linchpin.'

'And you, Hat Man.' She winced. 'Sorry, I—'

'Hat Man?' He laughed and ran a hand through his hair, as if to check he wasn't still wearing one.

'You were at Olga's stall,' Jess explained. 'The red felt hat?'

'Ah.' His gaze was amused. 'So you were watching me?'

'No! It's just that Olga's stall—'

'I'm joking,' he said. 'You work in the market, obviously. You're the linchpin.'

'Not me, my boss,' she told him. 'I'm just an extension of Wendy, so we get lumped in together.' She had still felt a glow of pride when Roger had said it, though. 'And you've done your good deed for the day.'

He shrugged. 'I didn't have a clue what I was doing, to be honest. Following him was pure instinct, then I thought I was going to be stuck there for ever, just trying to stop him wriggling out of my grip.' He frowned. 'You know the stallholder?'

'That's Roger,' Jess said. 'He used to be a policeman, and he'll know exactly what to do with Braden. I'm guessing . . .' she glanced over to see Roger giving the boy a firm telling off. 'He'll be lenient with him, despite what he's done.'

'He's about twelve.' Hat Man sounded outraged. 'I couldn't see his face properly before. I wish I'd had the balls to steal something in broad daylight from a crowded market when I was that young – not that I would have,' he added quickly. 'I was still playing with my train set.'

Jess laughed. 'You never grow out of train sets, from what I've seen.'

'Oh? Who's the guilty party in your life?'

'My dad,' she admitted, stumbling slightly over the word, as she often did with new people. She always wanted to add *adopted* on the front, get that fact in quickly, even though she was twenty-seven now, and Graeme Peacock had been nothing but fatherly to her. 'He has one in his garage – studio. That's what he calls it.'

'Sounds like he's serious about it. I'm Ash, by the way. Ash Faulkner, not Hat Man.'

Jess smiled. 'Ash, not Hat Man. Got it.' Should they shake hands? Her fingers flexed at her sides. This close, she caught a waft of something delicious, somewhere between coffee and chocolate. It could have been aftershave, or a lingering smell from something he'd bought at the food hall. A few dark locks curled in front of Ash's left ear, and she saw a faint mark on his lobe, as if he'd worn an earring a long time ago.

'I should really . . .' She thumbed in the direction of the market.

'Do you sell antiques, too?' Ash asked. 'On your stall?'

'I work in one of the shops along the edge. It's a gift shop – No Vase Like Home. I suppose one day, years from now, some of the items might become antiques.'

'No Vase Like Home?' He frowned.

Jess rolled her eyes. 'Try it in an American accent. Then you *might* get it.'

'No Vase Like Home. *Vase*. Vase? I see. Sort of.'

Jess laughed. 'It's one of my bugbears, that Wendy – my boss – thought it would work as a pun. But it's a talking point, I guess. Are you just here for the morning, or . . .?'

'I'm killing time,' he told her. 'The market's an interesting place to be, as this has proved.'

'You can lose hours to it,' she agreed. 'And it's a great place if you're waiting for an appointment, or to meet someone.'

'It's my third Sunday,' he said darkly, as if he was admitting to attending some kind of support group – and maybe he was; maybe that's what he was killing time until. He exhaled and glanced at Braden. 'I hope he figures it out.'

'Roger will do all he can,' Jess said with confidence. He wouldn't send a teenager like Braden back into the wild, free to steal another day – potentially from someone a lot less tolerant. He'd get in touch with his contacts on the force, social services, see what could be done. 'Braden might have a bright future ahead of him.' She smiled. 'I should be getting back.'

'You're here every Sunday?' Ash asked.

'Of course. Sunday's one of the market's busiest days, and the best for home sales.' He gave her a questioning look. 'People laze around at home on Sunday mornings,' she explained, 'and they think "I could clear out the spare room", or "we could do something different with the kitchen", or "wouldn't a creepy hare ornament look amazing next to the picture of little Billy on the mantelpiece?"'

Ash laughed, and even though it wasn't as loud as Olga's cackle, the earthquake was back, rumbling low in Jess's belly. She felt stupidly proud that she'd made him laugh. 'You sell creepy hare ornaments?' he asked. 'I'll have to come and have a look. Do you get a lunch break?'

She did, but she rarely took it. 'Sometimes.'

Ash glanced at his watch. 'I've got an hour now, if you're free? I need to be gone by one, but . . .'

Jess's pulse sped up. 'You're just killing time until then?'

'Exactly. We could do it together if you fancied. I could buy you a coffee?'

Jess was already shaking her head. 'I don't think so.'

'Why not?' Ash asked, a half-smile on his face.

'I just . . . why would we?' Why did two strangers ever get coffee together? His voice made her insides fizz. His face was open and friendly, and he was undeniably handsome, but they didn't know each other – at all. And she had to get back to the shop.

'You came to help,' he said, gesturing at Braden. The teenager was nodding at whatever Roger was saying, his sulking demeanour replaced by a spark of intrigue. Something warmed inside Jess's chest. Roger was a good person – and Ash, too;

he hadn't tackled the boy to the ground or shouted to alert a mob, and that might partly have been indecision, a *what the hell do I do now?* moment, but some had been instinct: that the boy deserved a chance.

'You helped more,' she told him. 'If it wasn't for you, Braden would have been long gone by now, and who knows who he might have tried to steal from next? I should buy *you* a coffee.'

'Excellent,' Ash said quickly. 'Let's do that then. Know anywhere good?'

Jess narrowed her eyes at him, and his smile widened.

'You clearly want to, deep down,' he said.

Jess pressed her lips together. 'I don't—'

'I'll let Wendy know,' Roger called, somehow managing to counsel Braden while also listening to their conversation. 'You hardly ever take a lunch break, Jess.'

'See?' Ash said. 'I'm doing you a favour. Breaks are important.'

Jess huffed, fighting against a traitorous smile. 'There's a café just round the corner. It's not fancy, but that means it's more likely to have a free table.'

'Lead the way.' Ash swept his arm wide, then looked over to Roger and Braden. 'Will you be OK?'

'We'll be grand.' Roger's smile was triumphant. 'I'm going to take Braden and introduce him to Wendy.'

'Oooh you're in for a treat, Braden,' Jess said.

'Fuck's sake,' Braden muttered.

She patted the teenager's shoulder as they passed, and wondered how much smaller her hand was than Ash's. She glanced at him, but he was waiting patiently, his hands in his jeans pockets so she couldn't see. Nerves and excitement bubbled up inside her.

14

'Ready to go and have a drink in a dingy little café?' he asked.

Jess laughed. 'That's not how I described it.'

'I was reading between the lines. And, honestly, I don't mind where we go. Sitting cross-legged on the pavement would be fine with me.'

'But not with all the people who were trying to get past you.' She could picture him sitting nonchalantly on the dirty ground while tourists and locals threw him angry looks, and her smile was back. 'Let me show you how *not* dingy this café is.' As she brushed past him to head away from the market and onto Greenwich's busy streets, she couldn't help noticing that Ash was smiling too.

Chapter Two

'What are you killing time until, then?' Jess asked, once they had found a table in her chosen café, The Tea Chest, albeit a tiny one crammed into the back corner, away from the glare of the windows. There was a tomato-shaped ketchup bottle on the scuffed wood next to a plastic cutlery holder, a pink sparkly pen with a fluffy top nestled alongside the knives and forks. The chatter of voices and clink of crockery was loud over the background hum of a radio playing chart songs. When Ash didn't answer, she leaned forward, ready to repeat the question.

'Just a thing I have to get to,' he said, his eyes shifting to take in the rest of the café. 'This place is great, even if we've been relegated to the naughty corner. Your local?'

'One of them,' Jess said. 'I'm spoilt for choice, working in Greenwich.'

'Those food stalls.' Ash shook his head. 'If I worked here I'd be eating constantly, picking something different each time, hiding food under the counter when customers came in.'

'You're not far off the truth,' Jess said. Her favourite was Kirsty Connor's Moreish Muffins, which offered a large range of sweet and savoury treats, something for every occasion and mood. She would have saved a lot more money by now without the temptation of Moreish Muffins so close by. 'This might be my favourite coffee, though.'

Ash's long fingers wrapped around the plain white porcelain of his mug. 'It's good.'

'I like that it has a lot of crema,' Jess added. 'It's not too thin.'

'Slight butterscotch taste.' Ash closed his eyes. 'A hint of smoke.' He hummed, and Jess's stomach flipped even as she laughed.

'A coffee connoisseur, I see. Glad you approve of my café choice.' She waited for him to open his eyes, then added, 'So your thing you're going to. Is it for work? Do you work on Sundays too?'

'No,' Ash said. 'I'm mostly a nine-to-five guy. Not as blond as Dolly Parton, though.' He ran his fingers through his hair, leaving it sticking up in the front. 'I work for a bank.'

'Oh?' That surprised her. 'A bank teller, processing cheques for people who still use them – do they even exist any more? Or are you a City Fat Cat?'

'Neither,' he said. 'I'm not actually a banker. I'm an occupational psychologist, working in the City.' He plucked a teaspoon out of the cutlery stand and stirred his coffee.

'That sounds fancy. What does it involve?'

He looked up from his stirring. 'Being an investment banker is a stressful, high-powered job, so I'm there to help with that. To ensure their working conditions are top-notch, and to try and get them to make sense of the volumes of money they're dealing with, and the responsibility that comes with it.'

'You're the person on the payroll the CEO can point to and say he's making sure his staff don't turn into greedy, selfish wankers?' She had meant it as a joke, mostly, but it sounded harsh spoken out loud.

17

Ash's lips kicked up at the side, but she couldn't tell if it was in amusement or displeasure. 'I'm not a box-ticking exercise,' he said gently. 'And I do think I actually help people, sometimes. The industry hasn't got a good reputation, and some of them are, undoubtedly, awful people, but there are some really good people, too. And that's the same everywhere, hey? Not everyone who works at the market will be a saint. You've probably got fraudsters, embezzlers, serial killers.' He picked up the fluffy pink pen. 'Whoever owned this, for example. They're clearly unhinged.'

'Hey,' Jess said, laughing, 'I like that pen. And I don't like the idea that I'm surrounded by serial killers every day.'

'There are no serial killers,' Ash said. 'Probably.'

Jess shook her head. 'I'm sorry.'

'What for?'

'For calling your colleagues wankers. It's easy to be judgemental when all you've heard is the stories in the press. I don't know anyone who works in the City.'

'I get it.' He sipped his coffee and sat back in his chair. He'd taken off his jacket, and was wearing a forest-green, long-sleeved T-shirt, three tiny buttons dancing down his sternum. 'And you do, now.'

'Sorry?'

'You know me,' he said. 'In the City.'

'I have known you for twenty minutes,' Jess pointed out. 'And I bet you're not the same there. Strutting about in a suit inside your glass-walled office, asking people about their moral compass. Do you have a clipboard? I bet you don't wear a red felt hat.'

She was gratified when he laughed, her inner panic fading. She so often managed to say the wrong thing, and was relieved he hadn't held it against her.

'It's better than not asking,' he said. 'Letting them get away with not thinking about it. Maybe wearing an elaborate hat would help them put things in perspective?'

'Perhaps one with a pigeon on it,' Jess said.

Ash's brows drew together.

'Didn't you see them?' she went on. 'Olga has these hats with felt pigeons on the brim. They're like something out of *Mary Poppins*. I've never seen anyone buy one, but she insists they're her most popular design.'

Ash shuddered. 'It would bring back too many bad memories.'

'Why? Were you the bird woman in an am-dram production of *Mary Poppins*?'

'No.' Ash did a good job of looking affronted. 'Are you a fan?'

'Of *Mary Poppins*? I like the kite-flying scene best. What's this with you and pigeons?'

Ash sighed. 'One landed on my head once, during an interview.'

Jess thought she'd misheard. 'What did? A pigeon?'

'Yup.' He rubbed his jaw. 'It was just after my degree. I was going for a role at a college, and they were giving me a tour of the site. I was talking to these two intimidating interviewers and then I just . . . I felt it land on my head. It made that cooing noise, and I—'

'Oh my God!' Jess laughed. 'You shook it off?'

'No.' Ash's smile was wry. 'I moved my head slightly and it held on tight. I could feel it scratching my scalp, so I just – I stood there.'

'You stood there,' Jess repeated. 'With a pigeon on your head. Still answering questions? What did your interviewers do?'

'They stared at me as if I'd sprouted wings, which I suppose I had.'

'It – I . . .' She couldn't say anything else.

'I was sure it was going to shit on my head. Can you imagine? "How did your interview go, Ash?" "Oh, it was fine, other than a bird *literally* did a shit on my head. I was a bird toilet."' A laugh sputtered out of him. 'Not my finest moment.'

'You can't end it there!' Jess squealed. 'What happened? How did you get rid of it? Did you even get the job?' A couple of people at the next table turned at her raised voice. She leaned forward and whispered, 'You have to tell me.'

'Glad you came for coffee with me now?' He raised an eyebrow, then sighed. 'A minute after it landed, the pigeon took off again and my tour resumed. My inquisitioners didn't mention it and, unsurprisingly, I was less focused after that. They didn't offer me the job, and I had to Dettol my head because the pigeon's claws had broken the skin.'

'The pigeon wasn't your fault,' Jess said solemnly. 'And I would have definitely mentioned it. I would have said, "Hey, Ash, did you know there's a fucking pigeon on your head?"' She dissolved into laughter again. 'I can picture you, standing there . . .' She wiped her eyes. 'Wearing this pigeon as a hat. I'm going to get you one of Olga's hats. A fond memento.'

'The pigeon interview.' He sighed again, then his smile broke through. 'It's a reminder that, however bad things get, they're very rarely as humiliating as that afternoon.'

Jess grinned at him, and the silence held between them, their shaded corner of the café suddenly a soft, intimate space. Ash was absent-mindedly twirling the fluffy pen, and the strong coffee was bitter and satisfying on Jess's tongue. It seemed unbelievable that she was here, with this man, and that he'd told her such an embarrassing story after only minutes of knowing her. She couldn't imagine admitting something like that to anyone, not even her best friend Lola. His openness felt like a special, rare thing.

'You know,' she said, 'In Greenwich Park, the pigeons are so used to being fed they'll land on your hand without any encouragement. Head too, I'm sure, though I can't remember seeing it. If the students at this college had been feeding the pigeons, then maybe it wasn't that unusual.'

'You realise you're making it worse?' Ash said. 'After all that, you're suggesting I wasn't even special? That I was just one of many resting posts the pigeon had?'

Jess held her mug in front of her smile. 'Of course you were chosen specifically.'

Ash narrowed his eyes at her. 'Are the pigeons like that all over the park?'

Jess sat up straighter. 'So you're not from Greenwich, then? I mean, none of this is local to you?'

He shook his head. 'I live in Holborn.'

'You just come here for your . . . thing. Every Sunday.'

'Right.' He sighed the word, then glanced at his wrist. His watch was classic, with a white, analogue face, a gold case on a brown leather strap. Some of the lightness left his eyes. 'I'll need to go soon.'

'Sure,' Jess said. 'Do you want me to . . . walk you?' It sounded ridiculous. Old-fashioned and entirely unnecessary.

Ash squinted at her, his lips kicking up at the corner. 'I'll be OK, but thank you. Next week, I was thinking we could go to the park, but not if I'm at risk of another pigeon ambush.'

'Next week?' Jess almost squeaked the words. 'You want to do this again?'

21

'Don't you?'

'I mean . . .'

'I have coffee with my neighbour, Mack, first thing every Sunday. I get his paper from the local shop, then he keeps me captive for at least an hour, and by the time I get down here—'

'From Holborn,' Jess added.

'Right. I get the Clipper, usually. If Mack has got one of his lunch dates – which he takes an inordinate amount of time to get ready for, considering he's had seventy-five years to perfect his look – then I'm released a bit early, so I take the scenic route.'

The Thames Clippers were the London Transport boats that deposited people between Barking and Putney, and sailed tourists and commuters past some of London's riverside landmarks, including the *Cutty Sark* – another clipper that hadn't felt water against its hull for seventy years, which was stationed only feet from where Jess and Ash were now.

'But you'll still have time before your appointment?' she asked.

'An hour. I like to make it down here with an hour to spare.'

'And it's every Sunday?'

'At the moment.'

Jess felt the twin sparks of intrigue and frustration. 'And you really want to meet up again?'

He held her gaze, his grey eyes suddenly sombre, contrasting with his smile. 'I have time to kill, you don't take enough breaks. I figure we could help each other out.'

'Help each other by spending time together?'

Ash laughed. 'It could work, couldn't it? This hasn't been too much of a disaster, I don't think.' He sounded nervous, and Jess's incredulity made way for something softer.

'It's been fun,' she said truthfully. 'I'm never going to forget your pigeon story as long as I live.'

His smile widened. 'Good. Great. So, I'll come and find you, then? No Vase Like Home.' He pronounced it in an American accent, so that Wendy's ill-advised pun worked, and Jess knew she'd have to tell her boss about him. 'I'll get to yours for midday, and we can spend an hour together.'

'For coffee?'

'Maybe,' he said, frowning. 'Maybe something else. I'll think about it.'

'I can't wait.' She had meant to be flippant, a bit sarcastic, but it just sounded eager. She drained the dregs of her coffee, and when she'd put her mug down, Ash held out his hand.

Jess stared at it. She wasn't sure if he was helping her up, or asking for her empty mug. She reached over and, before she could spend any more time analysing it, grasped his hand. It was warm, his fingers wrapping easily around hers, but he looked surprised too, as if he hadn't expected her to take it, or he hadn't expected it to feel like that. Her hand was tingling, a mini-shockwave, and she wondered if it was the same for him.

Jess stood up, and for a moment they stayed linked together. Then she dropped her hand, and Ash went to put the pink fluffy pen back in the cutlery stand.

He paused. 'Do you want this?'

Jess thought of her tiny, neat desk in the flat she shared with the landlord, Terence. The workstation where she created her Etsy prints, the pen pot with the colourful sharpies that she used for the handwritten notes she included with each order. The pen would match the overly fluffy Yeti cushions she had on her bed. But. *But.*

'You think I'm unhinged?' she asked him.

23

Ash grinned. 'I don't know, yet. Definitely no more than me.'

'The real owner might come back for it.'

'Good point.' He put it in the cutlery stand. 'After you.'

Jess wove through the tables and pushed open the café door, stepping out into the sunshine, Ash close behind her. They stood on the pavement facing each other, even though it was narrow and busy, and she heard at least one person make a pointed comment about *people being aware of what's around them.*

'So,' she said. 'Next Sunday.'

'Next Sunday,' Ash repeated. 'Midday at No Vase Like Home.'

She nodded. 'Thanks for coffee.'

'You're welcome.' His hand hovered for a second, then he squeezed her shoulder. She could feel the warmth of his skin through the thin fabric of her dress. 'Thanks for agreeing to it.'

'I hardly ever turn down coffee,' she said, then winced. 'I didn't mean that – that I only agreed because—'

'I know,' Ash said gently. Another glance at his watch, and he clenched his jaw. 'I need to go.'

'OK.' Jess wouldn't ask again where he was going. He might tell her next week, anyway. *Next week.* She had agreed to this stranger absorbing another hour of her time with hardly any protest, with so few questions to herself about whether it was a good idea. 'See you Sunday.'

'I'm already looking forward to it.' He gave her a final smile, and she watched him weave through the crowd for a moment, then turned in the direction of the market, hunching slightly against the wind. She wasn't quite sure what had happened. She didn't accept coffee with strangers; she had more than enough people in her life to be going on with. But Ash Faulkner, good citizen, pigeon magnet and all-round charmer, had woven some kind of spell around her, and now she knew how much bigger his hand was than hers because, for a few tingling seconds, she'd had it wrapped around her own. Already, she knew she wouldn't mind it happening again.

Chapter Three

By the time Jess got to Lola and Malik's flat, the sun had given up and the temperature had dropped, reminding her that the year hadn't fully shaken off the last traces of winter. She wasn't sure whether to tell Lola about her coffee with Ash, and their plans to meet up again. This would be big news, and Jess didn't know if she was ready for the full force of her best friend's excitement.

Lola answered the door, tendrils of her long blonde hair falling down either side of her face like curtains framing a beautiful view.

'Hey,' she said, breathlessly.

'Am I interrupting something, or . . .?' Jess raised her eyebrows, but Lola scoffed and turned round, heading back into the flat and clearly expecting Jess to follow.

Their living room was a haven of soft furnishings, the two rather threadbare sofas hidden beneath a sea of brightly coloured scatter cushions, most of which had been bought at the market. Malik, Lola's lanky, bespectacled boyfriend was jiggling up and down in front of the TV, playing one of his favourite shoot-'em-up video games, the sound turned low so that the gunshots were quiet, which somehow made them more sinister.

'Hey, Jess,' he said, barely looking up.

'We're getting our Fitbit targets,' Lola explained. 'He's been sitting down all day, so now he's trying to hit his ten thousand steps.'

Jess laughed. 'You could both – I don't know – just go for a walk? Not that *you* need any more steps, I'm guessing. You were working earlier, weren't you?'

'Yup. Sunday lunch shift, always a delight.' Lola went into the kitchen, filling and then flicking on the kettle. 'Tea?'

'I'd love one.' Jess followed her and leaned against the kitchen counter. 'The market's filling up with tourists now, so I expect the Gipsy Moth is the same.'

Lola worked at the pub closest to the *Cutty Sark*, which had a large, outside veranda looking out over the British clipper and the concrete foreshore that ran down to the river, a gloomy interior and a menu that stretched to several pages. It was always busy with a combination of locals and tourists, which meant that Lola rarely got a quiet shift.

'It was non-stop,' she replied, tipping her head back on a half-groan. 'There was a family of fifteen, four generations, from newborn baby to crinkly old great-grandma, behaving as if we were a Michelin-star restaurant. Could we supply them with jugs of iced, filtered water and gluten-free bread?'

Jess smothered a laugh. 'Gluten-free options are pretty standard these days. So is water.'

Lola's lips twitched. 'Yeah, well, my patience was frayed by that point. Then one of the women suggested it would have been nice if the napkins had been shaped like swans. I couldn't decide if she was winding me up, or if she was genuinely going to give us a two-star review on Tripadvisor for our serviette oversight.'

'And, after all that, you're adding to your twenty thousand steps by prancing up and down in front of the TV with Malik, who isn't even paying attention to you.' Jess tapped her fingers against her lips. 'Who lives in the flat below you again?'

'We were *both* playing that game before you arrived. He's switched to single-player mode now you're here, like a good boyfriend.' Lola grinned.

Jess liked to pretend that she was mad her best friend had found her person, but Malik was genuinely lovely: quietly geeky, unwaveringly patient, and committed to Lola 100 per cent. He had a well-paid job doing something in computer tech that she didn't understand – she wasn't sure Lola did, either – but mostly Jess loved that Lola was so happy, and had only been mildly miffed when it had meant, a few years ago, that she'd had to find somewhere else to live.

Lola and Malik had both said she could move into Malik's two-bedroom flat with them, but who wanted a third wheel rolling around their love nest on a daily basis? And who wanted to *be* that wheel, constantly walking in on moments of affection, always being in the way?

Jess had got used to her near-solitary existence in her shared flat with Terence. She was, for the most part, happier on her own anyway. For a long time, she had daydreamed about her future in those terms: about one day owning her own home by the sea, big enough for her to adorn with beautiful items (though not sinister hares) and perhaps share with a scruffy dog; going for walks along the beach; maybe one day levelling up from her Etsy shop to running her own gift shop.

Right now, she and Lola both lived in Greenwich and saw each other at least every other day, and that was what mattered to Jess. They very rarely annoyed each other.

'I was thinking of invading the market sometime next week,' Lola announced, her back turned as she drowned teabags in boiling water, and Jess remembered that it was actually very possible to be annoyed with her friend.

'For your video?' she asked.

Lola chuckled. 'I don't need any more cushions, do I?'

'You don't,' Jess agreed.

Lola's passion was playing the violin; after years of being first violin in a community orchestra, she wanted to branch out on her own, to do something more than play classical pieces as part of an ensemble. Jess knew she was biased, but she loved listening to her friend play, especially since she'd turned her focus to folk and rock music, transforming modern tunes that she knew well into pieces that sounded magical on the stringed instrument. She should be making a career out of it, not having it as a hobby while she worked all hours in a pub.

'You really think the market's the best setting?' Jess asked, for probably the tenth time since Lola had told her her idea.

'Of course.' Lola crossed her arms. She was wearing a thin grey long-sleeved T-shirt and navy jogging bottoms, and still managed to look chic. 'You're always going on about the weird and wonderful things that happen there, so what better place for my video? TikTok will lap it up.'

'Things do happen there.' Jess scrunched her nose up. After today, that felt like an understatement. 'It's just . . .'

'Just what?' Lola stirred milk into her and Jess's tea, leaving Malik's black.

Jess thought of the people who worked at the market. Gentle, quiet Enzo with his delicate filigree jewellery; Susie who ran Better Babies, all the items on her stall plush and desirable, her bright smile hiding her insecurities; Roger, who aimed for cavalier but was as strait-laced as they came. She wasn't sure how much they would love being thrust into the limelight in Lola's TikTok video – Lola, who was loud and confident and captivating. But then, Jess wanted her friend to get the success

29

she deserved; she wanted to support her. 'Are you going to prepare everyone first? Explain what you're doing?'

Lola put the milk back in the fridge. 'I'm going to do better than that, I'm going to get *you* to explain it to them.'

Jess closed her eyes. 'I knew this would happen.'

'Of course you did. I wouldn't be surprised if you've already primed them for my appearance.'

Jess huffed out a laugh, and her gaze fell on the digital clock on Lola's oven, the display stuck blinking at 00:00, as if it hadn't been reset after a power cut. She thought of the solid half-hunter in Braden's small hand, the way he'd clutched it possessively while Roger explained its provenance.

She accepted her tea from Lola, in a cream mug with *World's Best Friend* in rainbow letters on the side. It had been a birthday present, one Lola had insisted stayed here, the gesture – that she would always be welcome – meaning so much more than the mug itself. She followed Lola into the living room, her thoughts on fire.

The half-hunter. Ash and his ridiculous pigeon story. The reminder that she was seeing him again sent a swift, sharp thrill of excitement through her. She settled on the sofa and Lola held out a share-sized bag of Doritos that looked as though it might have been stuffed between the cushions for a couple of days. She hadn't eaten anything since wolfing down a peanut-butter muffin after she'd got back from her impromptu break, so she wasn't about to turn them down.

'Hellooo, Jess?' Lola waggled the crisp packet and she realised she'd had her hand in it, hovering, without actually taking any crisps.

'Just wondering how many dust bunnies I'm going to find in here.'

'We opened it last night,' Lola protested.

'And I had a clip on it until an hour ago,' Malik added, slightly out of breath from his spot in front of the TV.

'Five-star hygiene rating then.' Jess grabbed a handful and shoved it in her mouth.

'So, about my video,' Lola said. 'Let's do it together, OK? You can introduce me to everyone, I can sell the magic of featuring in my TikTok, and ask people if they're happy to be involved. You're, like, royalty there, so if they know I'm your friend, they're much more likely to say yes.'

Jess scoffed. 'You're overestimating my influence over everyone.'

'I bet I'm not. And anyway, I'll give them a demo.' Lola waved her hand as if it was a done deal – and perhaps it was: she was charismatic enough without a violin tucked under her chin. When she started to play, people went positively misty-eyed.

'Who's filming it?' Jess asked.

Lola's smile was slow and catlike, and Jess's stomach swooped.

'No,' she said. 'No way.' She didn't think she could shake her head any more vigorously. 'I have zero video skills. My Instagram reels for the shop could have been made by a child.'

It was Lola's turn to scoff. 'A child genius who's done an Instagram Secrets course. And this is TikTok. You hold up my phone, point and shoot. Ta-da!'

'Can't Malik do it?'

'I'm at work when the market's open,' he puffed. 'Lola needs you, Jess.'

'I absolutely do,' Lola agreed.

31

Jess made a grunt of protest. Introducing Lola to her market colleagues was one thing – one morning, over and done with. Doing the filming was a whole other level of involvement. 'You do not need me.'

'I'm doing this properly,' Lola told her. 'I've got release forms and everything, and I really want you to be part of it. You and me against the world, right?'

Jess buried her head in a cushion and groaned. Because that was it, wasn't it? She kept her social circle purposely small, and Lola was the most important part of it. She would do anything for the blonde, bold, slightly scatty woman sitting next to her on the sofa. The smile on Lola's face said she knew it.

'I'll think about it.' Jess sipped her tea. 'But I can't change anyone's minds if they don't want to be filmed, and I can't suddenly become Steven Spielberg.'

Lola squealed and wrapped her in a hug. 'Thank you so much. This is going to be *so* awesome!'

'Is it, though?' Jess muttered, but she hugged her friend back anyway. She hoped managing Lola's expectations as well as her colleagues' wouldn't be too much of a juggle.

'A thousand steps left,' Malik panted. 'Join me, ladies!'

Lola bounced up immediately, but Jess stayed put. It was one more thing she didn't need to be involved in. She didn't even *have* a Fitbit.

Then, before she could sink fully into the sofa cushions, Lola took her *World's Best Friend* mug out of her hand and put it on a side table, then pulled her up. Soon, Jess was jumping about on the old beige carpet to the sound of gunfire and the cries of animated people falling down dead, and she was laughing and sweaty and wondering if, actually, Lola and Malik knew a few things about happiness that she didn't.

Chapter Four

On Monday morning, Jess stood behind the counter in No Vase Like Home, in a staring contest with one of the hares, and thought about Ash. His eyes were grey, with a slight shift towards green, and for most of the time they were together his gaze was all-consuming, as if he could see past the creases on her forehead to the thoughts tumbling inside. It had been exhilarating and excruciating, but she also couldn't remember the last time she'd laughed so much. Her cheeks still ached with it. Wasn't it worth seeing him again, just for that?

Monday was duller, both in terms of the weather and the market's atmosphere, and while the chance to replay the pertinent bits of the previous day was welcome, Jess also felt more exposed. She could lose herself in a crowd, and everyone else would lose her too. When visitors were sparse, it was as if all the people who passed by the window of the shop turned to look at her, assessing and wondering about the woman behind the counter.

'That Braden lad isn't too bad under the surface,' Wendy said, putting the hare Jess was staring at back amongst its friends.

'I expect you and Roger showed him what's what,' Jess replied. 'Is he ready to put his criminal past behind him and be an upstanding, moral citizen?'

Wendy leaned her elbows on the counter and gave Jess an amused side-eye. 'We're not that good. But he apologised for stealing the watch, didn't try to make up an excuse, and he's coming here on Wednesday to help tidy the storeroom.'

'You're *employing* him?'

'Very much on a trial basis,' Wendy said. 'He knows I run a tight ship, and that if there's even the suggestion of something going missing, then Roger's original threat of calling the police comes back into play.'

'I'm sorry I'll miss it,' Jess said.

She had Tuesdays and Wednesdays off, because they were the quietest days at the market. It made sense for Wendy to give Braden a trial then – if at all. She wasn't sure she'd have been as charitable if she owned the shop. Her eyes roamed the clocks and ornaments, the selection of cushions: silky and fluffy, some pastel and soft, others with bold prints or clashing colourways. There was a tangle of sparkly rainbow twigs that Wendy had ordered by accident in a tall vase by the door. Nobody had bought them yet, much to Wendy's irritated acceptance and Jess's secret surprise. This was one of the places she felt comfortable in – a space she knew off by heart and loved like a second home.

'I hope he appreciates what you're doing for him,' she said.

'I'm sure he will eventually,' Wendy replied. 'If he's a hard worker, I might ask him to come in while you're here. I know you're secretly itching for a new project.'

Jess frowned. 'What are you talking about?'

'It's been ages since you helped Susie redesign her stall, and Jasmine said the mice haven't been back in Art Everywhere since you spent that afternoon chasing them round with bits of cheese and humane traps.'

'They weren't projects.' She tried not to sound affronted. 'They were just things that needed doing, and because you're so generous with my time, I was the one that did them.'

Wendy raised an eyebrow. 'If you say so. Anyway, I need sustenance to think, so I'm getting a coffee from Kirsty. Want anything?'

'Has she got her mini-muffins today?' Jess asked, her tastebuds coming to life at the thought.

Kirsty Connor was a few years older than Jess, and her Moreish Muffins stand was at the front end of the market, in one of two food-focused areas that ensured Jess was never far from the temptation of something delicious. Moreish was an understatement for the treats Kirsty sold: a standard blueberry muffin wouldn't even get a look-in. Hers were filled with buttercream or ganache in decadent or unusual flavours, gooey toffee sauce or, if you fancied something savoury, ham and melted cheese. Recently, she had been doing selection boxes of mini-muffins, where you could satisfy all your taste cravings in perfect, pocket-sized morsels.

'I'll check,' Wendy said. 'A selection box if she has them?'

'Yes please.' Jess went to get her purse, but Wendy waved her away.

'We'll sort it out later.'

Once she'd gone, Jess set about tidying the already pristine counter, her actions dictated by restlessness. Wendy had hired a shoplifter, Lola was days away from charming Jess's colleagues with her larger-than-life presence, and she had agreed to meet a man – basically a stranger, and one who upset her calm equilibrium – for a second time. It was as if there'd been some kind of rip in the space–time continuum and everything had been turned on its head.

She went into the storeroom to put the kettle on, hoping tea and a muffin would make her feel more at ease.

'Hello?' The voice was familiar, and Jess returned to the shop floor to find one of their regular customers hovering in the doorway.

'Hey, Felicity,' Jess said. 'How are you?'

'I'm very well, thank you.' The other woman was, Jess guessed, in her sixties, but still had beautiful skin and a perfectly coiffed grey bob, her blue eyes bright. She was wearing a silk blouse, cream with a bold pink flower pattern, and a long grey skirt and matching jacket. Jess had gathered from previous discussions that she lived in a large house close to Greenwich Park, which she shared with three cats but no other humans, and she was constantly on the lookout for elegant items to fill it with.

'Anything take your fancy today?' Jess asked. 'Other than the usual?'

Ever since she had worked in the shop, there had been a large oval mirror with an intricate gilt frame on one wall, and Felicity always gave it a longing look. She had bought plenty of other things, and it was a mystery to Jess what temptation the mirror held and why Felicity had never given into it.

She tried to imagine the room in which the older woman might place it: a hallway with black-and-white diamond tiles on the floor, where she could check her evening ensemble before a night of dancing and champagne; or in her bedroom, so she could perform her daily skincare routine, which would include Crème De La Mer; or in a separate, private dressing room, because even though she was in her sixties, she still treated herself to delicate undergarments – tasteful teddies and slips in shades called oyster and blush.

Felicity glanced at the mirror, then at Jess, and let out a tinkling laugh. 'I'm not quite *there* with the mirror yet,' she admitted. 'But I am considering this.' She ran her hand over the smooth globe of a water feature that wasn't turned on but, from the label Jess had put up, copying the words directly from the brochure, would provide a gentle, meditative sound once it had water running through it.

'That's a very popular piece,' Jess said, because she'd sold one last week. 'Especially with summer on the way. If you have a pond, the moving water helps keep mosquitos and midges away.'

'I don't have a pond,' Felicity said, 'but I am considering one.'

'Are you remodelling your garden?' Jess had spent far too much time daydreaming about what Felicity's beautiful house might look like. The garden, of course, would be tranquil, with the mature trees of Greenwich Park adding another layer of green beyond an elegant, red-brick wall.

'Potentially,' Felicity said. 'If I were to order this, would you provide a delivery service?'

'Uhm.' Other than the large mirror and the taller vases lining the wall below the window, the water feature was the only substantial item they sold; all the others were easy to take away in tote bags or strong carriers. They hadn't had to consider delivery before – the customer who bought the water feature last week had taken it out to his van, which was apparently parked around the corner.

'I'm only a five-minute walk away, but I couldn't manage it by myself.' Felicity held out her slender arms to demonstrate.

'Of course not.' Jess frowned when she noticed the cuff of the other woman's sleeve was frayed. Had she caught it on a wall on her walk here? She didn't know what she could offer without asking Wendy, so she walked around the counter, bent her knees and tipped the water feature, sliding her fingers under the plinth. When she lifted it, she found it wasn't as heavy as she had expected.

'Is shoplifting contagious?'

Jess almost dropped it on her fingers. She lowered it gently, smiling when she saw that Wendy had returned with a selection box and two large takeaway cups.

'I was seeing how heavy it was,' she explained. 'I think it's made of resin, rather than stone.'

'Goodness, of course it is,' Wendy said. 'Stone would be impossibly heavy, especially as we can't offer delivery. Hello, Felicity.'

'That's what I was wondering about,' Felicity said. 'Whether Jess would be able to deliver this to my house, if I bought it.'

'She'd walk it round for you, as you're one of our best customers.' Wendy put the cups on the counter. 'Wouldn't you, Jess?'

Jess held back her frustrated sigh. Hadn't Wendy *just* said they couldn't offer delivery? But she probably *could* walk it round, with only a couple of rest stops, as long as Felicity wasn't exaggerating about how close her house was to the park. 'Of course,' she said, because she couldn't exactly complain about being loaned out in front of the customer in question.

'Wonderful.' Felicity clasped her hands together. 'It'll make such a difference to the patio. And aren't these adorable?' She plucked one of the hares off its shelf. It was the most disturbing one, in Jess's opinion, with its front paws raised in what was perhaps supposed to be a coquettish gesture, but to her looked grasping.

'They're lovely,' she said, and Wendy's amused glance told her she hadn't sounded remotely sincere. 'Though I do prefer our glass ornaments. What do you think of these?' She showed Felicity the paperweights with swirling colour patterns and bubbles inside, some twinkling with suspended glitter. Felicity seemed charmed, even though she must have examined them on her previous visits.

Once she'd left, saying she'd be back in a few days to arrange payment and delivery of the water feature, Wendy passed Jess a hot chocolate and opened the selection box.

Jess took a strawberry cream mini-muffin.

'You're very tolerant with Felicity,' Wendy said.

Jess smiled around her mouthful. 'You're very keen to give me extra jobs to do.'

Wendy ignored her comment. 'You didn't want her to have a hare.'

'I don't want *anyone* to have a hare. They creep me out.'

'They're gorgeous.'

'They're sinister, and they have impure agendas.'

'They're inanimate objects.'

'That's what they *want* you to think.' Jess folded her arms, her back to the items in question. Her neck was prickling, as if they were all watching her, and she wondered if she was taking this flight of fancy too far.

'You have too much time on your hands,' Wendy said. 'That's why I have to give you extra jobs. And you should make yesterday a habit – take a proper lunch hour again today, and go and have a walk in the sunshine.'

Jess dropped her eyes to the counter. 'I would like to take one again next Sunday, if that's OK?'

'Of course!' Wendy said, laughing. 'You're supposed to have one *every* day.' She left a tiny pause, then asked, 'Anything fun planned?'

Her attempt at casual was piteous, and Jess would have found it amusing if her own attempt wasn't ten times worse. 'Just a thing I . . . have to see to.' She could feel heat blooming across her cheeks.

'Well,' Wendy said, her takeaway cup raised to her lips, 'enjoy your thing. And if you happen to take a bit longer than an hour, please don't worry. It's not as if you haven't got a whole lot of time in the bank.'

'Thanks.' Jess couldn't work out whose gaze she was least enjoying: Wendy's, or the creepy inanimate hares'. She definitely needed to take more advantage of her lunch hours away from the shop.

Chapter Five

Most twenty-seven-year-olds who lived five minutes away from the centre of Greenwich, and a short boat or train ride from the bright lights of Central London, would not be spending Saturday nights in their bedrooms unless they had company.

But then, most people who wanted a motivational poster on the wall above their desk, or pinned to their fridge, would make one using a free graphics app on their phone. Because some people *didn't* do that, Jess was spending her Saturday night alone, painstakingly changing font sizes on the design she was creating on her laptop while a Morgan Wade album played quietly in the background. She had built up a small income stream from her Etsy shop and, even though it wasn't anywhere near enough to live on, it gave her a sense of purpose outside No Vase Like Home.

She took photos of the soft green corners of Greenwich Park, or a blue sky dotted with clouds, or the river on its calmest, silveriest days, then she thought up a slogan, made sure the fonts and colours were aesthetically pleasing and, when someone ordered one, slid a piece of thick card into her printer and hit print. A quick trim, then she sent it out in a 'do not bend' envelope along with a handwritten note.

When she first came up with the idea for her prints – which was when Terence had said to her, 'Life gives you lemons, and do you know what? I fucking hate lemonade,' – she had wondered whether to create two separate shops: genuine motivation for people who were inspired by a positive slogan, and the more Terence-like sayings for those who had cynicism running through them like the place name on a stick of rock.

She had found, though, that a lot of her customers wanted both: that everyone was bitter *and* hopeful, in different amounts.

Tonight she was working on two side by side. *A chance encounter with a stranger could change your life: make room for the unexpected*, alongside *Eye contact with a handsome stranger means true love, or that his accomplice is about to steal your phone.* They needed honing, but sometimes it was easier to let the words shuffle into place in her mind while she focused on making them look pretty.

She loved the idea that little pieces of her creativity were scattered across the country, cheering up people's houses and making them laugh. Home decor was such a personal thing, and Jess felt strongly that people should be able to style their homes how they wanted – even though she had tried to persuade Felicity not to buy a hare earlier in the week.

Jess's own personal space consisted of the four walls she was in right now, and it was always tidy, with decorative items from No Vase Like Home that she'd bought with her discount: a large J with built-in LED spotlights on the shelf in front of her favourite paperbacks; a small stone with ears and the suggestion of a face, unidentifiable as any creature beyond a pet rock; a mother-of-pearl photo frame, the rainbow sheen glinting under her fairy lights, with a photo of her and Lola, arms outstretched, on a pebble beach. She liked bright colours against neutral backgrounds, and had created a space that was cheerful but soft, too.

It had been a long time since anyone other than Lola or Terence had been in here. Her last, short-lived boyfriend Warren had come over a few times, though, in hindsight, their relationship had never really got off the starting blocks. He certainly hadn't been around long enough to influence how her room looked.

She was close to finalising her new designs when there was a knock on the door. She clenched her teeth and called, 'Yeah?'

'I'm ordering from Golden Palace,' Terence said through the door. 'Want anything?'

Jess had been so busy at the market today – Saturdays were always frenetic – that she couldn't remember what she'd eaten. She opened the door to find her landlord and flatmate, his reddish-brown hair in its usual dishevelled state, wearing jeans and a loose blue T-shirt, leaning against the wall.

'I'd love a beef chow mein,' she said. 'And . . . do they do dim sum?'

'I've got the menu open on my iPad.' Terence went back to the living room, and Jess followed. 'Working on your Etsy stuff?' The wall-mounted television was showing some spangly Saturday night show with the sound off, which enhanced its inanity.

'I've got a few orders to fulfil, and I'm adding some new designs,' Jess said, as he handed her the iPad.

'Need more of your envelopes?'

'If you can wangle me a few, that would be great.' One perk of living with a postman was that he could get her stationery supplies at a huge discount which, on her spreadsheet of business incomings and outgoings, barely made a dent.

'No worries.' Terence was staring at the brightly clothed presenters on the TV as if he had an exam on the subject the next day. He was in his mid-thirties, and Jess might have considered him a loner, except that he went to the pub with friends at least three times a week, which was more socialising than she ever did. She very rarely saw anything spark joy in him, rarely saw deep emotion of any kind pass through him – though he seemed content enough. As two people who lived in fairly close quarters, they didn't share a whole lot, other than takeaway orders, milk, and a belief that Royal Mail was one of the country's greatest institutions and was being systematically destroyed.

'Thanks,' Jess said. 'And along with the beef chow mein I'd like some spicy chicken wings. Except – do you know *how* spicy they are? How long do you think they'd . . . linger?'

Terence looked at her as if she'd asked when he was next delivering mail to Mars. 'I don't get wings, so . . . no clue. Why? Have you got a hot date later?' He glanced at his watch, as if to suggest she was pushing it fine if that was her plan.

Jess's laugh was more of a manic titter. 'No, I . . . you know. Sunday tomorrow. We'll be busy at work. Who knows who I might encounter?'

Terence swapped his incredulous expression for a grin, and Jess was reminded that casual fibbing was not one of her skills. She was much better at staying silent, locking things away completely. She wished she hadn't asked him about the chicken wings.

'Who knows indeed,' Terence said. 'I reckon they won't blow your head off. Want me to add them?'

'Yeah. I've got some notes in my purse – let me get them.' She hurried back to her room, her laptop screen glaring at her from the corner. No psychologist would sweat to interpret the meaning behind her newest quotes: the mention of a handsome stranger; the reference to stealing.

Last Sunday's events would have played on her thoughts even if they hadn't had lasting consequences, but she was seeing Ash again tomorrow and, even if she wanted to back out, there was nothing she could do, because they hadn't exchanged numbers.

She dug in her handbag for her purse, and took out the crumpled notes. Ash had managed to knock down the defences she usually kept up around other people without so much as breaking a sweat. She had sat in a café with him, laughing at his stories about rogue pigeons and wondering what he was killing time until. His reluctance to tell her had only made her more curious, and she thought that maybe he'd done it on purpose, as a way to keep her on the hook.

'It's going to be an hour,' Terence called. 'Saturday night and all that!'

Jess went to give him the money, and told him she didn't mind waiting. She didn't want to be alone in her room any more, fiddling with her motivational quotes and thinking about tomorrow.

Terence was scrolling idly on his phone, the Saturday-night series still silent in the background.

'What's this, then?' Jess sat on the sofa and pointed her foot at the TV.

'Some shit,' he said without looking up.

'Let's find something less shit, then.'

'Good luck with that.'

Jess scrolled through the channels, looking for anything remotely interesting, and eventually found a Denzel Washington film that had only been going for three minutes, the cast names bouncing along the screen as a wide shot of an American city zoomed slowly in to find the inciting incident.

'How about this?'

Terence made a noise that could have meant acceptance or indifference, but he put his phone down and asked Jess if she wanted a beer. Jess nodded and thanked him, and wondered if she really would be able to forget about seeing Ash again for a couple of hours, distracted by a good film and a Chinese takeaway. At least she wasn't alone in her room on a Saturday night any more.

Chapter Six

At ten past twelve the next day, Jess decided Ash wasn't coming, and her stomach settled like a popped balloon: no more nervous bouncing, but also fully deflated.

It was a sunny day, the first weekend in May, and the light shone through the glass roof of the market, alighting on the coloured, see-through hearts that reminded her of the stained-glass biscuits she'd made two decades ago at Brownies. It had been one of the activities her parents had encouraged her to do, though she had much preferred swimming club, which had been less about false fun and more about competition. She had spent so much time with her head underwater that it wasn't a surprise when she hadn't found any firm friends by the end of the first term.

'I thought you wanted to head off for lunch,' Wendy said, talking over the sound of Jess drumming her fingers on the counter. Beyond the shop the market was busy, laughter and chatter and the smells from the food court batting up against the window. A scream filled the air, followed by a bellow that could have been anger or hilarity, and Jess found herself looking for running figures, for Braden again, for Ash.

'It doesn't matter,' she said, and was surprised by how flat she sounded.

'Roger told me about his saviour,' Wendy went on. 'The man who collared young Braden before you two got there. The one you went to coffee with.'

'He was just some guy.' Jess flicked through a supplier's catalogue, and wished that she could dismiss him from her thoughts as easily.

'Is that so?' Wendy didn't sound convinced.

'I'll be fine here for a bit.' She put down the catalogue and rearranged the pile of tourist maps next to the till, feeling Wendy's gaze on her. She was relieved when a large group of friends bustled into the shop, talking over each other and cooing at the display of cushions, and they were both kept busy answering questions, checking the storeroom for more stock of pomegranate room spray.

Jess wasn't surprised that Ash hadn't shown. He'd been fun but evasive, a bright spot in an ordinary week, and she'd made the mistake of getting her hopes up, letting in the spark of possibility that she could spend an hour with a handsome stranger and that he'd want to see her again.

The friends left with wide smiles and full paper bags, and the clocks ticked loudly in the quiet, telling her it was just after half past twelve. She tried to put her disappointment into a box.

'You still need to eat,' Wendy said, 'even if your plans have fallen through.'

'I'll get a muffin,' she said automatically.

'Good choice.' Jess recognised the deep voice, and she looked up to see Ash standing in the doorway, wearing his grey jacket, jeans and a dusty blue jumper. He was holding two takeaway coffees, and his smile was hesitant. 'I'm so sorry. Can you still take a break? I understand if I'm too late.'

'Ash,' she blurted. 'I—'

'I was just about to force her out of the door,' Wendy said. 'Take her, please.'

He didn't. Instead he waited, dipped his head slightly and said, 'Jess?'

She stood, frozen on the spot.

'I really am sorry,' he said.

She picked up her bag from behind the till. 'I can come for a bit, I suppose.'

His shoulders dropped, his smile widening. 'Great. I got you an Americano, because of last weekend, but I also have cappuccino if you'd prefer that.' He held up the cups. 'I love the shop,' he added, as Jess got her jacket.

'Thank you,' Wendy said. 'I'm Wendy. Lovely to meet you, Ash.'

'You too,' Ash replied. 'I particularly like the hares.' He gestured to the shelf where they sat, looking menacing, and Jess wondered if it was rude to push a man you'd only met once before. Instead, she tugged his jacket until he was facing the door and then, when he made no move to walk through it, she pressed her hand between his shoulder blades and nudged him forwards. His jacket was soft against her palm and she felt the thrill of putting her hand on him – like something forbidden.

'You did that on purpose,' she said, once they were in the narrow walkway outside the shop.

He looked at her. 'No I didn't.'

'You don't even know what I'm talking about. Can I have my coffee?'

'Not yet. It's busy in here, you might get knocked.'

'And you have a forcefield around you, I suppose?' She waited a beat, then added, 'I didn't think you were going to turn up.'

'I'm so sorry,' he said again. 'This morning didn't go as planned.'

49

'Aren't you going to be late for your thing? It's in twenty minutes, isn't it?'

'I can still have an hour with you. I called ahead, made sure I could be late, just this once.'

'For me?'

'For you.' He nodded, his smile a flicker and then gone. 'Shall we get going? We don't want to miss it.'

'Miss what?' Jess asked, but Ash was already ahead of her, weaving between parents with children so small you didn't see them until the last minute; couples who had decided Sundays were for strolling, no matter the crush; tourists looking at maps to determine which exit they needed for their next destination. Jess noticed that, as he passed the other stalls, Ash nodded hellos. To Olga – which wasn't a surprise considering she'd seen him goofing around with her hats – but then he said hello to Susie on the Better Babies stall, and Enzo as they passed his elegant display of earrings and necklaces, the gold winking in the sunshine. Jess waved and smiled too, of course, but she worked there.

'Where are we going?' she asked, once they'd left the alley at the top of the market, going past the baker's that smelled of warm, fresh bread, doughy and irresistible.

'I thought we'd make the most of my lateness.' Ash glanced at his watch. 'We've got ten minutes.'

'Until what?' They waited to cross the road, tourists banked up at the crossing like runners at the start of a marathon.

Ash nudged her arm with his elbow, still holding firmly onto the takeaway mugs. 'Patience.'

'Really?' Jess laughed. 'I already had to wait over half an hour for you. I didn't have to come.'

She was gratified to see a blush stain his cheekbones. Even embarrassed, he was unfairly handsome. 'I know,' he said.

'Sorry. We're going to the Meridian Line. There's a red ball on the observatory that drops at exactly one o'clock every day. You can set your watch by it.'

'I know about that,' Jess said. 'I live here, remember? But actually,' she softened her voice, 'it's been ages since I saw it happen.'

Ash smiled. 'See? It's a good plan. And it wouldn't hurt for me to make sure my watch is accurate.'

Jess rolled her eyes. 'You can stop apologising now. You're here, and you brought coffee.'

'And I'm taking you to the park where, only last week, you told me there were thousands of over-friendly pigeons, so I'm making a pretty big sacrifice.' The look he gave her suggested he saw their lunch date as anything but a sacrifice, and Jess gave him a reluctant smile.

They walked through the wrought-iron gateway into the park, everything technicolour under the May sun. The lawns were busy with dog walkers and families, relaxed strollers and focused joggers. An ice-cream van must have been parked up somewhere because people were clutching cones, taking satisfied licks. Jess loved how many different personalities the park had: open grass to laze on, an ornamental lake with ducks, a boating pond that ran pedalos in the summer months. You could find shade under the mature trees or hide away in the secret garden that was fit to bursting with seasonal flowers, a riot of colour that smelled as good as it looked.

'Can I have my coffee now?' She held her hand out, and Ash handed her a cup.

'We'll have to hurry if we want to see the ball drop.'

'I can keep up with you,' Jess said with a scoff, then worried it was a lie, because Ash's legs were longer than hers.

But she kept pace with him, even when they reached the steepest part of the hill, and they stopped inside the courtyard of the Royal Observatory, the brick building's white cornicing gleaming in the sunshine, the red orb like a model of Mars proud on the top.

'Here we are.' Ash was slightly breathless. 'We made it. And . . . there. Five to one.' They watched as the ball slid halfway up its mast, coming to a neat stop.

There were 'Ooos' of wonder from the tourists standing around them, and Jess laughed.

'What's so funny?' Ash was next to her, and there was a comforting warmth down her right side, where their arms touched.

'I don't know,' she admitted. 'It just looked a bit silly, the ball popping up like that.'

'It's a historic marvel. It's been doing it since 1833, did you know that?'

'I did not. No wonder Braden called you Dictionary Corner.'

He gave her an amused glance. 'I think today you mean *Encyclopedia Brittanica*.'

'Smart with words *and* facts.' Jess grinned. 'Thanks for my coffee.'

'Thanks for still coming with me, even though I messed up.'

'What happened?'

Ash looked away, to where people were standing with one foot either side of the Meridian Line, as if they were straddling two different lifetimes. 'I just wasn't sure,' he admitted.

'About your appointment?'

His burst of laughter was humourless. 'No, I'm very sure how I feel about that.'

Jess waited for him to elaborate. She could feel her pulse beating in her neck.

'I meant about this,' Ash said after a moment. 'Last weekend was so random.' He swallowed, his Adam's apple bobbing. 'It wasn't that I didn't want to see you – I haven't doubted that for one second since we left the café last week. I just wasn't sure it was a good idea.'

Jess sucked in a breath, trying to temper her disappointment. 'Why not?' she asked. 'Because I liked that fluffy pen? You were worried I was a serial killer?'

Ash laughed. 'No, I just—'

'There!' The ball had bounced to the top of the mast while they weren't looking, and now it dropped, like a stone, to the bottom. There was a smattering of applause and Jess said, 'Quick, set your watch.'

Ash fiddled with the crown on his watch, his coffee cup tipping precariously.

'Here.' Jess took it from him, her fingertips brushing his.

'Thanks. I almost missed it.'

'Then you would have been even later next week.' It had just popped out, her heart thudding along with the words, but she felt a spark of pleasure at the way Ash's face brightened.

'There.' He held his arm out, his elegant watch showing a minute past one on his tanned wrist. 'Come on, I'm going to test you.'

'On what?' Jess handed Ash his coffee cup, then he took her free hand, tangling their fingers together.

'You live here, so you must have this view burned into your retinas.' He led her to the railing at the top of the park's main thoroughfare, in front of the statue of General James Wolfe. Below them, the lawn sloped down to the Queen's House and the Old Royal Naval College, with the towering skyscrapers of Canary Wharf a gleaming contrast beyond. It was a magnificent view, especially with the Thames weaving through it, glittering like a sequinned serpent.

'You're going to test me on the landmarks?'

'I bet you know them off by heart.' Ash spoke softly, but his voice cut through the tourists' chatter, and the breeze dancing through the cherry blossoms.

As she stood there, with London spread out before her, he came to stand behind her. His body wasn't touching hers, but he was close, a wall of warmth sheltering her from the spring wind. He put their coffee cups on the low wall. 'You have ten seconds,' he said into her ear.

Jess felt a flash of panic and looked out across the park, then down at the illustration on the metal plaque at waist height, which had labels for all the notable buildings. She could hear Ash counting under his breath, and when he got to two, he said, 'Ready?'

'For what?'

He held his hands out in front of them, then brought them slowly towards her face. 'OK? he asked.

Jess swallowed. She already knew how warm his hands were. 'OK.'

He brought them closer, then very gently pressed them over her eyes. The darkness was tinged pink, and there was a floral scent from whichever soap he'd used last.

'What buildings are there?' he asked, his words gusting breath onto the back of her neck.

'The Queen's House, the Old Royal Naval College, the Gherkin.'

'You need to point, too.'

'I can't see, Ash. How can I point?'

'You know which direction they're in.'

'Fine.' She huffed. 'The Queen's House, the Old Royal Naval College.' She pointed straight ahead. 'Then that way, there's the Shard, the Gherkin, the Cheese Grater. St Paul's and the London Eye right over . . .' She swung her hand left. 'Then that way,' she pointed right, 'is the O2 and Greenwich Power Station.'

He laughed. 'This wasn't challenging at all.'

'I should have made *you* do it,' she said. 'That would have been more fun.'

'I would have managed the park,' he replied, and a second later she could see again, her skin immediately missing the warmth of his. She blinked into the sunlight, then turned around.

'The park isn't a building,' she pointed out.

'Nor is the London Eye, technically.'

Without discussing it, they picked up their coffees and walked over to the first bench they could see, a little way down the path, away from the groups of foreign students and day-tripping families. Here, the Queen's House and the river were shielded by trees, but above the canopy they could see the yellow spikes of the O2, and the power station's towers.

'I brought a muffin.' Ash reached into his jacket pocket and took out a familiar red paper bag.

'From Moreish!'

It was a lemon and poppy seed muffin, full of lemon cream – part of Kirsty's summer range – and she could barely wait for Ash to tear it in half. He handed her a large piece and she bit into it.

'Thank you,' she said around a mouthful of sugary sponge.

'Apology muffin, for almost not turning up.'

'The best apologies are made with food that's really bad for you.'

He gave her a sideways look. 'That is very true.'

'I've used those words in my shop.'

Ash frowned. 'No Vase Like Home?'

'No, not there. I have an Etsy shop.'

'You have a side hustle?'

She nodded. 'I make motivational prints. I took an arty photo of Kirsty's stall, all those muffins arranged in their little paper cases, and I wrote that over the top. *The best apologies are made with food that's really bad for you.* It sells really well, but not as well as the cynical version.'

'What's that?'

'*The best apologies are heart attacks in disguise. Are they really sorry, or just trying to kill you?*'

Ash's laugh was a guffaw. 'Are you worried I'm a killer, now? Do you want me to eat your half?'

'No.' Jess spun away from him, holding the muffin against her chest, then took another large bite to be on the safe side. 'I wrote a new one last night.'

'What did it say?'

'*A chance encounter with a stranger could change your life: make room for the unexpected.* Today has been unexpected, because first, I didn't think you were going to turn up, and then you did, and then . . .'

'I forced you to prove your status as a local by giving you a spot test on the sights of Greenwich peninsula?'

'Exactly.'

'I'm very glad I turned up,' he said. The conviction in his voice made Jess look at him more closely. He wasn't smiling, but his eyes were holding hers, inviting her to tell him all her secrets. 'I love the sound of your prints. The dark and the light.'

'I love making them,' she admitted. 'I like the thought that something I've created is making someone's home a bit brighter, whether I'm inspiring them or making them laugh. *A new dawn is a chance to make a hundred more mistakes; your oldest friends are the ones who haven't worked out how to get rid of you.*'

Ash laughed. 'Ouch.'

'Too bitter?'

'Too real,' he said. 'I think I prefer the positive ones.'

'OK.' She gave him a small smile, but inside, it felt as if the world was shifting around her. Ash touched her lightly on the knee, a gentle pressure through her dress, and she went very still, focusing on the sensation, the low rumble of her internal earthquake.

'Hey, I—'

He was interrupted by a small white dog rushing up to their bench. It reminded Jess of an illustrated edition she'd had of T. S. Eliot poems, the drawings in 'Growltiger's Last Stand' and 'The Pekes and the Pollicles'.

The dog bounced in the grass at their feet, scraping Ash's jeans with its tiny paws.

'Hey, little guy,' he said. 'Who are you?'

'She's a demon,' said a tall, thick-waisted woman wearing a cranberry red coat, striding up the hill to join them. 'It doesn't matter how securely I fix her lead to her harness, she always manages to escape.'

'She's adorable.' Ash ran his fingers through her candy-floss fur, his hand almost the size of the little dog's head.

'She's too sociable, that's her problem. Always looking for new friends. Come on, Diamanté, leave these people alone.'

Ash glanced at Jess, amusement shining in his eyes, and Jess put her coffee cup in front of her face to hide her smirk.

Diamanté yapped and then raced to her owner, dancing at her feet. The woman bent down, held a treat out on her palm and secured the lead in one swift movement.

'Sorry to have bothered you,' she said.

'You didn't,' Ash replied.

'She's cute,' Jess added, 'for a demon.'

The woman gave them a rueful smile and retreated down the hill with her unruly pet.

'Diamanté the Demon Dog,' Ash said. 'It sounds like a West End musical.'

'Or a nightmare,' Jess replied. 'Do you have any pets?'

Ash shook his head. 'My apartment block is an animal-free zone, except that the guy with neck tattoos who lives on the ground floor has two Dobermanns – unless he walks them for a friend every day.'

'He has neck tattoos and two Dobermanns?' Jess shuddered. 'I guess he's not going to be called out on it any time soon.'

'Certainly not by me.' Ash's grimace made Jess double over with laughter. 'What about you?'

'I have a Terence,' Jess said.

'Cat or dog?'

'Housemate, actually. And, in fact, my landlord. He's well-behaved most of the time.'

'Oh,' Ash said. 'He's . . . is he, uhm . . .'

Jess hid her amusement at Ash's loss of composure. Did he think Terence was her boyfriend? Friend with benefits? The thought was laughable – there was zero attraction between them – but she was tempted to keep Ash dangling. 'He's mid-thirties, a postman, and mostly keeps to himself. Eats jam out of the jar with a spoon, no toast required.'

Ash's pause seemed to last for eternity. 'You get on, though?'

'We don't antagonise each other, but that's mainly because we don't spend much time together. He's up and out really early, so he crashes early, too. My work days are more straightforward, but I spend a lot of time in my room.' She didn't know why she'd added that last bit, but spoken aloud it sounded lonely. 'Working on my Etsy things,' she clarified. She watched Diamanté and her owner disappear into the trees at the bottom of the hill.

Ash rubbed his hand over his jaw. He seemed distracted all of a sudden, no longer with her, then he glanced at his watch and his brows drew together.

'I have to go,' he told her. 'How would you feel about . . .?' He cleared his throat.

Jess realised she was sucking her cheeks in, that it must look like a bad impression of a duck. She released them. 'Same time next week?'

'Midday,' he confirmed. 'I promise I won't be late again. I'll bring you an Americano?'

'I'll get the drinks next time. What's your favourite?'

'Cappuccino.'

They made their way down the hill, along a narrow path that ran through the grass.

'You were saying hello to people in the market,' she said. 'On our way here.'

'I've talked to some of the stallholders,' he admitted. 'Just the last few weeks.'

'Only a few weeks, and you already know them enough to say hello.' It had taken her months to get to know the other vendors, but Ash had broken through boundaries in minutes.

'Places like the market, it's the people who hold it together, isn't it?' he said. 'What they sell is important, sure, and the muffins and jewellery are a draw, but Olga's hats are just hats without her jokes and the way she greets everyone like a long-lost relative. And the objects – they matter because you associate them with a happy memory, or they're the perfect gift for someone important. None of the items matter in isolation, there's always a story or a connection.' They broke through the trees, onto the clear expanse of grass with the Queen's House in all its splendour beyond. 'I didn't find your shop first, or get drawn in by the window display. I met you.'

'Only because we both chased Braden.'

'I would have found you,' Ash said. It was such a simple statement, but it made Jess's heart stutter and then start up again double time. 'It's not the *things* that matter – not the money that my colleagues make in horrifying amounts; not the hares and vases and cushions you sell that make your customers' homes cosy. It's the people they surround themselves with.' He shrugged, and she saw a tinge of pink on his cheeks. 'I come for the company, not the muffins.' He stopped on the path. 'I'm sorry, I need to run.'

'OK.' Jess took a breath. 'Bye, then.'

'Bye, Jess.' He strode away from her.

'Midday next week?' she called, needing to cement it in place.

Ash turned around. His hands were clenched into fists at his sides, and the lightness in his eyes had gone, as if he'd pulled down a shutter. But his smile, when it came, filled her up.

'We can get to know each other an hour at a time,' he called back.

'Works for me.'

She watched him walk away, then made her own way out of the park, her pace slower. She admitted to herself how glad she was that he'd turned up; that he'd decided she was worth his time. Being with him made her feel giddy, but it also left her with the heavy weight of satisfaction, like a flower, laden with petals, blossoming inside her.

They may only have had an hour together, but it was one of the best things she'd done all week.

Chapter Seven

As he left the bustling cheerfulness of the park behind, bypassing the centre of Greenwich with its beeping horns and narrow pavements in favour of the leafier, quieter streets, Ash didn't know what to think. Had it been a good idea, meeting up with Jess? Had his original instinct, to miss their coffee date altogether, been the right one?

If he'd been rating his own performance at being an approachable, warm human being, then he would have given himself six out of ten, and that was only because he had a tendency to be generous. What idiot put their hands over the eyes of a woman they'd only met the week before and asked them to recall every aspect of the view? He was lucky she hadn't walked away, or threatened to put her ex-policeman friend Roger on to him.

It wasn't fair of him. He'd known that last week when he'd approached her, leaving Roger to take charge of the young guy who'd stolen the watch. He should have just left, not let himself be pulled into her orbit. She'd looked so strong and open, though, and beautiful, with those clear, dark eyes and wavy brown hair to match, and the thought of leaving right then and going where he needed to – with adrenaline still in his veins from chasing the thief, mingling with shame at the way he'd frozen – felt impossible.

So instead he'd gone up to her, spoken to her, found himself laughing, feeling lighter than he had done in a long while. Then she'd surprised him by agreeing to go for coffee, and after they'd sat opposite each other at that intimate table, and she'd laughed at his pigeon story, which had been almost worth the abject humiliation for the way it had broken through any awkwardness between them, the idea that he could spend more time with her had been too much to resist. They'd hatched another plan – *he'd* suggested it, even though he couldn't be the best company right now.

He stepped off the pavement, looking up and then swiftly moving back when a taxi rounded the corner, golden light glowing, offering him an exit. But he couldn't: he had made promises. He was already an hour late; he couldn't bail altogether. So he crossed the road and walked up the hill, uneven paving stones beneath his feet, a row of tall trees in full spring foliage shielding the park from view.

His palms felt dusty from the muffin, and beneath that was the usual prickle of sweat he got every time he came here, no matter how much he rationalised with himself.

The white door was unassuming, a brass plaque announcing its name on the brick wall next to the frame, which was surrounded by a climbing rose that, Peggy had told him last week, was due to flower any day. The thought of her small talk and her humour, her way of making everything seem less monumental, was the one thing that made him feel calmer.

He didn't need to knock, so he just pushed open the door and walked into the airy reception space, with its curved white desk and a slight smell of antiseptic in the air.

He was told to take a seat, that Peggy would be along any moment, so he sat on one of the white leather benches. The magazines splayed out on the glass coffee table were the current editions which, more than anything else, told him this place was expensive; that it had the funds to keep its distractions up-to-date.

He took out his phone, expecting a notification, some indication that he hadn't invented the last hour. There was a message, but it wasn't from Jess – they hadn't even exchanged numbers. It was from Mack, his neighbour:

Supplement missing in today's paper. That newsagent is getting sloppy. M.

Ash rolled his eyes. He mostly got on with the older man and didn't begrudge their Sunday mornings, although, if he dropped off the paper and didn't stay for coffee, he could be with Jess earlier next week – earlier even than midday. Would she be able to get away for longer? What had started as a favour for the man who lived opposite him had become something of a burden, and wasn't that the story of his life at the moment?

'Ash Faulkner, as I live and breathe.'

Ash looked up, his smile automatic.

Peggy was, he thought, around the same age as him – late twenties or early thirties – with reddish-gold hair held back in a ponytail, blue eyes, and the air of someone who was born to look after other people. It didn't say Peggy on her name badge, but that's how she'd introduced herself, and how he thought of her. The first time they'd met he'd found her concern stifling, but at week four it was a comfort to know that she'd be here, a gatekeeper between him and what he had to face.

'Peggy.' He shoved his phone in his pocket. 'How are you?'

'Can't complain with this weather.' She pulled a stool across and sat opposite him. 'I'm glad you're here. After you called earlier, I thought "late" meant you weren't coming at all.'

He rubbed his jaw. 'It was tempting, but I . . . I had something to do. Before this. Thanks for letting me come now.'

She nodded. 'Everything OK?'

'Yeah,' he said. 'Yeah, it's good.'

'You were seeing Jess again. The woman from last week?'

'That's right.' He couldn't remember what he'd told Peggy about their coffee, how much of his feelings had spilled out. His thoughts always felt scrambled after leaving here, and last week had been no different.

'You like her.' It wasn't a question.

'I'm going to be here every Sunday for the foreseeable, so it made sense to find some kind of . . . connection, instead of just drifting about.' He thought of what Jess had said about him greeting everyone at the market. It was second nature to him – talking to people, finding out the reason behind their stall, how long it had taken them to turn a passion project into a business.

'And how was it?' Peggy turned when there were voices down the corridor, then, as if realising they weren't for her, gave him her full attention.

'I like being with her,' he admitted. 'I was late because I'd convinced myself I shouldn't see her, then I changed my mind and it was rushed . . . awkward. She wasn't happy with me to begin with, understandably. But I don't know if I should force her to spend time with me right now.' He gestured to the neat waiting area.

'You're forcing her, are you? Snuck some handcuffs out of your pocket? Put a gun to her head? She has no agency in your meetings at all, then?'

'You know what I mean. I haven't told her about this.'

'You've known her a week.' Peggy's voice was softer. 'Life stories can come further down the line.'

'You think it's OK, then?' He hadn't expected her to condone it, and he hadn't expected to care so much about her opinion. He'd only known her a couple of weeks longer than he'd known Jess.

'This is a hard time for you,' Peggy said. 'Whatever you need to do to get you through, as long as it's not harmful to you or anyone else, you should do it. I can't see how a drink in the sunshine can be hurting her, even if it *is* with you.' She smiled, a twinkle of mischief in her eyes. 'Do you want a coffee now?'

'I'd love one,' Ash said. 'Thanks, Peggy.'

'All part of the service.' She disappeared through a door, leaving him with a copy of *Country Life* to flick through, the bold headlines reminding him of Jess's side gig. Could he ask her to make him a print, something related to this situation, to give him the courage that he couldn't dredge up from anywhere? *Before you can embrace the future, you have to face down your past.* Or: *The hardest journey starts with a single step.* That one was a classic, but saying it silently to himself didn't make him feel any better.

Peggy came back with a porcelain mug, the cappuccino froth visible above the rim. 'I told John I had a real-life occupational psychologist coming in today,' she said. John, Ash knew from his first visit, was Peggy's husband.

'Did you also tell him that I can barely sort through my own thoughts right now, let alone anyone else's?' His smile was wry, but he worried that he'd sounded self-pitying. And he *did* feel sorry for himself, alongside knowing that he needed to man up and get on with it. 'Sorry, Peg.'

'No apology needed.' She flapped her hand dismissively. 'John said, and I think you'll like this, "it's much easier to make sense of other people's shit than your own." That's pretty much a universal statement, don't you think?'

Ash laughed. 'I do. Jess would love it, too.'

'Would she now?' Peggy raised an eyebrow. 'Are you seeing her again, then?'

'Next Sunday.' He felt a spark of something pure and bright as he admitted it. It cut through the murkiness he'd been drowning in since stepping through the white door. 'We're going to have another hour together.'

'Another hour,' Peggy mused. 'Must be serious, then.'

'It feels good,' Ash said simply.

Peggy looked at him, and the dread started to creep in. The mug felt unsafe in his sweaty grip. 'Are you going in, then?' she asked gently.

'In a minute.' His voice came out gravelly. It was the fourth week, and so far he hadn't made it beyond reception, despite psyching himself up. Last week he'd told himself it was because of what had happened with Braden and Roger, Jess and the stolen watch. This week, he had zero excuses.

'Take your time.' Peggy patted his knee, then got up. 'You have all the time in the world.' She told him she'd be back, then walked away down the corridor.

Ash stayed seated, clutching his mug like a lifeline, the heat of the coffee spreading through the porcelain and into his hands. The problem was, they both knew that he didn't have all the time in the world. In fact, he didn't think he had much time at all, and every moment he sat here was another moment that slipped away, where he wasn't facing down his past or embracing his future. He was stuck in limbo, dealing with absolutely nothing at all.

Chapter Eight

Jess spent the whole of Monday thinking about what Ash had said about people being at the heart of the market. Ash, who was an occupational psychologist, whose business it was to get inside other people's heads. His work days consisted of looking at employees' behaviour and trying to get the best productivity out of them while also giving them maximum job satisfaction and support (she'd looked it up, obviously). What did he think of her distrust of ornamental hares and her Jekyll-and-Hyde side project, where she enjoyed creating the mean quotes as much as the uplifting ones?

He smiled easily, laughed readily, and his eyes could, she thought idly while tidying the shop's stock of coloured tissue paper, convey an entire essay's worth of emotions. But there were also moments when he'd brought down the shutters, kept everything inside, his jaw tight. Already, she couldn't wait to see him again, to find that place right in the centre, the part of Ash she didn't think he showed to many people.

What would he think of what she was doing now? Her attempt to let go of her reservations about Lola's music video and allow her personal and work lives to collide? She wondered if he'd think she was brave, or if he'd think she was too sensitive for even worrying about it.

The Tuesday version of the market was a lot quieter than at the weekends, and was infused with a calm that Jess usually only found in the early mornings, when she opened up the shop. The smell of fresh coffee won out over exhaust fumes, and a bell was ringing somewhere, over and over, as if it had got stuck at its tipping point.

'I don't recognise any of these people,' Lola whispered as they edged up the side of the market, peering at the stallholders.

'You don't get the same traders during the week,' Jess explained. 'Some days have a specific focus like antiques or artwork, other people are full time, some just have a stall for one or two days. You can get some shots this morning, which will be easier while it's quiet, then we can bite the bullet and come back at the weekend, give your video the full market atmosphere, while also pissing off a large number of tourists.'

'They won't be pissed off,' Lola said. 'They'll all want to be *in* my video. I already have fifteen thousand followers on TikTok, just from some practice scales and bowing sessions. Think how many more I'll get posting a full-length track that's been professionally edited.'

'Professionally edited?' Jess waved at Susie, who was here full time with her Better Babies stall, and was currently eating what looked like a Pot Noodle for breakfast.

'You're filming, Malik's editing – doing all the cutting and splicing and whatnot.'

'Isn't TikTok meant to be more raw? All on-the-fly, in-the-moment sort of stuff? Authentic snapshots of real life?'

'That's what everyone *says*,' Lola told her with a huff, 'but think how many hours of practice those dancers must put in to get their moves in sync, how many takes they do. Most of the big hitters have been edited to death.'

'Fair enough. Let's come back to Susie in a bit. Why not . . .' Jess turned in a slow circle, wondering which of the vendors would be an easy introduction for Lola and her plans. 'Let's go and see Enzo.'

'He's a jewellery maker, right? Portuguese? He has all that intricate gold stuff on his stall?'

'It's filigree.' Jess led the way, ducking around a trader she thought was called Perry, who was in the process of shaking out his blankets before hanging them along the back of his stall. 'It's so beautiful, and all made by his wife Carolina. Although . . .' She frowned. Hadn't she overheard someone, possibly Kirsty, saying that Carolina had been unwell?

Enzo looked up as they approached, his warm smile lighting his dark eyes. Jess noticed that the delicate gold necklaces, earrings and bracelets were laid out sparingly on the white cloth, each piece nestled on a purple velvet cushion. It made the items seem exclusive, but Jess had been working at the market for four years, Enzo had been there six, and this wasn't what his stall usually looked like.

'*Olá*, Enzo,' Jess said. 'How are you?'

'*Olá* Jess, and Jess's friend. Hello.'

'This is Lola,' Jess said. 'Lola, meet Enzo.'

They shook hands. Enzo was wearing a navy shirt and black dress trousers, everything about him smart and respectful. He was one of the kindest, most courteous people Jess knew, and she felt a flash of guilt. She had come here first because she knew he wouldn't turn Lola down.

'Nice to meet you, Enzo,' Lola said. 'Your jewellery is stunning.'

'Ah. Thank you.' He dipped his head. 'My wife, Carolina, she—'

'Is she OK?' Jess blurted. 'I heard that she . . . that maybe she wasn't well?'

70

Enzo's smile was sad. 'She has been diagnosed with rheumatoid arthritis. She is only forty-two, so it has been a shock.'

'I'm so sorry,' Jess said. 'How's she doing?'

'That sucks *so* much.' Lola sounded angry on their behalf.

'She has good days and bad,' Enzo said. 'She is on her second kind of medicine, because the first, it gave her a rash – a . . . reaction.'

'She was allergic?' Lola asked.

'Exactly.' Enzo nodded. 'This new one seems kinder so far. But now we have to wait, to see how she will respond, how she will feel about getting back to work. She hasn't been able to make pieces for a long time.'

Jess looked again at the sparsely furnished stall. 'Shit.'

'We are managing, but—'

'It's all going to be groovy, Enzo dude. Hey, Jess.'

'Hello, Spade,' Jess said.

Spade draped his arm around Enzo's shoulder in a move that was half-hug, half-headlock. 'What are you doing here on a Tuesday? Wendy got you tied permanently to this place now as her little helper? Or, let me guess, you've done it to yourself, but you're pretending you don't know anything about it.' He chuckled, and Jess decided to get the attention off herself.

'Spade, this is my friend Lola. Lola, meet Spade.'

He sang the first line of the Kinks' song. 'Nice to meet you, *Lola*.' He held out his free hand, and she laughed and shook it.

'You too,' she said. 'You look . . . familiar?'

Spade tipped his top hat towards her. Beneath that he had a cloud of tangled curls, an even split between dark brown and grey, and was wearing faded jeans, a T-shirt that said *Crush the patriarchy*, and a navy blazer with sequinned lapels. A silver cross dangled from one ear, completing the aging rockstar look – a look that was entirely justified because that was exactly what he was. 'House of Cards?' he said.

Lola frowned, looking to Jess for explanation.

'House of Cards was his band,' Jess told her. 'They split up in the Nineties, but it still has a cult following.'

'Do you sell memorabilia, then?' Lola asked.

'Ah no.' Spade chuckled. 'I'm one of the market ghouls. Don't work here, but come for the intrigue – the entertainment. There's more of us than you think.'

Jess had never heard him refer to himself that way, but the phrase sent her mind skittering to Felicity, browsing the shop on a weekly basis, and then Ash, killing time here every Sunday. *Lost souls,* she thought, then pushed the idea away.

'Whatcha got there?' Spade pointed at Lola's violin case. 'Little Stradivarius?'

'This is Cecil.' Lola stood up straighter.

'Sweet. Fiddling's a proper talent.'

'I'm here to shoot a music video, actually,' Lola said. 'Jess is introducing me to everyone, getting you all onside so I can strut my stuff down the aisles without hundreds of complaints. The market's got such a great atmosphere – it's going to be the perfect backdrop.'

Spade rocked back on his heels, eyebrows raised. 'Shoot crew on their way?'

Jess and Lola exchanged a glance. 'I'm the shoot crew.' Jess held up her phone. 'We're doing it on TikTok.'

'It's the modern way,' Spade said. 'Need any help?'

'Oh *yes!*' Lola clapped her hands. 'An *actual* rock star? Yes please!'

Spade grinned. 'I'm a world-class consultant. Mostly on living the high life, but music at a push. What do you need?'

'Spade is an excellent friend,' Enzo said. 'He will help you, I am sure. And of course, please, I am happy to be in the background of your filming. I will do what I can.'

'Thank you, Enzo.' Jess squeezed his arm. 'That's so kind of you. And I'm sure it wouldn't hurt to get a couple of shots of your jewellery.' Could they help him, somehow? Lola was hoping this video would go viral, and with the market being featured, could it serve a dual purpose?

'What's your song?' Spade asked.

'It's a piece I've written,' Lola told him. 'Modern vibes. More *Two Cellos* than traditionally classical. It's the first time I've done this, though, so I'm just hoping that . . .' She cleared her throat, and for the first time in months, Jess sensed her friend's uncertainty.

'What is it?' she asked.

'Nothing. I just . . . Spade?' Lola said. 'Do you still play, ever?'

'The guitar?' He scratched his neck. 'Only about an hour a day, these days, and I've not played for an audience for a while, but you've got to keep your fingers flexible, keep up with the noodling.'

'An hour a *day?*' Lola sounded breathless. 'So would you . . . I mean, if I worked on the piece, do you think—?'

Lola's excitement was a physical thing, and Jess bit back a laugh. 'Aren't you trying to showcase your own talent?' she asked.

'But think of the views,' Lola said, spinning to face her. 'Me, alongside House of Cards' lead guitarist. Just imagine!'

'You want me to be in your video?' Spade asked. 'Your Cecil, my Axe?'

'Your *what?*' Jess said.

'He means my violin and his guitar.' Lola exhaled. 'I know it's asking a lot, and that I'm an amateur and I don't have a shoot crew or a director, and that this is all very sudden, but—'

'Nah, dude,' Spade waved her away. 'It sounds cool. Kooky. I've not played with a fiddle for twenty years, but it could really work. I'll limber up a bit, dust off the old skills.'

'Oh my God!' Lola was almost vibrating. 'Thank you. Thank you!' She hugged him, almost knocking his hat off in her excitement. Then she hugged Enzo, who let out a surprised chuckle, then she hugged Jess. 'OK, mission aborted. I need to go home and work on my piece, turn it into a duet. This is going to be *amazing!*'

'Here.' Spade reached inside his jacket and pulled out, of all things, a business card 'Want any input on the composition, just give me a shout.'

Lola held the card to her chest as if it was a shimmering diamond. 'I will,' she squeaked. 'I'll be in touch.'

They said their goodbyes, and Lola dragged Jess to the opposite side of the market. 'You didn't tell me you had a *rock legend* here!'

Jess laughed. 'Had you even heard of him, or House of Cards, five minutes ago?'

'That's not the point. I'm going to go home and look them up on YouTube. And anyway, he is *so* cool. I'm levelling up, Jess – I see viral TikToks in our future.'

'That would be incredible,' Jess conceded. 'And Spade's a good guy, even if he is a market ghoul. So filming's being delayed?' She tried not to sound too relieved.

'Until I've changed my composition,' Lola said. 'Want to come and watch old House of Card gigs with me?'

'As tempting as that sounds, I have a couple of errands to run.' She also needed to grab hold of the idea that had fluttered into her head while they were talking to Spade. 'I want to pop in and see Wendy, too.'

'Going into No Vase Like Home on your day off?' Lola raised an eyebrow. 'What a surprise.'

'Hey. I wouldn't even *be* here today if it wasn't for you.'

'Fine,' Lola said. Then a slow, catlike smile spread across her face. 'I am *so* glad we came when we did. This is going to be epic, Jessica Peacock.'

'It was always going to be,' Jess said, 'with you at the helm.'

'Next Thursday,' were the words that greeted Jess when she walked into the shop two minutes later. Felicity was standing next to the vase of unwanted rainbow twigs, wearing a coral-coloured dress and flat sandals, looking like she had just come from a garden party at Buckingham Palace.

'Hi, Felicity.' Jess looked past her, but couldn't see Wendy. 'How are you?'

'Very well, thank you. Next Thursday, if that's all right with you?'

'If – uh, if what's all right?'

'The water feature,' Felicity said. 'You're going to bring it to my house.' She was wringing her hands, her face serene but her body full of nervous energy.

'Of course,' Jess said. 'I'm working next Thursday, so as long as Wendy lets me escape for half an hour, then I'll carry it round. Except . . .' She was here right now, and by helping Felicity on her day off she wouldn't be leaving her boss alone in the shop. 'We could do it today, if you fancied?'

The older woman shook her head. 'It's not convenient.

I'm not . . . I need to prepare everything. Make sure the garden is ready.'

Jess held back a smile. She could tell Felicity was very particular about things, so this need to plan everything in advance didn't surprise her. It reminded her a little of her mum.

Edie Peacock, who was a lot younger and more vivacious than her old-fashioned name suggested, collected sunflowers: ceramic sunflowers attached to cutesy-looking milkmaids on plinths; glass paperweights with sunflower designs in the bottom; sunflower mugs and jugs and cushions; sunflower bedding. When Jess was growing up, their house had been a canvas for the large yellow blooms with chocolate-coloured middles. In summer, vases of real ones adorned the living room and kitchen, their oversized heads drooping after a few days. But Edie treated every one, real or designed, as if it was precious, finding it the perfect space in her home.

Sometimes, Jess had felt that her mum cared more about the sunflowers than she did about her: as if she'd collected her too, but then discovered she wasn't quite bright enough, didn't fit snugly into her collection. For years, she had thought that she was imagining it, that she had imposed that attitude on Edie and Graham because she hadn't been wanted, hadn't belonged anywhere, before them. Because the truth was, they had treated her like their own daughter from the moment she came to live with them, all the way up until that summer afternoon two years ago when she'd overheard Edie talking to their neighbour, Celine. Right up until that moment, she had thought—

'What time works for you?' Felicity prompted, bringing Jess out of her daydream.

'How about eleven?' Jess said.

'Eleven o'clock would be marvellous.'

76

As Felicity left, she gave her favourite mirror a longing glance, and Jess resisted the urge to ask her outright: if she loved it so much, then why didn't she just buy it? Why distract herself with water features?

'Jess!' Wendy emerged from the storeroom, the cordless landline in her hand. 'I was ordering more statuettes from Harbour's. What are you doing here?'

'Harbour's? Not more hares. I'm starting to think you actually hate me.'

Wendy grinned. 'They've got a new line of owls. Much less sinister.'

'Owls are not entirely *un*-sinister,' Jess pointed out.

'I think you're averse to the countryside, confused by its bucolic charms. If I brought in statues of scrawny city foxes, rats and pigeons, you'd be perfectly comfortable.'

'Not pigeons,' Jess said, feeling defensive on Ash's behalf.

'Give the owls a chance, eh? Why are you here on your day off, anyway?'

'I was introducing Lola to some of the stallholders,' she admitted. 'She wants to film a music video here, and now she and Spade have met the whole thing is, predictably, snowballing.' She thought of Enzo, and his struggle to keep his business going while Carolina was ill. Would he even be able to pay for his stall next month?

'Lola and Spade together, eh?' Wendy tapped her lips. 'There's some confidence worth bottling right there.'

'Don't I know it. Anyway,' Jess sighed, 'no filming for me today, at least. I'm off the hook until Lola's rewritten her tune.'

Wendy gave her a knowing look. 'Enjoying your time in the limelight?'

'I'm going to be *behind* the camera. That's what filming is.'

77

'All right smarty pants. Sort everything out with Felicity?'

'I'm taking the water feature to hers next Thursday, which is weirdly specific.'

'She's a weirdly specific sort of person.'

'Agreed. I just popped in to see how you were doing, anyway.'

'I'm surviving, just about.' Wendy gave her a gleeful grin. 'Something else on your mind?'

Jess bit her lip. 'Not really.' She hadn't really had an errand to run, she just felt as if coming into the market *without* visiting the shop would be a betrayal of some kind. 'See you on Thursday.' She stepped backwards through the doorway, nearly bumping into a couple who were walking past outside.

'Don't be too miserable away from the market,' Wendy called after her, in a tone that Jess chose not to analyse. Of course she had a life outside the market. Of *course* she did. It was inconsequential that she'd brought her best friend and her colleagues together, and that she'd struck up a coffee arrangement with a man she'd met here. Greenwich Market wasn't the centre of the entire world, and it certainly wasn't the centre of hers.

Chapter Nine

In only a few weeks, getting the Thames Clipper from Embankment down to Greenwich had become part of Ash's Sunday routine. It was a much better way to travel than the combination of tube and DLR, especially when the weather was good and he could make the journey in the fresh air. Today, the sun was bright and – thank God – there was a brisk breeze, turning the surface of the river into ripples of light and shade, chilling the back of his neck as he stood on the deck, holding the thing he'd brought tightly against his chest.

The boat was quiet, the majority of passengers travelling in the opposite direction in the mornings, up towards Central London rather than away from it, but there was a young family sitting in the front row of plastic seats, a little girl with pigtails watching him with curiosity. He ran a hand through his hair self-consciously, then realised what she was interested in – it was what he had brought for his hour with Jess.

She'd given him the idea during their first coffee, and then last Sunday – well, it had felt chaotic, with him turning up late, cobbling together a plan to go up to the Meridian Line. But somehow, it had worked out. He'd made her laugh, she'd made *him* laugh – and for an hour, his tension had gone. He had felt as if he was exactly where he was supposed to be, and he wanted more of it.

'Hello,' the little girl said to him.

'Hello,' he replied. He made eye contact with her parents, and they exchanged smiles, then Ash went back to staring at the water. They had passed the main landmarks now, the Tower of London and Tower Bridge, the Gherkin and the Shard, which he'd forced Jess to point out to him last weekend, and now the banks changed, the buildings becoming shorter, more domestic and industrial, London's grand epicentre behind them.

The sun glinted off the water, and there was the occasional waft of something deep and rotten on the breeze, but mostly the air was fresh, letting him breathe more deeply. He pictured Jess with her dark, wavy hair brushing her shoulders, the way she kept her smile mostly guarded, but sometimes it burst out of her unexpectedly; how, when she bunched her cheeks, it changed the shape of the freckle constellations below her eyes.

He had never imagined, when he'd first gone to Greenwich, following the directions in the email, that he'd find something like this. After that first week, when he'd left far too much time, adamant that he wouldn't be late on his first day, he'd stepped into the market – somewhere so much brighter than he was feeling – and let himself get caught up in it.

It was easy, the following weekend, to leave the same amount of time, to give himself that space before walking up to the white front door and all that lay beyond it. And then the third Sunday – the shout from Roger, Braden running through the market. Ash had chased him without thinking, then stood there, feeling like a fool without a plan. But then he'd noticed her standing there and, even though seeing a beautiful woman in that situation should have made him feel worse, should have heightened his embarrassment, somehow it had been the opposite. It was almost as if he'd been waiting for something more, biding his time at the market until it came along, and then Jess had appeared, and *she* was that more. He couldn't imagine ever not wanting more of her.

'I like your kite.' The little girl with pigtails pointed at it, and Ash was brought out of his reverie.

He grinned. It was a traditional, diamond-shaped kite with brightly coloured panels in pink, yellow, green and purple, the ribboned-tail a rainbow of neat bows. 'Thank you,' he said. 'I'm going to fly it on Blackheath.'

'We're going to the big ship,' the girl said. 'Can you fly kites there?'

'I don't think so,' Ash said carefully. 'But you can pretend you're sailing out in the middle of the ocean, surrounded by sharks and whales and giant squid.' He shot a glance at her parents, but they didn't seem alarmed by the picture he was painting. 'You can pretend you're a pirate.'

'Pirates don't have kites?' She sounded incredulous, as if that was the most ridiculous oversight.

Ash pretended to think for a moment, tapping his finger against his chin. 'You know what?'

The little girl nodded, her eyes never leaving his.

'I think they'd be worried about being dragged off the ship. One strong gust, and then . . .' He lifted the kite, unfurled it slightly and staggered towards the edge of the deck, as if the wind was going to pull him overboard.

The little girl giggled, wriggling in her chair.

'They wouldn't want that to happen.' The girl's mum wrapped an arm around her shoulder. 'Maybe kites and pirates don't mix.'

'Once they're back on land, though.' Ash moved back to the middle of the deck in case there *was* a sudden gust. 'Kite tournaments all the way, I bet.' He could see, on the bank, the familiar glass dome of the entrance to Greenwich's foot tunnel, the mast of the family's destination reaching up into a blue sky dotted with puffball clouds. 'Have a great day,' he said.

'Have fun with the kite,' the girl's mum replied, giving him a warm smile.

He folded it back up as best he could, tucked it half inside his jacket and made his way to the back of the boat.

The market was busier than he'd ever seen it, with people crushed into every aisle, and Ash held the kite tight to his chest, feeling more ridiculous with every step. This was a child's activity. He wouldn't be surprised if Jess shook her head, said they should get a coffee and a burger instead or – even worse – that they should leave it this week, perhaps not bother next time either. The thought made the band tighten around his chest, and he picked up his pace as much as he could.

He bought two coffees, and could feel the stare of the woman who'd served him as he tried to work out how best to hold them, how to pin the kite to his chest with his upper arm. To squash the embarrassment, he grinned up at her and said, 'I might be being a bit ambitious. How did Mr Poppins manage it?'

'I don't think Mr Poppins bought coffee for everyone.'

'Right,' Ash said. 'Well, first time for everything, I guess.'

'Good luck!' she called after him, as he tried to negotiate the packed market with the addition of hot coffee.

No Vase Like Home was busy with people browsing, picking up the hares that Jess seemed to hate so much, a couple of customers waiting to be served at the counter. Ash looked over their heads, but he could only see Jess's boss, Wendy, her reddish-brown hair cascading over her shoulders. He stood in a corner, felt the press of cushions at his back, and tried to get his pulse to settle.

While Wendy served, Ash watched the doorway behind the counter, waiting for Jess to step out of it. The coffees were starting to burn his palms, but he didn't dare put them down in case he spilled them on something precious.

'Ash?' He looked up. Wendy was peering at him over the head of the woman she was serving.

'Hey,' he said.

'She's not here. She's . . .' Her attention was drawn back to her customer. 'Oh no,' he heard her say. 'I can wrap it for you, so . . .'

'Right,' he said to himself, disappointment settling in his stomach. He thought she'd had fun last week, amidst the chaos of the park. 'Thanks,' he called as he left the shop. He thought he heard Wendy say something else, probably some kind of apology, but she was busy, and he didn't want to get in the way any more than he had already.

He chose the least busy aisle and walked slowly, looking at the stalls, feeling like an idiot with two coffees to drink and a redundant kite. How was he going to fill the hour without Jess? Before he had met her, he'd found it easy. Browsing, chatting to the stallholders. Now, his mind felt empty, his ability to joke and laugh robbed by disappointment. He'd only been in her company for two hours, and already a part of him had decided spending time with her was essential to him. How long would it take him to unlearn that? To face what came next without her?

'If I can help you with anything, please just ask.'

Ash looked up. He'd stopped in front of a jewellery stall, the sparse pieces beautiful and intricate. The vendor stood behind the table, watching him with kind brown eyes.

'Thanks,' he said. 'I'll let you know.'

'Best jewellery in all of London.' The man who'd sidled up to him was wearing a shimmery grey jacket over a Mr. Men T-shirt, a red fedora perched on top of a wild mane of curls. 'Like your kite, dude.'

'Thanks,' Ash said again, and relaxed a fraction.

'Can I see?' The man tipped his hat back and held his hands out. 'I'll take the coffees.'

'You want to see my kite?'

'Not been up close and personal with one of these in years. I'm Spade, by the way. One of the market ghouls.'

'A ghoul?' Ash laughed, confused, but he was already handing over the coffees, unfurling the kite from where he'd had it tucked under his arm. Perhaps he'd be able to hang out here after all, and maybe he'd even forget about Jess for upwards of thirty seconds at a time. Maybe, he thought, as he untangled the ribboned tail, and Spade whistled in a way that he didn't think was ironic, there was hope for him yet.

Chapter Ten

Susie had had a disaster, followed swiftly by a meltdown, and Jess was trying to sort it out.

A teenager had gone past her stall on a skateboard, hit an uneven patch of floor, and let go of their coconut-and-lime smoothie, which had upended and landed in a giant, creamy splat all over her Better Babies stall. The girl had been apologetic, but Susie had turned up at No Vase Like Home with tears in her eyes. *I'm sure Jess can help*, Wendy had soothed, and Jess had glanced at all the clocks, seen it was only half an hour until Ash was due, and tried not to groan out loud.

She'd made a mad dash to the nearest hair salon, borrowed one of their water sprays and a hairdryer, and for the last forty minutes had been cleaning and then drying the cuddly toys, changing bags and soft blankets until she was overheated, Susie was smiling serenely, and the fluffy items looked as if they'd been through a round of electric-shock therapy. By the time she'd finished it was ten past twelve and panic had set in.

'Thank you *so* much,' Susie cooed. 'Can I buy—'

'I have to run,' Jess said. 'I need to get these back to the salon, and then . . .' She swallowed. 'And then I've got lunch, so—'

'Another time?'

'Another time,' Jess agreed, though she didn't know what, exactly, she was agreeing to. She pushed through the tourists, gritting her teeth – why was it so *busy* today? – and gave the salon back their things, thanked them profusely, and almost got a faceful of hairspray as she passed by the chair closest to the door on her way out.

By the time she got back to No Vase Like Home, she was flustered and frantic, and the look Wendy gave her did nothing to improve her mood.

'I tried to tell him you wouldn't be long, but it was so busy in here.' They both looked around the empty shop. There were signs of a rush: items left haphazardly on shelves, a blanket pulled out and dumped in a heap. Someone had discarded a crumpled paper bag in the sparkly twigs by the door, but Jess didn't care about that now.

'He just left?' He hadn't waited for her.

Wendy looked apologetic. 'I only managed to tell him you weren't here. I didn't have a chance to explain why.'

Jess bit her lip. She should go and get a muffin, try to forget about him. Clearly, it was a one-time – two-time – thing. But then . . . 'He might still be in the market.'

'You'd better go and find him then,' Wendy said softly.

Jess grabbed her bag and raced out of the shop.

She didn't know where to go. She stood, floundering, hoping the answer would come to her. He wasn't trying on hats at Olga's stall, and she knew he wasn't in Susie's aisle because she'd just come from there. She couldn't see him down towards the food court, except it was all so *busy,* so how was she ever supposed to— She heard laughter, deep and rumbling, and her stomach flipped. That *had* to be Ash. She followed the sound, weaving between tourists and trying not to shove them out of the way, holding on to her last thread of patience. She rounded the corner, saw Spade's familiar red fedora and also—

'A kite?' A laugh bubbled out of her, and the kite, which had legs, was lowered to reveal Ash. His dark hair was untidy, his grey eyes wide with surprise. Her breath caught.

'Jess? I thought . . .' His expression softened. 'I thought you weren't here.'

'I had to help Susie at Better Babies,' she said. 'A smoothie disaster. It's all sorted now, but I'm . . . I'm sorry I wasn't there.'

'You still want to spend time together?'

She stood in front of him, with the beautiful, brightly coloured kite between them. 'If you do,' she said. 'Are we going to fly this?'

Ash's smile tipped into a grin. 'That was the plan.'

'It's nearly twenty past twelve.'

'We can have an hour from now.' His words came out in a rush. 'But we'll have to get going. Come on.' He held the kite out, and she took it. He picked up the two coffees that Spade had balanced on Enzo's stall.

'Hey, Enzo,' she said. 'Hi, Spade.'

'You have been busy then, Jess,' Enzo said.

'She's always busy.' Spade slung his arm around her shoulders, pulling her into his traditional half-headlock. 'Always helping someone out. She scowls about it, but she can't stop herself. Ash is your man, eh? I always trust a man with a kite.'

Jess burst out laughing, but her heart skipped at his words. 'What does that even *mean*, Spade? I'm sorry, but we have to go.' She extracted herself from his grip.

'Get going, you young things.' Spade shooed them away. 'Great to meet you, Ash.'

'You too,' Ash called over his shoulder.

'We're going to Blackheath?' Jess asked, once they could walk side by side. 'Can I fold this up?' She thought she'd already jabbed him in the arm with one of the kite's corners.

'Shit, of course,' Ash said. It looked like he was about to balance one coffee on top of the other so he could help.

Laughing, Jess turned away from him and folded the kite, then wound its tail up so it couldn't trip or stab anyone. They waited at the lights, the gusty wind pushing Jess's hair into her face as they dodged people on the narrow pavement, then walked through the gateway into Greenwich Park.

Jess's legs burned and her breaths shortened as they strode up the hill. They went past the observatory – too early for its ball drop today – then down the long, wide driveway, with parking spaces either side and trees framing the lawns that stretched away from them, leading to the bandstand and pond, the formal gardens.

'Did you buy this specially?' Jess asked, once the ground had evened out and her breathing had slowed.

'There aren't many places to fly a kite in Holborn,' Ash said.

'But you did when you were younger?'

He frowned. 'I mean, we must have done, once or twice. I don't really remember.'

'So if you're not doing this to show off your skills, then why did you bring it?'

Ash stopped suddenly, then turned to face her. A woman walking two sleek Dalmatians changed course, shooting them a glare over her shoulder. Ash didn't notice, and Jess ignored it. 'I have come here today with a brightly coloured kite, decked out with rainbow bows and ribbons, and you think I brought it so I could look cool in front of you?'

Jess laughed even as she shrugged. 'OK. Maybe not.'

'I made a friend on the boat,' he said, as they started walking again. 'She had pigtails and red patent shoes. I think she was five.'

Jess's cheeks hurt from smiling. 'OK,' she said again.

'I bought this because I thought it would be fun,' he told her. 'But if we get onto the heath and there's some guy with a stunt kite, wearing proper sports gloves and mirrored sunglasses, you bet I'm going to try and compete with him. Get our kite to fly higher than his.'

'Oh God,' Jess said. 'I really hope there's a professional kite-flyer now. I would *love* to see that!'

Ash made a disgruntled noise, but when Jess glanced at him, he was smiling.

There were two other kites dancing in the sky above the heath, but neither looked like stunt kites. One was shaped like an octopus, with huge eyes and tentacles wiggling in the wind, and the other was a diamond like theirs, its red and blue design distinctly patriotic. They found a spot close to the park gates, the spire of Blackheath Church hazy in the distance, a cluster of rooks pecking through the grass nearby.

'Are you going to challenge him?' Jess pointed at the small boy in a blue parka, taking the reins of the octopus.

'It wouldn't be fair,' Ash said. 'He's too young to be gifted the arrogance of flying against us. I'm not sure we're even going to get this thing in the air.'

'Of course we are,' Jess said as she unfolded it. Even this low to the ground, the wind was whipping the tail into a fervour.

'Here,' Ash said. 'Let's swap. Americano.'

He passed Jess the cup, and she was surprised that there was no telltale leakage darkening the stiff cardboard. 'Is this a skill of yours?' She handed him the kite once he'd put his own cup on the grass. 'Holding onto coffee in unstable situations?'

He unwound the kite's string, gripping the handle firmly as he gave it more slack. 'Maybe it is,' he said. 'I've never monitored my ability to not spill coffee, but I'm as surprised as you that we haven't lost more. Now, I guess this is what we're supposed to be doing?' The kite was trailing along the ground, catching in the grass.

'Didn't you look it up?' Jess was laughing again. 'I think I should hold the kite until enough of the string's unravelled, then . . . throw it up, see if the wind catches it?'

'OK,' Ash said, 'that sounds good.'

Jess put her cup next to his and went to rescue the kite. She held it in both hands, and walked backwards while Ash unspooled the string. She could feel the wind tugging at the thin fabric in a hopeful sort of way.

'Now?' Ash called.

'I'll throw it up?'

'Yes! Go!'

She braced her legs wide and threw the kite into the air. It shimmied for a second then plummeted back to the ground. 'Ouch,' Jess said, on the kite's behalf.

'Never mind,' Ash shouted. 'We'll try again. I'm not letting Mary Poppins get the better of us!'

'No way!' Jess agreed, fighting to make her voice carry above the wind. 'Let's do this!'

They tried again and again, Ash letting out more string, Jess waiting until she felt a tug of wind, then throwing the kite into the air. Sometimes it went up a few feet, then came crashing back down. Sometimes it didn't even catch the wind, sinking sadly to the grass without even trying. A couple of times it swerved towards Jess and she had to jump out of the way.

By the time Ash came over to her, she was sweaty and giggling, and the kite was lying limply on the ground.

Ash flopped into the grass next to the forlorn toy, his breaths staccato. 'This is harder than it looks,' he said, as Jess sat next to him. 'How are those kids doing it?'

She looked over at the young family with the octopus kite, their heads angled upwards, staring at their soaring sea creature. 'Maybe they just *believe* they can do it?'

'I think *we* can do it,' Ash said, handing her her coffee. 'It's probably cold by now.

'It doesn't matter.' Jess took it gratefully. 'A break, then we'll try again in a minute?'

'Definitely. I'm not giving up.'

'It's a good superpower to have,' Jess said, after a minute.

'Flying a kite?' Ash asked. 'Surely flying *like* a kite is better.'

'No, the ability to not lose coffee. We came all the way from the market, up the hill, through the park, and my cup's still full. It's not life-changing, but it's still impressive.'

Ash stretched his legs out on the grass. 'Maybe everyone has a superpower, but most of us have small ones, like not spilling coffee, always arriving at the bus stop just as the bus turns up, being able to tie the perfect tie. Maybe it's only a few, very select people who get the world-saving superpowers, like flying and X-ray vision.'

Jess grinned. 'Aren't these small superpowers you're talking about just skills?'

Ash shook his head. 'Turning up at the bus stop just as the bus pulls up isn't something you can learn. I'm not talking about memorising the timetable, I mean you get there at the perfect time even when it's late. And we dragged ourselves all the way up this hill, out here, and *you* were the one who pointed out that I've not lost you any coffee. Under the circumstances, it seems beyond the bounds of normal human skill.'

'So it's a mini-superpower?'

'Yes! Or . . . how about a subtle superpower?'

'I like that,' Jess said. 'A subtle superpower.'

'What would yours be?' Ash turned to face her, his knee unapologetically nudging hers where she was sitting cross-legged on the grass.

'My subtle superpower?' Jess asked, stalling for time.

'What small but incredible thing are you able to do, to improve your life or other people's?'

She had thought that it was to bother nobody, to exist quietly by herself, but that hadn't been working out for her too well recently.

'Do you know all the lyrics to a song after you've only heard it a couple of times?' Ash suggested. 'Can you tell what time it is without looking at a watch? I had a teacher who could do that; she instinctively knew what time it was, down to the minute. She wowed us all.'

'*Wowed* you?' Jess asked. 'With being able to tell the time?'

'Wowed the nerdy kids,' Ash corrected with a sheepish smile. 'Most of my fellow pupils didn't give a shit, but I thought it was cool.'

'Are you sure she wasn't tricking you?'

'She used to do it in the playground, with her hands behind her back.'

'And there were no clock towers nearby? No classroom window she could see into that you, as small, impressionable children, didn't notice?'

'I don't think . . .' Ash frowned. 'You're about to turn my whole world on its head.'

'Let's forget about it,' she said. 'It was her subtle superpower, not a trick.'

Ash stared at her with a hurt expression.

Jess couldn't help grinning. 'Maybe my superpower is to break hearts, dash hopes, crush dreams?'

'That's not a superpower. And it's not something you would do.'

'I'm not sure you know me well enough to decide that,' Jess said, and the teasing, jovial atmosphere evaporated.

Ash looked at her a beat longer, and Jess turned away, gazing at the expanse of the heath. There were lines of cars queuing like shiny ants on the roads that cut through the space, and the couple with the blue and red kite were packing up, folding their toy into a swanky-looking carrying case.

'OK,' Jess said, desperate to recapture the lightness Ash brought with him. 'Let's do quickfire questions. What's your favourite holiday destination?'

'Seattle, no question,' he said. 'Yours?'

'Aldeburgh,' she replied, even though her trips to the Greek Islands growing up had been more exotic.

'In *Suffolk*?'

'I like the bleak East Anglian coast. And this is quickfire: no time to dwell or delve. Your favourite TV show.'

'*Friends*,' Ash said, his smile widening when Jess opened her mouth, desperate to know more, but was banjaxed by her own rule. 'Yours?'

'*Antiques Roadshow*,' she admitted. 'When they get those people who've paid twenty pence for something at a jumble sale, and it turns out to be worth fifty thousand.'

'Deeply satisfying,' Ash agreed. 'Right, my turn. Favourite food?'

'Japanese gyozas,' Jess said. There was a stall in the market that she visited far too often on her way home. 'Yours?'

'It depends if we're doing a single item or a whole meal. If it's a meal then a Sunday roast with beef, Yorkshire puddings, thick gravy and golden roast potatoes. If it's a single item, then Yorkshire puddings.'

'All on their own?' Jess laughed.

'If they're crispy, they need no embellishments.'

'You don't have a hint of a Yorkshire accent, but maybe you lost it working with all those posh bankers. Are you a secret northerner?'

'I'm actually half Italian,' Ash said.

'Oooh.' Jess used his admission as an excuse to stare at him. His brown hair was glossy, but not as dark as hers, and his grey eyes were undoubtedly striking, but even though his skin looked as though it would tan easily, she wasn't sure she would have picked Italian heritage for him. But then, she wasn't an expert, by any means: she didn't know much about her own background, had found it too painful to go looking for more after that first, horrible revelation. Edie and Graeme had both been brought up in southeast London, so that was how she thought of herself, too. 'On your dad's side, or your mum's?' she asked him.

'Dad's.' He ran a hand from the top of his head, down over his neck. 'But I got more of Mum's features. My dad didn't get much of a look-in.' His smile was tight and quick, gone in a second. 'What about you?'

Jess tensed automatically. 'I'm adopted,' she told him. 'I don't know a whole lot about my birth parents.' She sipped her tepid Americano.

'Have you . . . do you want to look for them? Find out more?'

'I did, once,' she said, the memory tightening her throat. She swallowed. 'I haven't really got that far.' She didn't want to tell Ash the whole sorry story – not now.

'Do you feel part of a family, though?' Ash asked. 'With your adopted parents?'

'Yeah, I guess.'

'A glowing endorsement,' Ash said, but he wasn't laughing. His gaze was sharper than it had been a moment ago. 'It must be tough, growing up like that. I mean – if you're happy, then they're as real as any family could be. But still, I know that my dad is from a village on the Amalfi coast, just outside Positano, and that my mum grew up an only child in Stratford-upon-Avon. I can't imagine not having those pieces of my history.'

'It's not so bad,' Jess said. 'You can invent your own history, if you want to: pretend you're the daughter of film stars whose affair was secret and then scandalous, who couldn't possibly keep you. Or that you were left on a church doorstep in a snowstorm, after your mum had an affair with the lord of the local manor. Maybe I'll discover that I'm the progeny of a world-class opera singer, and that with some coaching I could have an incredible voice.'

'You think that's likely?' Ash asked. 'Because I am here for having a famous opera-singing friend. I'd want VIP tickets to all your concerts.'

'If karaoke nights with my friend Lola are anything to go by, that might not be my origin story.'

'Shame,' Ash said. 'And I'm sorry.'

'What for?'

'Despite your insistence that it gives you freedom, I don't think being adopted can be all sweetness and light. All families have their issues – believe me, I know.' His laugh sounded

95

slightly bitter. 'But adoption, I always thought it must add another layer of complication, of . . . rough edges, to the family dynamic.'

'Like when people put crushed biscuit in tiramisu?'

'Exactly like that. Who puts biscuit in tiramisu?'

'Do you have a nonna who makes it for you? I bet proper Italian tiramisu is very different to what you get in Prezzo.'

'My nonna died when I was little,' Ash said. 'I have had tiramisu in Italy, though. A long time ago.' Jess watched him swallow, and then, a second later, he was on his feet, holding out his hands to her. 'Come on, we haven't got much time left, and I'm determined to get this kite in the air.'

Jess let him pull her to her feet, and this time she took the handle, making sure there were no kinks in the string as Ash walked backwards, holding the kite in both hands, its ribboned tail trying to wrap around his long legs. Jess didn't blame it.

They tried again, Ash thrusting the kite into the air when there was a strong gust of wind, then darting out of the way when it came slicing back down, its sharp edges aiming for his head. He sighed at it, his hands on his hips, as if he was a forlorn parent who had been let down. Jess started laughing again, and this time she found it hard to stop, every gesture or expression Ash made setting her off again. By the time they were on their fourth try, she was struggling to focus, holding the handle limply, her gaze fixed firmly on him, so when the kite tugged and then lifted, she almost let go. She had to use both hands to get it under control, staring as the bright diamond soared up into the sky.

'Yes!' Ash punched the air and raced towards her, glancing back every few seconds to check it was still flying. 'You did it!'

'*We* did it,' Jess said. He stood next to her, and they gazed up at their achievement, the ribbons dancing happily against the blue.

'Here.' Jess's heart was in her throat as she took Ash's right hand – the one furthest from her – and placed it over hers on the handle. It felt clichéd, like something out of a film, and it made his position awkward, unless he came to stand behind her, which was what he did.

'This OK?' he asked gently, bringing his left hand round her too, until she was cradled in his arms, her back pressed to his front, while they both held onto the kite's handle. She tipped her head up, nestling against his chest. He smelled like coffee and chocolate, something dark and spicy underneath.

'Yeah.' It came out scratchy. She could feel her limbs softening, while everything inside her tightened, tingled, at the sensation of Ash's strong body around hers, sheltering her from the wind. 'Yeah, this is good.'

They watched the kite in silence for a few moments, then Ash said, 'Can I have another one of your quotes?'

Jess inhaled. 'You're putting me on the spot. It usually takes me ages to come up with them.' She didn't tell him that her brain was entirely scrambled from being so close to him, even though she'd orchestrated it.

'OK,' he murmured, his breath warm against her head. Jess stared at his feet. He was wearing a pair of battered blue Vans, and she wondered how long he'd had them, where they'd been. To Italy, perhaps? Up and down the river a few times, certainly. And to his next appointment, which she still knew nothing about. 'How about . . . Flying isn't as hard as it looks; just make sure a part of you stays tethered to the ground.'

Jess smiled. 'That's pretty good, considering you just came up with it.'

'Or . . . We all have superpowers, you just need to believe in yourself to discover what yours is.'

Jess sucked in a breath. She let go of the kite's handle, and turned in his arms. 'That one's *great*. Please let me have it? Let me use it in my shop?' She stared up at him, his jaw dusted with stubble, his grey eyes close to hers as he looked down at her, surprised. 'We'll seal the deal with this kiss.'

'What?' Ash swallowed. 'Jess—'

Before he could say anything else, she pressed her hands into his chest, leaned up and kissed him on the cheek, brushing her lips against his warm, slightly prickly skin. 'There,' she said, feeling bold and terrified all at once. 'It's mine now.'

'Really?' he whispered. His eyes had dropped to her mouth. 'You realise I almost let go of the kite?'

'I would have bought us another one,' Jess told him, and as Ash smiled down at her, some of the surprise leaving his face, she had to work very hard not to kiss him again, not to tuck herself against him and let his arms come properly around her, letting the kite fly off into the sky, no longer tethered to the ground. 'For next time.'

'Next time,' Ash echoed, as he started to pull the kite in, letting it down gently. It felt like a promise.

Chapter Eleven

'You look chipper,' Peggy said, when Ash walked through the pristine white door and into the airy reception room, five minutes after leaving Jess at the gates of the park, twenty minutes after he should have been here. The space smelled unusual, and he wrinkled his nose. 'Ah,' Peggy went on, 'Mrs McBride dropped a glass bottle of lavender pillow spray. I've dealt with the glass, but the lavender . . . we'll be lucky if all our visitors don't fall asleep.'

'It doesn't smell particularly soporific.' Ash took off his jacket and put the slightly bedraggled kite on a chair. 'It's more . . . suffocating.'

'Not a whole lot of difference between sleep and suffocation.' Peggy grinned when he gave her a shocked look. 'Coffee?'

'I'd love one.' This routine was so familiar now, the dread and shame creeping over him at his imminent, almost certain failure. He sat down and took out his phone, but he couldn't send Jess a message to thank her for their hour, to ask if he'd imagined that brief brush of her lips on his cheek, because they still hadn't exchanged numbers. Some further communication with her would have calmed his nerves, would have made this feel more possible.

'I went to the heath with Jess,' he called. There was nobody sitting behind the reception desk, but it always had a vase of fresh flowers on it. Today it was a bouquet of soft pink roses and carnations, their buds just beginning to open. It made him think of the cherry blossom on the trees in Greenwich Park.

'I didn't miss the kite,' Peggy called back. 'So that's how you're wooing her, eh?'

Ash smiled. 'I'm not wooing her,' he said, which was partly true. 'We've just been having coffee together. I thought kite-flying would be fun.'

'You could woo someone with your eyes closed.' Peggy's scoff carried from the kitchen. 'Do you remember Miss Dennison from last week? She was wearing a purple jumpsuit.'

'She turned up not long before I left?'

'That's right.' Peggy brought him a mug brimming with frothy coffee and a packet of chocolate digestives. 'When you'd gone, she asked if you were a hired actor.'

'An *actor*? What role was I supposed to be playing?'

Peggy put the mug and biscuits on the coffee table. 'I think her exact words were . . . *Surely that gorgeous hunk of a man was here as a distraction? He took my mind off everything.*'

Ash exhaled. 'Where's my actor, then? My distraction?' He hadn't meant to sound so bitter.

'I'm here, and I'm not acting,' Peggy assured him. 'Besides, she only said that because you didn't go through: just talked to me for a bit, then left. Are you doing that again today?'

'Not today,' Ash said firmly. 'I'm going in.'

'What's changed?' Peggy hadn't sat down, and he assumed she was anticipating being called away.

'Nothing really,' he said. 'I had a good time with Jess. *She* took my mind off everything for a while. And she made me see that . . .' He thought of what she'd said about being adopted, and the sense he got that she felt as if she didn't really belong.

'She reminded me that things could be worse. That all this . . .' he gestured around him, 'that I'm lucky, in lots of ways.'

'To have somewhere like this to come to?'

Ash nodded. 'That he's here, being looked after. That I had him at all.'

'That makes sense,' Peggy said softly. 'But just because someone else has had it worse, it doesn't belittle your experiences. You don't have to be grateful for a bad version of something because you think it's better than nothing.'

Ash dug a biscuit out of the packet. 'It's just good to get other people's perspectives; realise what they're dealing with. I've been so caught up in my own situation – my self pity – that it's easy to lose sight of everything else.'

'Jess has given you some insight, then?'

'Insight, fun, laughter. She's the best thing about Sundays, and I still look forward to coffee with Mack, even though it can be a sparring match sometimes.'

'It's turning into a three-coffee Sunday, then.' Peggy laughed. 'And you know, you wouldn't have met Jess if it wasn't for your visits here.'

'I wouldn't have met her if I hadn't gone to explore the market,' Ash corrected. He didn't want to give what he was doing here credit for his life colliding with Jess's. He had to keep the two things separate.

'Fair enough,' Peggy said. 'So she's your new favourite Sunday thing. She's pretty?'

'She's beautiful,' he admitted. 'Beautiful and challenging. She makes me think in a way I haven't for a while, as if I'm waking up from a long sleep. We've come up with this subtle superpowers idea.' He grinned, remembering the way she'd turned in his arms when he'd come up with the affirmation about them, and insisted he let her have it. And then that kiss. As chaste as it had been, he'd felt it everywhere. He could power himself for days on the memory of it.

'Subtle superpowers?' Peggy repeated.

'The amazing things you can do that won't change the world, but will have an impact on you and the people around you. I made it to the heath without losing any coffee from those flimsy takeaway cups. Jess looks after people instinctively, so they feel safe and cared for, but I don't think she sees it as a big deal. I thought she wasn't going to turn up today, but it turns out she'd gone to help one of her friends at the market. Apparently she does it all the time.'

'Intriguing,' Peggy said. 'What about me?'

'Well, you definitely look after people, but that side of you is fully on show: you're a caregiver. So there must be something else. What do *you* think?'

'I can make a delicious sandwich out of the most eclectic selection of ingredients. John is frequently amazed by what I come up with.'

'Give me an example.'

'Chickpeas and lemon curd.'

Ash stared at her. 'No.'

'I promise you, Ash. Take two slices of white, pillowy bread, crush the chickpeas with a bit of salt, add a thick spread of lemon curd, and it's a treat for the tastebuds.'

'I can't . . . I refuse to believe that.' He rubbed his cheek. He couldn't think of anything worse, apart from a big pile of haggis. He wasn't an offal fan.

'See, now you've laid down a challenge. I know what you're getting instead of a choccy digestive next week.'

'If I tell you I believe you, will you let me off the hook?' He hugged the biscuit packet to his chest.

Peggy folded her arms. 'I'm not sure. I might leave it as a surprise: what will you be treated to next week? A boring old McVitie's, or one of my special creations?'

'It's hard enough for me to come here as it is.'

Peggy smiled. 'I can't wait to see the look on your face.'

'The look of abject horror?'

'The look of wonder. Right. Come on, bring your coffee. We're going in.'

Ash stiffened. She'd lulled him into a false sense of security and now he was desperate to run for the door. And this was despite the mantra he'd been silently reciting since he woke up this morning, despite the fact that seeing Jess, finding out more about her, had made him even more determined to take this next step.

'You can do it, you know,' Peggy said gently. 'It feels like the hardest thing in the world, walking through the next door, but you're strong enough. And think about your mum, and Dylan all the way over in New Zealand. They're counting on you, in their own ways.'

Ash nodded. He was doing this for his mum, and Dylan – well, he didn't feel quite the same way Ash did – but he still couldn't be here, with his young family in Aukland. Ash had to do this for all of them, and so far he had failed spectacularly. The only updates he'd been able to give them ran along the lines of: *The waiting room is nice and the staff are great*, and *no, I haven't made it further than that but I promise you I will*. It was time for him to keep his promise.

He stood up on legs that felt as if they had run up and down the Greenwich Park hill multiple times, instead of walking up and down once, and followed Peggy down a calming corridor, the walls a soft blue. Doors lined the hallway, brass numbers attached to the white-painted wood, as if they were normal flats with normal people and straightforward lives beyond them.

Ash imagined he could hear the muffle of low-spoken voices, confidences and apologies being shared, and the rhythmic beep of machines. But it was also entirely possible that he was imagining these things. Mostly, he could hear his heart pounding in his ears, the way his breath had shortened.

He wondered, stupidly, what Jess would think of him right now. She was tough, and slightly reserved – in a way that made him think she kept walls up to protect herself. It made sense, hearing about her upbringing. Would she tell him he was being pathetic, that he should get a grip? The thought of her shaking her head, rolling her eyes, or – this was far too much to hope for – wrapping her arms around *him* this time, telling him it would be OK, spurred him on.

Peggy stood next to the closed door like a sentry woman. 'OK?'

Ash laughed. 'Not really. But I need to do this.'

'You'll feel better, I'm sure. And once you've broken the seal, you can come back as often as you want. Say anything you want to.'

'And will he . . .' He cleared his throat, ashamed at the way fear churned up his insides. 'Is he awake? Will he be able to hear me, if I speak to him?'

'He does sleep a lot,' Peggy said gently. 'When I checked on him five minutes ago, he was sleeping. But even if he doesn't wake up, he might be able to hear you. And, honestly?' She waited for him to acknowledge her with a nod. 'The important thing – for you – is that you get to say what you need to, in his presence. But if you're not ready for that, if you just want to sit next to him, then that's fine too. Ease into it as slowly as you like.'

Ash gripped the door handle. 'I didn't think I had a whole lot of time.'

'We don't know how much time there is. But you're here, that's what matters. And if you can only be in the room for five minutes, well – that's more than last week.'

'Right.' Ash exhaled. 'Right, let's do it, then. Ready?'

He looked at her, needing reassurance, a sense of camaraderie, even though it wasn't Peggy's battle. His mum and Dylan were behind him, they wanted him to be here, but they weren't here themselves, were they? He pushed down the surge of anger, and for a second let himself picture Jess's face as they'd finally got the kite up in the air; the way she'd watched it soar, her eyes bright and her smile wide.

'I'm ready,' Peggy said. A reddish curl had escaped her neat ponytail and fallen over her face. She squeezed his arm.

Ash pushed down the handle and let the door swing inwards. He took another beat, another moment to compose himself, then walked into the room where his dad was waiting for him.

Chapter Twelve

The weather had been bright and cheerful all week, mirroring Jess's mood. Wendy had commented on it when she'd found her humming a Taylor Swift song while tidying the stacks of soft, colourful blankets on Monday, an unnecessary task because they were mostly overlooked at this time of year.

Jess had told her it was just an ear worm, because if she gave her boss even a hint of how happy Ash made her, Wendy would pounce on her and delve deeper until Jess told her everything. And it felt precious, something she wasn't ready to share: the kite-flying; Ash coming up with affirmations for her; the kiss. He'd been so distracting that, even when they'd talked about their families and she'd sensed him shutting down, heard a sudden brusqueness in his words, she hadn't asked him about his appointment. She had wanted to hold on to the fun they were having, and not let anything ruin it.

On Wednesday she'd come back to the market, filming Lola and Spade as they filled the space with their music and their self-belief, bouncing ideas off each other, getting stallholders and visitors involved. They worked well together, the ultimate double act, and Jess had been happy to hide behind the phone and stay out of the spotlight, filming take after take, even though it was supposed to be spontaneous.

'Looks like the video's going well,' Kirsty said on Thursday, from inside her Moreish Muffins food truck. It was a tiny, old-fashioned van painted a soft cream colour, whimsical illustrations of muffins, coffee cups and flowers adorning the side. 'Everyone's talking about it.'

'Lola and Spade aren't exactly introverts,' Jess replied. 'They got a whole book club group – six women all over seventy – dancing to their music at one point.'

Kirsty laughed. 'They were trying to come up with a name after you left. Now that it's not just Lola on her own.' She leaned on the counter, her blonde-brown curls swaying gently.

'I can't wait to hear what they choose.' Jess grinned, then thought of Enzo, the kindness and enthusiasm he'd shown for Spade and Lola yesterday, the worry lines creasing his forehead when he thought nobody was looking. 'What do you think about using their TikToks to help Enzo?'

'What do you mean?' Kirsty glanced over Jess's shoulder. 'And what do you fancy?'

'Sorry, you're busy. Could I have . . . one of your bacon and cheese muffins?'

'Sure thing.'

'I just wondered,' Jess went on, needing to bounce her idea off someone, 'if Lola and Spade are aiming for this video to go viral, and Enzo's struggling because Carolina isn't well—'

'Yeah, it's awful. He's been here years.'

'Exactly. So do you think there's some way . . . I don't know.' She shrugged. 'We could use Lola and Spade's plans to help them get back on their feet?'

'What about a petition?'

Jess turned around, and recognised Margaret, who often came into No Vase Like Home, loved anything green, and was like a bright bubble of cheerfulness. Jess only knew her name because one day she'd come into the shop wearing her nurse's uniform, her name badge pinned to her chest.

'Or – no,' she went on. 'If he's struggling to make ends meet, could you set up a Just Giving page for him?'

'That's a great idea,' Kirsty said. 'We could link to it on TikTok, as long as Lola and Spade were happy for Enzo's jewellery to feature.'

'Don't they have fundraising buttons on TikTok?' Jess said.

'I think you need to be a registered charity for that,' Margaret replied. 'But you could still link to the page on their profile.'

'That could work.' Spade and Enzo were good friends, the ex-rock star – soon to be current rock star? – always hanging around his stall, making him laugh. 'Lola's keen to raise her profile, but now she's got Spade on board, I think they'd both jump at the chance to help Enzo if they can. Thanks for the suggestion, Margaret.'

'No worries. What's good today?'

'Everything.' Jess laughed. 'I've gone for the bacon and cheese.'

'Oh God, great choice. I'm going to copy you.'

'Enjoy!' Jess called, waving goodbye to her and Kirsty.

In the shop, Wendy was flicking through a catalogue and humming to herself. She looked up when Jess came in. 'Fuel to get you through carrying a water feature to Felicity's?'

'A muffin because it's Thursday.' Jess shrugged. 'But I am off to Felicity's in a bit.' She glared at the hares, as she always did when she walked in the door. 'She seemed nervous when she gave me her address on Monday.'

'She lives on her own,' Wendy said, 'so maybe having you round to her home, even briefly, is a big thing for her. Just follow her lead.'

'Of course. I'll finish my muffin, then get started on the new display before I leave. The owls aren't in yet?'

'Next couple of days,' Wendy said. 'I promise you'll love them.'

'Don't make promises you can't keep,' Jess said, suppressing a shudder.

At ten to eleven, with Felicity's address and the route from the market memorised, Jess went to get the boxed water feature from the storeroom.

'Bend your knees!' Wendy called, and Jess rolled her eyes.

She tottered onto the shop floor, her hands clasped under the box, her chin resting on top. 'I've got it.'

'Are you going to be OK carrying that?'

'It's not heavy, just awkward. Felicity definitely wouldn't have managed it.'

'She wouldn't have been brazen enough to nudge people out of the way, either.'

'That too,' Jess agreed. 'Right, I'm off.'

'Take as long as you need,' Wendy said.

'You always say that!'

'I always mean it.'

Jess walked carefully through the market, trying *not* to nudge people with the sharp corners of the box. Whenever visitors shot her curious glances, she glared back until they looked away.

The last part of the journey was uphill, on a residential road that ran parallel to the park, and the houses were large and well kept, with tiny front gardens sporting manicured rose bushes or potted marigolds, front doors gleaming white, sage green or pewter grey. There was no cracked plasterwork, no wheelie bins on show. Kerb appeal was clearly an important factor in this neighbourhood.

109

Number sixty-seven was smart too, though not quite as polished as its neighbours. The door was a glossy primrose yellow, but there were weeds creeping up between the pathway flagstones, and all the blinds were drawn; no vases of peonies visible in the windows, no high ceilings on display. The door was the only welcoming thing about this house, and Jess felt a spike of unease.

She walked slowly up the path and lowered the box onto the porch, then lifted the brass knocker and slammed it down twice. She waited, listening for footsteps, and wondered if Felicity had forgotten. Then the door swung inward, making her jump.

Felicity was wearing biscuit-coloured linen trousers and a thin, grass-green jumper. Behind her, Jess could only see darkness. 'Hello Jessica,' Felicity said, smiling thinly. 'Are you sure this is all right? You taking time out of your day to bring this to me?'

Jess wanted to laugh, because she was already here. She wasn't about to say it was inconvenient and walk all the way back to the market with the box tucked under her chin. 'Of course,' she said brightly. 'Shall I bring it in? I can help you set it up too, if you like.'

Felicity bit her lip like a self-conscious teenager. 'Yes, please. Do come in. And please excuse the mess.'

Now Jess did laugh, because 'mess' to Felicity probably meant a book left out on a coffee table, or mugs upside down on the draining board. But then Felicity pulled open the door, letting sunlight flood into the house, and it was . . .

Jess clamped her jaw shut so hard it hurt. The entrance hall, which was wide and high-ceilinged, a staircase with a wooden banister running up the left-hand side, was full of . . . stuff.

She could see piles of newspapers, clothes or fabric shoved into plastic bags that were tearing at the seams, a stack of tatty-looking wicker baskets. As she left behind the fresh May morning and stepped into Felicity's house, the mustiness was a scorch in her nostrils, the stale air cloying and thick. The walls, she could just about see, were covered in wallpaper: little white daisies on a blue and green foliage background, but most of it was obscured by clutter.

'I'll just get this.' Jess bent to pick up the box again, not recognising her own voice.

'Absolutely. Of course!' Felicity was back to the strong, in-control woman Jess had got to know a little in No Vase Like Home. 'I'll take you to the garden.' Was it denial? It had to be denial.

This turned out to be the hardest part of her journey, because there was only a narrow walkway through the mess, and she couldn't see her feet. She tripped a couple of times, but Felicity didn't turn round, though she slowed her pace, never leaving Jess behind.

The kitchen was a bright room, with a long window that looked out over the back garden, but the sunlight showed that this space, too, was buried under detritus. Jess tried not to wince at the piles of papers, books and leaflets, unopened post in towers next to the hob. There was no area to prepare a meal or sit down to eat one. Panic and claustrophobia clawed at her, tightening her throat.

'Felicity.' It came out as a scratch.

'This way, Jessica.' She walked through the narrow gap she had left herself, and unlocked the back door.

Jess followed, the box colliding with papers and bin bags, threatening to send them toppling into the limited space that remained. She breathed an audible sigh of relief when she was back in the fresh air, in a garden closed in by high, red-brick walls, the space a colourful tangle of unkempt trees and shrubs. The patio, hosting an iron table and single chair, was the most looked-after part of the house so far.

'On here?'

'Perfect.' Jess put it on the flagstones, and Felicity opened it.

'Can I help?' Jess asked.

'Could you show me how to set it up? I have an outdoor tap over here that we could connect it to.'

'You don't need that,' Jess told her. 'It has a built-in water tank, so once you've filled it for the first time, it will just cycle through. It's not going to use a huge amount.'

'Wonderful,' Felicity said. 'Come on then – let's get to it!'

Jess read out the instructions, then helped Felicity attach the pump and the water tank, making sure it was all secured properly, while a blackbird dug worms out of the long grass.

She had seen tiny chinks in Felicity's armour whenever she'd been in the shop: her frayed hems, the slight dishevelment, but she'd never once imagined she'd be living like this. It was clear that the house was going to remain the unmentioned elephant in the room, but that didn't mean she couldn't come at it sideways.

'How long have you lived here?' she asked.

'Twenty-seven years,' Felicity said. 'Twenty-three of those on my own. With my cats, of course.'

Jess hadn't seen any of the cats yet. She swallowed, wishing she'd brought a bottle of water with her. It was awful to think it, but she wasn't sure she'd want a cup of tea from Felicity's kitchen.

'Are any of your cats twenty-three?' Jess widened her eyes, trying to find some levity.

'No, dear.' Felicity chuckled. 'But I've never been without one. Not since – not for a long time.'

'That's good.'

'I don't know what I'd do if they weren't here.'

Jess tried, and failed, to stop her mind straying down horrifying pathways. Were the other rooms in the house as bad as the ones she'd seen? Did the cats bother to come outside to relieve themselves? Did Felicity even care? And how – how could she *not* care about what was happening in her hallway and kitchen? How did she justify it to herself?

'And you . . . you're happy, living here?' she tried.

There was a beat of silence. She looked up to see Felicity scrutinising her. 'I know it's not the tidiest house,' she said, 'but I've been so busy recently. I simply haven't had the time to keep things pristine. Life, you know. It gets in the way.'

Jess was incredulous. Was this really what she thought? But then, what could she say? *Felicity, I'm terribly sorry but you're living in a death trap. You're in complete denial. You need help.* She didn't know her well enough to say these things, so instead she said, 'Of course. It's a beautiful property. And so close to the park, too.'

'Indeed,' Felicity said. 'Now, where does this cable go?'

Jess checked the instructions and got back to work.

Once there was a soothing bubble of water flowing over the globe at the centre of the sculpture, Jess hovered, her hands in the pockets of her dress. Should she ask for a drink, then try and get Felicity to open up? Should she request a tour of the house, so she could see how bad it was? Or should she say nothing, go back to the shop, and ask Wendy what to do? Her boss was bound to have some kind of solution.

An image of her mum flashed into her head, with her soft brown curls and green-framed glasses, saying: *You can come to me about anything, Jess. Nothing is off limits.* But it was: it *was*. And in the last couple of years, the distance between them had grown, and Jess felt as if she could barely speak to her mum about anything.

'This was incredibly kind of you,' Felicity said. 'I know you have to get back to work, but you're always welcome to come for tea – whenever you want to. It'll give me an excuse to have a bit of a tidy up.'

'I'd love that,' Jess said, trying not to collapse in nervous laughter at the thought of Felicity having a *bit of a tidy up*. 'Thank you, Felicity. And come to the shop again soon. We've got some new stock arriving in the next couple of days.' It felt important to keep the connection with her, now she'd seen what was going on.

'Of course,' Felicity said. 'I'm always on the lookout for new pieces.'

Her lips clamped firmly shut, Jess let the older woman lead her, hopscotch style, to the front door, with its cheery yellow paint and glass panels.

On the doorstep, she turned. 'See you soon, I hope.'

Felicity nodded, and the look she gave her might have been a whisper of desperation or plea for help, or simply a silent request for Jess not to judge her. 'See you soon, Jessica. Thank you again.'

'Any time.' She squeezed Felicity's thin arm.

As she walked back to the market, past all those beautiful houses, the wealth evident in every blooming hanging basket and sleek car parked outside, she felt physically unburdened – without her awkward box – but emotionally weighed down.

114

She had three distinct thoughts running through her head. One: she understood, now, why Felicity had never bought her coveted mirror. There was no place for it in that house. Two: Felicity needed help, but Jess was almost 100 per cent sure that she wasn't the one to give it. Three: if this was what happened to an intelligent woman after two decades of living alone – a beautiful house turned into a hoarding nightmare, cats that were probably buried under piles of stuff with mice or rats or God knew what else – was that going to be *her* future, too?

She almost bumped into a woman carrying a potted plant, apologised and stepped out of her way, then nearly walked straight into a lamppost.

'Fuck,' she muttered.

Today had not gone as she had expected, and now her mind felt almost as cluttered as Felicity's hallway. She inhaled the welcome scents of the market's food stalls, and realised that she had yet another thing to add to her to-do list. Her urge to run away and live by herself was even stronger than usual, but today had been a harsh reminder that that wasn't always the solution. People were complicated, always demanding *something*, but – in some cases at least – being alone, relying on nobody but yourself, refusing to let other people in, could have some alarming repercussions.

Chapter Thirteen

'You must come across some sights, as a postman,' Jess said, the moment Terence walked through the door. She was making what could loosely be described as a stir-fry in the flat's tiny kitchen. It was so easy to buy food from the market on her way home, but she would never have a hope of moving to her own place one day if she spent her entire salary on gyozas and stone-baked pizzas.

'You must come across some things, working in one of London's tourist hotspots,' Terence parried, dumping his rucksack on a chair. 'Celebrities. Buskers. Weirdos.' He shuddered.

'Everyone's weird.' Jess stirred her onion, mushroom and red pepper round the frying pan, and hoped the addition of diced chicken breast would make it more appealing. That was another thing about the market – it threw her cooking inadequacies into a stark light. 'You can't call people weirdos.'

'Some are weirder than others.' Terence took a beer out of the fridge. 'Want one?'

'They're yours.'

'Which is why I'm *offering* you one. You don't have to accept.'

'No – I'd love one, thank you.'

Terence opened the bottles with the shark-fin opener that lived on the fridge, and handed her one. She took it and they clinked, then both took a long sip. The bubbles danced in Jess's mouth, cool and refreshing.

When she'd made it back to No Vase Like Home after the shock of seeing Felicity's house, Wendy had already had her bag over her shoulder, waiting for Jess to return so she could keep an appointment with a local company who made unusual ceramic bowls. There hadn't even been time for Jess to give her the highlights. She'd been alone in the shop all afternoon – apart from a bunch of customers, most of whom didn't buy anything – then she'd locked up and come home.

Her disquiet needed an outlet, and Terence was all she had.

'Do you want to share my stir-fry?' she asked him.

He was leaning against the counter, scrolling on his phone. He looked at her paltry vegetables frying in the pan, and the chicken breast she hadn't even diced yet. He sighed, then opened the fridge and took out a large broccoli floret and a packet of bacon.

'Only if we make it more interesting,' he said. 'And shouldn't you have done the chicken first?'

'Probably. I haven't been that focused,' Jess admitted. 'Are you sure?'

'I reckon we can make something passable. I'll do the chicken separately.'

They worked alongside each other, chopping and stirring, adding seasoning. Jess's nervous energy began to dissipate.

'Why did you ask about my job?' Terence said, once the chicken was sizzling gently. 'And I do – I see all sorts. Nasty arguments and people coming to the door in hardly any clothes; dogs snarling, children screaming. Sometimes, when I post letters with red reminder stamps on them, the house owner opens the door and tries to give them back, so they can pretend they never got them.'

'Denial.' Jess nodded. 'I bet that's a big one.'

'Not as frequent as the bloody dogs. They try to rip my trousers sometimes. It's a cliché because it's true. Who's denying what, anyway?'

'Oh, a . . . customer, at the shop.' Jess suddenly thought that Terence might have Felicity's street on his round, and it wouldn't be fair to betray her confidence. She wanted to talk to Wendy because she thought she'd be able to help, but telling Terence identifiable details felt like overstepping a line. 'But it's fine,' she went on. 'No problem. Tell me about your strangest encounter of all time.'

Terence laughed. 'It's not as exciting as you think it is.'

'But you see naked people.'

'That's your idea of excitement?' He raised an eyebrow, and she blushed. 'It's not all six-packs and smooth skin, let me tell you. I wish I could un-see most of it.'

'Do lots of people live on their own?'

'I suppose so,' Terence said, after a moment. 'I go to lots of places where the letters are addressed to a single name, where the same person always answers the door. People *do* live on their own, though. Young guys and gals who haven't settled down yet, old folk who have lost their other half, middle-aged people who've decided they prefer the solitude. You and I rub along all right, don't we? But we're only living together because London rent is off the charts, so I couldn't afford this place on my own, and you couldn't afford anywhere by yourself, either. We've been brought together by necessity.'

'But we make a good stir-fry between us.' Jess felt comforted by his matter-of-fact observations.

'We've not tasted it yet.'

'It looks and smells great, though. The component parts.'

'Sure.' He sipped his beer. 'You OK?'

She looked up. 'Of course. Why?'

'The questions, the ruminating. You're being more . . . share-y, than usual. There's something on your mind.'

'There's always something on my mind.' She shrugged. 'But today it is a very specific thing, and you've helped a lot.'

'Great. I have no idea how, or with what, but I realised a long time ago that sometimes it's best not to ask. Let's get this on some plates, and see if it tastes as good as it smells.'

It did taste good: well seasoned, crunchy and satisfying, with slippery noodles underpinning it all. While they were eating it and chatting about nothing in particular, Jess wondered if Terence was right. *Was* it best not to ask? To leave Felicity to get on with her way of life? The only problem was, the moment Jess had seen that hallway, she had felt, deep inside her, that the older woman inviting her there had been a cry for help. A sign that, however long she'd been hoarding for, a small part of her had had enough. Jess didn't think she could live with herself if she didn't try to do something about it.

Back in her room, she was restless. Lola was working at the pub, and calling Wendy out of work hours would alert her to how much this had distressed her, and would make her boss treat it with a level of importance that Jess didn't want to give it – more for Felicity's sake than her own. She still didn't have Ash's number, and the strength with which she wished she could call him and talk to him about Felicity, ask his advice, scared her. But she couldn't, so she did the only other thing she could think of.

It was her dad who answered the phone, surprise and warmth in his voice. 'Jess, love, how are you? Everything OK?'

'I'm good, thanks. How about you and Mum? You're both well?' She sounded so formal. She waggled her shoulders, trying to shake it off.

'We're grand,' he said. 'Your mother's on a redecorating kick. New carpets, new colours on the walls. She wants grey and blue, Duck Egg or Pea Flower Tea – there's a colour called Pea Flower Tea, would you believe? – and she's making noises about replacing the suite in the front room. It's taken me twenty years to get the perfect dent in that cushion.' He chuckled, and Jess laughed with him.

'What about the sunflowers?' she asked. 'Is this . . . is she—?'

'Of course not, love. Their place in this house is safer than mine. Shall I get her?'

'Sure.' Jess ran her finger over her laptop's trackpad, checking the status of her Etsy orders. She had created one with Ash's suggestion – of course she had – and only a couple of days in, it was already selling well. *We all have superpowers, you just need to believe in yourself to discover yours.*

'Darling.' Her mum's voice had a slight echo, telling her they'd put the phone on speaker. 'How's No Vase Like Home? And Wendy? And lovely Lola and Malik, who we haven't seen for ages?' Edie Peacock liked to reassure Jess, whenever they spoke, that she hadn't forgotten the important elements of her daughter's life. Jess didn't know if that was to prove how much she cared, or a subtle dig at the fact Jess didn't let Edie in much any more.

'Work's great – busier now we're getting close to summer, and Wendy's the same as ever. Lola's making a music video at the market, using one of her original pieces, and is getting everyone involved, unsurprisingly. Malik's doing very . . . Malik-y things.'

'That sounds exciting,' Edie said, 'about Lola's music video.'

'It is. And I'm good, too, if you were wondering.' Shit. She hadn't meant to say that.

There was a weighted pause. 'That *is* what I was asking.' Edie matched Jess's firm tone. 'I'm glad everything's going well. We think about you a lot, don't we, Graeme?'

'At least once a fortnight.' He chuckled again, trying to dispel the awkwardness.

Jess closed her eyes in frustration. It had been a mistake to call them. Since that day, almost two years ago, when she'd overheard Edie say that she wasn't wanted, she'd hadn't been able to think of them as her mum and dad. She'd been twenty-five at the time, and shouldn't have relied on them much any more anyway, but it had tainted everything that had come before. All their demonstrations of love couldn't erase what she'd learnt that day.

'What do you know about hoarders?' she said now. Maybe they would help her, even though she couldn't behave like a loving, eager daughter.

'That programme off the telly?' her dad asked.

'Is this about our house?' Edie said at the same time. 'The sunflowers? What has your dad told you? I'm *de*cluttering, if anything, though I do think the study could do with more soft furnishings.'

Jess rolled her eyes. 'It's not about *you*, Mum, and it's nothing to do with the TV programme, but it is the same thing as they talk about on that show. Just . . . in real life.'

'Is this about you, darling? Are you worried you have a problem?'

Jess surveyed her room, everything in it comforting and necessary, meticulously tidy, down to the smallest make-up brush. She dusted every Tuesday morning, though she wouldn't admit that to anyone.

'No, Mum,' she said faintly. 'It's someone I know through work. I had to go round to their house today, and it's this really beautiful place near the park. They're so elegant and proud at the shop. But when I went inside, there were stacks of things – all kinds of things – everywhere! Piled high up the walls. I saw a . . .' She tried to recall the details, the things she'd noticed in the chaos: a crimper still in its box, as if Felicity had a hankering to style her hair like an Eighties disco princess; several sets of Russian dolls, all the inner dolls spilled outside their bigger friends, scattered along the kitchen windowsill, some inside saucepans; five – she had counted them – packs of thirty-two toilet rolls stacked next to the dishwasher, which had its door open, plastic bags spilling out of it like a monster spewing up its lunch. 'I saw a whole load of batshit crazy stuff.'

Her mum made a noise of disapproval at the swearword. Jess didn't care. Now she'd said it out loud, she felt lighter. This was no longer a secret shared by only her and Felicity, and even though she wouldn't tell her parents who it was, and even if they couldn't help, the mere fact of having told someone made her feel marginally better.

'You could go to social services,' her dad said, tentatively. 'The council? It must be a fire risk.'

'It's all kinds of risks,' Jess said. 'But I don't want to get this . . . person in trouble, either. They live on their own with their cats, and I think if they were told they were doing something wrong, it would mortify her.'

'What's the alternative, then?' her dad said. 'If she needs help?'

122

Jess was annoyed that, right at the end, she had revealed it was a woman. Not that her parents often came to the market, or would have an inkling who she was talking about, but still.

'You help her,' Edie said. 'If you don't want to get someone else involved, if you think that would be counterproductive, then it's down to you, isn't it?' There was still an edge to her voice after Jess's earlier barb.

'But I have no clue what to do! I've never seen anything like this in real life, and I don't think three half-watched episodes of *Britain's Greatest Hoarders* qualifies me to give advice. Besides, I don't know her that well.'

'You know her enough to care about her,' her dad said.

'You care about her enough to call us for help,' her mum added, laughing. 'That says a great deal.'

Jess winced. 'Yeah, I guess. I'll . . . have a think.' She felt as if she'd done nothing *but* think since she'd stepped through Felicity's door that morning. 'Thanks Mum, Dad.'

'Of course,' her mum said briskly. 'You know we're here for you.'

'And it might be nice to see you, once in a while,' her dad added.

'I'd like that,' Jess said quietly, and for once it felt like it might be true. 'It's just hard, with me working on the weekends.'

'You have evenings off.'

'I do,' Jess conceded. 'I'll look at some dates.' Was there a more obvious brush-off than that? Still, it was all she could say right now.

They said goodbye, and she flung her phone aside and lay on her bed. She couldn't help Felicity; she had no idea where to start. Until that morning, she had looked up to the older woman as a role model, someone independent, elegant and in control of her life. Jess had imagined that her home was as polished as her appearance, but it was clear that there were two very different sides to her, and now all she could think about was how unhappy Felicity must be, to live such a chaotic, fractured existence, and how she might somehow end up like her. Before, that thought had filled her with hope; now, she felt nothing but dread.

She would speak to Wendy tomorrow, see if, together, they could come up with a way to help her. And tomorrow was Friday, which meant that, in only a couple more days, she would get another hour with Ash. Ash, who was easy to talk to and made her laugh, who was a nice distraction during a busy morning. Ash, who she suddenly wanted to tell all her problems and fears to, who she was desperate to phone up on a Thursday night, so she could ask his advice, listen to him reassuring her in his deep voice.

Groaning, she got up and looked at the new quotes she had created. Did she have any about falling into a deep pit that she'd dug entirely on her own? About being sent off course from a perfectly acceptable life plan of relying solely on yourself by a man with grey eyes? If not, it might be time to add a couple more to her collection.

Chapter Fourteen

Ash appeared in the doorway of No Vase Like Home at ten to twelve on Sunday, wearing a black shirt over jeans and a grey trilby with a peacock feather sticking out of the band.

'What's this?' Jess was smiling already. 'Dress-up Sunday?'

'Not quite.' Ash had a coffee carrier in one hand and held out the other hand to her. 'But this is for you.'

'I don't think so.' Jess shook her head, a laugh spilling out of her. 'A cherry red flat cap?'

'It's raspberry, actually.' He waggled it and, reluctantly, Jess took it and put it on, pulling the brim down low. 'How do I look?'

Ash's smile was slow, his eyes lighting up. 'Stunning,' he said. 'Shall we go?'

'Have fun kids!' Wendy called from behind the counter.

Ash led the way through the market, slipping easily past people while Jess stayed close behind him. Now they were together again, she felt an electric charge. She couldn't stop thinking about last weekend, and how she'd recklessly manoeuvred his arms around her.

'What's with the hats?' she asked, when they were clear of the market and Ash was leading her in the direction of the Queen's House.

'There's a Greenwich film tour, did you know that?' Ash slowed down so she could catch up with him, then handed her a coffee. The sun was hiding behind a slate-grey sky, a darker churn of clouds to the north threatening rain.

'And it requires hats?' Jess had heard of it. Greenwich, with all its stunning architecture and history, was a popular filming location for big budget productions, and the museum service ran a tour showing off the prime spots. She had never heard of participants needing costumes, though.

'The original film tour doesn't start until half twelve,' Ash said, 'and we only have an hour, so I've devised one of my own. Welcome to the Ash Faulkner tour of outstanding Greenwich filming locations.' He doffed his trilby at her, bowing low over his outstretched leg, and a woman walking behind him muttered, 'For God's sake', as she had to change course to avoid tripping over him.

'You're taking me on my own personal film tour,' Jess said. 'With hats.'

'I thought, as the guide, that I needed to stand out somehow.'

'From your audience of one?' Jess sipped her coffee.

'Exactly. And *then* I thought, how unfair that I got a great hat, and you didn't. Thus, the raspberry baker-boy cap, which really suits you.'

'A film tour with added flattery?'

'Aren't they the best kind? Come on.' Ash walked up the wide gravel walkway between decorative hedges shaped like spirals, and Jess followed. The Queen's House was starkly white even on this gloomy day, with blank windows and curved, symmetrical staircases leading up to the ground-floor veranda.

'So, this is the Queen's House.' Ash kept glancing between his phone and her, managing to look both ridiculous and incredibly dashing in the ostentatious hat. 'It was used in the recent Netflix production of *Bridgerton*, which I watched in great detail in preparation for today.'

Jess smirked. 'Are you going to reenact the scene that was filmed here? All the best film tours have reenactments.'

'They do?'

Jess nodded.

'Right. OK, then. The – uh – main characters are arriving at a grand ball,' Ash said. 'It's not one of the more intimate scenes. So we could . . .' His brows pulled low as he turned in a slow circle. It was busy despite the weather, with groups of visitors dotting the golden pathways and manicured lawns. Ash's smile widened and he pointed. 'There.'

Jess followed his finger. A woman was pushing two children in a sleek black double buggy, a King Charles spaniel trotting happily on a lead at her side. 'That's your reenactment?'

'Just imagine it.' He tapped on his phone screen and a piece of music, familiar to Jess, filtered out of the tiny speakers. It was the string version of Taylor Swift's 'Wildest Dreams' that she'd heard in the series. She glanced at him, but he was looking ahead.

'The sky is darker, full of stars instead of clouds, and the pillars have vines and fairy lights wound around them. The air is filled with the summer scent of jasmine, and the string quartet are playing while champagne glasses clink like bells.' He lowered his voice, and Jess had to strain to hear his words above the swoop of the violin. 'There's an undercurrent of anticipation. Everyone feels it, low in their stomachs, wondering who they're going to meet tonight.' He pointed at the mum pushing the buggy. 'There's Lady Violet Bridgerton.'

127

'Was that a *guess?*' Jess asked loudly, trying to ignore the pit of anticipation he'd put in *her* stomach at his words. 'Who are the children?'

'Daphne, of course. And . . . Colin. The small boy playing with the plastic tractor is obviously Colin.' They watched as the family walked slowly in front of the house, the little girl turning in her seat to say something to her mum.

'You've actually seen *Bridgerton?*'

'A good tour guide does his research,' Ash told her. 'And the dog is their faithful steed, Midnight.'

'I don't remember a horse being named.'

'Everyone calls their horse Midnight, don't they? That or Blaze.'

The family stopped in front of the wide steps and then, to Jess's incredulity, the mum took her little girl's tiny hand and, carefully, helped her out of the buggy. She was wearing a pink dress, the skirt floaty with a lace trim. The spaniel skittered on the gravel, letting out a single bark, as if cheering her on.

'There you go,' Ash said smugly. 'The Bridgerton family arriving at the ball. It would probably be a footman that helped Daphne out of the carriage, rather than Lady Violet, but let's go with it.'

Jess laughed. 'How could you possibly . . .?'

'I'm just lucky.' Ash grinned at her.

'The dog is probably called Dave, you know.'

'Dave sounds quite similar to Blaze,' Ash pointed out, and Jess shook her head in mock despair. He adjusted his hat. 'Right. Next stop, the colonnades.' He pointed at the long walkways running either side of the Queen's House, shaded by proud, sturdy pillars. 'They're used for a fight scene in *Bridgerton*, and also in the film adaptation of *Sense and Sensibility*. Follow me.'

Ash kept up a happy patter of information – some of which Jess was sure he was making up – as they strolled along the colonnades and then down to the Old Royal Naval College, which stood between the Queen's House and the Thames, a gap left between the buildings so whichever monarch was on the throne would have an unobstructed view of the water. Today it was gunmetal grey and slow moving, devoid of shimmer.

'There's a huge fight scene in *Thor: The Dark World* that was filmed over here,' Ash said, leading her towards the baroque buildings.

'Are you going to reenact that one, too?'

Ash circled his right shoulder slowly. 'I hurt my rotator cuff playing rugby, so flipping cars might be a step too far today.'

'Such a shame,' Jess said.

People were glancing at them, probably because of their hats, but she didn't mind: her cap was warm and smelled comforting, and Ash had said she looked stunning in it.

'Do you know what else was filmed here?' He spread his arms wide. 'One of the greatest movies of all time.'

'*Les Misérables*? *The Queen*? *Sherlock Holmes*?'

Ash narrowed his eyes. 'Have you been on the film tour before?'

'No,' Jess told him. 'And definitely not *this* film tour. I don't care about the other one – there's no way this one isn't the best.'

'I'm glad you think so, because I bet the *other* tour doesn't talk about *Muppets Most Wanted*.'

Jess almost choked on her coffee. 'Seriously?'

'They used the Old Royal Naval College as a stand-in for Berlin. If we're talking about films I *have* seen, then *Muppets Most Wanted* is near the top of my list of all-time favourites.'

Jess clutched her hand to her heart. 'I'm giving up my Sundays to spend time with a Muppets fan?'

Ash looked affronted, and Jess's stomach flipped at the stern expression, his eyes shadowed beneath the hat, which suddenly didn't look ridiculous at all. She let her gaze trail over his wide shoulders, the way his black shirt clung to him. She wondered if he'd meant it about his rotator cuff, and if so, how sore it was.

'Do you prefer horror films?' he asked.

'I would argue that all Muppets films fit into that category. Apart from *The Muppet Christmas Carol*, which is a yearly tradition, obviously.'

'At least there's one thing we both agree on. We have one more stop, but it's a bit of a walk.' He glanced at his watch. 'I think we have time.'

'I'm up for it,' Jess said, and they fell into step alongside each other, walking a few paces in silence.

'How has your week been?' Ash asked, and Jess felt a strange mix of relief and sadness that he'd dropped his tour guide persona.

'It's been all right,' she told him. 'Though I had a shock, the other day.'

Ash's steps faltered as he looked over at her. 'What kind of shock? Are you OK?'

'I'm fine. But I found something out about someone, and it's shaken me a bit, I suppose. Made me re-evaluate things.'

'Do you want to share?' he asked gently. He moved closer to her as a cyclist clad in shiny red Lycra sped down the inside of the road, next to the pavement.

'I don't want to betray any confidences.'

'I don't know everyone at the market,' Ash said. 'But if it's someone you know I've met, then don't tell me.'

'You haven't, as far as I'm aware.'

'You can unburden yourself, then.'

'OK,' Jess said. 'I'm going to call her . . . Tina, just to make things easier.'

'Disguising her identity like in a Panorama documentary.' Ash nodded. 'Very wise.'

'Shush. This is serious.' She fought a smile. 'Behave.'

'I always behave,' Ash said, in a low rumble that suggested exactly the opposite.

Jess's breath quickened. 'And stop distracting me. I'd actually love to know what you think, as a psychologist. You might be able to help.'

'Shoot,' Ash said, his teasing tone gone.

So Jess told him everything about Felicity – Tina – from their interactions in the shop, her longing for the mirror, then the water-feature purchase, followed by Jess's trip to her house. They were skirting round the market, heading towards the river, and she wondered if Ash even remembered he was supposed to be taking her to a final film destination. He offered the odd comment, a couple of murmured swearwords when Jess described the state of Felicity's house.

'What did Wendy say?' he asked, when she'd finished.

'Wendy said, "hmmmm" a lot, then told me I had to give her time to think.'

'Entirely noncommittal, then.'

'The thing is, I'm not sure it's really any of our business. It's Tina's life, and she hasn't asked for help. She didn't want to talk about it when I tried to bring it up while I was there.'

Ash took a few moments to reply. 'It could be that her inviting you to her house, to deliver this item, was her way of asking for help. You said she was quite strange about it – specific about the time and date?'

Jess nodded.

'She would obviously have known that you'd see how she's living, so it might have been her first attempt at trying to do something about it.' He sipped his coffee, his brows furrowed. 'The main thing is to keep the dialogue going, keep talking to her, show her that she can trust you. That way, she might get to the point where she wants to bring it up herself.'

'What if she doesn't come into the shop again? What if she panics?'

Ash shook his head. 'If you go down the *what-ifs* path, you'll send yourself round the bend. Give it a couple of weeks, and if she hasn't been into the shop again, we'll rethink. Maybe plan a follow-up visit to see how the water feature's working. It's got moving parts, so it's not a totally stupid idea.'

'It would definitely be harder if she'd bought a statue,' Jess agreed. 'Although, if it had been one of the hares, I could have done a welfare check to make sure it hadn't murdered her.'

Ash's laughter burst out of him. 'I'm going to have to examine those hares properly. I'm always so keen to see you, I forget that the shop exists.'

'Oh.' Jess's cheeks burned. 'It's so kind of you to help, with Tina. I feel better now I've shared it with you: it's like a weight's been lifted.' She hadn't missed that he'd said *we'll rethink*. He'd made it sound like it was their problem, not just hers.

'I'll always help, if I can.'

Jess glanced at him, and all her nerve endings tingled to life. Their laughter had faded, and even though they were down by the river, the *Cutty Sark* a proud silhouette behind Ash, the space busy with visitors, Jess felt like it was just the two of them. She wanted to step closer to him, to find another way to orchestrate herself into his arms.

'Thank you,' she said quietly.

'Of course,' Ash whispered. Then he looked around him, as if he'd forgotten where they were, and cleared his throat. 'Here we are.'

'The final stop on your film tour?'

'I've saved the best until last.' Ash strode over to the small, red-brick tower with the glass-domed roof.

Jess followed, intrigued. 'Who used the foot tunnel in a film?'

It was a historic piece of Greenwich architecture, joining the south and north banks of the river, and was used every day by pedestrians and cyclists. But while Jess appreciated its purpose, and the engineering that must have gone into it, it wasn't her favourite place. It was cold and bleak, and she wouldn't even think about using it at night. Then she remembered what Ash had said by the naval college. 'Ah. A horror film.'

'A little-known zombie film called *Twenty-Eight Days Later*.'

Jess grimaced. 'Are you going to go down into the tunnel and chase people as if you were a zombie? Because I'd have to film that.'

Ash laughed. 'It would make a grand finale for my tour. Has Hollywood done a zombie in a trilby?'

'I don't know, but I do know the tunnel is supposed to be haunted. People see ghostly Victorian figures, rather than flesh-eating zombies.'

'Are you a secret ghost hunter?' Ash asked. 'There's a lot of important history around here. Maybe I should have done a ghost walk instead.'

133

'Maybe,' Jess murmured, but she didn't want to go into the tunnel, to get submerged in the gloom.

A tourist boat was gliding serenely down the grey river, and an aeroplane powered overhead on its way to City Airport. 'Do you know what's been missing on your tour?' she asked.

'What's that?' Ash had stepped closer, and it didn't look like he had any intention of taking the stairs that led into the tunnel either.

'A kissing scene,' Jess said, her heart lodged in her throat. 'We've had sparkling balls and superhero fights and Muppets and zombies, but Greenwich is romantic, too. Why aren't there any kissing scenes on your tour?'

'I don't know,' Ash said. 'Maybe I didn't visit the right websites. Maybe—'

'We could create one of our own?' Jess finished.

A smile lifted Ash's lips. 'That would be a better grand finale. And I've been thinking about last week, on the heath. I know it was just a peck, but—'

'Me too,' she cut in, elation and relief shortening her breath. 'I've been thinking about it a lot, too.'

'You can live off happy memories all week,' he murmured.

Jess huffed out a laugh. 'Ash Faulkner, are you inventing more quotes for me? I'm going to have to start paying you commission.'

'One kiss is worth a thousand words,' he whispered.

'Sometimes the anticipation is better than the reality,' she said, feeling a flicker of uncertainty, now that she'd set this in motion.

Ash's soft expression hardened into intent, into something that looked a lot like desire. 'Let's see if I can prove you wrong with that one.'

He tipped her cap back, the cool air rushing to her forehead, and with his other hand, adjusted his own hat. Jess thought how ridiculous this was: their silly hats, Ash using children in a buggy to represent a scene from a show he might or might not have watched; but the truth was she'd loved every single, stupid minute, had thought about nothing but Ash and what he was telling her, what was coming next and how much she was laughing, and then he leaned forward, his fingers stroking down her arm, and pressed his mouth against hers.

He tasted of coffee and certainty, and Jess, so overcome by how good he felt, how the sensation of his lips and his hands on her body woke it up in ways she hadn't thought about for eons, let her mind empty. She wrapped her arms around his neck, closed the gap he had left between them, and felt his palms press into her lower back.

They were cinched tight, the kiss slow and exploring, and Jess thought that if he let go of her now, she wouldn't be able to stay upright. She felt as if Ash had some kind of power over her, some fundamental element within him that she was unable to resist. Spending time with him had been bad enough, but now she knew what he felt like pressed against her – all those important bits of him; lips and fingers, the jut of his hips – she was worried she wouldn't be able to let him go.

An hour, she thought frantically, as he pulled back slightly, looking down at her with a dazed, happy incredulity that she knew she was mirroring, was soon going to feel like nowhere near enough.

Chapter Fifteen

Time had got away from them. He was surprised it hadn't done before now.

Their fourth Sunday together and it felt like Christmas, only Ash hadn't enjoyed Christmas after the age of twelve, when all the idyllic, rosy fantasies he had lived out, with two parents and a brother he adored, too much food and stockings hanging over the arms of the sofas, wrapping paper everywhere, had disintegrated, replaced by stretches of silence, his mum too heartbroken to make an effort, he and Dylan creating their own fun. He had felt responsible. It was his job to step up and make things OK, to make his mum and his brother smile again, even though he hadn't known how to at that age. In lots of ways, he still didn't.

No, being with Jess, kissing Jess, was better than Christmas. It made him feel as if he'd done something right in all of this, had found some impossibly bright spark that still felt too fragile to grab hold of, in case he crushed it in his palm.

He arrived at the gleaming white door out of breath, his heaving chest mirroring the chaos of his thoughts, the bliss replaced by the usual dread and regret, and also resentment that he'd had to leave her. They'd realised the time, had rushed back towards the market, laughing, their fingertips brushing, other people throwing them looks of consternation or curiosity as they literally held onto their hats. Making it back to No Vase

Like Home, they'd hovered in the doorway, and he hadn't known what to do.

Jess had, though. She'd stretched up and kissed his cheek, and he'd relished the feel of her lips against his skin again, brushing his Sunday stubble. She'd said, 'Same time next week?' He'd nodded, told her *of course* and then legged it, moving faster through the market than he'd done before.

'Ash Faulkner, you're cutting it fine,' Peggy said, when he stepped inside and closed the door.

He glanced at his watch. It was three minutes past one. 'Hardly,' he puffed out.

'Did you forget about today?' Peggy scrutinised him. 'Nice hat.'

'Thanks.' He put it on the chair beside him. 'As if I could forget about this. No, Jess and I got . . . carried away.'

She raised an eyebrow. 'No details, please. This is a family space.' She gestured around the empty waiting room.

'I didn't mean . . .' he started, then stopped. Because that kiss had felt like a prelude, and even though they had been in public, it had been a struggle not to pull her even closer, to whisper everything he wanted to do with her in her ear. She had matched his kiss, but maybe telling her how frantic she made him, how much closer he wanted to get, would have sent her jumping over the wall into the river just to get away from him.

'Coffee?' Peggy asked. 'I'll give you a moment to sort yourself out.'

He glanced down, but his shirt and jeans looked unruffled.

Peggy tapped her temple. 'In here. I expect it's a big switch, coming from Jess to here.'

'That's all I've ever done with Jess,' he said. 'Come straight from her to this place.'

137

'I know. Let me get you that coffee. And,' she called over her shoulder, 'I've got one of my special sandwiches, as promised.'

Ash groaned, but his thoughts were already back with Jess. Was it right that she didn't know where he came after seeing her? He was so desperate to keep her separate from this, but now that they'd kissed, now that their companionable hours were becoming more, should he tell her the truth?

Peggy brought over a cappuccino and a packet of Bourbon biscuits. 'I couldn't do it to you. My tuna and peanut butter masterpiece will have to wait until another time.'

'Thanks.' Ash took a biscuit.

'No witty comeback?'

'I kissed Jess.'

Peggy didn't seem surprised. 'A quick peck goodbye, or . . .'

'More of an *I really like you, hello* kind of kiss.'

'Oooh. And I'm guessing a "hell*ooooo*" rather than a "hey".'

Ash laughed. 'Yep.'

'Then you had to put her down and race over here. No wonder you're all at sea.'

'It's fine – it's not like I haven't kissed a woman before.' Why had he said that? He took a second Bourbon and bit straight into it, not even removing the top layer of biscuit with his teeth so he could scrape off the cream.

'I don't doubt it, you absolute cad,' Peggy said indulgently. 'You know I should get paid extra, as your therapist?'

'I do know that,' he said. 'Sorry, Peg.'

'Nonsense.' She patted his knee. 'But I do have some news for you, actually. And I'm here, however you want to take it: cry, use me as a punchbag, scream. If you try and run out of the door, though, I will block you.'

'That sounds ominous.' Ash's muscles tensed, the knot that lived permanently between his shoulder blades tightening painfully.

Peggy gave him her gentlest smile, her tone matching when she said, 'He's awake.'

Ash stood in the doorway, looking at him.

He'd seen him last week, of course, and had been able to catalogue all the changes: how much his dark hair had thinned; how pale his face looked whereas, when Ash was a boy, there'd been no mistaking his Italian heritage; the way the skin on his forearms was loose and wrinkled now, lying on top of the blanket on the bed. It wasn't the man he had worshipped growing up, and then come to hate. That had made it easier, somehow.

Now, however, he was sitting up against the pillows, the machines beeping in the background, monitoring or assisting various parts of his body.

His head turned slowly, and Ash watched his eyes widen. It was a small movement, as if he wasn't that surprised, but Ash sensed that it was just that everything about him was smaller. He was no longer the gregarious, physical man Ash had grown up with. His cancer was in charge now.

'Ash.' His voice was barely there, but his strong Italian accent twisted the word into a name Ash hadn't heard for years. He had stopped being *that* Ash the moment his dad had left them, and when his mum had reverted to her maiden name, he had too – becoming Ash Faulkner instead of Ash Lombardo. He hadn't wanted anything to do with him, then. He didn't feel a whole lot different now.

'Hey, Dad,' he said.

He felt a small, almost imperceptible nudge in his lower back. He turned, and Peggy nodded him forwards. He frowned, and she – she *stuck her tongue out at him*. He was outraged, comforted, calmed. He squeezed her wrist, then turned his attention back to the room that, with its large window and lush greenery outside, the earlier cloud thinning to reveal the blue of the afternoon beyond, was the real waiting room.

He sat in the chair next to the bed, squeezing his hands between his knees, and tried not to let panic overwhelm him. What could he say? Not *how are you?* Or *How's life been treating you?* because both those things were obvious. He closed his eyes, casting about for a subject, and found one: something that would help him edge towards the end of this window of time, when he could see the man who should have meant everything to him, but had come to mean nothing. A voice whispered that it was a very complicated nothing, but he pushed it aside.

'Dylan says hey,' he said to Nico Lombardo.

'He's in Aukland?' Nico scratched out.

'With his wife Sadie and two boys, Zack and Eli. Your grandkids.' He didn't put any emphasis on the last words. His dad knew all the ways in which he was lacking.

'What about you?' Every word was a struggle, and Ash knew he would have to do the heavy lifting in the conversation.

'I haven't given you any grandkids,' he said. 'I work in the City as an occupational psychologist. I have a flat in Holborn, I play rugby out near St John's Wood when I can get there. My neighbour, Mack, makes me get the Sunday paper for him, then rewards me with a coffee and a lecture about whatever outrageous headline is on the front page, as if I'm personally responsible for the state of the world.'

Did his dad's lips twitch upwards? It was disconcerting that this whole, stilted exchange was happening against a soundtrack of beeps. He couldn't help thinking of it as a countdown.

'Don't shoot the messenger,' Nico said.

'I think that's part of the fun for him,' Ash said. 'He called me a whippersnapper, once. Young and overconfident, which isn't true. I'm not that young any more.'

'Twenty-nine.'

'Well done, Dad. Glad you've been keeping tabs.' It was out before he could rein it in. He glanced guiltily at Nico, but he had his eyes closed. He wasn't going to apologise.

'How's your mother?'

Ash gritted his teeth. *Not fully put back together after you left her with two boys to bring up on her own. Too gracious for her own good.* 'She was the one who asked me to come and see you,' he admitted. 'She couldn't face it herself, which I hope you understand, so she asked me to.'

'And you – you wanted to?' His voice was quieter, and one of the machines gave a quick, high beep, more attention-grabbing than the rest.

How unfair it was, Ash thought, that he couldn't be honest; that he couldn't shout and scream, fling all the rage and guilt and despair inside him at the man who was the root of it all, because you couldn't do that to someone who was dying.

'I wanted to come for her,' he said, instead. 'She asked me to, so here I am. And I'll come back next week, and the one after, until . . .' He stopped. This was worse than he'd imagined it could be.

'Don't worry,' Nico said, his eyes closing again. They had been warm and full of humour when Ash was little, deep brown

141

irises he used to wish he'd inherited. 'It won't be for too much longer.' He went still, only the shitty, irritating beeps letting Ash know he was still alive.

Ash ran a hand over his mouth, then got up and turned away. He stood in front of the closed door, not sure he could face Peggy's empathy and her soft, warming smiles. Right now, he didn't think he deserved her kindness.

How was it that his dad had been the one to walk out on them, to disappear into a new life, barely stay in touch and then wind up here, in this expensive place – no doubt paid for by one of his few madcap schemes that had actually worked – and yet it was Ash who felt like the guilty one? Like he wasn't a good enough son because he didn't want to be here, and couldn't hide it from Nico?

He pulled open the door and stepped into the corridor, sighing his relief when he saw it was empty. Today had been both his best and worst Sunday since he'd started coming to Greenwich, and while he was desperate to go back to the market and see Jess again, mostly to remind himself that she was real, that their kiss had happened, he couldn't.

It was more important than ever that he didn't tell her about this, that he kept his miraculous, stolen moments with her separate from the time he had to spend here. He had to hold on to the good things, and being with Jess was *so* good. The only problem was, it was always followed by one of the worst things he'd ever had to do.

Chapter Sixteen

Jess was at the market on her day off. Again.

She hadn't been prepared for the knock on her door at half past eight, and with Terence at work, she was suddenly faced with the possibility of exchanging small talk with one of his friends. But when she'd opened the door, a bowl of cereal in her free hand, she'd instead found Lola, holding out her phone with an excited look on her face.

'We've gone viral,' she said. 'Me and Spade.'

'What?' Since that first day of filming, which Jess thought had gone fairly well, even if she did say so herself, Lola had worked on the composition, and Spade had worked his charm on a friend who was a cameraman, and they'd reshot the whole thing without Jess, until their TikTok video was more like something you'd see on an online music channel.

Jess had watched it when it first went up, and Lola had been updating her on view numbers via WhatsApp, but Jess had had other things on her mind. Guilt gripped her, both because she hadn't been paying attention to her friend, and because she hadn't got any further with her vague plans to help Enzo.

'Eighty-nine thousand views so far,' Lola said. 'So many comments. People already want our next track.'

'That's brilliant, Lols.'

'We still haven't come up with a name,' Lola went on, but she looked pleased with herself. 'Anyway, Kirsty said you wanted to do something for Enzo, so that's what's happening today.'

'What?'

Lola rolled her eyes. 'Come on, Jess. You spend your whole time grumbling about the demands of other people, about how we're all too needy, but everyone knows you're the helper. Kirsty said you wanted to use our inevitable popularity' – she spread her arms wide – 'to help solve Enzo's predicament, and now we've proved we *are* popular, so we've called a meeting, and it can't happen without you. Finish your cereal, get your shoes and let's go.'

Her protests had fallen on deaf ears, so now here she was, at one of the high tables next to the food stalls in the market, with Lola and Spade, Enzo, Susie, Roger and Kirsty, who was still manning Moreish Muffins but was within shouting distance. The market was quiet, but Lola didn't seem to notice, holding court with a voice loud enough to reach the river.

'The response on TikTok has been amazing,' she said. 'And I know I started this to showcase my own music, but it's clearly become bigger than that.'

'You're the star,' Spade said magnanimously. 'I'm just happy noodling in the background.'

'Your noodling is magnificent, though,' Susie said. 'Almost a hundred thousand views. And with the market as the backdrop!'

Lola nodded. 'We're already thinking about the next one, aren't we?'

'That we are, dude,' Spade said. 'And we agree with Jess: we can use our platform to do good things for Enzo.'

'Like a scaled-down version of Live Aid,' Roger suggested.

'*Exactly* like that!' Spade pointed at him.

'But how will the music help Enzo?' Susie asked.

'I do not know if this is necessary,' Enzo said, his voice quiet but firm.

144

'We can use the popularity of the music to promote you,' Kirsty called over, making the woman who was waiting for her summer berries muffin jump. 'We can put a link in the TikTok profile that highlights your stall.'

'How about a fundraising page?' Roger said. 'If we could cover your market rent for a few months, would that take the pressure off?'

Enzo looked down at the table. 'I do not want charity.'

Jess's heart squeezed. She understood his desire to hold on to his dignity, his pride, alongside the need to provide for his family. Sometimes, though, people needed a bit of support. She thought of Felicity, how she'd tentatively reached out to her. Jess still hadn't come up with a plan to help her, either.

'Totally understand, Enzo, mate.' Spade slapped him on the back. 'Everything's doable though, right?'

'What if we raise the money?' Jess said. 'We do things to *earn* it, rather than just asking for handouts. Bake sales, baked beans in the bathtub, some kind of run – or dance – in hats!' God, how often had she thought about Ash's tour? His silliness, his grey eyes sexily shadowed by his trilby. That kiss. She cleared her throat. 'We use Lola and Spade's popularity to get word out, but instead of just asking for donations, we get sponsored for things – or we sell something specific, maybe?'

'Are you still trying to come up with a name?' Susie asked. 'How about the Greenwich Market Musicians? Something that ties it all together.'

Lola chewed a fingernail. 'Do we have time to organise a sponsored run?'

'The Market Melody Makers,' Roger suggested. 'Alliteration is always good.'

'I can bake some muffins,' Kirsty said. 'Sell them separately for the cause.'

'Not sure about Melody Makers.' Spade drummed his hands on the table. 'We need to be immediate, catch everyone's attention right from the off.'

Jess watched everyone pitching in, trying to find all the answers, while Enzo sat quietly, looking forlorn. They needed to come up with the right way of raising the money, something that wouldn't make him feel powerless. 'We just need to be proactive,' she said, 'fix on something that can work quickly. It's about propping you up, Enzo, not taking over.'

'That would be . . . good,' he said tentatively. 'Thank you.'

Spade clicked his fingers at Jess. 'A sponsored kite tournament. What d'you think of that nugget of genius?'

'What?' Jess coughed a laugh, her cheeks burning. 'I don't think . . .'

'How is your boy, anyway?' he asked. 'Art, isn't it?'

'I think he was called Ash,' Enzo said helpfully.

Jess resisted the urge to dive under the table as all eyes turned towards her. One pair was more hawklike than the rest, so she studiously avoided meeting Lola's gaze.

'We should all go away, have a think and then reconvene,' she said. 'When are you planning on posting your second video, Lola?'

'Spade's cameraman, Deano, is free on Sunday,' Lola said, 'so how about we meet again on Sunday morning? We can plan the fundraising, decide on a name, get some shots under our belt. I have a shift later in the afternoon, but we could meet here at twelve?'

'Sounds great,' Spade said.

'Good for me,' Roger added.

'I'm here.' Kirsty waved.

'Sunday will be far too busy,' Jess said. How had Lola managed to fix on the *one* time of the week that Jess categorically couldn't do? Had Wendy let it slip? Had Spade or Enzo said something when she hadn't been paying attention?

'We need to show the market at its busiest,' Lola replied. 'If we get Enzo being mobbed by customers in the background, that'll help. You could bring your *boy*, Jess.' She pinned her with a stare. 'I could get him to sign a release form, in case he wants to be involved.'

'I guess,' Jess said faintly. She knew this wouldn't be the end of it, that Lola was going to get her back for keeping Ash to herself.

'In fact,' her friend went on, 'how about we use your side project as part of the fundraising? You could create some motivational prints specifically for the market. They're not that expensive to produce once you've got the design finalised, are they? Maybe we could sell some of them on Enzo's stall?'

'You can't change what you sell without consulting the management team,' Susie pointed out.

Jess was too stunned to speak. Lola had *outed* her?

'What are these motivational prints, Jess?' Roger asked.

'It's just something I do in my spare time,' she scratched out, glaring at her friend. 'Quotes on an attractive background. Some funny, some inspirational. I could create some more, and . . . we couldn't sell them here, like Susie says, but I guess we could promote the link to my Etsy shop?'

'Are you sure?' Kirsty asked. 'You'd be giving up some of your profits.'

Jess shrugged. 'Lola's right. They're not that expensive to make or send, and once I've come up with the design, they're easy to mass produce. I'd be more than happy to do some extra ones.'

'Surely Wendy would love to have a selection in No Vase Like Home?' Roger said. 'Put them in frames, give them some additional heft. Haven't you spoken to her about it?'

'Oh no,' Jess said. 'I'm not sure—'

'We'll add it to the agenda for Sunday,' Lola said, 'but this sounds really promising.'

'Great,' Jess said quietly, but she felt a bit sick. She'd never told Wendy – or anyone here – about her Etsy shop, because she didn't see herself on the same level as them. They were all professionals: artists and bakers, true creatives, not just making up whimsical signs in their bedroom. But now, in one fell swoop, Lola had announced it to everyone.

'Let's meet outside the pub,' Spade said. 'They'll be open by twelve.'

Everyone agreed, and Jess's stomach clenched. She could tell them that she wasn't free, that they'd be fine without her, but now Lola had put her firmly in the centre of their fundraising efforts, and she would be working here anyway, so she couldn't get out of it. And she wasn't giving up Ash. They only had an hour as it was, and she wasn't prepared to relinquish that.

That left only one option: bring Ash along, and introduce him to Lola. Make whatever they had together even more real. It felt like all of the parts of her life, that she had worked so hard to keep separate from each other, were colliding, and it was out of her control.

The group disbanded, everyone drifting back to their stalls to relieve whoever was covering for them. Spade was already talking to Brad who ran the hog roast stall, whatever story he was telling him involving some serious air guitar.

'Jessica Peacock.' Lola folded her arms. 'Who is this boy Enzo and Spade were talking about, and why do I know absolutely nothing about him?' Jess opened her mouth to reply, but her friend kept going. 'We need a proper powwow. This evening at your place, with a bottle of wine. Is the lovely Terence going to be in?'

'I've got no idea,' Jess admitted. 'But we can go to my room if we have to. Do you think that would also be a good time to talk about how you've just told everyone about the secret side project that I have purposely, for over a year now, kept to myself?'

'You've just been waiting for the right moment,' Lola said smoothly. 'And now it's going to help Enzo, this is *exactly* the right moment to share your talents.'

'You're unbelievable.' Jess shook her head, but she was smiling.

'It's one of the reasons you love me. And let's not forget, you've got more explaining to do than I have. I'm not the one who's been hiding an entire male person from her best friend.' She pressed her hands against her chest. 'I need to go and practise with my bandmate before Sunday. We want over a hundred thousand views next time, so we need to get it right.' Lola kissed Jess on the cheek, then went to interrupt Spade's air guitar.

Jess slipped quietly out of the market, not even passing No Vase Like Home on her way, and headed for the safe haven of Waterstones, where she could lose herself amongst a thousand different stories that had nothing to do with her. She had less than a day to decide which bits of Ash she wanted to share with her best friend, and which parts she was going to keep to herself.

Chapter Seventeen

'I'm really sorry about outing your Etsy shop,' Lola said. 'But I was just shocked to hear about this Ash person from Spade, rather than you. And it *is* a good idea, letting everyone know about your prints, because they're amazing and you shouldn't be hiding them.'

She was sitting cross-legged on Jess's bed, while Jess sat backwards on her armless desk chair, twisting left and right, because she couldn't settle enough to sit still. They had goblets of rosé wine, and Jess had set the fairy lights over her headboard to a soft pink, the mood cosy and subdued.

They could have been fifteen again, talking about boys in one of their bedrooms, posters unfolded from magazines Blu-Tacked to the wall, the crowd sounds of a televised football match echoing from the other room. Women, Jess realised, would sit in rooms and discuss love at every age: it was only the naiveness of their outlook, the nature of their sighs – from hopeful to world-weary – that changed.

'I don't mind really,' she said. 'I don't think, anyway. I'll get back to you once Wendy fires me for conflict of interest.'

'She'll probably set aside half the shop for you and your posters.'

'Doubt it.' Jess flung a screen-cleaning cloth at her friend, but it only just made it to the end of the bed.

'Anyway, enough of that. I need to hear all about Ash. I am so, so happy for you.'

'We're not even a thing,' Jess said. They'd had one kiss. Two, if you counted the kite-flying moment (and Jess *was* counting every moment, each one as precious as a priceless gold coin). 'I've known him a month. We've had four hours together.'

'But you like him? Who is he? This is all very important.'

'*Why* is it important? It's not like I need a guy to be happy.'

'You need people to share things with,' Lola said. 'People you're close to, who you can trust, and you're not a natural sharer. You have me, and Wendy, but you *don't* have your parents, because you've bottled up a whole mare's nest of misinterpretations, and held grudges for far too long.'

'Can we not,' Jess said, because they'd been over this ground so many times it was nothing more than a muddy, churned-up puddle.

Lola made an exasperated noise. 'They're your *parents*, Jess. And I know what you heard her say, but if you just take *my* interpretation of it—'

'I know what she meant,' Jess said. 'It fits, OK? It all fits.'

'With your warped, insecure sense of—'

'Get back to the sharing thing,' Jess said. She didn't really want Lola to go on about this, either, but anything was preferable to talking about what Edie Peacock had said about her.

'You're impossible,' Lola moaned. 'I'm going to write you a long WhatsApp about your mum later, when you can't cut me off. But Ash is important because you need another person to share with. Wendy and I, we're not enough for you.'

'I've never said that.'

'No, of course you haven't, because you'd rather stay in your tiny bubble where you think you only need your best friend and your boss. I'm saying it. *Me.*' She sipped her wine. 'I didn't think *I* needed anyone else either, until I went to collect my order from the McDonald's counter and realised, horrifyingly, that I'd picked up a bag with a Filet-o-Fish in it. Malik had my double cheeseburger, they'd somehow got the order numbers wrong, and in doing so inadvertently created the greatest love story of this century – and that's *despite* Malik liking Filet-o-Fish.'

'Getting their Fitbit steps together until the end of time,' Jess said dreamily. 'Nothing more romantic than that.' Lola threw one of Jess's colourful, yeti-fur cushions at her, which was much more effective than a screen-cleaning cloth, and almost knocked her wine out of her hand.

'It was fate, karma, magic – that's what I'm saying. I didn't know that being with Malik would change anything, but now I've got him, I can't imagine being without him. How will you ever know if you need something, if you don't give it a chance?'

Jess's thoughts went immediately to Ash, pressed up against her, the cool wind coming off the river at her back, contrasting with the inferno she'd become the moment he had pushed her hat off her forehead. The raspberry baker-boy cap was hanging on her headboard. Lola hadn't noticed it, or she would have commented on it.

'I met Ash at the market four weeks ago,' she told Lola. 'It was completely by chance – we both went after a shoplifter – and he asked me for coffee.'

Lola held out her hand. 'Picture?'

'I don't have one,' Jess said. She hadn't got a selfie with him, she was only now telling Lola about him, and yet she already thought of him as an integral part of her life.

Lola looked aghast. 'Tell me about him, then.'

Jess closed her eyes and conjured him easily. He wasn't by the river, now, but standing on the heath, holding the handle of the kite while she stared up at him and he looked down.

'Flying isn't as hard as it looks ... Just make sure a part of you stays tethered to the ground.'

Had that been a prediction about spending time with him, because she was starting to feel more and more untethered in his presence?

'You're smitten,' Lola said.

Jess opened her eyes. 'What?'

'You were grinning,' Lola told her. 'Sappily. You have never done sappy in your life. Not even on that holiday in Suffolk, where you met Scott and spent a lot of time banging—'

'He was a holiday fling,' Jess cut in quickly. 'We had an expiry date before we even said hello.'

'And what about Ash?'

Jess shrugged. 'He doesn't live here. He's got a flat in Holborn.'

'Oh my God, then why are you even *bothering*? A couple of miles up the river, and on the north side, too? No long-distance love affair has ever survived such a chasm.' She pressed her hands on either side of her face, doing an excellent impression of Munch's *The Scream*.

Jess threw the cushion at her. Lola caught it and grinned at her over the top. 'Continue, please.'

Jess scowled, but she couldn't hold it in, now. 'He has an hour at the market every Sunday, and—'

'Why?'

Jess chewed her lip. 'He hasn't told me that, yet. He has this appointment he has to get to, every week. I've asked him

153

about it, but he always changes the subject.' Or distracted her with a tour, a kite, an unspilled Americano, frothy with crema. 'But before that, we have an hour together. We've been to the park and flown a kite on Blackheath. Last weekend he made up this film location tour, about Thor and the Muppets . . .' She broke off, laughing.

'Holy shit,' Lola whispered.

'What?'

'A minute ago you said *we're not even a thing*, but you're cracking up at the memories. You've flown a *kite* together. This isn't just a thing, Jess. This is more than a thing.'

'It's just fun,' Jess told her. 'He's easy to be around, and whenever I think about him, whenever we spend time together, I'm full of happy, nervous anticipation. I can't wait to see him again the moment he leaves, and it's like . . . when you only have a small amount of time for something, you make the most of it, don't you?'

'Like me and Malik on a Monday night,' Lola said. 'There's only a small window between him finishing work and his online World of Warcraft game. Monday night sex is the best sex as a result.'

Jess shook her head slowly.

'So you and Ash, you've kissed?' Lola asked.

'Last Sunday,' Jess said. 'But I think . . . I mean, I like him a *lot*. And he must like me too.'

Lola rolled her eyes. 'He didn't put his tongue in your mouth to get a bit of lettuce out of your teeth, did he?'

'I am running out of things to throw at you.'

'I know. That's why I said it. Seriously, though, what's next?'

'Next is the fact that you've arranged a Market Misfits meeting when we usually meet up, so unless I abandon you to manage Spade and Susie and our fundraising for Enzo all by yourself, then Ash is going to have to spend his Sunday morning helping us.'

'Whoop!' Lola clapped so enthusiastically the fairy lights shivered. 'I meant it as a joke when I said he should come along, but I *knew* there was a reason I wanted to do it on Sunday. I must have had a secret intuition.' She tapped her temple.

'Yeah, well. This is when it all falls apart.'

'Why?' Lola laughed incredulously. 'Because he'll get to meet your market friends, and *me?* Is it me you're worried about?'

'Of course not,' Jess said. 'And he knows everyone at the market already.' She didn't know how to explain it. Her hours with Ash felt like a precious, almost fantastical bubble, and the moment she brought him into the real world, with Lola and her voracious enthusiasm, all the ways in which he might find out that she was less than perfect in comparison to her best friend, that she was often a grumpy, cynical person, it was likely to burst. An hour a week felt contained, like nothing could go wrong. 'It's just new and . . . a bit precarious,' she said. 'We're just meeting for coffee, so—'

'And kisses,' Lola reminded her.

'*One* kiss,' Jess said. 'And I don't know if it'll be more. You can't have a proper relationship in one hour a week.' Perhaps that was why she'd let it happen.

'So break through the boundaries,' Lola said. 'Meet him one evening; take him to the cinema or to dinner, or bring him here.' She patted the bed. 'Be honest with him, see what he wants, and if it turns out that he wants what a long,

155

fiery-hot kiss suggests he wants, do all of it with him. Enjoy every moment. Don't confine this thing, Jess – and don't confine yourself. You don't have to put all the bits of your life in separate little boxes, or . . . Russian dolls. What are they called?'

'Matryoshka,' Jess said.

Lola looked surprised, and Jess shrugged. She couldn't tell her friend that she'd Googled it after seeing the chaotic collection on Felicity's kitchen windowsill. That was another thing she'd yet to come up with a plan for, and the reminder was like an itch, somewhere on her body she couldn't quite reach.

'Right,' Lola said. 'Don't separate your life into matryoshka dolls – that's not how it works. Things are messy, they overlap all the time. Embrace the overlap!'

Jess managed a smile, but she wasn't convinced by Lola's suggestion. Ash was the one who had put a one-hour limit on their time together – coffee with his neighbour beforehand, the thing he wouldn't talk about afterwards. But maybe that's how they worked best. An hour of doing silly, fun things, having the occasional kiss, not letting themselves ask too much of each other.

'How did it go with Spade?' she asked, wanting to change the subject.

'Oh great,' Lola said. 'He is the definition of chillaxed. And he's an amazing guitarist. I get the feeling he could have kept going with his career all these years, but he'd made more money than he knew what to do with, so he gave up. He's been so generous, giving me his time and knowledge – he's really changed things for me. So many of the comments on TikTok are excitement that Spade's playing again. I don't think he even realises what a favour he's done me.'

'Or what a favour you're doing Enzo by using your popularity to help him,' Jess pointed out, because Lola hadn't pushed back once; she had instantly accepted it as something worthwhile.

'The market's a community, isn't it?' Lola said. 'And it's your place, Jess. You moan about it sometimes, you pretend you want to spend your life hibernating from everyone, but I can see how much you care about them all. If I can help even a little bit, then I will.'

'It's lovely of you, that's all. More wine?'

Lola thrust her empty glass forward. 'Yes please.'

Jess topped up their glasses to the gentle patter of rain against the window, the shush of tyres on wet tarmac, the faint sounds of Terence's football match on the TV in the other room.

'Also,' Lola said, when her glass was full, 'you have just come up with the best name for us.'

'I have?'

Lola laughed. 'Do you not pay attention to yourself? The Market Misfits. It's brilliant, Jess. I'm changing my TikTok handle now. Spade is going to fall off his chair in delight.'

'The Market Misfits,' Jess repeated. She'd said it as a joke, but now she thought about it, it was the perfect name for all of them: Lola and Spade, who were part of their group but didn't work there; Roger, Susie, Kirsty and Enzo with their stalls; her and Wendy in the shop. Perhaps their haphazard group really could make a difference to Enzo with a few music videos and some motivational signs.

She felt a sudden sense of camaraderie, an unusual happiness at the thought of being part of something, and for the first time she wasn't apprehensive about Ash joining their

157

meeting on Sunday, she was actually looking forward to it. But then she always looked forward to seeing Ash. She was coming to think of him as essential to her happiness and, as much as she wished she could be braver about it, that felt like a very precarious place to be.

Chapter Eighteen

At first, Jess hadn't believed that a violin and a guitar could work in harmony. In her mind it had always sounded discordant, the bringing together of Lola's melodious strings and the electrical twang of Spade's Fender. The first video had swayed her – Lola had worked her magic with the composition, and Jess had been impressed – but now, sitting on a bench outside the pub in the corner of the market, their latest live performance was shattering all her assumptions like a boot through a pane of glass.

'Oh my God,' squealed Susie, right in Jess's ear. 'I can feel it in my bones!'

Jess nodded vigorously. She didn't want to talk; she wanted to listen.

Spade was wearing a glittery silver baseball cap and a blue velvet jacket, and Lola had her blonde hair tied back in a bun, a navy jacket with large brass buttons over her *Where the Wild Things Are* T-shirt, and a look of serene concentration on her face. Jess had always known her friend was talented, and had never tired of listening to her, even when she'd been part of a distinctly mediocre school orchestra. Lola had stood out, her confidence and skill palpable, treating the violin like an extension of her body and soul.

But here, standing in a small space between the picnic benches and the market stalls, with a crowd steadily gathering, she and Spade were a force of nature. Jess was sorry she'd suggested the Market Misfits – a name which they had told her they loved – because it didn't seem right: they were musical magicians; melodious maestros. Misfits didn't do them justice.

Lola's composition soared to its crescendo, the sound so beautiful Jess found herself holding her breath, then the violin and guitar came tumbling down together, a thunderous finale of strings. Lola raised her bow in triumph as the final note reverberated through the market.

There was a beat of pure, stunned silence, then the applause and cheers erupted, Jess clapping above her head, Kirsty bouncing up and down from her position on one of the tables. Spade's cameraman friend Deano was filming on his phone, even though this was a trial run.

'If that was the practice,' Jess said, leaning over the table so the others could hear her over the whoops, 'then TikTok is going to have a meltdown.'

'One hundred thousand views doesn't seem entirely out of reach,' Roger agreed.

'It is amazing,' Enzo added quietly, and Jess wondered if he was thinking the same thing she was: if the Misfits used their videos to promote the group's fundraising ideas, then surely, soon, he would be able to stop worrying. Since their meeting on Tuesday, Jess had added five new print designs to her Etsy shop, and they were selling well – without any more marketing than she usually did. At this rate she would have to get Lola or Kirsty to come round and help her pack up orders.

The musicians put away their instruments, while customers asked them questions and showered them with praise. Eventually they extracted themselves, and Lola slid onto the bench next to Jess and accepted a coffee, her smile tinged with incredulity at all the attention. Spade sat opposite and Roger handed him a pint. It was a bright day, the light drizzle Jess had woken up to whisked off elsewhere, the intense blue sky peppered with fuzzy white clouds visible through the glass roof of the market.

'You're a genius, Lola,' Kirsty said. 'And you're both crazy talented.'

'When are you filming the final take?' Susie asked.

'After this,' Lola said. 'I just need to work out who's going to be in the background, and get any additional release forms signed.' She lifted a thin cardboard folder out of her battered leather satchel.

There were murmurs of assent round the table, and Jess said, 'Sounds good.' But she couldn't stop her gaze wandering, looking for a familiar face, a head of thick dark hair in the crowd. Wendy had pushed her out of the door at twenty to twelve, clearly having had enough of her shifting things aimlessly around on the shelves and whistling tunelessly.

'So,' Lola said, 'the plan is that we put up the second video today. I've changed my account name to the Market Misfits, so we won't lose momentum from the first video. The market background as before, but we'll perform most of it in front of Enzo's stall.'

'We could sliiiiiide aside at the end.' Spade stretched his arms out wide.

'Which will set things up nicely for our next performance.' Lola grinned, cradling her mug in both hands.

'Which is?' Roger was the first to crack, unable to hold Lola's deliberate pause for long.

'In No Vase Like Home,' she said. 'When Jess's motivational prints are on display.'

Jess squirmed on the bench as everyone looked at her. She resisted the urge to put her hands over her eyes.

'You've actually told Wendy, then?' Kirsty asked. 'That's great. You should be putting your stuff out there.'

'I'm *going* to tell her,' Jess corrected. 'Today. After . . .' After she'd had her nerves soothed by Ash, was what she was thinking. She didn't say it. 'Hopefully she'll let me stock a few, and the money we raise can go towards Enzo's rent.'

Enzo fiddled with the top button of his shirt. 'I do not know if I am comfortable with this.'

'Why not?' Jess asked gently. 'You're not asking people to give you handouts. We – your friends – are raising it legitimately. It isn't even fundraising, it's just straight-up selling.'

'But the profits should be going to you, and to Wendy.'

'This is what I want,' Jess said. 'And I'd bet you anything – a million pounds – that Wendy will feel the same.' Her pulse raced every time she thought about speaking to her boss, asking to bring her frivolous designs into the real, physical world of No Vase Like Home.

'I am almost out of stock,' Enzo said. 'Carolina is still not well enough to work, and if I have nothing to sell, then having rent money will make no difference.'

There was a beat of silence, and a rowdy hen party clattered past, the women wearing tight dresses in bold colours and gold feather boas.

'Oh Enzo,' Susie said, 'I'm so sorry.' She'd brought one of her fluffy ducklings with her, and was kneading it like a stress toy.

'That's raw, man,' Spade added quietly.

'There has to be something we can do.' Kirsty sent her wide-eyed gaze around the table.

Enzo stirred his tea. 'My wife's sister, Sofia, can make the jewellery too: they learnt together, growing up. But she has three children, and works as a supply teacher four days a week. I can't ask her to reduce her hours, or to pay for childcare, just to help us.'

'She's family, though. Surely she would want to help out?' Susie squeezed the head of her duckling so tightly that Jess winced.

'There's a difference between wanting to and being able to.' Spade shrugged. 'The cost of living's through the roof right now.'

'So if we could raise enough money for you to pay Sofia, then she could reduce her school hours and make some pieces for you to sell?' Jess said.

'She could.' Enzo rubbed his eyes. 'I feel as if *I* should be doing it, that I should have got Carolina to teach me, but she has the fingers . . . the dexterity. I have always been in charge of the business side of things.'

'You can't do everything, Enzo.' Lola covered his hand with hers. 'And even if you could, there aren't that many hours in the day.'

'I've already sold some of my new designs online,' Jess told him, her cheeks heating. She felt like an intruder, because all these people were so much more creative than she was, making a living from their work. 'If Wendy lets me display some in the shop, and Lola and Spade do their TikTok thing, then we might be able to raise enough for you to offer Sofia some work.'

'It's a good plan,' Kirsty said quietly.

'We've got to give it a shot.' Spade ruffled Enzo's hair. 'We're here for you, dude.'

There were solemn nods around the table, and Enzo gave them a weak smile. Jess knew he was embarrassed, but what else could he do? He couldn't risk losing his livelihood at a time when they were most in need of support. If Carolina's arthritis was too bad, then getting Sofia to make their traditional jewellery until she had a working treatment plan in place was their best bet.

'Bloody hell, have I stumbled on a wake?'

Jess's head shot up, and despite the sombre mood she grinned and bounced out of her seat. Ash looked as casual as she'd ever seen him, in a Pop Art T-shirt and faded jeans. His forearms were tanned, and his hair looked wind-ruffled, as if he'd stood on the deck of the Clipper for the entire journey.

'Hey,' she said. 'Happy Sunday.'

'Happy Sunday.' Ash came round the table and squeezed her arm, then brushed his lips over her cheek. 'Hey, everyone.'

There was a chorus of hellos, and Jess realised that he knew them all – apart from Lola.

'Ash, this is my best friend, Lola. Lola, this is Ash.'

'Hello, Ash.' Lola stood and gave his hand a firm shake. 'Jess has told me a whole lot about you.'

'You, too,' Ash said. 'I'm glad I found you: I didn't realise this was our activity for today.'

'I asked Wendy to send you here when you got to the shop. Lola and Spade are planning a new TikTok video, and we're going to . . . uhm, I'm going to see if Wendy will let me sell some of my prints in the shop, to help Enzo out.'

It had been after their kite-flying on the heath, as they'd been walking back to the market, that she'd told Ash about Lola's music, and the way her plans had expanded once Spade had got involved and Enzo's predicament had become clear.

'You're going to sell your work in the shop?' His face lit up. 'Jess, that's brilliant.'

'Only if Wendy agrees to it.'

'Of course she will,' he said. 'Is there anything I can do to help?'

'You can sign a release form, in case your pretty face ends up in one of our videos and we start getting international acclaim.' Lola waggled a piece of paper at Ash.

He took it with a rueful grin. 'Of course. Wouldn't want me suing you for a cut when you get your five-album record deal.'

Lola laughed. 'He's smart, your man.'

Jess felt her cheeks flame. 'We're nearly done here,' she said to Ash. 'You don't mind?'

His gaze softened, his voice low when he said, 'As long as I'm with you, I don't mind what we do.' Then, to the whole table, 'Anyone want a drink? I could do with a coffee.'

'Treat yourself, get a beer.' Spade pointed at the pub. 'They do a great local ale.'

Ash glanced at his watch. 'Better not, but I'm happy to get one for anyone else.' He collected tea orders from Susie and Kirsty, and went inside the pub.

'OK,' Lola murmured to Jess while Spade regaled the others with a story about a brewery tour that had got out of hand, 'you didn't tell me he was utterly gorgeous.'

'I thought it would be better for you to see for yourself,' Jess said, her insides fluttering.

'Are you going to take it outside your hour, like we talked about?'

'At the very least, I'm going to get his number.' There had been so many tiny, inconsequential things Jess had wanted to tell him over the last week, and not being able to had felt like

165

an emotional strait-jacket. She was on the verge of having to start a *Dear Ash* journal.

He returned with the drinks and sat next to her, sliding his long legs over the bench.

'Hey.' She turned towards him.

'Hello.' He smiled. 'Good week?'

'It's been full of meetings,' she said. 'This is our second in six days, so I'm worn out.'

Ash laughed. 'That's far too many meetings. What about—'

'Felicity!' Jess blurted, cutting Ash off. The other woman had appeared behind Spade and Kirsty.

'Hello, my dears,' she said. 'This looks like fun.'

'Come and sit down, Felicity,' Susie said. 'We're helping Enzo out, having a nice chat. You should join us.'

'Oh, I . . .' Felicity clutched the collar of her jacket.

Jess tried to quell her panic. It wasn't surprising that the other traders knew her; it made sense that Felicity didn't just visit No Vase Like Home when she came here. But the confirmation made Jess nervous because of what she knew, and now here was Ash – who she'd told everything to – and Felicity in the same place. But what could she do? She didn't want to leave her out. 'We'd love you to join us,' she said firmly.

Spade patted the bench next to him. 'I've seen you around. Are you another market ghoul, like me and Ash?'

'A ghoul?' Felicity looked shocked.

'We haunt the market,' Ash explained. 'Because it's more interesting than our own lives.'

'There is nothing ghoulish about me,' Felicity said, lifting her skirt to step over the bench. 'I would much prefer to be a wraith. Hello, everyone. I know most of you, but not all.'

166

She smiled and gave Jess a little nod. Spade jumped up and went inside the pub without asking her what she wanted.

'Do you want to be in our TikTok video, Felicity?' Lola asked. 'We're shooting it here in a little while. We need people in the background, to show the market off to its full potential. Would you be up for it?'

'I'd love to be a part of it,' Felicity said. 'As long as you allow me to do a little touching up beforehand.' She patted her perfect bob, and Jess marvelled again at her poise and elegance here, how at odds it was with the chaos of her house. But she could see a long dark smudge on Felicity's peach shirt, visible beneath her jacket when she shifted in her seat.

Jess glanced at Ash, and saw that he was frowning. He'd worked it out *already*?

'Jessica,' Felicity said, once Spade had placed a cup of Earl Grey tea reverently in front of her, 'I was wondering if you wouldn't mind another little visit to my house?'

Jess froze. Below the table, she put her hand on Ash's thigh. It felt bold, but she had to convey, somehow, that he shouldn't say anything. She had to treat Felicity like a rabbit frozen in headlights, so they could tiptoe in slowly and catch her, not let her run off into the darkness where she'd be alone.

'Of course,' she said. Ash pressed his warm hand over hers, slid his fingers between hers, and it felt equal parts reassuring and incendiary, so she had to concentrate extra hard on the conversation. 'When would you like me to come round? Is everything all right with the, uh . . .?'

'The water feature is marvellous,' Felicity said. 'Twiggy, Bond and Artemis love it. They paw at the stream, and have started to drink from there rather than their water bowls.'

'Your cats,' Jess said.

167

'My companions,' Felicity corrected. 'Since being on my own, they're invaluable to me.'

'I bet.' Jess's voice came out scratchy.

How many cats would *she* end up having in her future, solitary life? She'd always pictured being by the seaside, running her own gift shop, selling trinkets for families to adorn their homes with. But the picture had changed recently, and in the living room of her imagined house, instead of a cosy sofa and polished coffee table, there were piles of newspapers, old towels, broken Tupperware boxes. Her dream was slowly morphing into a nightmare, and the thought of not helping Felicity made her feel frantic.

'But there are some things they're unable to do,' Felicity went on, 'so I wondered if you might help me decide where . . . where I could put that mirror, should I end up buying it from No Vase Like Home?'

Jess sucked in a breath. This, surely, was her asking for help.

'I love a frothy mirror,' Spade said. 'The snazzier the frame, the better.'

'This one is intricate and beautiful,' Felicity told him. 'It's unlike anything else I've seen. But I am *hopeless* at knowing where to place things, and Jess is the expert.'

'Oh, I don't know . . .' Jess started, and Ash squeezed her hand. 'But of course, I'd love to help you decide.'

'You can come too, Ash, if you'd like.' Felicity gave him a warm smile. 'If you're at that inseparable stage.'

'We're not—'

'You look super cute together,' Susie said, holding the fluffy duckling against her chest.

Jess swallowed. 'It's just that—'

'I'm afraid I can only get down here on Sundays,' Ash said.

'And only for this hour: I'm bookended either side. Although, for a special occasion, I could get here a little earlier.'

'And I would be a special occasion?' Felicity asked.

Ash's laugh was so warm that Jess wanted to press herself against him and feel it rumble through his chest and into hers. 'You and Jess don't need my help with the mirror – she's the expert, as you say, and it's your home – but if you're inviting me, I won't say no.'

'Well I . . . I am!' Felicity said, and Jess watched her expression go from pleased, to horrified, to uncertain in the space of a few seconds. She must know what she was opening herself up to, but maybe she'd found the courage to tackle it. And Jess knew the impression Ash could have on people, because she'd fallen under his spell, too.

'That's settled, then,' she said.

'Next Sunday,' Felicity confirmed. 'Around eleven?'

'I could do eleven,' Ash said. 'Count me in.'

By the time the meeting had broken up, they had fifteen minutes left. Lola gathered up the completed release forms and shot Jess an amused glance as Ash took her hand and dragged her away, to the narrow alley that led from the market to the busy roar of Nelson Street.

'Felicity trusts you,' Jess said, as he pulled her against him, even though it was one o'clock on a Sunday afternoon and their alleyway was a popular cut-through. 'It took her two seconds to realise you were a good person.'

'Well, I'm glad,' he said. 'Felicity's your friend "Tina", obviously.'

'Was it the mention of the water feature that gave it away?' Jess raised her eyebrows.

Ash laughed. 'I'm a veritable Sherlock,' he murmured, as he lowered his head. 'This feels way too short.'

'I'm sorry, it was out of my hands. I tried to get them to have their meeting at any other time, and in the end there wasn't even much to do. You missed Lola and Spade's practice run, which was insane.'

'You don't need to apologise,' Ash said. 'And I saw their first video: I downloaded TikTok specially. It's great that you're going to sell your prints in the shop.'

Jess groaned. 'Is it, though? My silly side hustle, it's—'

'*Not* silly,' Ash said. 'You know it isn't. Come on, Jess. Don't underestimate yourself.'

'So you . . . you'd like one, then?'

He frowned. 'Like one what?'

She reached into her handbag and took out the item that had been sitting there all morning, almost burning a hole through the leather. It was wrapped in her favourite tissue paper from the shop: blue with little gold clocks on it. She handed it to him.

'What's this?'

Jess laughed. 'Open it and you'll see.'

She watched him unwrap the tissue paper, watched his brows rise, his mouth fall open as he revealed the print, secured in a chunky white frame. '*We all have superpowers, you just need to believe in yourself to discover yours*,' he read out. 'Jess, this is—'

'I went back to the heath,' she told him. 'I waited for a windy day, and there was someone else flying a kite, so the photo – it's not *our* kite, but it's similar.' It was another diamond, the panels gold, green and red, its shimmery fabric glowing. It looked, almost, like a superhero costume. She'd put the text next to it, over the blue sky, but matched the font colours to the kite. The design was one of her boldest, the words were Ash's, and it was selling well online, already making money for Enzo.

'You made this for me?' he asked.

'I did,' she said. 'I'll put it in the shop, too. I hope you don't mind, but—'

'Of course I don't.' Ash laughed. 'Thank you. I love it. I'm going to put it up at home, and it'll always remind me of you. Of that day on the heath.' There was something sad about his smile, and Jess had the urge to push; to get him to open up.

'You have to go to your next appointment in a bit?' she asked.

'Yeah.' He exhaled.

'You're not looking forward to it?'

'It's not a whole lot of fun,' he admitted.

'So what—'

'But I'm glad we get this time, now. Before I have to go.'

Jess paused. The subject change had been obvious, but they'd had so little time on their own, and she didn't want to ruin their goodbye. 'And next week,' she said instead, 'we'll have two whole hours.' She felt giddy at the thought. 'Though we won't be alone, and it's going to be challenging, helping Felicity face her demons.' She leaned into him, and he brought his arm around her waist. 'You didn't have to offer to help.'

'Felicity invited me,' Ash said, his mouth close to hers. 'And I don't want you to have to do it alone. If we can work together to make things easier for her, then why not? And, like I said earlier, I don't mind what we're doing, as long as I get to spend time with you.'

Jess's throat squeezed. 'Don't think I didn't notice that Felicity got you to sacrifice your coffee date with Mack, while I haven't been able to.'

171

Ash grinned. 'I'm testing the boundaries. I can see Mack any evening after work, whereas this time in Greenwich – it's only on a Sunday. An hour isn't enough any more. Not because of Felicity, but because of you.'

'So you're saying,' Jess said, as two small boys flew through the alley on scooters, followed by their jogging, harassed-looking dad, 'that you would have given me two hours next weekend whatever?'

'That's exactly what I'm saying.' Ash cupped her face, his touch delicate, fingers brushing her cheek. His kiss, when it came, made her feel weightless and beautiful.

'I need your number,' he said, pulling back an inch. 'I can't believe I don't have it already.'

Jess laughed. 'I was thinking the same.'

They swapped phones, typed in their numbers, then handed them back with the new, precious information safely stored.

'So many boundaries broken,' Ash said.

'*So* many,' Jess agreed. 'Maybe one day you'll be able to stay with me past one o'clock.' She smiled up at him, and while Ash returned it, there was something in his grey eyes, a haunted look, that echoed what he'd told her a moment ago. *It's not a whole lot of fun.*

'Maybe,' he murmured. 'But this week, I have to go.'

'I know,' she said. 'I'm sorry, if—'

'Don't apologise.' He brushed her hair behind her ear. 'Please. Just leave me with another kiss?'

'Not a *total* hardship,' Jess said, trying to take them back to light and flirtatious, to dissolve the black cloud that had fallen over them.

Their goodbye kiss started out gentle, then Ash slid his fingers into her hair, and she twisted hers in his T-shirt, and it was only a loud 'harrumph' that broke them apart, both of them flushing under the glare of the sturdy older woman with a shopping trolley, who had stopped in front of them as if they were blocking the entire alleyway.

'Sorry,' Jess murmured.

'Please.' Ash pressed himself against the wall and gestured for her to go past them.

The woman kept her eyes trained on them as she walked slowly past, the wheels of her tartan trolley squeaking painfully.

Once she had gone, they dissolved into laughter, Ash pressing his head into Jess's neck, his warm breath dampening the collar of her dress.

'We should make it our aim to appal old ladies as often as possible,' she said.

'For as long as possible,' Ash added.

'Agreed.' His words made her pulse dance unsteadily in her throat.

'Same time next week?'

'Nope,' she replied gleefully. 'An hour earlier than usual.'

'Of course!' He laughed. 'Your kiss wiped my mind clear.'

'Exactly my plan.' Jess blew him a final one to send him on his way.

At the end of the alley, he turned and held up her print, which he'd carefully wrapped up again. 'Thank you for this.'

'You're welcome,' she called, and watched him turn right and disappear from view.

Jess walked back into the market high on desire, her mind still scrambled by their unexpectedly earth-shattering kiss. Most of the other traders had gone back to their stalls, and Lola and Spade had their instruments out and their heads close together, debating something with Enzo, while Deano set up his large, professional-looking camera on a sturdy tripod.

Other people were sitting at the picnic tables outside the pub, full pints in front of them, and Jess's eyes were drawn to the blackboard next to the door, the scratchy chalk writing in pink and blue, the penmanship slightly slanted.

Written at the top, in capitals, were the words 'HAPPY HOUR!' Beneath it, instead of the deals for two-for-one cocktails and a pint and a chaser for £7, she wanted to write *Jess Peacock and Ash Faulkner,* because that was exactly what she had with him. A time of the week she looked forward to, where she could feel lighter and less inhibited, drunk on laughter and lust, her whole body flushed with enjoyment. Being with Ash on Sunday mornings – that was her happy hour. She wouldn't replace it for all the Espresso Martinis in the world.

Chapter Nineteen

Mack isn't speaking to me because I'm abandoning him on Sunday. He says I've betrayed him.

Uh oh. Can you do another time? One evening, like you said?

I offered Friday night, actual FRIDAY NIGHT, when I should be out getting drunk, and he said no because he wants his Sunday paper and coffee combo.

There's no pleasing some people.

Then, Jess couldn't help adding:

You go out and get drunk with a whole crowd of banker friends on Fridays? I wouldn't have thought that about you.

I don't really. Sometimes I have a few pints with the personnel team. Mostly I stay in by myself and fire up Netflix. A sad indictment of my life.

You could ask Mack if he wants to Netflix and chill, then get his Sunday paper just before you come here, and see if that appeases him.

I AM still getting his Sunday paper, but that's not enough.
I am too young and stupid for my own good – his words.
He knows how to flatter me. Also, how am I going to
scrub that Netflix and chill image from my head, Jess?

Sorry. 😄 Why not imagine it's not Mack, but someone
else with the Netflixing and the chilling?

Who would you suggest?

No clue. Sure you can think of someone. 😊 xx

Jess often spent Thursday tidying the shop, checking orders
and stock levels. It was never as busy as Fridays or the
weekend, but sales of their smaller items were consistent –
the paperweights and candles that weren't a big financial
investment, the dinkier vases which – due to it being in the
shop's name – there were a lot of. But today was the (very
soft) launch of Jess's motivational prints, so there was no calm
tidying, no checking of stock levels.

'I can't believe I didn't know about this,' Wendy said for
at least the fiftieth time, rearranging the framed prints on the
prominently positioned shelf she'd designated for them. She
had also, when Jess had told her about the plan they had all
concocted, decided that whatever profits Jess was giving to
Enzo, she would match. She said it shouldn't all be on Jess's
shoulders to help Enzo out financially. Everyone was offering
moral support, but it had only been Jess's prints – so far – that
had made it over the fundraising finishing line, and Wendy, as
self-designated mother hen of the market, hadn't wanted her to
be the only one contributing. 'They look wonderful here,' she

went on. 'I'm going to buy this one for starters.' She chuckled, then read aloud: '*If at first you don't succeed, try a new way of annoying your nemesis.*'

'Oh God.' Jess pressed her hands into her eyes. 'And Lola and Spade are coming in a minute, to prance about and play their instruments.'

Wendy laughed. '*Prance about and play their instruments?* I've heard them, Jess.'

'OK, I'm not being fair. It's a whole lot better than that.' She tipped her head back. 'My designs are going to be on TikTok.'

'You say that like it's BBC One.'

'It has more viewers,' Jess pointed out. 'Can we just . . . I'm not sure about this one. Could we put it at the back?' It was one of her earlier, clumsier designs, created when she had been feeling particularly grumpy, that read: *Live, Love, Laugh and then Leave.* She didn't know why she'd chosen it for the shop, except it had a photo she was proud of; the river on a slate-grey morning, the water shrouded in a thin blanket of mist. She went to move it, but Wendy slapped her hand away.

'No. No hiding anything. They're all staying and they're all going to sell.'

'Shit balls,' Jess said with feeling. 'Why the fuck did I agree to this?'

Wendy waggled a tenner at her. 'Stop swearing, go and get some muffins, and calm your nerves until the musicians get here.'

Jess sighed and took the note, felt a brief surge of glee at the thought of stuffing some mini-muffins in her face, then saw Lola, Spade and Deano heading in their direction. 'Oh God,' she said, and then, when she saw who was with them, added, 'What the hell?'

177

'Ah. Yes.' Wendy folded her arms. 'Braden asked if he could come in today. He wanted to hear Spade and Lola perform; he's actually very musical himself.'

'He is?' Jess said faintly. She knew that Braden was still working in the shop on Tuesdays and Wednesdays, and that Wendy thought he'd proved himself. No items had gone missing – not even any hares, sadly – and he was a hard worker. And now, here he was, hoody-clad and grinning.

'They look *great,*' Lola said, zeroing in on the display of Jess's prints immediately. 'Really professional.'

Jess sold them unframed online. She didn't have a lot of space to store frames, and it made posting them more effort and more expensive. They were printed on glossy, good-quality photo card and that was it. But for the shop, she'd put each of her designs in a white wooden frame. People came to No Vase Like Home for trinkets and decorations, not DIY projects.

'You're just saying that,' Jess mumbled to herself, but Lola heard her.

'No, I'm not.' She looked Jess straight in the eye. 'You have to start believing in yourself.'

'All talents are valid talents,' Spade added, as he took his guitar out of its case. It was a glittering peacock blue, and Jess was drawn to it whenever he had it with him. The musicians, their cameraman and Braden had taken up the whole shop – one of the men was wearing overpowering sandalwood aftershave – and Jess felt on the verge of claustrophobia. She wondered if she could hide in the storeroom until they were done.

'You need to be in the background,' Lola said, as if she could read her mind.

'I don't,' Jess protested. 'Just focus on the prints. Nobody cares who made them.'

'We care,' Lola said. 'And everyone else will too.'

'What am I going to do, though? Just stand there like a lemon? Gesture to the pictures like some kind of QVC model?'

'Hold one up,' Lola suggested. 'Smile for the camera.'

'I don't—'

'Do you know what you're doing, Braden?' Lola asked him, cutting Jess off.

'Fuck yeah I do!' He punched the air, his fist hidden by his oversized sleeve.

'What's your role in all this?' Jess asked, curiosity overriding her nerves. 'Do you have an instrument, or are you their official cheerleader?'

'Cheerleader!' Braden scoffed, then tapped his cheek. 'It's all in here.'

'You're a singer?'

'Nah, man. Beatboxer.'

'Oh!' Jess said. 'OK. With a violin and a guitar?'

'He's really good,' Lola told her. 'We've made it work, our little trio of misfits. Right. Deano, are you all set up?'

'Just about.' Deano had long, dirty blond hair in a ponytail, and his skinny jeans looked painted on, but he clearly knew what he was doing.

Jess gritted her teeth, let herself be manoeuvred into position next to the display of her artworks, and hoped that Lola, Spade and Braden would block her from view.

Braden, it turned out, was a revelation. The moment he joined in, Jess wanted to stop him and ask how he did it. Did he have a tiny electronic speaker hidden in his cheek? She didn't know how anyone could be a walking percussion section with only their tongue and soft palate.

179

Lola and Spade were unfazed, and Jess watched from her awkward spot as Deano panned round the shop, zoomed in on the prints, and hopefully left her out of it. Their music filled the shop and reverberated through her bones, while the lights on Spade's portable amp danced like a mini disco. It flowed through her like electricity, making her fingers and toes tingle: Lola's soaring violin, the growling Fender, Braden adding structure with his beats. It made her think of her last kiss with Ash, the desire and desperation growing between them, her certainty that, if they had been somewhere more private than an alleyway, they wouldn't have stopped.

The music cut off all of a sudden, and Jess swayed slightly on the spot.

'That was marvellous.' Wendy clapped, her voice raised as if the music was still ringing in her ears.

'Thank you.' Lola gave them a low bow, then straightened. 'Is the landing page all ready to go?'

Jess nodded. She had written a blurb telling Enzo and Carolina's story, the long tradition in their family of making delicate filigree jewellery, Carolina's sudden illness and how sales of the prints would go towards getting them back on their feet. She had checked Enzo was happy with the wording, emphasising that it was a temporary measure to get them through a tough time, *not* begging for handouts, and she hoped that a combination of the Misfits' music, TikTok's ability to latch onto the unusual, and some brightly coloured wall prints could make a difference to the couple's future.

The Misfits left as noisily as they'd arrived, and then it was just Wendy and Jess and their empty shop, and the whole thing felt surreal and a bit anticlimactic.

'You just wait,' Wendy said. 'In a few hours' time there'll

180

be a mad rush, and you'll have to leave early and make more of these for tomorrow.'

'I doubt that,' Jess replied, but she felt a small blossoming of hope. Maybe they *would* all sell out, and it wouldn't only be Enzo's business that got a boost, but Jess's side hustle too.

'Oh God, I *love* these!' The familiar voice snapped Jess's head up. She had been sneakily looking at her phone below the counter, waiting for Lola to send through the video. The shop had been unusually quiet, as if laughing at Jess for letting herself believe she might make some sales.

'Hi, Margaret,' she said.

'I adore these prints. You've got a new supplier?'

'Sort of.'

'Some of them are so funny!' Margaret picked one up, and Jess's palms prickled with sweat.

'Our new supplier,' Wendy announced, arms outstretched towards Jess as she came out of the storeroom.

'Really? You made these?'

'Yup,' Jess admitted. 'Profits from every sale are going to help Enzo, one of the stallholders here whose wife is unwell.'

'Even more reason for me not to resist.' Margaret grinned, then went back to examining each print, letting out little bursts of laughter as she flicked through them.

Wendy and Jess exchanged a hopeful look. If Margaret bought one, it would be the first shop sale Jess had ever had, the first time she'd broken beyond the bounds of Etsy. It didn't matter that she was giving the profits to Enzo – and she wouldn't want to do anything else right now – if she exchanged money with a customer who had deliberately chosen one of her designs, wanted it inside their home or office or caravan, then she would feel triumphant, as if she could accomplish anything.

'Oh now, I really like this one.' Margaret held it up, and Jess's heart thumped. It was Ash's first quote: *Flying isn't as hard as it looks, just make sure a part of you stays tethered to the ground.* 'It really resonates, right?'

'I think so,' Jess said.

'Sort of like, *reach for the stars, but also don't get ahead of yourself.* Obviously yours is worded better, which is why it's on a poster.'

'A friend of mine came up with it,' Jess admitted, as Margaret handed it to her and she wrapped it in tissue paper. She was aiming for nonchalance, but wasn't sure she had managed it.

'Lovely to see you,' Margaret said, once the sale had gone through.

'Come back again soon,' Wendy replied.

'I'm sure I will!'

When she'd gone, Jess squealed and flung her arms round her boss, breaking all her own rules about respecting personal space.

'I'm so proud of you, Jessica Peacock,' Wendy said.

'I'm proud of me too. One sale down, only about thirty more to go.' They swapped grins.

'Want a celebratory muffin, seeing as we didn't get a chance earlier?'

'Always,' Jess said.

Once she was alone, she picked up her phone, but there was still no video from Lola.

She realised that her life felt very different now to how it had done a month ago. It was busier, brighter, more full of people, and it made her think of one of her earliest quotes, one that would never make its way into No Vase Like Home: *Being alone doesn't always mean you're lonely*. She still stood by that – she still valued time by herself – but she did wonder if, before the separate parts of her world had started to converge, she had been a bit lonely, too.

Her phone beeped and she glanced at the screen, the smile coming easily to her lips.

Know where else in Greenwich is haunted besides the tunnel? There's a whole load of spooky history. Some of this stuff is fascinating. 😨 x

Jess rolled her eyes and tried to think of a reply to Ash's message. She was still smiling when Wendy returned with two bacon and spinach muffins in one of Kirsty's red gift boxes, their tantalising smell filling the shop. As she thanked her boss and bit into the fluffy, gooey centre, she wondered how wise it was to rely on Ash for her daily dose of happiness when, around a month ago, she had tried very hard to rely on nobody but herself.

Chapter Twenty

Ash turned up at the shop on Sunday wearing jeans with rips in the knees and a grey T-shirt darkened by rain. The damp cotton clung to him, giving Jess a tantalising glimpse of a body that was lean but strong: collarbones and biceps and defined shoulders she wanted to feel beneath her palms. He looked ready for his starring role – hot guy doing battle with a house full of mess – and a delicious shiver ran down her spine.

'I have no idea if Felicity likes coffee, or if she'll be offended that I've brought drinks,' he said.

Jess had come to look forward to his beverage-related greetings. 'And yet here you are with your cardboard cup carrier.'

'I couldn't turn up empty-handed. How are you?' His grey eyes were bright with anticipation, no sign of the dread Jess had felt all morning at the thought of going back to Felicity's house.

'I'm OK,' she said. 'Are you sure you want to do this?'

He glanced at Wendy.

'Don't worry, I know,' she said from behind the counter, where she was flicking through a homeware magazine.

'I know you know about Felicity,' Ash told her. 'I just wasn't sure how honest to be in front of you.'

'I would say not at all—' Jess started.

'You were about to admit that you didn't mind helping Felicity, but that you'd much rather spend the next hour kissing the sense out of my very best colleague, is that it?'

Jess gasped out loud, then felt like an idiot.

Ash laughed. 'I can be completely honest, then.'

'Nothing gets past me.' Wendy smiled at him. 'But I think it's great, what you're doing. Not just the kissing, but with Felicity. Especially as you have some experience, Ash. Not necessarily with this particular issue, but . . .'

'Yeah, this is a new one for me,' he said. 'But as long as we're careful, and let Felicity lead the way, I hope we can help her see things differently.'

'And you'll look after Jess?'

'I don't need looking after, *Mum.*' Jess picked up her bag from the storeroom.

'Of course,' Ash said seriously.

'Have a lovely time,' Wendy called gleefully as Jess turned Ash around in the doorway – he was entirely pliable – and pushed him out into the market.

'She's great,' he said, as they navigated the throng. The rain drummed steadily on the roof, and even though the sky was grey, the market was still colourful, with its dangling hearts and cheerful stalls, visitors in their weekend-bright dresses and jackets. It was never a monochrome place.

'She's a challenge,' Jess replied.

'But you love her.'

'She's all right.' Jess couldn't have sounded any more like a petulant teenager, and Ash laughed gently.

'Did you get away OK?' she asked, after they'd left the market behind.

'It was fine,' Ash said. 'I got Mack his paper, stayed for twenty minutes so he could rant about the latest climate change conspiracy' – he rolled his eyes – 'then escaped. And now, we have two whole hours.'

'You remember what we're spending the next two hours doing, don't you?'

'Of course. But it doesn't mean that's *all* we're doing.' They'd reached a quieter, residential road, and Ash put the coffee carrier on the low wall of the house they were outside.

'What's happening?' Jess asked.

'Come here.' Ash's voice was soft, and as she stepped towards him, he put his hands on her hips.

'It's raining,' she said, but it had faded to a barely there drizzle. She was in her own pair of tatty jeans and a navy T-shirt, a thin hoody slung over the top, but she might as well have been naked for the way sensation shivered through her at Ash's touch. His kiss was gentle, and she closed her eyes so she could focus on feeling, on living in this moment: kissing Ash in the rain, in broad daylight, in the street. She didn't even care if people were looking, judging, disapproving.

'I feel much more prepared now,' she whispered, when they pulled apart.

'Good,' Ash said roughly. 'Me too.'

'It's just up here.'

'Lead the way.' Ash retrieved the coffees, and they walked up the hill together.

Felicity opened the door wearing a dove-grey dress and pearl earrings, as if she was off to have afternoon tea at the Langham. Ash looked a little taken aback, and Jess wondered if she should have spent more time explaining how complete Felicity's denial was.

'Jessica, Ash – thank you for coming. Do come in.' She stepped back, into the narrow space left in her hallway. Jess threw Ash a quick smile and walked into the house.

186

'Lovely to see you, Felicity,' Ash said, following her in. Jess heard something fall behind him – a stack of papers, perhaps, as he'd brushed past it.

'You've brought coffee, too.' Felicity clasped her hands. 'How wonderful of you. Shall we go into the living room?'

'That sounds great,' Jess said, but she had to stifle her gasp when she stepped through the door. With high ceilings and a large bay window, it was a proud, elegant space that could have been gorgeous. As it was, she could just make out a sofa, one cushion exposed beneath the piles of things, a white cat lying on it, curled up asleep. There was the narrowest of walkways, a clear line of sight to a television, the screen covered with a thick layer of dust, and then books and papers, heaps of folded clothes, boxes of biscuits, crackers and chocolates everywhere, everything in high, teetering piles.

Jess thought there must be a fireplace against the far wall, but it was obscured by a row of dining chairs, several plastic storage crates resting on top of them.

'This is . . .' she started, then noticed one of Wendy's hares standing on top of a box. Felicity must have bought it on a day when Jess wasn't working. It looked smug, as if ending up here, overseeing this chaos, had been its goal all along.

'Who's this guy?' Ash put the coffees on the floor and bent to stroke the white cat.

'This is Twiggy,' Felicity said. 'He's a sweetheart.' She stood next to Ash and chucked the cat under the chin. 'I don't know where Bond and Artemis are.' She smiled at Jess, then her shoulders sagged. 'I do feel as if I could have been a better hostess, but I haven't had the time to tidy, lately. Life gets so busy.' Her laugh was high and anxious.

'Have a coffee,' Ash said. 'I have cappuccino or Americano. I wasn't sure if you took milk.'

'Cappuccino would be wonderful,' Felicity said. 'Thank you.'

He handed her a cup. 'I don't think I spilled any of it on the way here.'

Jess gave Ash a secret smile as he handed her an Americano.

He returned it, then said, 'Can I sit next to your cat, Felicity?'

'Twiggy would love that.' Felicity perched on a low pile of books, and Jess wondered if she knew the towers of stuff like a well-trodden obstacle course: which were safe to sit on, which were too precarious. Jess glanced around, looking for somewhere she could sit that wouldn't be a catastrophe, and found a duvet bunched up in an opaque bin liner. She lowered herself gingerly onto it.

'Tell me about the cats.' Ash stroked Twiggy, his tanned hand dark against the cat's white fur. 'Are they rescues?'

'Bond is,' Felicity said. 'My friend Coco found him, abandoned as a kitten outside her apartment block in Lambeth, and she isn't allowed pets, so she asked if I'd like him. I'd recently lost one of my older cats, Marigold, and I was feeling all at sea.'

'Losing pets is always hard,' Ash said. 'They're part of the family.'

'Do you have any?'

'Unfortunately not. We're not allowed them in my apartment block, either. I think my contract says I could have a goldfish, but they're not the same, are they?' He ruffled Twiggy behind the ears, and she purred loudly. 'What about the other one? Twiggy, Bond and . . .'

'Artemis,' Felicity said. 'Oh, now he is a *real* terror. The leader of the bunch.'

As they talked, Jess noticed the way Ash spoke to Felicity, gently teasing details from her while also making her feel comfortable, softening her apprehension. Outwardly, he seemed entirely relaxed, but she knew him well enough now that she could see a tightness in his jaw, as if he was on a mission; in professional mode, determined to help.

He was almost too good to be true: certainly too good to let go. This kind, funny man who wanted to spend his Sundays with her, who had so readily agreed to come here today. She didn't want to rely on him – she didn't want to rely on anyone, entirely – and even though he wouldn't tell her what it was, she had a sense that, whatever he did after seeing her, the reason he was in Greenwich in the first place, wouldn't go on for ever. She had let herself enjoy it because there was something about it that felt temporary.

But today he'd arrived at the shop looking so gorgeous and necessary, already an essential part of her Sundays, and she'd realised that giving him up would be like finding a winning lottery ticket and gifting it to someone else, or throwing it off a bridge so the wind caught it and snatched it away.

'Oh, I don't know,' she heard Felicity say, and tuned back into their conversation.

'Only if you fancy it,' Ash said gently. 'It's impossible to know where to start, sometimes. You get focused on other things, and then the job seems too big. But three pairs of hands are better than one.' His smile was so warm and inviting, Jess didn't think anyone would be able to resist it, but Felicity had put her coffee down and was wringing her hands.

'I'm not sure.' She looked around with wide eyes, and Jess realised Ash had decided to tackle the hoarding head on. 'I just . . . all these things, they have a purpose.'

Ash nodded. 'Of course. They're your belongings. We wouldn't have to get rid of a thing, I just wondered if you'd like our help to organise them a bit better. We could focus on one space, perhaps clear these few bits off the sofa, so your cats could snuggle up together.' He tapped the cushion next to him, which was buried under plastic takeaway containers.

Jess couldn't imagine Felicity eating a chow mein or a vindaloo, but she could see what Ash was doing: framing it as a way to help her cats, her saviours. She decided that this man, who had stopped a thief and then approached her in the market all those weeks ago, was some kind of miracle. He sipped his coffee, stroked Twiggy, and waited.

'I just . . .' Felicity tapped her fingers on her knee. Ash stayed quiet, so Jess did, too. 'I suppose we could,' the older woman said eventually. 'Just these few things, if you think that Bond and Artemis would like it?'

'I'm sure they would,' Ash said evenly. 'We'll take it slowly.'

He waited . . . waited, until Felicity got up and wove through the clutter to the sofa, then stopped in front of the piles of boxes, a few tatty magazines sticking out like the most chaotic game of Jenga.

'All right,' Felicity said. 'What shall I . . . how shall we . . .?'

Ash stood and picked up the nearest thing. It was a green cool bag, the National Trust logo sewn onto the front. 'Is this for picnics?'

Felicity nodded. 'But it . . . the lining is damaged. I put a knife in it one time, and it sliced clean through. But it could be mended, do you think? It seems a shame to throw it away.'

Ash took his time examining the bag. 'You know, I think this might be beyond repair. We could put it to one side, see if you have any others? But if it were me, I might well decide that I'd used it enough, that it was time to let it go.'

Felicity looked anxious. 'Are you sure?'

'It's your decision,' he said. 'We could come back to it later?'

'Oh yes, I . . . I think we should . . .' As she spoke, Ash stuck his finger through a hole that went all the way through the bag. 'Oh!' She pressed her hands to her cheeks when Ash waggled two fingers through it, a goofy grin on his face. 'Oh, of course let's not keep it!' She laughed, and this time it sounded genuine.

'Where shall I put it?' Ash asked, and Jess decided he was the most patient person in the world.

'I just . . .' She looked over at Jess, her expression pleading.

Jess turned an equally pleading, though she hoped more subtle, gaze on Ash. His smile was barely there, his nod tiny, but she felt his approval, felt as if she *could* help, if he thought she could.

'Why don't we make a pile by the front door?' she suggested. 'Then Ash and I could take the things you don't need any more when we go.' On their way here, just before they'd reached Felicity's road, Jess had noticed a double garage, the concrete space in front of it containing a clothes bank, a cardboard bin and a general waste bin. She thought that, if Felicity agreed to get rid of anything, then it should go as quickly as possible, or it would get subsumed back into the house.

'If you're sure,' Felicity said.

'We're happy to help,' Ash said lightly, and handed Jess the damaged bag. She took it into the hallway, then opened the front door and put it on the porch. One item down, she thought, as she watched a bee fly lazily to a tangle of white roses, their petals sparkling with raindrops, that were creeping up the side of Felicity's house.

When she got back to the living room, Ash was holding a mug with a large chip in the lip. At this rate, it would take thirty years to go through everything. But, perhaps, if they helped give Felicity the confidence to do it, things might get a little bit easier, a little bit quicker, over time.

An hour had passed, leaving only half an hour until Ash needed to go wherever he went, and Jess had to get back to the shop. They had made decisions about a dozen things, and Felicity had agreed that she no longer needed seven of them. Ash was being unwaveringly patient, and Jess was battling a surge of feelings for him that were almost as overwhelming as the piles of clutter in Felicity's house.

'What about this?' He picked up a purple blanket made of a soft, fleecy material. It was crumpled, and he shook it out then began folding it, tucking it under his chin so he could reach the bottom corners.

Jess stepped forward to help, but he'd worked quickly, and she knew she was being hopeless. Still, he flashed her a smile, then turned his attention to Felicity.

'My husband bought that for me,' she said, her uncertainty replaced by steeliness. 'About a week before he left.'

'Oh,' Jess said. 'I'm so sorry, Felicity. That must have been awful.' But – alongside sympathy – she felt a wave of relief. It explained so much, her being abandoned by the man she loved. Couldn't something like that trigger behaviour like this? The urge to hold onto things? If you *decided* to be on your own, if you were in charge of your solitude, then this wasn't destined to be your fate.

'He was an ambitious man,' Felicity told them. 'He wanted to go everywhere, see *everything*, meet new people all the time. He was a whirlwind of outlandish ideas, and I couldn't keep up. I never truly felt a part of his plans.'

'That's terrible—' Jess started, but then she glanced at Ash. He'd gone perfectly still, and was staring at the blanket in his hands. His chest rose on an inhale, and she was about to go over to him when he looked up. His expression was blank, his lips pressed into a thin line.

'Ash? Are you—'

'Could I have some water, Felicity?' he asked, speaking over Jess.

'Of course. The kitchen's at the end of the hall.'

Ash held the blanket out for Jess, catching her eye for barely a second. When she took it he slipped past her, and she could hear the slow, soft pad of his Vans as he manoeuvred down the narrow walkway in the corridor.

Jess tried to swallow past the lump in her throat. 'This is soft,' she murmured, because she couldn't think what else to say.

Felicity's gaze was sharp. 'You should go and check that he's all right. I would wager that he's not, and that he wants you there.'

'You can't know that.' Jess wondered how Felicity could be so astute about other people, and still have got herself into this disastrous state.

'Go and hug him, Jessica. He might not want to talk, but that was a man who needed a hug, if ever I saw one.'

'OK.' Her voice sounded pathetically small.

She handed Felicity the blanket and crept down the crammed corridor, into the kitchen with its Russian doll army and a million other things. She saw Ash through the window, standing next to the water feature with his back to the house.

She pushed open the door and sucked in a breath of crisp, rain-damp air. The water feature was bubbling away, competing with the pitter-patter of raindrops, and Jess took a step towards Ash, his shoulders a rigid, unyielding line.

'Hey,' she said gently.

He glanced at her then looked away. 'Sorry. I just needed a minute.'

'You're so amazing with Felicity.' She took another step forward, until her front was almost pressed against his back. 'It must take a toll, though.'

He shook his head. 'It's not that.'

'Can you tell me what it is?'

He cleared his throat. 'I don't . . . this isn't about that.'

'What isn't about *what*?'

He turned around, and she saw that his eyes were red. She had no idea if he'd been rubbing the dust out of them, or if the water on his cheeks was raindrops. There was a tiny bit of purple fluff from the blanket caught in his stubble, and she reached up, teasing it out, smoothing her fingers along his jawline.

'Thank you for bringing me here,' he said.

Jess laughed quietly. 'Are you kidding? My heart feels like it's been pummelled. Poor Felicity.'

'I know. But she's open to working through it, so I think . . .'

'If we commit to doing this for the next decade, we'll make some progress? Maybe unearth the carpet in the living room?'

'Accepting it, making the first move to face something, is the hardest part.'

'You sound like you're speaking from experience.'

Ash dropped his head, and Jess waited. The rain picked up its pace, and she could feel the ice-cold pellets on the back of her head, sliding down her neck. But she watched Ash, breath held, until he looked up.

'I'd do this for the next decade,' he said, 'if it meant spending that time with you.'

Before she had a chance to process what he'd said, to come up with something to defuse the weight of it, he wrapped his arms around her. Instead of bending his head to kiss her, he dropped it onto her shoulder, burying his nose in her neck and breathing her in.

Jess ran her hand over his soft, wet hair and down his neck, and slid her other arm around his waist, pulling him tight against her. He was taller than her, but they fitted together perfectly: he felt so right tucked against her, both soft and solid, like Rodin's sculpture of the kiss.

He pulled back eventually and murmured 'thank you' and then, 'I need to go.' He squeezed her hand before walking back into the house.

Jess followed him to the living room, and found Felicity folding up another blanket, this one red and green tartan. 'I do wonder if the charity shop could make use of a few of these things,' she told them.

Jess wanted to jump for joy, but Ash was calm and noncommittal when he said, 'I expect they could.' It was as if he'd wiped the last few minutes from his brain, tucked his hurt into a box. 'We have to head off now, but do you want us to take the things we talked about?'

Felicity put the blanket down and gave them an anxious look.

'Come and double check.' Ash gestured for her to accompany him.

They went out onto the porch and, apart from a mug with a broken handle that she insisted she could use as a vase, she allowed them to take the handful of things with them.

'You should come for afternoon tea, or for dinner one time,' Felicity said, her hands clutching the skirt of her dress.

'I'd love that,' Ash assured her. 'And I'm sure Jess will see you again soon.'

'Of course,' Jess said. She knew he meant that they should keep up the momentum, but she wasn't sure she could do it without him, without his calm presence and his instinctive way of knowing exactly what to do.

They said goodbye, and she and Ash carried the broken items to the bins at the end of the road.

'That went better than I thought.' Ash glanced at his watch.

'I didn't think she'd get rid of anything. You were wonderful.'

He shrugged. 'I had a few techniques I could call on. And she loves you, Jess. She looks up to you.'

'Are you OK?' She laced her fingers through his. 'You know that I'm here, that I'll help if I can.'

'Thank you.' He swallowed. 'But nobody can help with this. And what we have, what we're doing – that's what matters. Getting to spend Sunday mornings with you.'

Jess wanted him to open up to her, wanted to force him to talk about it, but they were always running out of time. 'Two hours next week?' she said instead.

'It's a risk,' he replied, mock-solemn. 'Mack might turn on me, but I'll try and work something out, OK?'

'OK.' She wanted more time with him. She would need to use his own tactics, coax the truth out of him slowly, just like he was doing with Felicity. 'You'll let me know when you can come?'

'Of course. I need to head off in this direction, so . . .'

'Sure. Bye, then.'

'Bye, Jess.' He cupped her cheek and pressed his lips against hers, and she couldn't help thinking that it felt a little desperate, that there was something raw and untethered about his kiss. She was drunk on the feel of him, reluctant to let go, his hand warm and firm against her jaw.

They broke apart and he turned and walked away. Jess watched him until he was out of sight.

As she returned to the market, her rhythmic footsteps seemed to tap out a phrase: *He's. Mine. He's. Mine.* It was as if all of his smiles, his deep laugh, turning up in the doorway of No Vase Like Home with coffee every Sunday, and even – perhaps especially – that moment in Felicity's garden, where he'd clung to her like she was his life raft, every one was a new link in a chain, and those links had banded together, tying *them* together in a way that was impossible to break. As she reached the alley where they'd kissed like teenagers the weekend before and the heavens opened properly, she realised that, whatever they had together, whatever these hours turned into, she wouldn't be able to let Ash go, even if she wanted to.

Chapter Twenty-One

He almost didn't go. He almost walked down to the jetty beyond the *Cutty Sark*, got on the boat and went home. He wanted to go back to the market and find Jess, but then he'd have to give her an explanation that went beyond burrowing into her like she was his security blanket, and muttering a lame excuse about it not being relevant to what they had.

It wasn't Felicity and the terrible state she'd got herself into – though of course it wasn't easy to see someone so broken. He actually felt like he'd helped a little, that he'd shown her it was OK to work through it slowly, that she could get there, however long it took. That was the key with so much of what he did: being careful, letting them find the answer or come to a realisation in their own time. He was the trail of spotlights that lit up a pathway in the dark, switching on whenever someone approached, guiding them to the end. But they needed to do the walking, travel down that path, themselves.

No, what had got to him, threatened to undo all his careful composure, was what Felicity had said about her husband. She could have been talking about Nico Lombardo, not her ex.

It made him wonder how *he* was broken, because if hoarding was her way of coping, then what was his? Was it working too hard, spending too much time alone in his flat? Was his inability to find any empathy for his dad, even though he was dying, proof that he was fucked up? He'd told himself that seeing Jess, finding that connection with her, was healthy;

a sign that, now his dad was here and he'd committed to seeing him, he was working through things, healing himself. Now, he wasn't so sure.

He stopped at the end of the path, staring at the white door and the brass plaque that read *Cherry Blossom Lodge*. It conjured up a memory of the bench in the park, Jess and him laughing about Diamanté the demon dog, which he supposed was the point: it sounded more hopeful than the reality you got once you stepped over the threshold.

He cared too much about Jess. He had, less than half an hour before, clung onto her in sheer desperation. He wasn't sure that the amount of time he spent thinking about her, the overwhelming way her touch and her words affected him, was that healthy, after all.

'Hey, you.' Peggy was standing in the open doorway, staring at him. 'You look like hell, and I don't know if it's just because you're drowned. I should take pity and come out there, but it's pissing it down, so you'll have to come to me.'

Ash felt the tightness in his neck loosen a fraction. He hadn't even noticed how hard it was raining. He walked up the path, trying to conjure up some courage.

'Difficult day with Jess?' Peggy hurried to the desk and returned with a towel so he could dry his face and hair.

'We've been helping one of her friends.' He kept it vague because Peggy lived in Greenwich, and he wasn't sure if the rest of the area was as tight-knit as the market. 'She's struggling right now, so Jess and I are supporting her. So it was . . . But I mean, it's never hard seeing Jess.'

Peggy frowned. 'Are you sure you should be adding that to your day? Not being with Jess, but whatever is going on with her friend.'

He sat heavily in a chair. 'I can help, though.'

'You need to help yourself right now.'

He let himself remember Jess stroking his hair, how he'd felt ridiculous – like one of Felicity's cats – and also unbelievably calmed. 'I am getting help,' he said. 'Being with Jess helps.'

Peggy looked unsure, but – unusually for her – she didn't push him. 'Now, I have some Jammie Dodgers, or we've got piccalilli and Nutella on sourdough. What do you fancy?' She tapped her chin thoughtfully and Ash laughed.

'Peggy, you're one of the most delightful people I've ever met, but you are also a monster.'

'I like to show my dark side occasionally,' she said. 'Keep things edgy.'

She waggled her eyebrows then went into the small kitchen, and Ash thought how he had come to see this routine, where she went and got him coffee, as invaluable. Then he thought about how he'd started doing that on the way to see Jess, getting them a drink before he met her at her shop, and how, already, it was a ritual he didn't think he could do without.

He had wanted to impress her from that very first day, to show her that he was someone worth knowing. Only a few weeks in, and he didn't think he'd be able to find happiness without their Sunday mornings just behind him, so he could replay them, or ahead – keeping him going through the rest of the week.

But this part of his life, inside Cherry Blossom Lodge, had an unknown but inevitable end date. There were so many reasons he couldn't think about that now, including the sense he got that Jess liked their meetings because they were contained, with a structure and boundaries, and he didn't know if she'd be willing to change that. They'd had two hours this morning, but that had been for Felicity, not them. And Ash wanted, more than anything, for a 'them' to exist: one that wasn't tied to his visits to this depressing place. He wanted Jess to spill over into every part of his life, but he wasn't that confident that she felt the same way.

'Why do bankers need emotional . . . support? If they have committed to that job, they have no real emotions.'

Ten minutes later, Ash was by his dad's bedside. His breathing was painfully laboured, but it was the first time he'd seen some of the old Nico spark, as if he was getting better, rather than deteriorating.

'That's not . . . you can't say that, Dad.'

'Why not use your skills to help more worthy people? Trauma victims. Nurses.'

Ash clenched his jaw. There were so many things he could say: how everyone deserved support; that you couldn't define anyone by their job, assume they were devoid of humanity because of how they earned a living; how Nico had spent his life chasing wealth, that his get-rich-quick schemes had helped only himself when they worked, and hurt others when they didn't. But time within these four walls was limited, and his blanket of guilt would be even more suffocating if he didn't show some kindness.

'Did you go to the park much, Dad? The museums? I get the boat down from London, and the view from the river . . . it's so different.'

His dad stuttered out a laugh.

'What?' Ash took a sip of his quickly cooling coffee.

'You were always good at deflecting,' Nico rasped. 'Whenever Julie and I got in an argument, even when you were little, you'd thrust a toy between us, or pull me into the garden to show me something. Like you couldn't bear us fighting.'

'Do you blame me? No kid wants to grow up in the middle of warring parents. And Dylan was always so upset.'

'You knew the right thing to say, even then. How to change the subject, turn to something happier. Sometimes you'd do a silly dance, so that Julie and I couldn't help but laugh. I suppose this is what you do with your bankers, too?'

'I don't dance in the office, that's for sure.' He shook his head. 'We work through things. You can't skirt round your problems, you have to walk right through the middle of them: examine them in detail, destroy them, whatever. I couldn't fix you and Mum; I could *only* deflect.'

'To *accept* your deflection, then, I haven't been to the park, or the museums. All this promise beyond the window, and I am stuck here for whatever time I have left.'

Ash looked at a bland painting of a tulip in a frame on the wall. 'Why Greenwich, then?'

'This place was the best,' Nico said. His voice was fading, the wheezing more pronounced. 'I searched, and this was top, and I had the money.'

Ash's first thought was *thank you*. If his dad had picked somewhere else, then he never would have met Jess. But he was also indignant on his mum's behalf, on Dylan's, because they could have done with money after Nico left. Julie Faulkner had brought them up, juggling long hours at two jobs with looking after them, no question of childcare or nannies because they would have taken what little salary she was bringing in. It had meant that Ash, at twelve, took care of Dylan after school, had never had playdates with his own friends or joined the school football team.

202

'The park's great,' he heard himself say, and Nico scoffed. 'I'm not bragging, I'm just telling you. The views over London, the river – when you get to the top of the hill – are impressive. You can see so much of the city. And there are cherry trees, and parakeets, and people walking hundreds of different breeds of dog. There's the Meridian Line, which runs over the observatory courtyard and people are always standing across it, taking photos, so it turns into a bit of a scrum.'

'Tourists are stupid,' Nico said.

Ash couldn't help grinning. 'Only because they're excited to be somewhere they've heard about. We see the photos and we want to be a part of it. There's so much to see out there.'

Nico shook his head, and Ash recognised the tightness in his dad's jaw, because he saw it in the mirror so often: when he was shaving, or after a long day – or after being here. He wondered if he'd fucked up.

'You did— you've done a lot with your life, Dad. Travelled the world, done some pretty outrageous things.' *Left your family behind*, he didn't add.

'You don't need to cosset me in your therapist language. Past tense is fine.'

Ash rubbed his cheek. 'Tell me about Positano the last time you were there.' He wouldn't let his dad fall into bitterness so he could use him as a punchbag. It was self-preservation, sure, but wasn't it only fair to Nico – to anyone, really – that the last conversations he had were as bright as they could be? His mum and Dylan weren't coming, so it was up to Ash: he was the custodian of some of his dad's final hours, and that felt like a big responsibility.

'What do you want to know?' Nico was still breathing heavily, but Ash could see a glimmer of his old steeliness, and knew he wanted to keep talking.

'The people you met, the deals you made. The nights when you stayed out until the sun came up. It's been a long time since I had proper Italian food, so tell me about that.'

And, as he watched his dad's jaw unclench, and the look in his eyes turn misty, Ash tried to listen to what he was saying, to appear entirely engaged, while also thinking about what Jess was doing right this moment, and whether she'd greet him with a grin or an eye roll the next time she saw him. It didn't matter what it was, what mood she was in – it was always so much better than this: stoking the embers of a relationship that had died a long time ago, trying to rekindle them again for appearances' sake and knowing that, before they fizzled out for the final time, it was more than likely that he'd end up getting burnt.

Chapter Twenty-Two

J ess walked into the Gipsy Moth with the sun hanging low and golden in the sky outside, and wondered if her happiness was visible; whether she was lifting her feet up higher, adding a sashay to her hips as she walked.

She went through the dark pub and out to the covered veranda, where her friends had pulled several tables together. Enzo and Spade were next to each other, Enzo folding a paper napkin into smaller and smaller triangles; Susie had her hair in a high ponytail, and a small, fluffy, whale-shaped bag on the table next to her. Kirsty, wearing a thin crimson jumper, was sipping a huge glass of white wine, and Roger and Olga were laughing over full, frothy pints. Lola was there – of course – and Felicity sat on Spade's other side, wearing a rose-coloured top that was looser than her usual prim outfits, and made her look softer.

'Jess!' Lola's wave was exaggerated, as if she was a hundred feet away rather than three. 'What do you want to drink?'

'I'll get it,' Jess said. 'You're all settled. Anyone need a top-up?'

'A pint of lager, ta.' Spade raised his nearly empty glass, then glanced at Felicity. 'Or a . . . vodka and lime, maybe?'

Enzo frowned at him.

'I'll get you a Stella.' Jess grinned as she went back inside. She had also felt the urge to be a more polished person in Felicity's presence, but that was before Felicity had shared the darkest parts of herself with her and Ash.

They'd had three more Sundays since that first morning, when Ash had stood in the rain to gather his emotions about something he still wouldn't talk to Jess about. In literal terms, they had made very little progress, and Jess couldn't see much of a canyon opening up in the mountains of things. In emotional terms, however, it felt as if they had performed miracles. Or, more accurately, Ash had.

His patience was infinite, and his kindness with Felicity and her cats – even though Artemis was an aggressive bruiser of a tabby, as territorial about the items in the front room as Felicity – was what made the whole thing work. His gentle humour kept Felicity and her going, even when the going got tough, and it recharged Jess's batteries. It was as if, during the week, her energy slowly drained, and then she saw his face and his dark, messy hair, and he pulled her into a hug, brushed a kiss over her lips, and she was fully topped up again.

'What would you like, love?' The burly man behind the bar was Lola's boss, Milo, who was kind and fair, and the only reason Lola put up with the busy, chaotic shifts.

'Vodka tonic please,' she said, glancing at her phone. 'And a pint of Stella.'

Ash had sent her a photo. It was the view from the window of his flat, which looked out over the rooftop of the shorter building opposite, where someone had stuck a couple of loungers and a few potted plants. Beyond it, between two London skyscrapers, there was a thin slice of sky, a burning orange glow, as if the sun was trying to squeeze through the narrow gap like Indiana Jones.

Not too bad, he'd typed. **Bet it's better where you are. Ax**

She replied while Milo filled her glass with tonic from a tiny bottle.

We're at the pub. The sunset over the river is pretty, but I'd have to go outside to take a photo and I can't be arsed. x

Milo put her drinks on the counter, she paid for them and thanked him, then snapped a picture of her glass.

Have this instead. xx

It looks like a G&T? Not filling me with awe, tbh.

I'm cheersing you, Ash. Cheers! 🥂

Oh right. Cheers!

He added a photo of a mug of what looked like too-milky tea.

I'll message you later.

Can't wait. Have a good night. xx

She felt an ache that he wasn't with them. She could easily imagine herself snuggling up to him while everyone chatted around them. Because, while they'd been busy at Felicity's house, they had also found the time, the quiet corners, for kisses that felt even more delicious because they were stolen.

All Jess's plans for where she'd take Ash – the parts of Greenwich she wanted him to see – had fallen by the wayside in light of Felicity's needs, and while she didn't want to stop helping, she missed having him to herself.

She took the drinks back to her friends and found Felicity holding court, a large canvas bag in the middle of the table.

'What are these?' Susie asked, as Felicity took items out of it. 'Photo frames?'

'This is mother-of-pearl.' Olga lifted one up and ran a finger down the edge.

'I don't need them any more.' Felicity's tone was slightly defensive.

Jess felt a surge of pride as she slipped in next to Lola. Even a fortnight ago, she couldn't have envisaged Felicity doing this – voluntarily giving away any possessions – but, having learnt from Ash, she didn't make a big deal of it. 'How's TikTok fame?' she asked her friend. 'Judging by my online sales, your popularity is skyrocketing.'

She basically had two jobs now: working at No Vase Like Home and fulfilling orders on Etsy. On a couple of occasions, she'd had both Lola and Malik helping her pack up prints, taking over the living room, which had led to Terence pitching in too as they worked to clear the backlog. Added to that, she'd already had to restock the framed prints in No Vase Like Home, while Lola, Spade and Braden continued to delight people in the public spaces of Greenwich, and on social media. It meant Jess had been able to donate money to Enzo for rent and, with Wendy matching her contribution, he had also been able to pay for Sofia to spend a couple of days making more jewellery. It wasn't enough to keep them going for ever, but it was a start.

'Over half a million views on our last video,' Lola said proudly.

'Which featured the Better Babies stall,' Susie added. 'I even made up a little dance.'

'I saw it,' Jess said, laughing. 'You looked great, Susie. I just hadn't checked the numbers in a while.'

'Next stop record company, baby.' Spade raised his glass.

'You've achieved so much.' Felicity handed the last photo frame to Kirsty and took her empty bag off the table. Jess noticed Spade tap the back of her hand, as if in approval.

'I am very grateful,' Enzo said. 'From the sale of Jess's prints, the money she and Wendy have given me, Sofia has been able to help us a little. The stall is full of new pieces.'

'You're fucking magic, Jess,' Spade said.

'Absolutely!' Felicity laughed. 'An absolute fucking superstar.'

Jess almost spat her vodka tonic over the table. She was about to comment on Felicity's swearing when she noticed the adoring look Spade was giving her, the little bubble of admiration they seemed to have sunk into, and kept quiet.

'A proper superstar,' Enzo agreed. 'Thank you. But I do not want to take your charity for any longer than I have to. It's your work, not mine.'

'You know I'm happy doing this,' Jess said. 'Me *and* Wendy. It's just until you're firmly back on your feet. And you're helping me out too, because I never would have brought my designs into the shop without this push.'

'It's very generous of you,' Olga said.

'*So* generous,' Kirsty added. 'I think we need another round to celebrate. Susie, come to the bar with me?'

'Of course.'

'I'm surprised Ash isn't here,' Felicity said. 'Was he busy tonight?'

Jess opened her mouth to reply, then realised she couldn't. How could she tell this group of lovely, sensible people that she hadn't even considered asking him to come to the pub because he was a Sunday morning thing? Except that was no longer true,

209

because he was in her thoughts and her dreams and lighting up her WhatsApps constantly. He was so far beyond Sunday mornings for her, even though those were the only times they'd seen each other.

'Yes,' Olga added. 'It would be good to get his take on all this.'

Lola laughed. 'You want to know what Jess's part-time boyfriend thinks of her fundraising for Enzo?'

'He's not my—'

'He's a solid dude.' Spade sounded indignant. 'He'd be a good drinking buddy, I'm sure.'

'He caught Braden when he stole that half-hunter from my stall,' Roger added. 'And look how far Braden's come since then. Ash seems like an incredibly competent young man.'

'I don't know what I would have done without him,' Felicity said quietly.

'He gave me a new muffin idea the other day,' Kirsty announced, as she and Susie returned to the table with trays full of drinks.

'What was that?' Olga asked.

'Pistachio, vanilla and lime. He told me it was his favourite gelato combination, and I'm trialling the cream now. It's going to be a bestseller, I can feel it.'

'Wow.' Lola sat back in her chair, her phone discarded. 'Sounds like Ash is a pretty integral part of the market.'

There were nods and murmurs around the table.

'One of the coolest ghouls we've ever had,' Spade said. 'You should invite him next time, Jess.'

She nodded, surreptitiously looking at everyone while she accepted a new drink from Kirsty. She had known that Ash could charm anyone, but she hadn't realised quite how fond her fellow marketeers were of him; how he'd worked his way into their lives, probably without even trying.

She felt bad for keeping his visits tucked into their Sunday morning box, but there was also a possessive voice inside her that said he could share flavour ideas and catch criminals and offer opinions as much as he wanted, but *she* was the one he was kissing, the one she wanted him to think about – at least half as much as she thought about him, if possible.

When she glanced at Lola, her friend's smile was soft and knowing, as if she realised just how hard Jess had fallen for her happy-hour man.

She finished her new drink in three large gulps, told everyone she needed to nip to the loo, and hurried away from the table, desperate for a moment to herself.

She sent him a message when she was safely back in her room, her head swimming slightly from the vodka.

> Missed you tonight. But I didn't invite you because it wasn't Sunday. That's stupid, isn't it? xx

His reply appeared almost immediately.

> I do exist outside Sundays, but I get it. It's not how it's worked between us. Good night?

> It was fun, and everyone asked after you. You should have been there.

> It's fine, Jess. Really.

WhatsApp told her he was typing again, and Jess kicked off her shoes and sat cross-legged on her bed. Her fairy lights were scrolling through a pastel rainbow, red to yellow to blue to purple to pink. His message appeared.

But we could meet up one evening, just you and me. What do you think? I'd still come to Greenwich.

Jess's fingers fumbled as she typed.

> Really? I'd love that.

You would?

> Of course! Sundays are Felicity's now, anyway. Let's go out one night. Just the two of us. 😊

What about Friday? I finish at lunchtime this week, some training thing I'm not needed for.

> I can get off at four! Must be serendipity.

She chewed the inside of her cheek. Was she being too eager? Her heart was pounding.

Let's take the serendipity and run with it. 😄

> So we're really doing it? 😲

Jess thought of their kisses, of how he turned her on and made her feel safe, and how much she wanted to kiss him with abandon, when they didn't have Felicity waiting for them or people watching them in alleyways. They had never, she realised, been truly alone. She typed again: not a question this time.

> We're really doing it.

I'll come to the shop at 4 on Friday.

> Friday. So weird.

212

I'll bring coffee. Americano?

What else? We have to hold on to some of our traditions.

Naturally. It already seems too far away.

I've added it to my calendar.

She hadn't, but he sent back the 😊 emoji, and she felt a giddy rush of excitement and anticipation. She didn't know how she was supposed to get any sleep now – or at all, before Friday.

Sweet dreams, Jess. Ax

You too. 🌙✦ xx

She put her phone on charge and, with her elation overriding the flicker of unease that told her she was getting carried away, that she was letting him too far in, that the vodka had made her reckless, she went to clean her teeth in the tiny bathroom she shared with Terence.

Chapter Twenty-Three

'I just don't know, Mum,' Jess said, her phone tucked under her ear. 'I can't say when I'll be free. I haven't asked Wendy for any weekends off for ages.'

'Surely that means you could,' Edie suggested.

Frustration bubbled to the surface. She didn't need this pressure now: arranging to see her parents, changing up her weekends. She had so much work with her Etsy shop, packing up orders had become a nightly thing to stay on top of it all, but weekends were just as busy. Wendy wouldn't be able to cope without her on a Saturday, and she couldn't send Ash off to see Felicity alone. The thought was both unsettling and preposterous, because Sunday morning was *theirs*. Except they were branching out. Tomorrow.

'I'll talk to Wendy,' she said, trying to ignore the butterflies. 'But I've got such a lot on at the moment. My print sales are really taking off.'

'We've seen Lola's TikToks,' Edie said. 'They're wonderful. And it's so good of you to give some of your Etsy profits to that young man.'

'Enzo,' her dad replied. 'Enzo and Carolina Vela. It's on the landing page. We shouldn't forget their names.'

'They're not the forgotten victims of some terrible crime,' Edie said.

'But they have names,' Graeme pressed.

Jess almost put the phone down and got on with her work while they bickered in the background. She was working on a print that said: *Boundaries are made to be broken through, unless you're next to a field of angry bulls*. It wasn't quite right, but she'd found a beautiful photo of Highland cattle at sunset that was available for commercial use, and she'd tinker with the wording later on.

'We'd love to see you, Jess,' her dad said. 'You're not far from us, but sometimes you act as if you're on a different continent.'

'We're a couple of miles away,' her mum added. 'And what we're saying is that *we* can make the journey. It doesn't always have to be the chick flying back to the nest.'

'I'm just busy,' Jess said lamely.

'With any boys?'

'Mum.' She sighed the word. 'Work's full-on, and anyway . . . Terence's flat is so small.'

'But Greenwich has endless possibilities, for lunch or dinner or walks. We don't expect you to cook for us.' Edie's laughter was sharper than it needed to be.

Jess remembered what Lola kept telling her. Edie and Graeme Peacock had chosen her. She hadn't been an accident, something unexpected or thought about in abstract terms. They had gone through a rigorous adoption process, court orders, home visits and questionnaires and scrutiny, to have Jess as part of their family.

'I'm working tomorrow,' she said. 'So I can ask Wendy then, and let you have some dates.'

'Marvellous,' Graeme said, in a tone that meant he thought the conversation was over.

'What about your Friday nights?' her mum asked. 'What about tomorrow? Are you and Lola hitting the town?'

Jess winced at her mum's phrasing. Of course, it would be today that she asked. 'I don't think so,' she said. 'I'm not sure yet.' It wasn't a lie, because she *didn't* think she and Lola would be hitting the town, and she also wasn't sure what she was doing, because Ash had been teasing her with hints about where they were going, but had refused to tell her outright.

'Well, look after yourself,' Edie said, when Jess failed to be more forthcoming. 'And let us know when we can come and impose on you. We miss our daughter!'

'Sure,' Jess said. 'I'll let you know. Bye, then.'

'Bye, love,' her dad said.

'Take care, sweetie.'

Jess hung up and flung herself dramatically onto the bed, groaning and pressing her hands into her eyes.

'Didn't want to tell them you had a hot date?'

She sprung up again and glared at Terence, who was standing in the doorway, a pot of pesto in one hand, a teaspoon in the other. 'Are you putting that on pasta, or is that your dinner?'

Terence shrugged. 'I'm cooking some potatoes, so thought I'd check it was still good.'

'Fair enough. Anyway, how do you know I have a hot date?'

'I heard you talking to Lola on the phone, something about arranging it after the pub. This guy Ash?'

'Has he come and helped out on your round?' Jess asked.

'What?' Terence frowned. 'I don't know him, I don't think. Why?'

Jess sighed. 'Sorry. He's just... everyone loves him at the market, and speaking to Edie and Graeme always makes me snippy.'

'Your mum and dad, you mean?' He raised an eyebrow, ate another teaspoon of pesto. 'Surely it's a good thing that everyone loves him. It suggests your radar isn't totally off and you're probably not going to end up on a late-night, one-way date with a serial killer.'

Jess laughed. 'Maybe.'

Terence leaned against the doorframe, as if settling in for the long haul. 'Come on then, out with it.'

'Out with what?'

'Your reservations. The reason going out with a popular guy is giving you hives.'

'I think of beehives when you say that.'

'It's a swelling on your skin, like an irritation. I watch a lot of American TV, whatever. I can see it's worrying you, is my point. Would you prefer to go out with a loner?'

Jess narrowed her eyes, but Terence was unmoved.

'Fine,' she said eventually. 'It's worrying me because . . . everyone knows him. They love him! What if we go out and it goes wrong, and then I get blamed because I've scared off this amazing guy that they all adore. Or – worse! What if it goes really well, and then suddenly I'm at the pub with them all every night, and my life turns into this social whirlwind?' She shuddered.

'You were at the pub the other night,' Terence pointed out.

'Yeah, and I used up all my battery.'

'Also,' Terence went on, 'everyone at the market loves you too, and has known you longer. You really think they'd be loyal to the new guy?'

'But he's so lovely, and kind, and generous. He's patient, and—'

'And he wants to go out with you,' Terence said. 'So you shouldn't worry about it. He wants this, too.'

217

Jess dragged one of her yeti pillows onto her lap. 'That wasn't what I was worried about.'

'That's not what you *said* you were worried about.' Terence pointed his teaspoon at her, a blob of pesto dangling precariously on the end. 'What you're really worried about is that you won't be good enough for him, that he won't hang about and he'll take all your market friends with him, and you'll be left all alone. None of which is plausible, by the way.'

Jess stiffened. 'I'm not thinking any of that.'

'Sure you are. You're adopted, you keep your folks at arm's length, you think you're on this dusty road to perpetual abandonment so you make it your business to push people away before they push *you* away, but you never let on. You're the queen at coming up with reasons why relationships won't work out.'

'What?' It came out as a scratchy whisper.

'I watch *Long Lost Family*. These are common abandonment insecurities. But you've got it worse than most. Being brittle is your shield.'

'I do not . . .' She felt hot all over. 'Terence!'

'I haven't kicked you out yet, have I?'

'No, but we never—'

'And Wendy, your boss – right?'

Jess nodded dumbly.

'She's kept hold of you too, for like . . . four years. And all these market people you mention, Enzo and Olga and Kirsty, you pretend you barely know them, but all your little stories . . .' He waggled his fingers, put the teaspoon back in his mouth, then took it out again, 'Your nights at the pub with them. So much denial.'

'This is unhelpful.' Jess resisted the urge to throw the cushion at him.

'You think you're this lone soldier, battling away by yourself, but you're not. If all these other people like hanging out with you and sharing their problems with you, so you end up sorting out TikToks and prints, *giving away your profits* to help them fix whatever bullshit the world has chucked at them, then why not believe that the guy likes you enough to hang around for a while, too?'

'I . . . I don't know,' she said, her anger dissolving. This was more than she'd heard Terence say in all the time she'd been living with him. 'Have you been analysing me?'

He laughed, the sound warm and kind, despite his hard truths. 'I'm a postman, not a psychologist. But we do share a tiny flat, we've shared a few meals recently, too, and I'm not entirely unobservant. All I'm saying is, give it a chance; don't write yourself off before you've gone on one hot date.'

'We've had some Sundays,' she said.

'That's not the same as Friday night, though, is it? Weird how the day of the week makes a difference, but it does, right?'

'It does,' Jess agreed. 'And I'm meeting him straight after work, so I can't even get changed first. I have to get ready tomorrow morning, which feels so hard, somehow.' She was spilling it all out, wondering, even as she spoke, why Terence was suddenly her confidant.

'You always look great,' he said simply. 'Don't stress about it.'

'OK,' Jess replied. 'Thanks.'

'Sure. Come and have some pesto potatoes. I've done sausages too, and there's enough for both of us.'

'Really?' Jess swallowed the lump in her throat, the turn of events so unexpected she felt as if she'd got whiplash.

'I promise I won't psychologise you any more. There's one of the earlier *Mission: Impossible* films on in a bit, if you want to watch that?'

Jess nodded, and then, because she couldn't be too real with him, said, 'Are you sure there's enough pesto left to put on the potatoes now you've had it as an aperitif?'

'I've got another jar in the fridge,' he said, and went back down the corridor, his footsteps gentle on the carpet.

Jess buried her head in her fluffy cushion. Were her insecurities really that obvious to everyone? Terence's reassurance that people liked spending time with her should have made her less nervous about seeing Ash, but now all she could think was that he saw right through her, too. He was an actual psychologist, after all. It made her wonder if he was being genuine with her, or if he'd been the version of himself that he thought she wanted: fun and silly, good at deflecting serious questions. Had he been worrying that *she* wouldn't stick around, because it was obvious that she didn't form connections easily?

She threw the cushion against her headboard. Ash liked spending time with her, and he liked kissing her, but he still hadn't told her what he did on Sundays after their time was up. She suddenly felt as if he was a solid, impenetrable form, and she was this opaque, wispy thing, all the hidden parts of her on show. Would an evening together change that? Would he open up more now that they were breaking through their original boundaries?

The whole thing felt more nerve-wracking than it had before Terence had decided to psychoanalyse her. She should be annoyed with him – his speech had come after she'd had to deal with her parents, as well – but she couldn't be. And there was one thing he'd said that she completely agreed with. The day of the week shouldn't make a difference, but it did. There would be no lunch hour to squish into, no Felicity, no mysterious appointment for Ash to race off to afterwards. They were going to spend unrestricted time together – a date with no countdown attached – and Jess was both elated and terrified.

Terence was right about another thing, too. Pesto potatoes and Tom Cruise playing Ethan Hunt were what she needed right now. Otherwise, she would spend the next twenty-four hours watching the seconds pass, waiting for a date that felt both full of possibility, and riddled with hazards.

Chapter Twenty-Four

The sun shone all day on Friday, keeping the market, and No Vase Like Home, busier than usual. At four o'clock, the light was more intense than it had been at midday, and Ash was even more beautiful in the golden glow of an afternoon that was tripping towards evening, his skin tanned, threads of amber in his brown hair. He was wearing jeans, and a deep blue shirt in a fabric that looked soft enough to sink into. His hands were empty.

'I thought we could get a drink after,' he said, and she was pleased that his eyes swept up and down her body, and that there was a flicker of desire she recognised, because she was feeling it, too. She was wearing a red dress with a puffin print, and the curls she'd put in her hair that morning had mostly stayed in place.

'After what?' she asked.

'After we've been where we're going.'

She grinned. 'Enlightening.'

'It's a surprise.'

'I can't wait.'

'You don't have to.' He gestured to the shelf adorned with clocks. 'You said you could get off at four.'

'Before she'd even asked me!' Wendy called from the storeroom.

Ash's eyes widened. 'You mean—'

'It's fine,' Jess cut in. 'I would have texted you if she'd said no.'

She hoisted her bag over her shoulder as they left the shop, emerging into a market with the frisson of almost-drink-o'clock, nearly at the end of its countdown to the weekend. The voices and laughter were boisterous, Olga showing a customer her Indiana Jones-style hats, Roger holding up one of his more expensive trinkets for another – a porcelain scene of a country house with a large oak tree outside, tiny porcelain people standing in front of the tiny front door.

Without his customary coffees, Ash had his hands deep in his jeans pockets, and Jess had the absurd thought that if he tripped, she would have to catch him.

'So, Friday,' she said unnecessarily. 'Did it feel weird?'

'Coming here?' he asked.

She nodded.

'I thought it would, but the journey has become like muscle memory. Except . . . it's also the opposite.' They stopped at the lights on Romney Road.

'The opposite how?'

'I always remember every step of it,' he explained. 'You know how you can take a familiar journey and your mind drifts, so you reach your destination without really noticing it? It's easy to do on public transport, but I can also do it driving to see Mum or a friend, which is scary.'

'I often don't remember my walk to work,' Jess said, 'but that's only ten minutes.'

'Exactly. But with my trips here, whether I take the train or the boat, it's as if I'm hyper-aware the entire time.'

'Why is that, do you think?' They were threading through groups of people on the busy pavement, grand buildings on either side of them.

'Because I have stronger emotions associated with this place than I do with work, I guess.'

'And why is *that*, do you think?' She glanced at him, expecting him to be smirking – that he'd been referring to her, and their kisses – but he looked anxious. 'Oh,' she said. 'The thing after.'

'Not just that,' Ash said hurriedly. 'But . . . anyway. It didn't feel weird coming here today, it just felt good. I've been looking forward to all this time with you.' He gestured to the right, and Jess walked through the gate.

'The Queen's House? Are you going to reenact an entire episode of *Bridgerton* for me this time?'

'Did you know there's a famous ghost here?'

'One photo, taken in the Sixties.' Jess laughed. 'Is this your plan?'

Ash looked affronted. 'I thought we could investigate the Tulip Stairs.'

'For . . .' she looked at her watch. 'Forty-five minutes?'

'A quick tour, then I'll take you for dinner.'

'Zombie tunnels, ghostly staircases.' She shook her head. 'Do I need to worry about you, Ash?'

'And where have you been taking me for the last four weeks? Is that really date material?' He brushed his hand down her back, leading her along the path to the beautiful white house. Greenwich park rose up behind it, visible in slices through the colonnades on either side. The grass was impossibly green, the sky blue with white clouds scudding through it. The rosy sun kissed the white stonework and turned it peachy pink, and the whole thing was glorious. Ash, most of all, with his dark hair and late-in-the-day stubble.

'We've really helped Felicity.' She didn't regret it, but she had often wondered what they could have been doing if it was just the two of them; how much more they would know each other by now.

'I'm joking,' Ash said, gesturing for her to go first down the stairs that led into the basement, then up into the main house.

Inside, visitors were admiring the black-and-white tiled floor in the great hall, and the famed tulip staircase rising above it, its blue, wrought-iron banister shining in the afternoon light. The whole thing was magnificent, but Jess thought it was cold. It needed twinkly lights, some soft furnishings, a few well-placed prints on the walls. A guide gestured them to the start of the tour, the first information plaque, but neither she nor Ash was interested.

'You do realise that we'll have to leave long before it gets dark,' she said. 'Our ghost-hunting efforts aren't going to be very credible.'

'It's a bit . . . echoey.' Ash sounded disappointed.

'It's all very shiny,' Jess said, as a group of teenagers in shorts and vest tops went past them, giggling. 'And it's important, historically. This staircase is the first of its kind.'

'I should have taken you to the proper *Bridgerton* house.'

'The Ranger's House? I wouldn't have been bothered about that, either.'

Ash ran a hand through his hair. 'I'm sorry. I've got this all wrong.' He looked so forlorn, Jess couldn't bear it.

She noticed a closed doorway in the far corner of the hall, its heavy frame creating a deep alcove, the area in shadow. 'Come on.' She took his hand and led him to it.

'What's this?' he asked, as she turned so her back was against the door. Ash hovered in front of her. 'What are we . . .?' She let go of his hand and grabbed his shirt, pulling

225

him forwards. He smelled amazing, his aftershave smoky and delicious, and she watched his pupils dilate, the grey consumed by black as he looked down at her.

'I'm interested in you,' she said softly. 'I don't mind where we go, or what we do.'

'Are we going to stay here until five o'clock,' he murmured. 'Hope nobody spots us and get ourselves locked in, so we can hunt for the ghost?'

She grinned up at him. 'You don't have to get back home?'

'For who? Mack, or the cactus that lives on my windowsill? They're mostly self-sufficient.'

'Great,' she whispered. 'I wonder what the bedrooms are like here.'

'If we really do get locked in, we can explore.' He cupped her chin and tilted her face up, and then his lips were on hers, the kiss more gentle than usual, as if they were both aware of the evening stretching ahead of them. Jess felt every nerve ending in her body fizz to life, and she pulled him closer, biting back a moan as his body pressed so perfectly against hers.

'This was a good idea,' she said in between kisses, her hands sliding up his back, into the soft hair at his nape. She felt drugged, dizzy.

'It's a good doorway,' he murmured.

'I mean *this*,' she whispered. 'Friday night. Seeing each other outside our hour.'

'I think that was *my* idea.'

'I'm looking forward to seeing what else you've got planned,' she said.

Ash raised an eyebrow, and then kissed her so thoroughly that all her words were lost. They could have gone on for hours

226

– Jess was getting worked up, wishing that she hadn't started this in a fucking *doorway* of all places – if it hadn't been for a very loud, very annoyed '*Excuse me*' that echoed through the space behind them.

'I'm not sure Henrietta Maria would have appreciated this behaviour.' It was the guide they'd passed on their way in. 'And we're closing shortly.'

'We got carried away,' Ash said, stepping back from Jess. 'It's a very romantic building. Henrietta Maria wouldn't have begrudged us a few stolen kisses, surely?'

'That may well be.' The guide hoisted his belt up, as if he was a small-town sheriff with a gun instead of a walkie-talkie. 'But my boss will have my guts if he finds out I've let you engage in illicit acts in here.'

'Hardly illicit,' Jess said, though she couldn't believe that she, of all people, had been caught kissing in a historical building. Ash was addling her brain.

'Hardly appropriate, either. There are kids here, pensioners. What if one of them has a heart attack?'

'I don't . . .' Ash started.

'That was pretty much rhetorical,' the guide said. 'Go and roll about on the grass in the park. It's a gorgeous evening, and nobody will bat an eyelid there.'

'Understood.' Ash took Jess's hand and pulled her towards the exit.

'Thanks for not arresting us!' Jess called behind her, and Ash picked up his pace until they were out in the sunshine again.

'So, that went well,' he said as they walked down the path, Jess getting her hand comfortable in his, not letting go. 'Where next on our disastrous date?'

Jess traced a finger over her lips. 'It was hardly disastrous.' She gave him an impish grin.

'Let's go and get a drink. Do you know the Trafalgar Tavern? It's got great views of the river, apparently.'

'Oh, I love it there,' Jess said.

'Excellent. I'm going to stop trying to be quirky and just aim for traditional. Let's pretend the last half-hour never happened, that I am capable of planning a vaguely successful date with a woman I care about.'

'I don't think I can do that,' Jess said, but her heart skipped at his words. 'Didn't you enjoy – oh, hello Margaret!'

The woman who had bought her first-ever print in No Vase Like Home was walking towards them along the pavement, and Jess added a cheery wave to her greeting.

'Hello . . .' Margaret said, then her smile fell away, replaced by confusion. 'Ash?'

Ash's steps faltered, then he came to an abrupt halt, dropping Jess's hand. 'Peggy.'

Jess looked between them. *Peggy?*

'It's good to see you,' Margaret said. 'Both of you. I just hadn't . . .' She laughed awkwardly. 'Things hadn't clicked for me. But they should have. I should have realised – the print with the kite on it!' She shook her head. 'But I need to be off now, anyway. Take care.' She hurried past Jess, their shoulders brushing, and Jess got a wave of peony perfume.

Once she'd gone, Jess and Ash stared at each other in silence. Jess couldn't work it out. Ash knew Margaret. From the place he went after seeing her on Sundays? But wasn't she a nurse? The uniform Jess had seen her in looked like a nurse's uniform. She wished she knew more about her – but she didn't need to wish: she could just ask.

'You know Margaret?'

Ash had stiffened, his curls blowing in the breeze the only soft part of him. 'I know her as Peggy.'

'From where?'

'From the thing I . . .' He glanced behind him, but Margaret – Peggy – had disappeared into the Friday evening crowd.

'What is your thing?' Jess asked. 'Can you tell me now? I feel as if we've gone way beyond stolen moments of time.'

'What about back there?' He thumbed in the direction of the Queen's House. 'That doorway felt like a stolen moment.'

'You know what I mean.' They were in the middle of the path, people swarming around them, and Ash took her arm and pulled them to the side, against the metal fence that surrounded the grounds of the Old Royal Naval College.

He looked away from her for several long moments, his jaw tight. Then he met her gaze. 'I don't want to tell you.'

Jess scrunched her hands into fists. 'Why not?'

'Because tonight is about *us*.' Ash sounded as frustrated as she felt. 'And I don't want that to . . . to *infect* this.'

'*Infect* it?' She laughed. 'Are you part of a disease control study? A strain of blood poisoning that turns people into zombies to be used as weapons for the state? Are you, Ash Faulkner, part zombie? Is that why you wanted to take me into the tunnel?'

'Don't be flippant!' he snapped.

'Don't keep things from me,' she shot back.

He leaned against the fence. 'This is our time, Jess. We don't get enough as it is, and I don't think it's wrong of me to keep this to myself.'

She swallowed. She didn't want this to fall apart. 'But if tonight is about us, then don't you think we should be sharing more of ourselves? I don't want . . .'

'What?' His voice was softer.

'I don't want you to be the version of yourself that you think I need.'

'What do you mean?'

'I want all of you, Ash. I know I have this need for self-preservation, and that I like being on my own sometimes, but I've opened up to you more than I have to anyone else in a long time. I want you to feel comfortable enough with me to do the same.' She took his hand and squeezed it gently.

He huffed out a breath. 'I *am* comfortable with you. I don't hold anything back, except . . .' He shook his head. 'Look, you don't want me to talk about this, believe me. It isn't first-date material, and I don't want to . . . to burden you with it, or the part of me you'll get when I open the floodgates.'

'I just said I want all of you. And I know we haven't had much time, but tonight's supposed to change that.'

'It is changing it,' Ash said. 'The Queen's House was a crap idea. Let's go and get a drink in the Trafalgar, start again.'

Jess looked past him, to where the sun had fallen further, burning amber around the edges of the statuesque buildings. 'But it's obviously a big thing for you,' she said. 'I want you to trust me with it.' Edie Peacock's words from two years before echoed in her head. *It's hard to feel loved when you're not wanted or needed.* She wanted Ash to want her, to want to tell her.

'I will,' he said. 'But not now.'

'And Peggy?'

He shook his head. 'Not now, Jess.'

Her chest tightened, her nose prickling with the telltale warning of impending tears. 'Fine,' she said. 'Sorry to take up your time. Have a safe journey back.'

'What? Jess, no!'

She was already walking away, wishing that she could get swallowed up by the crowds, become invisible just like Margaret had.

'Jess!' Ash was following her, calling her name, and she heard him swear when he met the same wall of tourists she had, but couldn't get through them as quickly.

She had almost reached the market when he caught up with her, his warm hand finding hers. She had been anticipating it, but his touch made her jump, and she bashed into someone with a sharp-cornered briefcase.

'Ow!' She bent and rubbed her shin, but Ash didn't let go of her hand. 'Go away, Ash.'

'I'm not going anywhere. Are you OK?'

'I don't want to do this with you.'

'And I don't want our first real date to be this much of a disaster. I thought I'd hit a pretty low point with the stupid ghost-hunt idea, but this is . . . this is so much worse.'

'So you'll tell me where you go on Sundays, after you've seen me?'

He swallowed. 'I will, I promise. But can we – can we not do that tonight? It's fucking miserable, and I just . . .' He made a low growl in his throat. 'I need this, us, to be stronger before I land it on you.'

'What—'

'But I'm not a criminal,' he said hurriedly. 'And I'm not already married, or with someone else. It's family shit, and I just want to have fun with you tonight.'

She couldn't look away from him, could see nothing but honesty in his grey eyes. He was desperate, and she knew that partly because she was, too. She didn't want to walk away from him; not really. She just hated the low, whispering voice that said she wasn't important enough: how could she be, if he didn't trust her with his secrets? But he'd told her he would, in time.

'OK,' she said, and took his other hand.

'OK?' He sounded as if he didn't believe her.

'OK.' She stepped closer to him.

'God, Jess—' He bent his head, brushed his lips over hers.

'One day soon, if we're not careful, we're going to get arrested.'

'What do you suggest?'

She squeezed his hand and smiled up at him. 'I have an idea. I hope you're going to like it.'

Chapter Twenty-Five

They bought a bottle of cheap Prosecco at the nearest Tesco Express, and waited ten minutes for Jess's favourite Italian restaurant to cook them a pizza with black olives and chargrilled peppers, gooey melting slabs of mozzarella, and the aroma of fresh oregano wafting off it.

'We're really doing this, then?' Ash carried the pizza box in one hand, and held onto Jess with the other as they walked towards her flat.

'We've kissed down by the river, in an alleyway, on several roads, next to some bins, in amongst Felicity's clutter when she's been in another room and then, tonight, in the doorway of a famous historic house. Before I met you, I struggled to hug my best friend in public.'

'Clearly I'm irresistible,' he said, and she gave him a look that made his smile falter. 'How far to your flat?'

'Here we are.' Jess gestured to the nondescript black door, then dug in her bag for her keys. She opened it and led the way up the narrow stairway to the first floor. 'Terence?' she called.

'Oh great, I get to meet your pet,' Ash said into her ear, and she giggled, remembering when she'd told Ash about him, how satisfied she'd been that he was clearly jealous.

'Hey,' Terence called, the sound of tennis balls being hit back and forth coming from the TV. 'I thought you were on your hot date!'

'Fuck's sake,' Jess muttered. She could feel Ash's shoulders shake with laughter. 'Here's my hot date,' she said, because what could she do but brazen it out?

Terence turned his head, looking over the back of the sofa. 'Hey, man. I'm Terence.'

'Ash.' He put the pizza box on the kitchen counter and went to greet him. Terence shook his hand, and they stared at each other for a cringe-worthy moment. 'Good to meet you.'

'Ditto. There's beer in the fridge, and you can come and watch the tennis if you like? It's some random celebrity tournament, not as good as Wimbledon, but it's better than what's on the other channels.'

'We're fine,' Jess said. 'Thanks, though.' Watching tennis, squashed between Ash and her flatmate on the sofa, was not how she wanted this to go.

She got two wine glasses from the cupboard – not proper flutes, but they would have to do – a couple of plates and some kitchen towel.

'This way,' she said, leading Ash down the corridor. She felt like a student taking him to her room, with its fairy lights and her Etsy workstation – still tidy, despite the increased orders – but the evening hadn't gone as planned, and this was better than all the other options she could think of.

She stepped inside and took a deep breath. He followed her in, then closed the door gently behind him and leaned against it. She watched him take it all in: the bed and the trinkets, the colourful lights and the fluffy cushions; everything about it so much softer than she was.

'This is great,' he said. 'And obviously, I love the hat.' He gestured to the raspberry cap hanging on her bedpost. He'd been so funny that day, taking her on his ridiculous

234

film tour. Now, everything was different. He was nervous, clearly – as nervous as she was – and she relished seeing another side of him.

'Someone pretty important bought it for me,' she replied, as she cleared a space on her desk for the plates and glasses. Ash followed with the Prosecco and the pizza. 'This is my sanctuary,' she told him. 'Terence is a nice guy, and we watch films together sometimes, but—'

'Everyone needs their own space,' Ash finished. He stepped towards her.

'Exactly.' Her throat had gone dry.

Ash took another step. 'Only so much comfort an alleyway can offer.'

'That doorway was a bit sparse, too. But I have some really fluffy cushions.' She gestured at the bed, and watched him swallow, falter, even though the tension between them was thick. She was surprised her fairy lights hadn't blown, or at the very least started flickering.

'Ash?' she said.

'Yes?'

'The pizza will be good cold, the Prosecco will be OK warm, and I would like you to come here, right now, so I can put my hands all over you. If you're not a fan of yeti cushions, even luminous pink ones, then—'

He stepped forwards and kissed her, sliding his arms around her back and then lower, cupping her bum, lifting her carefully off her feet and walking them backwards. He put her gently on the bed, then stood between her legs. Jess undid his shirt buttons, silently marvelling at how dexterous she could be while still kissing him, as if this was a romcom and she was a seductress, when really the only reason she was managing

235

it was that she was so desperate to feel his warm skin against hers, to see all of him.

'I love yeti cushions,' Ash murmured into her shoulder, as he gathered the skirt of her dress and pulled it up her thighs. She leaned back on her elbows and lifted, so he could slide it up her torso, then over her head, until she was only in her underwear. He took her in, lips parted, his pupils dilated. 'If you look at my search history, it's 80 per cent yeti cushions.'

'Twenty per cent the ghosts of Greenwich,' she said, then gasped as he kissed her neck, laughing into it. The sound made heat pool low in her stomach.

'Can we not talk about that?'

'It was great, all of this is great.' She was breathless now, because she'd dragged his shirt off his shoulders, and when he sat back on the bed she saw that he was strong and toned, a smattering of dark hair over his chest, two moles on his collarbone that were usually hidden.

His gaze clouded. 'Not all of it.'

'Shush.' She sat up and pulled him towards her, then found his belt buckle, slipped her fingers in to undo it. 'We're not talking about it.'

'Thank you,' he murmured, and she almost combusted when he reached up to undo the clasp of her bra, the pads of his fingers trailing along the sensitive skin of her back.

'Save your gratitude.' She snagged his gaze, held onto it while he slid her bra down her arms and then off. 'You're going to have a whole lot more to thank me for soon.'

She saw the desire spark in his eyes, and then he was helping her tug down his jeans, and settling his body over hers, her yeti pillows cushioning them, his skin smooth and hot and so delicious pressed against her own.

'You're so beautiful, Jess,' he whispered, as he kissed her neck, her collarbone, and then lower, squeezing her breast with just the right amount of pressure. 'Is this OK?'

She swallowed, trying not to gasp. 'It's a good start,' she managed, as his lips brushed softly over her nipple. She could feel how hard he was, and she wanted to whimper, to make some high, uncontrolled noise at how perfect he was, the pleasure of every sensation, and so she let herself. She stopped trying not to gasp or moan or arch her back, and when he asked her what she liked, she told him, letting her words guide him to everywhere she wanted him. She did the same for him, until she was coaxing low moans from his throat that only made her more needy, made her want him more.

She let go of her worries that she wasn't enough, her concerns that he wasn't giving her all of him, and let her need for Ash overrule everything else. He kissed her and stroked her, reverent and hungry all at once, and she gave into her desire to see and touch all the parts of him she hadn't had access to before tonight.

Each tingle was deeper and brighter than the last, until she was nothing but sensation. She bared all of herself to him, and Ash gasped against her neck, her lips, kissing her with a desperation that he hadn't shown her before. It felt natural, and right, and more than she'd imagined it could be. She wondered how she'd ever thought of Ash as temporary, a fleeting Sunday distraction, when he'd so quickly, so thoroughly, become one of the most important people in her life.

Chapter Twenty-Six

J ess had had one guy in her room in Terence's flat before Ash, but things hadn't lasted long or been particularly great even while they were happening – Warren was always on his phone, or working out some deal for his property business, and she'd never been more than an item near the bottom of his to-do list.

Lying in her bed in Ash's arms, as the Saturday morning sunshine crept beneath her thin blue curtains, she felt only bliss. It was as if her mattress and her duvet, her yeti cushions, had all become softer in the night, while Ash's warm skin and strong arms wrapped around her, even while he slept. She felt as though everything was in exactly the right proportions, nothing off-kilter. It was safe, and too perfect, and terrifying, and she had to force herself not to slide out of his embrace so she could go and make coffee and think about it with some distance between them.

Ash's arm shifted from her waist to her hip, and a low rumble came out of him as he turned, burying his head in her neck.

'Hey,' she said.

'Hi.' The affection in his voice made her forget about coffee. 'You OK?'

'Better than OK,' she said truthfully. 'I'm happy, and I'm tired.' They hadn't got a whole lot of sleep. 'Do you have to go and . . . do things?'

'I'm supposed to be playing rugby this afternoon. I've missed the last couple of weeks, and my friend Jay is on my back about it.'

'I didn't know you played rugby.' She thought immediately of high tackles and shoulders being used as battering rams.

'It's just casual, not a league or anything, so they still play over the summer. It's a laugh, and I get to burn off some energy. You're working today? Have we got time for breakfast first?'

'Not cold pizza,' Jess said. They'd wolfed down a couple of slices the night before, though they hadn't allocated a whole lot of time for eating, and the Prosecco remained untouched. 'We could go to a café?'

'I'd like that.' Ash shifted on top of her and threaded his fingers through hers, pushing her arm above her head on the pillow so he could kiss her. 'Probably none of them are open yet, though.'

It was half past six, and she knew at least two of the greasy spoons would already be serving tradesmen, but she kept that information to herself. 'OK,' she said. 'So we could have some more sex before we go.'

Ash laughed, rewarding her by sliding his lips slowly from her ear lobe down the column of her neck, then pressing kisses into her collarbone. 'Were my intentions not clear enough?' he murmured as he reached her breast.

She smiled, arching her back at his touch. 'Just making sure.'

Ash gave her an intense, incendiary look, and proceeded to show her that they were, most definitely, on the same page.

They went to a café called Daisy's that was tucked into a side road, and ordered fry-ups.

Jess found herself watching Ash while he ate, the way he was careful, methodical about everything, as if he considered each mouthful before he put it on his fork. In bed he'd been the same, thoughtful and purposeful, responding to every move and sound she made, only losing control when he was close, as if it was the only time he let his thoughts switch off. She'd loved watching him come apart, collapse on top of her, knowing she'd been the reason.

Now, even more, she wanted to crack him open and see inside. While they ate and talked, she thought of the first time they met, how he'd seemed so calm and capable with Braden, even though he'd told her, afterwards, that he hadn't had a clue what he was doing. She wanted all those admissions from him, perhaps because she felt a tugging need to share her own.

'Do you visit your mum and dad?' he asked. 'I know you told me you're not particularly close, but do you ever see them?'

'Sometimes,' Jess said. 'They live in Bexleyheath, so it's not exactly a stretch. And they're angling for a visit – either from me, or to come here and take me to lunch.'

'You're not keen?' Ash speared a mushroom with his fork.

'It's just complicated,' she said, and here was a moment when she could be vulnerable with him. 'We never really knitted together, after I went to live with them. And I . . . I told you, didn't I, that I could invent where I came from, because I didn't know for sure?'

Ash put his fork down. 'I remember.'

'Well, that's not entirely true. I tracked down an aunt, through Genes Reunited. Once I could look at my records, when I was eighteen.'

'You found your birth parents?'

'My mum. Through her sister, who'd added her family tree to the site. I double- and triple-checked the details, and even when I was sure it was the right Holbrook – that's my birth surname – it took me two months to pluck up the courage to email her. She replied a couple of days later, and we decided on a phone call, first. And I was excited, as well as terrified. But then she phoned, and she told me . . .' She broke off, and stared into the dregs of her coffee.

'Jess?' Ash slid his hand over hers.

'She told me my mum, Catherine, had died two years before. She was still young, but she hadn't been well for a while.'

'Shit. I'm so sorry, Jess.'

'My aunt, Elizabeth, said there was no point in me meeting anyone else. Not without my mum there. She made it sound like they hadn't been that close, and so much time had passed.'

'Fuck,' Ash whispered. He squeezed her hand. 'I can't imagine finding that out – at all. Let alone over the phone, from a stranger.'

'The thing was, she didn't even consider whether there was any point for *me*. There was none for her, because she had her family: she knew who she was, and I wasn't worth the effort.' Jess could remember it so well. She'd been sitting on her bedroom floor, and Lola was there beside her, cross-legged, their arms linked. After her aunt had delivered the news kindly but brusquely, as if she had only allotted a specific amount of time to speak to her long-lost niece, Jess had felt numb. It had taken longer for the anger and sadness to come, and then there had been resolve. She was better off on her own. She didn't need anyone else. 'It wasn't the best day.'

Ash ran his palm up and down over the back of her hand. 'Would you have wanted to get to know your aunt? Despite her abruptness, despite not being close with your mum, if she had agreed to see you, would you have wanted to?'

'I don't know,' Jess admitted. 'It was Mum I was looking for, and so when I found out, it just felt . . . it was too hard. I didn't want to go looking for Dad and discover he was gone, too. And so – you know. I'm lucky to have Edie and Graeme. Mum and Dad.'

'But you don't feel that close to them? They're not very affectionate?'

'Oh no, they are,' she said. 'It's me who struggles. I just . . . I feel stronger on my own.' She pushed her toast about in the juice from the tomatoes, watching it go soggy. It had been harder to talk about than she thought, those deep parts of herself covered in rust, so rarely brought out and examined. When Ash didn't reply, she looked up.

'Nobody's stronger on their own,' he said quietly. 'I already knew you were strong, and now . . . You've been through so much. But even if you're happy and confident, you still need people you love and trust around you. If you don't have anyone to reflect against, I think it's hard to have a sense of yourself.'

'Do you have lots of people?' she asked, because she'd always got the impression that Ash, like her, was a bit of a lone wolf.

He took a deep breath. 'I'm close to my brother Dylan,' he said, 'but he lives in New Zealand with his wife and two boys. Mum's in Hampshire, so I see her every few weeks, and we speak on the phone. There's my neighbour Mack, who you know about, Jay and my rugby friends, and now Felicity, and you.'

'I'm one of your people, am I?' Jess asked quietly. Happiness and dread coiled together inside her.

Ash lifted her hand off the table and squeezed it between both of his. 'How could you not be?' he said, laughing gently. They stayed like that until a server came to top up their coffees.

Jess walked with him to the jetty, where one of the sleek Clippers was waiting for passengers to board it before it headed up the river.

'It's a lot more fun than the DLR and the tube.' Ash put his hands on her hips and pulled her closer. 'One day soon, you should take time off work and come with me.'

'I do need to see your flat,' she told him. 'And meet Mack. But you're still coming tomorrow, aren't you?'

'Of course,' he said. 'I could . . .'

'Could what?'

'Nothing.' He gave her a quick smile. 'I'd better go, or they'll leave without me.'

On cue, the boat's horn tooted, and Ash gave her a final, firm kiss and then let go of her, racing down the ramp to where a woman dressed in navy waited next to the open door. He went inside, then appeared on the deck, and Jess waved at him until the boat had steamed up the river, a ripple of waves in its wake, and Ash was no more than a dark silhouette, his grey eyes too far away to look in to.

The next day they tried very hard to focus on helping Felicity, but the fact that they couldn't touch each other made Jess want to even more, and from the looks Ash kept giving her, she knew he felt the same. She was slightly concerned they might cause a fire to spark amongst the piles of clutter, but there were fewer piles, now, and though the space they'd unearthed looked tired and dirty, it also had some beautiful features.

After working this way for several weeks, Felicity had started to take control – evident by her photo frame gifts at the pub – and now Jess followed Ash's lead, taking a step back and letting the other woman run the conversation.

'What do you think of this?' She held up a desktop chest of drawers that looked like an elaborate jewellery box. It was covered in green silk that was marked in some places, ripped in others. Jess opened her mouth to say something, but Felicity spoke over her. 'It was glorious once, but now it's ruined. I don't even think a charity shop would want this.'

'On the chuck pile?' Ash asked, and when she nodded he put it with the other things that he and Jess would take with them when they left.

'I do think, though,' Felicity went on, her hands on her hips, 'that a lot of these things are still good.'

Jess's heart sank. Maybe they weren't making as much progress as she thought. 'But still—'

'I could sell a lot of it, and help Enzo in the process,' Felicity went on. 'Roger's given me some advice about the best antiques dealers and vintage shops, but there's just so much of it.'

'What are you thinking?' Ash sat on the sofa, and Artemis moved across the cushion and lay next to him, his big, furry body stretched out along Ash's side.

'I'm still pondering.' Felicity tapped her lips. 'You know, Richard leaving all those years ago might have been a blessing in disguise.'

'Really?' Jess laughed. She glanced at Ash, expecting to share her incredulity with him, but his jaw was tight, his gaze trained on where he was stroking the large tabby, over and over. 'Why do you say that?'

'Because if I hadn't ended up like this, I would never have found you or Ash, or . . . everyone else at the market.'

'Everyone else?' Jess grinned as Felicity's cheeks turned a delicate shade of pink. She thought there was one person in particular she was referring to.

'*Everyone* else,' Felicity repeated. 'The world works in mysterious ways.'

'It certainly does,' Jess said.

'What about right after he left you?' Ash asked. 'All those years in between? You can't have been happy.' He gestured around the room. 'He ruined your life.'

Jess knew he was trying to keep his voice level, but she could hear it – the way it frayed at the edges, his anger visible in the tight line of his shoulders.

'Ash, darling.' Felicity crouched in front of him and put a hand on his arm. 'Nobody gets through unscathed, do they? But I can spend this time lamenting all the years he took from me – that I let him take from me – or I can focus on how things are now. With your help, I'm getting myself together, finding ways to be happy, people to be happy with. I'm very much looking on the bright side.'

'You've been so strong,' Ash told her, then glanced at Jess. 'You both have.' His anger had gone, and now he just looked hollow.

Felicity patted his knee. 'But I wouldn't have been, without both of you. Think of all you have to be grateful for, and whatever's left – whatever is still hurting you – let it fade into the background as much as possible.'

He sighed, but it was accompanied by a smile. 'I wish it was that easy.'

245

'One day it will be.' Felicity stood up. 'Now, do you think I can sell this hideous candelabra, or is it fit only for the scrapheap?'

They didn't get a chance to be alone until they'd left Felicity's house, carrying armfuls of items to take to the bins at the end of the road.

'I see the rugby went well,' Jess said, when their arms were empty and the bins were full. She stroked her thumb gently over the red line above Ash's left eyebrow. He flinched, then leaned into her touch.

'It was a rough game,' he said. 'I have aches in muscles I'd forgotten existed.'

'I wish I could kiss it better.'

'Me too,' he murmured.

'I finish work at four thirty on Sundays. You could stay in Greenwich, come and meet me afterwards? If your . . . thing is done by then?'

'It will be, but I can't. I have work tomorrow, so I need to get home tonight. But I could see you on Friday again?'

'I'd like that.' She didn't push, didn't offer to come up to central London and meet at his place on her days off. Instead she kissed him, ran her hand through his hair and watched him walk away from her towards some unknown mission, as she'd done every Sunday since the day they met.

Chapter Twenty-Seven

That week Jess felt supercharged. She was the perfect saleswoman in No Vase Like Home on Monday, even selling some of the hated hares and their new, equally sinister owl friends, with a smile on her face. On Tuesday and Wednesday, she got fully up to date with her overflowing Etsy orders, and started to think of some new designs.

She and Ash messaged constantly, and she began to imagine how the next few months might go. Friday nights spent with him, Saturday breakfasts – she could make him scrambled eggs and bacon, or they could eat croissants in bed (as long as she remembered to hoover up the pastry flakes), and then Sundays helping Felicity, who was becoming more confident every week.

On Thursday morning, Wendy messaged to say she had to drop one of her teenagers off at the airport, so Jess opened the shop, made herself a coffee and surveyed the shelves. She indulged in tidying what was left of her latest batch of prints, turning them all outwards, putting her favourites at the front. She realised she was humming tunelessly and went to turn on the radio, to add music to the July sunshine. Outside, the stalls were already buzzing with customers, and she felt open to anything – ready to embrace what the day had to offer.

She heard the shop door open, heard someone say, 'This is them,' so she came out of the storeroom and stepped behind the counter.

A young couple, dressed in T-shirts and shorts and carrying smoothies in see-through plastic cups, were over by her print display.

'The ones from TikTok?' the woman asked.

'Yeah.' The man rubbed a hand over his scruffy goatee. 'Bit shit, aren't they?' He put his drink on a shelf and picked one up.

'Anyone could make these,' the woman said. 'Just google motivational quotes, slap one over a photo, print it out. How are they raising money for that jeweller?'

'He needs to go back home an' all,' the man said. 'Course he's losing his business. Nobody here wants the rubbish he makes.'

Jess gripped the counter, her knuckles turning white. She closed her eyes, wishing fervently that Wendy would storm through the door in the next five seconds.

'You going to buy one?' The woman giggled. 'Look at this: *We all have superpowers, you just need to believe in yourself to discover yours.* What a load of sentimental shit! Who are these idiots?'

'Fucking artisan crafters. They're all just—'

'Excuse me!' Jess swallowed. Her whole body was hot, sweat prickling down her spine.

The couple stared at her, the man's eyes flinty. 'Yeah, love?'

'Are you going to buy anything? Or are you just going to stand there and bad-mouth everything in the market? Because if you don't like it, you don't need to even *look* at it. Just go somewhere else.'

The man smirked. 'Touched a nerve, have I?'

'Let's just go.' The woman tugged his arm.

'Why are you even here?' Jess went on. 'Being rude about my prints, saying unforgivable things about the people who

248

work here, who are just trying to make a living selling the art they've put a whole lot of time and effort into. *Unforgivable* things!' Her voice cracked, but she kept going. 'Enzo is one of the kindest people I know, he works *so* hard, and all you can do is insult him! Can you get out now, please.' She pointed at the door.

'We have every right to be here—'

'Let's just go, Matt.'

'Yes,' Jess said. 'Just go.'

He glared at her for a second, then flung the frame he was holding into the display, the loud crash making them all jump. Then he and his girlfriend left the shop, the woman hooting with laughter. As she went to see what the damage was, Jess realised her hands were shaking.

'I'm OK,' she said into the phone, half an hour later. 'I feel a lot better. Wendy's been looking after me.' She was sitting on a stool in the storeroom with a cup of tea and a muffin that Wendy had got her. She still felt a bit trembly, but some of the shock had worn off.

'Shit, Jess.' Ash's voice was tight with anger. 'Are you sure you're all right? Do you want to go home?' He let out a long breath. 'I wish I was there.'

'I'm fine.' She pressed her forehead against a pile of soft blankets. 'It was a surprise, that's all.'

'What the fuck is wrong with people? Nobody has a right to come into your workplace and insult you, scare you like that. Are you going to report it to the police?'

'Wendy's told Roger, but I don't want to do anything else. Only one of the frames got broken, and I'm not sure how we'd find them again, anyway. I just want to forget about it.'

There was a pause, and she listened to the quiet on Ash's end of the call. Did he have his own, cushy office? What would it be like to work in such a peaceful space?

'I can come and see you tonight,' he said. 'Not for long, but—'

'That's OK,' she cut in. 'You have work tomorrow, and my Etsy orders are still coming in. Despite what those idiots said, lots of people *do* like my prints.' Her laugh sounded hollow.

'Jess,' Ash said softly. 'I'm so sorry this happened to you.'

'It's OK,' she said again.

What she didn't add was that this phone call felt almost as frightening as what had happened earlier. Despite everything she'd told herself when they were having breakfast together, she was afraid of Ash breaking through the last few boundaries. She didn't want to rely on him when things got hard. A phone call was bad enough, but if she depended on him for comfort and reassurance, got needy for his hugs and kisses, then what? She didn't know that he was going to stick around, so she had to hold on to her independence; she had to be able to survive on her own. 'I'm almost back to normal now,' she told him.

She heard Ash sigh, heard him fiddle with something metallic on his desk. 'I'm here if you need me. You don't have to do this on your own, Jess.'

'I know,' she whispered, even though that was *exactly* what she had to do to keep her heart intact.

Chapter Twenty-Eight

By the end of the day, Jess was exhausted. Wendy had been keeping a close eye on her after she refused to go home early, providing her with an endless supply of hot drinks, enticing snacks and, when Jess allowed it, hugs.

'Pamper yourself this evening,' her boss said, as Jess got her handbag out of the storeroom at closing time. 'Do something nice.'

'Sure,' Jess replied, giving her a smile, and let Wendy inflict a final hug on her before she left.

What she really wanted to do was go home and think of nothing much at all, maybe watch a Gerard Butler film with Terence. She said a weary goodbye to Olga and Susie, who were both tidying their stalls away. It always felt strange walking through the market when it was closing, the sounds of shutters being pulled down, items being put into boxes more prevalent than talking or laughter. Tonight it felt extra sombre, even though she knew – of course she did – that there would always be people who were less than kind about artists and small business owners, who got their fun from making others feel bad. She'd never been personally insulted before, that was all.

An afternoon rain shower had been and gone, and Jess put her head down and walked quickly along damp, shiny pavements. She didn't usually get into her pyjamas straight after work, but today she might.

She took her key out of her bag, looked up, and came to a stumbling stop.

Ash was leaning against the door to her flat, typing something on his phone, his navy tie loosened over a white work shirt. Her body's reaction was instant desire, but her brain stuttered.

'Ash?'

He looked up, and even his smile couldn't break through the emotional wall that had just come up. 'Hey,' he said. 'You look worn out.'

'What are you doing here?' Her bag slipped off her shoulder, and she hauled it back up.

'I wanted to see you,' he said. 'I wanted to make sure you were OK.'

'I'm fine. I told you not to come.'

His smile faltered, but didn't fall. 'I know, but I was worried about you. You sounded so upset, and we were going to see each other tomorrow anyway—'

'I haven't got any food in. I was going to get a takeaway.'

'We could get one together, if you want. Or I could—'

'I didn't expect you to be here.'

Ash pushed off the door as she approached. Her fingers tingled with the urge to touch him, but she resisted.

'I'm sorry I didn't tell you,' he said. 'I thought it'd be a surprise. A *good* surprise.'

'It's very thoughtful of you.' She stopped in front of him, but she didn't let herself reach for him.

'You sound like a robot.' Ash laughed, but some of the warmth had left his voice. 'I'm sorry, are you busy tonight? I just thought, after what happened, that you might not want to be on your own. I wanted to check you were all right.'

252

'You did check, though, on the phone. And I told you I was.'

'Jess, I'm sorry—'

'You keep saying that.' She put her key in the lock and pushed the door open, then looked at him. 'Are you coming up?'

He pressed his lips together, then nodded. She heard his steady footsteps behind her, could feel pressure building up inside her. This was all wrong. She'd told him not to come, and he'd come anyway, and she wanted to . . . to fold herself into him, but she couldn't, could she? It was too much, too soon, and he hadn't listened to her.

'Do you want a beer?' she asked him. 'I have some Budweiser.'

Ash stopped just inside the door. 'Am I staying?'

She shrugged. 'I don't think that's down to me, is it? I mean, I told you not to come, but here you are.'

'I thought you'd want to see me. I thought our problem was finding time to see each other.'

'Yes, but today has been hard, and—'

'I know, and I thought I could comfort you, or take your mind off things, or . . .' He ran a hand through his hair. 'When bad stuff happens, you usually want to be with the people closest to you.'

'You meaning me, or a general you?'

Ash shrugged. 'I mean . . . everyone?'

Jess shook her head. 'I just want to put it out of my head.'

'I get that.' He took a step towards her. 'We can do anything you want.'

'I don't . . . I just – I want to be on my own, OK?'

Ash stopped. He looked surprised, and Jess felt as if she was shrivelling to nothing. She was a yo-yo, trapped halfway between an outstretched hand and the floor, because he was Ash, and he'd been nothing but wonderful to her, but she couldn't let herself need him.

'I'll go,' he said, and now *he* sounded like a robot.

'Ash.' She was wavering. She'd never wavered this much before.

'It's fine, Jess.' He turned to the door.

'It's not— it's . . .' Could she tell him how much this scared her? How the strength of her feelings for him went against the rules she lived by; how she stayed happy and safe and heartbreak-free? 'I don't often let people in.'

He turned back round. 'I know,' he said gently. 'And I understand. But I felt helpless, sitting at work, knowing what had happened to you. I'm here for you, whenever you want me. It's OK to need someone.'

It wasn't, though. Not for her. And . . . how could he say all this, when it wasn't OK for him to need her, either? 'What about Sundays?' She leaned against the kitchen counter and folded her arms. Terence wasn't here, and the room was gloomy without the TV flashing bright colours in the corner.

'I still want to see you on Sunday,' Ash said.

'No, I mean, what about *you* on Sundays? You say it's fine to need someone, and you're here for me now, as if you've picked yourself to be the person I turn to when things go to shit, but you won't tell me *anything* about what you do after we say goodbye, even though it has directly impacted our time together, every single week, and it obviously affects you a whole lot.'

'That's different.'

'How is it?'

'You're such a good thing in my life, Jess, and—'

'So I just get the fun bits? You're filtering yourself for me?'

He shook his head. 'All the things I feel with you – I don't want to ruin it.'

'But you want me to let you in when I'm dealing with crap? I can depend on you for comfort, but for you I'm only this fun-time girl? Don't you trust me to be able to help you, too?'

'Of course I do.' He yanked at his tie, loosening it further. It made him look dishevelled, his eyes slightly wild, and she realised how much she wanted to take care of him. Never mind that she'd resisted him doing the same thing – maybe once he told her what he was dealing with, she'd feel like they were on an even footing. 'It's awful, Jess,' he said. 'The whole thing. I don't want you to have that burden.'

'I want to, though. You can't dictate how we work, Ash. You can't ignore me when I tell you I don't want to see you, because your instinct is to come and look after me, then keep everything dark and gnarly about yourself hidden. Where's the fairness in that?'

'Life isn't fair, OK? It's just not!'

It was like an explosion, so different to the funny, charming Ash she knew. She felt the bite of the kitchen counter against her lower back as she leaned away from the shock of it. Ash stepped back, too, his hands pressed to his cheeks.

'I'm sorry.' He said it to the floor. 'Jess?'

'I need to go change.' She pushed herself off the counter and walked to her room, not sure what she was doing, why she'd left Ash standing there. She kicked off her shoes, switched on her fairy lights, flung her phone on the bedside table.

She felt him in the doorway before she saw him.

'My dad's dying.'

She turned around. He looked blank, as if he'd wiped his mind of all emotions in order to be able to tell her.

Her stomach clenched. 'Oh Ash, I'm so sorry—'

'He walked out on Mum, Dylan and me when I was twelve. He went back to Italy for the most part, though I know he travelled around, too. We got sporadic birthday cards, occasional phone calls, but it devastated Mum. She brought us up, working long hours, while he did whatever he wanted, running money-making schemes that usually failed. When they succeeded, Mum didn't see any money. No child support. No emotional support. No Dad, really.'

'That's terrible.' She felt sick that she'd forced it out of him this way.

'Now he's in Greenwich, in a private hospice, dying of lung cancer. Mum can't bear to see him, but she thinks he should have *someone*, some family, in his last few months, and Dylan's not here. So. It's me. I come here every Sunday and, after you, I spend an hour with him. Sometimes he talks, sometimes he can't get the words out or he's too drugged up. The last couple of weeks, he's mostly been asleep.'

He leaned against the doorframe, looking as exhausted as she felt. 'And I can't tell him how angry I am – how much he hurt Mum, how he fucked up my childhood – because he's sick. But I still have to sit there. Peggy, who we bumped into – she's one of the nurses. She's looked after me.'

Jess could only nod. He still came, even though his dad had abandoned him? Even though it was clearly torture. 'You could tell him, though.'

'What would be the point? Who would feel better if I did that?'

'You might,' Jess said, but Ash shook his head.

'I wouldn't. Maybe I'd feel better for a second, then the guilt would be even worse. And I didn't want you to know, because you were this sudden, bright part of my Sundays. I could look forward to coming here, because I got to see you before him. I still had to see him, but there was more – a better reason for being here.'

'You could have told me.'

'I didn't want him to leach out of Cherry Blossom Lodge and fuck this up for me, too. I've tried so hard to stop him fucking me up now, as much as he did then. And I know that's a shit way to think about a dying man, but I do.'

She walked over to him. 'You could just stop going. Spend Sundays with me. I'll speak to Wendy, change my work days. Braden's ready to take on more responsibility anyway.'

'I have to see him,' Ash said.

'Why?'

'Because I promised Mum.'

'If she really wants someone to see him, then why doesn't *she* do it?'

'Because he ruined her life,' Ash said. 'He broke up our family for some whim, some scheme back in Italy. Mum wouldn't go because we were settled in school, in our house, and she knew it wouldn't work anyway. He left her to struggle, so I get why she doesn't want to drag it all up again with him.'

'But she's happy for you to have to go through that, even though you were only twelve when he stopped being your dad?'

'I'm stronger than she is.'

'But you're allowed to be weak, too.' She put her hands on his shoulders, but he didn't relax into her touch.

'Not with this. It's my responsibility.'

'It *isn't*, Ash. My parents said some things about me that I wasn't meant to hear, and it changed the way I saw them. So I still speak to them sometimes, but I don't *need* them, and I don't feel any kind of responsibility towards them, and you shouldn't either. Your dad – you don't need to see him, and your mum shouldn't have asked you to go. It's not fair.'

'Life isn't fair,' he said again. 'You might feel no loyalty to your parents, and I understand why, but my mum did everything for me and Dylan when he was gone. This is the least I can do for her.'

Jess shook her head. 'What about you? What about looking after yourself? Who do *you* talk to about all this? Because it hasn't been me, has it?'

'I'm fine on—'

'On your own?' Jess finished. 'That's what I said to you, but you still turned up here, insisting that I was wrong. Am I allowed to tell you that you're wrong, or is this another example where I have to do what you say?'

He stared at her. 'This is *different*.'

Jess circled back to her bed, picked up her yellow yeti cushion and squeezed it. It was going to take all her strength to put his anger aside, to tuck her own fears away so she could examine them later, but she was going to, because what Ash was dealing with was awful. They were both stubborn, they both wanted to survive by themselves, but the truth was, they'd found each other; they cared about each other. She could let him in, and if she did that, then surely he would do the same for her?

'Come here.' She put her cushion down and stepped towards him, giving into her wants: to kiss him and wrap him up, let him bury his head in her neck just as he'd done

258

in Felicity's garden all those weeks ago. 'Let me take care of you, Ash.'

A flicker of longing crossed his face.

She smiled. 'I'll get the takeaway menus, and we can—'

'I need to go.'

'What?' She thought she'd misheard.

'I need to go.' His voice was flat. 'I can't do this right now, and you said you didn't need me, that you wanted to be on your own, so I'm going to go.'

'Ash!' she laughed, incredulous. 'Come on. I know you're hurting, and—'

'You don't get it,' he said. 'You don't understand this. You have no family loyalty because you have no real family, and . . .' He stopped, sucking in a breath, his eyes wide.

Jess pressed her lips together. He wasn't wrong, and it had been her choice to push Edie and Graeme away, but it still hurt that, of all the ways in which he could have shown his anger, this was the one he chose. 'OK, then.'

'Jess—'

'You can leave now.'

'I'm sorry, I—'

'This is a disaster, obviously. We're good at having fun together, and the sex is – was – amazing, but when it comes to feelings, we're clearly better on our own.' It was a good little speech, especially on the spur of the moment, and she worked hard to keep her tone cold, her expression blank when Ash met her gaze, his eyes bright with horror. He stared at her for a moment, then his shoulders slumped.

He nodded and turned around, and she listened to him walk down the corridor, heard the front door open and then close, way too gently, behind him. Why didn't he slam it? Why wasn't he raging and throwing things and shouting right now? That was what she wanted to do, the anger and sadness bubbling up viciously inside her.

She stared at her cosy duvet and fluffy cushions, and decided she didn't deserve their comfort. It was ironic that she'd told him – that she'd decided for both of them – they couldn't do feelings, when he'd made her feel more than she had ever allowed herself to before.

But it was fine – good, even – because now everything could go back to normal. She could return to the happy little solo island of her existence. Except, right now, with the echo of Ash's too gentle exit playing in her head, and his words about family loyalty like a bitter pill she'd swallowed in the back of her throat, her island felt like a very, very lonely place to be.

Chapter Twenty-Nine

'Did you know you have a spider in the corner of your ceiling?'

Jess was lying sideways on Lola and Malik's sofa, swinging her legs over the arm, a cup of tea going cold on the floor beside her. Lola was curled up in the armchair, looking at Jess with far too much concern, and Malik was in the kitchen, cooking his famous spaghetti bolognese that Jess was so fond of.

'He's called Marvin,' Lola said. 'We're friends now.' She sipped her tea, then rested her mug on her knees. 'I'm so sorry about Ash. Are you sure it's over?'

Jess closed her eyes. 'I haven't heard from him since he left the flat on Thursday.'

'Have you messaged him?'

'No.'

'But you called in sick to work, yesterday *and* today? A *Saturday?*' Lola sounded as incredulous as Jess felt. She never called in sick; not even when she had sprained her ankle running to get to Waterstones before they closed one evening last year. She'd just hopped about, then hobbled, sat in the storeroom more than usual, and fulfilled all Wendy's wholesale orders.

'I just felt so . . . hopeless.'

'Because you told Ash to go.'

'He was going to go anyway, and that made me so angry. He'd just told me this awful thing about his family, and I could see how upset he was, even though it was all tight muscles and defensiveness instead of tears. Then, when I tried to get him to stay, he said this thing about me not having a proper family, and I know he's right, so—'

'He's not,' Lola said.

'Then I told him to go, so I guess it was mutual.'

'You *do* have a family,' Lola said. 'You might not be that close to them, but . . .' She smiled, and Jess returned it.

'You know how I feel about Edie and Graeme.'

'Your mum and dad.'

'Guys, do you want red pepper in the bolognese?' Malik called from the kitchen.

'Yes!'

'No thanks,' Jess said at the same time.

Malik appeared in the doorway. 'Entirely unhelpful,' he said with a grin.

'Just put peppers in her bit and not mine.' Jess shrugged, which didn't really work when she was lying down.

'Always a delight to have you here, Jessica,' Malik said.

'I bought wine!' Jess shouted as he retreated to the kitchen.

'I told you, you're a delight!'

Jess laughed, then her smile fell. 'Thank you for putting up with me.'

'Never a chore,' Lola said immediately. 'But if you come round, you have to let me say some things.'

'Always.'

'Do you think, as mutual as you said it was, that you pushed Ash away like you've been doing with your mum and dad? Because, other than your incredible best friend,' she pressed a hand to her chest, 'you don't like letting anyone get close?'

Jess pulled herself to sitting and picked up her cold tea. 'You know what Edie said.'

'And I know how you interpreted it.'

'We've been through this a million times.'

'It seems worth repeating, especially when something like this happens.'

'This?'

'Ash,' Lola said. 'I've only met him once, but he seemed so . . . whole. A kind, funny, well-rounded person, which shouldn't be a rare thing, but I think when it comes to age-appropriate single men, it actually is. And I also have to mention – though this is the least important thing – he is completely gorgeous.'

'He's not whole,' Jess said. 'He's dealing with this horrible situation with his dad, and he's kept it from me for *months*. He only told me about it because we were having a fight about how I wouldn't let him in, and he hadn't realised he was doing exactly the same with me.'

'So you're as bad as each other? You like helping everyone, as long as the attention is focused on them and you're in the background. As long as you don't have to rely on anyone for anything or ask for help yourself.' Lola shook her head. 'And I understand that it was the hardest thing ever, finding your birth mum, being told she'd died, and for your aunt to respond the way she did.'

'That was a decade ago,' Jess said.

'I am 100 per cent sure it doesn't stop being traumatic,' Lola replied. 'And then, what you overheard Edie say: you interpreted it to fit your insecurities, and you've let it dictate all your relationships since then.'

'Lola.' Jess put a warning tone in her voice.

'Spaghetti or tagliatelle?' Malik called.

Jess let Lola answer, because the memory was replaying itself.

It had been just under two years ago, late in the summer, and Jess had been at the Peacocks' Bexleyheath home, helping Graeme build shelves in the alcove in the spare bedroom. Jess had stayed upstairs after Graeme had let their neighbour Celine in, and as she'd come downstairs to get a drink, she'd overheard them talking.

'Jess is better at DIY than me,' Graeme had said. 'She'll probably build you shelves too, if you ask her. She likes the practical things.'

'Always trying to be useful?' Celine had replied.

'Until she stops coming round altogether.' That was Edie.

'What do you mean?' Celine had asked.

'She's beginning to distance herself. We've tried our best, but she's never really acted like she wants to be a part of the family, has she?'

'She just gets by on her own, love,' Graeme had said. 'She's independent, and there's nothing wrong with that. Most twenty-five-year-olds haven't even considered leaving home yet.'

Edie had sighed, then said the words that had branded themselves on Jess's consciousness. 'It's hard to feel loved when you're not wanted or needed.'

Jess hadn't waited to hear more. She'd gone back upstairs, had busied herself with the shelves for another hour until Graeme had forced her to call it a day.

It had been another three months before she'd confessed what she'd overheard to Lola, when they'd gone away for a weekend to Aldeburgh, renting a tiny cottage with the money they'd saved up. Lola had been shocked, but not for the same reasons as Jess.

'She meant it about *her*, you doofus!' Lola had thrown a cushion at her, narrowly avoiding knocking a figurine off the table. 'She meant that you don't want or need her, so she doesn't know if you love her. She didn't mean that *you* weren't wanted.'

'You can't know that,' Jess had said. 'Maybe they *never* really wanted me. What if they wanted to adopt a younger child and I was all that was left? A Raggy Doll from the rejects bin.'

'No way.' Lola had been adamant. 'Every time we go round to theirs, it's so obvious how much they love you. Your mum thinks you don't need her, that you've always preferred being on your own. *That's* what she was saying.'

But Jess hadn't been able to convince herself, and it had turned into a self-fulfilling prophecy. She had begun to do what Edie had accused her of: she'd stopped visiting and phoning as often, slowly extricating herself from the family unit. She had never confronted them because she knew they would say the same as Lola – they wouldn't admit the truth. Instead, she'd let the rejection calcify inside her, alongside her aunt's: another tick in the column titled, *The only person you can count on is yourself*. She even had that as a print in her shop, though it was one of her worst sellers. She refused to remove it out of principle.

'You can't just hang out with me and Wendy for the rest of your life,' Lola said now.

'That's not what I do and you know it.'

'But you really like Ash. He's different, Jess – in a good way.'

She shrugged. 'It's Sunday tomorrow, so I'll know then, won't I?'

'Know what?'

'If it's properly over. If he turns up at the usual time, we can talk about it. If he doesn't, then that's it.'

'You're going to let him dictate what happens between you?' Lola went to get the bottle of red wine Jess had brought round. 'I thought that was part of the problem: that he showed up when you told him not to, that he decided to go when you asked him to stay. What will you do if he doesn't turn up? Just accept he's in control, or do something about it?'

Jess didn't reply. She didn't have an answer. Instead, she closed her eyes and listened to her best friend struggling with the corkscrew, and Malik singing in the kitchen, and inhaled the delicious, tomatoey smells.

Lola squeezed her shoulder and, when Jess opened her eyes, thrust a glass of wine into her hand. 'The best cure for heartbreak.'

'I'm not heartbroken,' Jess scoffed, then took a sip. 'It's not like Ash and I knew each other very well, anyway.'

Lola sat next to her. 'That's because you didn't let him, not properly. I get that you didn't want to rely on him, but sometimes you have to admit that people are worth holding on to. They're worth fighting for, even when things are hard. I would bet you anything that he turns up tomorrow.'

'You would?' Jess didn't want to admit that, since he'd left her flat on Thursday, that was the one thing she'd been hanging on to. Because she did care about him, and she wanted to fight for what they had.

'I would.' Lola's nod was firm. 'Now, come and help me lay the table. Malik's spag bol is worth clearing off all the piles of crap for – no eating off our knees tonight. We can celebrate the fact that you've found someone you really like, and that you're prepared to do the hard graft to make it work.'

'OK.' Jess let herself be infected by her friend's positivity. She let herself believe that, the following day, Ash would appear in the doorway of No Vase Like Home with two coffees and an apology, and she would tell him that he didn't need to apologise, that *she* was the one who needed to say sorry, and they'd go to Felicity's house together and Jess could get rid of this awful, tearing ache inside her.

With a smile, she went to help her friend clear the tiny dining table, so they could sit down and have a meal together.

Chapter Thirty

Midday on Sunday came and went without any sign of Ash, and all Jess's hope from the previous day drained out of her like water down a sink.

He had decided that they were over, that their argument had been enough to give up not only on her, but on the other friends he'd made at the market, and on Felicity. Jess had done that with her antagonism, her challenges, her lack of sympathy for him.

'I'm sorry,' Wendy said, as the shelves of clocks ticked round to quarter past twelve, the time displayed whichever direction Jess looked in.

'It's OK,' she said. 'It doesn't matter.'

Her gaze fell on her prints, the photographs of the kite she'd watched on the heath, and that was all it took for the memories to assault her: that first meeting, his grey eyes bright with humour despite the situation; the way – one week when they'd talked about Wendy's punny shop name – he had tried out umpteen different pronunciations of the word 'vase', each one more ridiculous than the last; how their first kiss had felt both shocking and inevitable, the wind coming off the river contrasting with Ash's warm palms pressed into her lower back, his body crowding hers and her melting in the middle, like a marshmallow toasting on an open fire on a frosty night. Then Thursday at her flat, and the things she'd said to him, their harshness making her wince even now, when some of the immediate horror had faded; the salt of her tears mingling with body-wash bubbles as she'd let herself cry in the shower for the last three mornings.

'Are you still taking a break?' Wendy asked. 'Will Felicity be waiting for you?'

'Oh . . . yes. She will be.'

'Take at least an hour, Jess. Get back here sometime before two.'

'Thanks.' She got her bag and left the shop. The market was heaving, the blue sky – unbroken by cloud – visible through the glass roof. She felt like a fawn skittering on new legs, everything unfamiliar and off-kilter. She had been convinced that, despite everything, Ash would turn up. A hopeful voice suggested he'd gone straight to Felicity's, and Jess clung on to it the whole walk there.

But it wasn't Ash who answered the door when she knocked, and it wasn't Felicity.

'Jess, my dude! Felicity thought you weren't coming. Is that man of yours with you?' Spade was in an old Proclaimers T-shirt, and without a hat his hair was especially wild.

'I'm sorry I'm late,' Jess said. 'Ash isn't here?'

'Not yet. Come through.'

He walked back into the house and, when Jess followed, it took her a moment to register the difference. The hallway wasn't clear, but there was a narrow pile of items along the wall, rather than a disorganised mountain range. She stepped into the living room, and couldn't stifle her gasp. The fireplace was there in all its original glory, though it looked scuffed and in need of painting. The grey carpet was dirty and dusty, and would probably need to be replaced, but Jess could see it enough to notice, and that was huge.

'Wow,' she said, then thought of how Ash had always played it, his casual understatedness putting Felicity at ease. 'Spade really fits in here, huh?'

He grinned, and Felicity turned from where she was examining the piles of stuff that still took over the back half of the room. 'He offered to help me with a few things, and I thought it made sense, with you working so much and Ash only being available on Sundays. Spade has more . . .'

'I'm a lazy layabout,' he finished. 'I don't need to work any more, so I don't – Market Misfits aside. But playing with Lola and Braden has given me a new enthusiasm for being part of the local scene, so I thought I could offer my services – which amounts to my two hands, my sturdy back and my smaller-than-normal brain – elsewhere. This seemed like a good enough *where*.' He glanced at Felicity, and from the way his eyes darted away again, the pinpoints of colour on his cheeks, Jess knew that Felicity was far more than just 'a good enough *where*' to him.

'Nonsense,' Felicity said. 'You're a marvel, Steven.'

He chuckled. 'Let's not stand on ceremony. Spade, please.'

'Steven?' Jess shot him an amused glance.

'A name from a different century.' He gave a dismissive wave.

'Is Ash coming?' Felicity asked. 'I had expected the two of you sooner. I've got the teapot out – with four of us here, I thought *that* level of ceremony was warranted.' The smile she gave Spade was so mischievous, so youthful, that Jess's heart squeezed. She hated having to let Felicity down. She felt Ash's absence keenly, but she knew she wouldn't be the only one.

'He's not coming today.' She perched on the sofa that was now fully uncovered, and currently home to tabby

Artemis and the sleek black moggy Bond. 'He's tied up with something.'

'Those life ties get you in a bind,' Spade said cheerfully. 'Shall I make the tea and open those fancy biscuits you bought, Felicity?'

'If you can find them in amongst the nursery of dolls,' she replied, and Spade loped out of the room, laughing.

Jess blinked. Felicity was making *jokes* about the hoarding now? She hadn't just turned a corner, she'd gone through the entire maze and found the exit.

'Ash is tied up with something?' Felicity asked her gently. 'Or you and he have had a falling out?'

Jess sagged, and Artemis, who ruled the back gardens of Greenwich with a sharp paw, raised his head and then crawled onto her lap, the sound of his purrs rivalling a low-flying aircraft. 'Is it that obvious?'

Felicity put down the jacket she was holding. It was plum-coloured, with a jewelled brooch on the collar. Jess wondered how anyone could lose something like that, then reminded herself that she and Felicity were very different people. Today, the older woman was wearing jeans and a loose grey shirt, its shoulders far too baggy. Was it . . .? She tried to remember if she'd ever seen Spade wearing something like that, as opposed to one of his slogan T-shirts.

'You look tired,' Felicity said, 'and your smile isn't reaching your cheeks, let alone your eyes. There's none of your usual perkiness, and you're usually so punctual. Both of you. It's not just that he's busy doing something else, is it?'

Jess stroked the purring monster on her lap. 'We had a fight – but all couples fight, don't they? One argument shouldn't mean the end.'

271

'How do you know it's the end?'

'He's not picking up my calls or answering my messages.' After leaving Lola's flat the night before, she had tried to contact him, but everything had gone unanswered. 'And he didn't come to the market today. It used to be his sanctuary, before . . . before the other thing he had to do, before we even met. But he's not here.'

Felicity crouched in front of her. 'Do you know that he didn't go to the market today?'

'I . . . Oh.' Jess swallowed. 'You mean he could have come as usual, and just avoided seeing me?'

'I don't know what's happened between you, but if he's hurting, then he might have wanted that familiar routine, even if he's not ready to speak to you.'

Jess nodded, but the idea went against everything she knew about him. He was, above all things, kind, and – even if he was still angry with her – she thought he would have popped his head round the door, acknowledged her at the very least.

'How did you cope?' she asked Felicity. 'When your husband left you. When you ended up on your own so unexpectedly.'

The older woman lowered herself to the carpet and crossed her legs. She looked pointedly behind her, then raised an eyebrow at Jess.

'Oh.' Jess's cheeks coloured. 'Shit. I mean . . .'

'I think we can both agree that I didn't cope. This has been years of insecurity, years of . . . well, not facing the feelings I needed to face. Hiding behind possessions instead. Every purchase gave me a rush of adrenaline, a moment of knowing who I was, because that object was a little piece of me: I'd chosen it, and I could keep it as long as I wanted, even if it was just a Sunday newspaper. It's laughable, because a *thing* can't define anyone, but when you're lost, you look for anything that might show you which way to go.'

'It makes sense,' Jess said. 'You'd lost your husband.'

'That wasn't what happened,' Felicity said softly, as Spade came into the room carrying a tea tray, the crockery and teapot jingling. Jess did a double take at the chintzy floral apron he was wearing, its lace trim giving him a rakish air. 'You're a darling,' Felicity told him.

He gave a curtsy and put the tray down. 'I'm gonna go and see about that pile of LPs in the bedroom.'

'Steven – Spade – thinks he's discovered a treasure trove.'

'I have,' Spade said. 'Felicity is a dark, dark horse.'

'I'm beginning to see that,' Jess replied.

He poured the tea out, added milk and brought them each a mug, along with a plate of biscuits, then he squeezed Felicity's shoulder, his fingers lingering at her neck for a moment before he left the room.

Jess took a sip of too-hot tea, counted silently to five and then said, 'You were saying?'

'Oh yes. Richard. He had a heart condition, and at one point, I thought I was going to lose him. But after the operation he made a complete recovery, and then he decided life wasn't about domesticity; it wasn't about routine, or lazy mornings with coffee and newspapers under the duvet. He wanted adventure, new experiences.'

'You didn't agree?'

'Not at all. I wanted to focus on our family and friends, spend time with the people we cared about. At that point, I was still young enough to have a baby, and I thought that we could grow our family. But Richard wasn't interested, so—'

'He left you,' Jess finished.

'No.' Felicity laughed. 'I kicked him out. I told him that if he wanted a round-the-world ticket and an Indiana Jones hat, then he should fill his boots. And, after only a couple of hours' protest – where his main argument was that I should go with him – he left. He never came back, not even for his things.'

Jess's pulse raced. 'But I thought . . . you said that he left you.'

'He did leave,' Felicity said. 'But only because I told him to go.'

Jess blew on her tea, picked up a biscuit. 'Right,' she said. 'OK.'

'You're wondering how I could have ended up like this, accumulating a city's worth of things, when I made the decision?'

Jess nodded. 'I thought that – that if you were in control, if you *chose* being on your own, then you'd – I'd – be OK. I thought that . . .'

'You can say it: you won't be saying anything to me that I haven't thought about myself a thousand times.'

Jess swallowed. 'I thought this was a response to trauma. I never thought it could happen to someone who was fine, and—'

'But I wasn't fine,' Felicity said. 'I didn't really want Richard gone, but I was angry that his priorities weren't the same as mine. I threw my husband out with the bathwater, then I stayed angry, and I didn't let anyone else in for a long time. I tried to fill the hole up with objects, instead.'

'Ash hasn't been letting me in.' The words rushed out before she could think about them.

Felicity nodded. 'What about you, Jess? You've been such a help to me, and Spade was telling me how turning the TikToks towards Enzo's plight was your idea, in the beginning. You're always projecting outwards. Do you let people look after you, too?'

'Sometimes.' It came out as a mumble. 'Not if I can help it,' she added, when Felicity didn't fill the silence.

'So you and Ash pushed each other away?'

'I think that . . . that if he cared about me as much as I care about him, he would have shown up today.'

Felicity took a biscuit and snapped it in half. 'You can tell yourself that story until the cows come home, but you're not inside his head. You don't know how he rationalises things. You won't know until you talk to him.'

'I want to,' Jess said. 'But how can I, if he's not answering my phone calls and messages, and I can't find him?'

'In that case,' Felicity said, 'It's time to call in a few favours. Let the people you've helped, help you back.' She rubbed Jess's arm, took an iPhone out of her pocket and unlocked the screen. 'I want to have a house sale, here. Get rid of most of these things; the ones that are good enough. If I help you, will you help me?'

Jess's brain stalled. 'You want to let people in here, so they can rake through all your things?'

'There's very little I need,' Felicity said. 'Whatever I sell, the money can go to Enzo – as much as he needs. When he and Carolina are on sturdier ground, we'll find another good cause. Are you in?'

'Of course I'll help you organise it,' Jess said. 'I'm sure everyone at the market will want to be involved, too. And you don't need to help me, Felicity. I'm not actually sure what you can do.'

'You'd be surprised,' Felicity said, glancing up from her phone screen.

Jess sat back on the sofa. 'You know when Spade said you were a dark horse?'

Felicity nodded, a slow smile brightening her eyes, making her look carefree.

'I think he was right.'

Chapter Thirty-One

Monday felt more like November than July, and when Jess accompanied Lola to the Gipsy Moth that evening, she had to zip her jacket up to the neck. Going to the pub was the last thing she wanted to do, but Lola had insisted and, after Felicity had messaged to tell her she wanted to talk to everyone about the house sale, she could hardly fail to turn up. But there would be no terrace for the group that evening, unless they were prepared to risk hypothermia.

'My, my, my, if it isn't Jess and Lola.' Spade's announcement was accompanied by a wave, his other arm slung around Felicity's shoulders. Enzo was on his other side, and Jess might have been imagining it, but he seemed less pensive than usual, the dark smudges under his eyes less pronounced.

'Hey, everyone.' She smiled at Kirsty, Susie, Roger and Olga. Wendy was there too, and she tapped the empty bench next to her. Jess slid along it and sat down. 'How's Carolina, Enzo?'

'She is a lot better,' he said. 'Since Sofia has been helping us, and our stall is looking brighter, she is less anxious. We have another meeting with her consultant on Friday, to review the medication she's been taking.'

'That's brilliant,' Jess said. 'I'm so glad, Enzo.'

'I've told everyone my house sale idea,' Felicity added. 'Including Enzo. They're all on board.'

'I'm going to make muffins to entice people in,' Kirsty said.

'And the Market Misfits are going to play a set, if you're up for it, Lols?' Spade raised his eyebrows.

'Of course I am. We can't disappoint our fans, can we?' Lola laughed.

'It'll be a market away from the market,' Susie said.

'And it will mean Sofia can work for Enzo as long as necessary,' Felicity added. 'Carolina won't need to rush back before she's ready.'

Enzo shook his head. 'I cannot thank you all enough. Your kindness and generosity – it's almost too much.'

'Nonsense,' Roger huffed. 'You would have done it for any of us. Us marketeers, we stick together.'

'Ghouls included.' Spade grinned at Felicity.

'Of course,' Felicity said. 'But we're not the only ones who are part of that club.'

Jess caught Kirsty's eye, and got a sympathetic smile in return. She thought the baker had been acting oddly when she'd bought her muffin selection box that morning.

'This isn't just about the house sale, is it?' she said. 'I thought we were here to plan it.'

'There isn't much to do,' Felicity admitted. 'Wendy and Susie, particularly, have been marvellous. It seemed daunting at first, but knowing how you've all rallied to support Enzo, I knew I could ask for help, too.'

'Teamwork makes the dream work.' Kirsty held her wine aloft.

'But I . . .' Jess said, as they all clinked glasses. 'You only told me about it yesterday.'

'You've done so much for me already, Jess,' Felicity said. 'And we're here tonight because *you* need help.'

She winced. 'There really isn't anything—'

'We all love Ash,' Susie cut in.

'And, more importantly, we love you and Ash together,' Felicity said.

Jess topped up her cider, watching it tumble over the ice in her glass. She couldn't remember the last time she'd felt so uncomfortable. 'We can't Crowdsource me a boyfriend.'

'Not just *any* boyfriend,' Kirsty said. 'Ash.'

'Ash Faulkner,' Olga added in a dreamy voice.

Jess folded her arms. 'You can't make a video saying how much you miss him and post it on TikTok. He only set up an account so he could watch the Misfits' videos. He's probably deleted it by now.'

'You mean you haven't checked?' Kirsty sounded horrified. 'What about his other social media accounts?'

Jess stared at the table.

'Of course she's checked,' Lola said.

Jess rolled her eyes. 'He has Instagram and Twitter, but he hasn't used either of them for over four months, and his TikTok account has no activity. There's no recent reel of him strolling through Covent Garden with a kooky backing track, so I can race up there and fling my arms around him.'

'He's a great guy,' Spade said. 'You didn't have to spend much time with him to know that.'

'He was so kind when I was worried about my new changing bags,' Susie said. 'He told me they were wonderful, let me give him a demonstration of all the compartments, even though he admitted he hadn't spent a lot of time around babies.'

'He came up with my latest bestselling flavour combo,' Kirsty added. 'My pistachio, lime and vanilla muffin is so popular.'

279

'He looked good in every one of my hats, which is a pure anomaly.' Olga shook her head.

'If it wasn't for Jess and Ash, I would still be living in an arsonist's dream,' Felicity admitted. 'Without them, I would never have faced it.'

'They may have started it, but the hard work has been yours.' Spade planted a kiss on her forehead.

'You've been amazing, Felicity,' Jess agreed. 'It's a huge transformation.' Her heart swelled as Felicity sat up straighter, basking in the praise. She waited for someone else to chip in, but it seemed as if, right now, she wasn't going to escape the spotlight. She sighed. 'I do miss Ash,' she admitted.

'You miss him because you love him.' Susie pressed her clasped hands to her chest.

'Oh, I don't think . . .' She cleared her throat, then took a long, slow sip of her drink. Did she love Ash? The fact that she'd taken two days off work because she was feeling too sad to play Happy Sales Assistant made her think there was something pretty cosmic going on inside her. She had tried not to examine it too closely, but she hadn't felt this miserable for a long time.

'We need to track him down, basically.' Kirsty made it sound like the easiest thing in the world.

'He's not answering your calls?' Spade asked.

'He hasn't even read my WhatsApps,' Jess admitted.

'He could have turned off the read receipts,' Lola suggested.

'He could have thrown his phone in the river,' Susie offered. Everyone looked at her like she'd sprouted wings. 'If he was upset, I mean.'

Jess sighed. 'I don't think we can find him. Thank you – all of you, but—'

280

'Roger is an ex-cop,' Spade said. 'Roger, mate, you can pull some strings, can't you? Get his address?'

'You think I should just turn up at his *door*?' Jess said.

'That would be highly immoral, not to mention illegal.' Roger frowned at Spade.

'Address?' Lola's shout cut through the chatter. 'You need his address, right?'

'That seems a bit desperate,' Jess admitted.

'Things done in pursuit of true love are never considered desperate,' Wendy said. 'They're charming and romantic, but never desperate.'

'Surely that depends on the outcome,' Susie said.

'I have his address!' Lola slammed her palm on the table. 'I have Ash's address!'

'You do?'

'You *do*?' Jess echoed.

'Yup. That day in the market, outside the pub. I asked Ash and Felicity for their release forms, remember? In case they ended up in the video.'

'Woah,' Spade said. 'The best friend comes to the rescue.'

'I don't *technically* think this is an appropriate use of the private information he's given you on his video release form,' Roger said.

'It's in pursuit of true love,' Felicity reminded him. 'Nothing is considered either desperate or illegal.'

'I'm not sure the Met's finest would agree with you—'

'I can't just go to Ash's flat and knock on the door, tell him I'm sorry for pushing him away and ask him to give me a second chance.' Jess laughed, expecting her best friend and her work mum, and all the other people she'd got close to despite her best intentions, to laugh along with her.

Instead, she got expectant, hopeful gazes.

'Why not?' Lola asked.

Jess looked at the table. She missed Ash, more than she had admitted to anyone. She missed their Sunday mornings, talking about ghosts and pigeons, flying kites. She missed him asking her for motivational quotes, then offering examples himself. Whenever she'd come up with a new idea for the shop, she'd sent it to him and asked him what he thought. Since Thursday, she hadn't even sat at her desk.

He had left her floundering, with too many thoughts and without access to the person she wanted to tell them to. She missed his warm skin pressed against hers, the pressure and taste of his kisses. If she'd known that night and morning they'd had together in her flat would be the last – the only – one, she would have held on more tightly. She thought they were at the beginning, that it was the first fumbling, deliciously imperfect time they'd be with each other, learning how they fitted together. She had thought it would be the first of many.

Now the people around this table were taking her fatalist approach – the one she'd always used that ensured her connections were temporary and all the better for it, so she didn't end up getting her heart pulverised – and they were telling her it wasn't the only way.

'Why not, Jess?' Lola repeated. 'Why can't you go up there, knock on his door and just be honest with him?'

Jess shrugged, her insides knotting tighter, making her restless. But it wasn't sadness this time; it wasn't the grief or guilt of losing him, of saying those things to him and telling him he had to go. It was the restlessness of possibility, the anxiety and anticipation that came with putting herself out there –

fighting for someone, accepting she still wanted what they had. It was the panic that came with admitting love was sometimes worth the pain it caused, and Jess couldn't remember the last time she'd felt, so strongly, that that was true. Now she wanted to put it on one of her prints and sell it in its thousands across the country, brand it onto her skin. But first, she had to go and get Ash back. Or, at the very least, she had to try.

Chapter Thirty-Two

J ess caught the Clipper late in the afternoon, the sky a bright blue canvas peppered with puffy white brushstrokes, yesterday's autumn-like chill entirely forgotten. She had spent the day in a state of fidgety irritation, almost wishing Wendy had let her work on her day off, to keep her mind on something other than the scenarios playing on a loop in her head.

On the way home the night before, she had gone to Lola's flat and waited while she burrowed through her release forms for the one Ash had filled in. His handwriting was bold, slightly spiky. There was his name, signature and, in the middle, his address. She and Lola had been silent while she'd typed it into her phone, and she knew her friend felt guilty. But Jess had also known that, if at any point while they were spending time together she had asked for his address, Ash would have told her. He'd been to her flat. On the second occasion, he'd turned up announced, so she was just going to have to do the same. What other choice did she have, if he was still refusing to answer her calls?

'This'll be a funny story to tell your grandchildren,' Lola had said, as she walked her to the door.

'I promise I won't tell him you helped me,' Jess had replied. 'I'll say I saw the stack of forms when I was here for dinner.'

'It doesn't really hold up, considering I announced to all your friends that I had the means to track him down.'

'They're all behind . . . this,' Jess had said.

'I know.' Lola laughed. 'No pressure, then. It's not just your and Ash's happiness you're going after, but all of theirs, too.'

'Great.' Jess's mouth had dried out. 'Thanks for that.'

Now she stood on the boat's outside deck, the wind whipping her hair, and felt like the figurehead secured to the *Cutty Sark*: moving forwards, but exposed to all the elements. If she wanted to get Ash back, she would have to tell him everything she was scared of, and she'd have to convince him to do the same. Getting him to let her in was the part she was most afraid of, because if he refused, there was nothing she could do.

They passed by London landmarks and under famous bridges, and when the boat went beneath Tower Bridge, with the Tower of London a hulking, impenetrable shadow to her right, Jess was crowded on all sides by other passengers eager to drink it in. From the water, the city gleamed. Buildings rose up, proud and statuesque, above the grey-green surface of the Thames.

She tried to imagine what it would be like to travel in the opposite direction, passing ships and cathedrals and towers, knowing that your dad, who you hadn't seen for years – who you no longer knew – was waiting for you, dying slowly without anyone by his side. The fear, the responsibility, would be overwhelming. Jess pushed the thought aside, and waved at three small children in colourful sou'westers standing on the deck of one of the city's packed tourist barges.

She walked from the Embankment up to Holborn, the streets as busy as Greenwich Market on a Sunday, flocks of workers crowded outside pubs, shirtsleeves rolled up and jackets discarded, filling the air with laughter. She checked her phone, following the gentle dings as it gave her directions to Ash's apartment block and then told her she'd reached her destination. It was a tall grey building that must have started out smart, but now looked grimy from years of traffic fumes. But there were pollarded trees outside the entrance, woven through with LED lights, and the foyer beyond the glass door looked spacious.

Jess hovered her finger over the button to flat twenty-seven, remembering the man Ash had told her about who walked his scary dogs. She pressed it, holding it down a few seconds too long. She waited, but there was no answer. She tried again, her insides clenching at the thought that, even now, he was rejecting her.

A figure walked across the foyer, the shadowed silhouette becoming a woman in a green coat. She opened the door and then held it for Jess, giving her a warm smile. Jess thanked her and slipped inside, even though a part of her wanted to shout after the woman – tell her she could have been anyone, a thief or a drug dealer. But she was in now. She walked over to the elevators, wearing her imposter status heavily, glancing behind every few seconds while she waited for one to come.

She got out on the fourth floor and followed the flat numbers down the corridor, treading on carpet patterned with brown and grey geometric shapes. At the end there was a window with frosted glass. Flat twenty-six was on her left, number twenty-seven on her right.

She reached her fist up to knock, then paused. It was after six, but he could still be at work, or perhaps he was one of the shirt-clad drinkers outside a pub near his office. How would she ever know, though, if he didn't answer her messages? She rammed her fist against the wood, hammering until her hand hurt.

'Ash! Ash, are you in there?' She paused to listen, but couldn't hear anything from inside. Not footsteps, or the low murmur of the television. But then there was a sound behind her, a *clunk*, and she turned to see the door of flat twenty-six opening, revealing a tall, silver-haired man with a slight stoop and a steely gaze, wearing a merlot-coloured sweater over grey trousers.

'Ash isn't here, I don't think,' the man said, his words slightly clipped.

'Is he usually back from work by now?' Jess asked.

His eyes narrowed. 'I'm not his keeper, young lady.'

'Of course not. I'm sorry. I'm – I'm Jess.' She held her hand out, and the man's eyes widened a fraction.

'I've heard about you,' he said. 'I'm Mack.'

'Oh – of course!' She barked out a laugh, and Mack looked affronted. 'Sorry,' she said again. 'He's told me about you, too. About your Sunday mornings.'

'He's a kind young man. He takes the time to check on me, to make sure I have all I need. I may look as strong as an ox, but two hip replacements means walking to the newsagent is a trial, rather than an amusing jaunt.'

Jess nodded. 'I know he likes spending time with you.'

Mack waved a dismissive hand. 'He thinks of it as a duty. Perhaps he's come to be fond of our time together, but he's very big on duty, isn't he?'

The way he said it made Jess think Mack knew everything, but she didn't want to betray Ash's confidence if she was wrong. 'He is,' she said. 'And you . . . you don't know where he is right now?'

'I'm afraid not. And he didn't come for his Sunday coffee. I had a message, crying off with no explanation.'

287

'Is that unusual?'

'He's been telling me about the market, about you and the woman living in that grand old house consumed by decades' worth of clutter.'

'Oh.'

'So, yes, it was unlike him to be so unforthcoming. I haven't seen or heard from him since then. I'm sorry I can't help you more.' He said the last part gently, as if he could sense how desperate, how unhappy, she was.

'You've been kind to talk to me at all,' she said. 'I snuck in, I'm afraid.'

Mack rolled his eyes. 'Some of the residents of this block are far too trusting, or simply have their heads in the clouds. It's not your fault.'

'Thank you. And—'

'If I see him, I'll ask him to call you.'

She nodded.

'I'll tell him,' Mack continued, 'that you made the effort to come all the way here, and that the least he can do is give you a few minutes of his time.'

She managed a smile. 'Thank you, Mack. Is there anything I can get you? Do you have everything you need?'

'I have a few backups when Ash isn't around, so I'm fine, thank you. It pays to still be this handsome at seventy-five.'

Jess laughed. 'I'm glad,' she said, and turned to leave. Mack squeezed her wrist, so quickly she thought she'd imagined it.

'He cares about you,' he said. 'Whatever's happened, I know that much.'

'Thank you,' Jess said again, and wondered if, from this point forward, her vocabulary would be at least 50 per cent *sorry* and *thank you*. She walked away from him down the corridor, and heard Mack's door snick quietly closed behind her.

It rained hard that night, grey cloud sweeping in to obliterate the blue. Lola had messaged her to ask how it had gone, and she'd replied with a simple:

He wasn't there so, no luck.

But she realised, as she lay on her bed, her fairy lights pulsing from pink to gold, hugging her lilac yeti cushion, it wasn't about luck. It was about her destroying a relationship that she'd valued. Perhaps she had been blasé because of her parents. It didn't matter how much she pushed them away, how often she refused their invitations to go round for dinner, they had never disappeared on her. She had taken that for granted.

She fell into a fitful sleep, the rain drumming against the glass like small hands trying to get in, the air humid despite it. She dreamed of Ash in the places they had spent time: on the bench in Greenwich Park; surrounded by all that space on Blackheath; at Felicity's house. Then she dreamed of him in places they hadn't been together: her beloved Waterstones; the long table in a shadowy corner of the Gipsy Moth. On the street, a few steps ahead of her.

She startled awake, glanced at the clock and saw it was only five past midnight. She'd been asleep for less than an hour. The heat in the room was almost unbearable, and she got up, pulled back the curtains and opened the window. The air, when it met her skin, was stultifying, but the raindrops were cool and she leaned out, letting them hit her bare arms, her shoulders.

And then she saw him, standing near the kerb, half hidden behind a van that was parked haphazardly, its front wheel up on the pavement. He had the same dark, ruffled hair, the same lean figure, but he was too far from the glow of the street light, a collection of black and grey shapes masked by the rain. It was only the tightness in her chest, the certainty in her bones, that convinced her it was him.

'Ash?' She called out, and he moved. But he didn't look up; instead he turned, quickly – unsteadily? – and walked away. 'Ash?' A few more steps, and then he was gone from her view, even when she leaned as far out of the window as she dared. She rubbed her face and then, leaving the window open, went back to bed, lying on top of the covers.

The dawn light was grey, and Jess woke to a damp breeze caressing her skin. She thought there must have been a thunderstorm in the night, though she hadn't heard it. She got up and walked to the window. The van was still there, parked like someone had been running late or looking at their phone, then not bothered to correct their position.

She had been dreaming about Ash a lot, but she couldn't work out if last night had just been more vivid than the rest, or if he'd really been there, in Greenwich, standing outside her window. By the time she'd showered and dressed, had toast and jam for breakfast and was on her way to work, she decided it had been a dream. It was such a long way for him to come, so late at night, and she didn't know if the DLR ran that late – the Clippers certainly didn't. And if he *had* made the journey, like she'd done earlier that day, then why hadn't he called up to her, pressed the doorbell? She'd checked her phone as soon as she was awake, but there were no missed calls or messages. No hint that he'd changed his mind about getting in touch.

She decided, as she walked to No Vase Like Home, that she was going to have to do something about this. No good would come of having such vivid dreams about him, especially if he was really gone from her life for good.

Chapter Thirty-Three

The rest of the week passed as sluggishly as the weather had been before the storm broke. On Wednesday, Jess worked feverishly on her Etsy shop, fulfilling all the new orders she had ignored over the last few days. She came up with a couple of new quotes which were, unsurprisingly, on the cynical side. *A new dawn is a chance for a hundred new disappointments* and, *If a shark stops swimming, it'll die. If a person stops swimming, they have to worry about drowning* and *the sharks*.

On Thursday, her spirits were lifted when Kirsty came into No Vase Like Home trialling a new muffin flavour: sausage and red onion relish.

'The chunks of herby, caramelised sausage really make it.' She held the box out to Wendy and Jess, who each took one. 'I'm expanding my breakfast range.'

Wendy looked at Jess. 'I feel like that's a dig at us.'

Jess smiled. 'Or a compliment about our dedication to breakfast muffins?'

'That one.' Kirsty pointed at her. 'Any luck with what we talked about on Monday night?'

'You mean tracking Ash down?' Wendy said before Jess could reply. 'It was a failure, unfortunately.'

Kirsty looked stricken. 'He didn't want to see you?'

'He wasn't there,' Jess said. 'And his neighbour told me he'd made an excuse not to have coffee with him on Sunday – so he wasn't here, but he wasn't *there* either.'

'Wow.' Kirsty rearranged the last muffins in her box. 'You must have really done a number on him.'

Jess's indignation flared. 'He did a number on me, too! At least I'm trying to get in touch with him.' She thought of her strange dream-not-dream, and wondered again if it had been real. But if he *was* trying to see her, then why not call? Why not reply to the messages she'd sent, that had started out apologetic, then aimed for jovially laid-back, and then, if she was honest, had got a little bit desperate?

Wendy tore her muffin in half. 'Don't give up on him yet.'

'Definitely not,' Kirsty said. 'Think about how close Enzo was to losing everything. Now his stall's full of beautiful new pieces, Sofia's planning on splitting her time between jewellery making and teaching for the foreseeable, Carolina's treatment is finally working out, *and* she's going to be working with her sister. They're all better off than they were before. So much good, from what was a horrible situation.'

'Exactly!' Wendy held her hand up, and Kirsty high-fived it. They both held their hands out to Jess, and she high-fived them at the same time, nodding and smiling. But the thing with Enzo was different: anyone could see that. When it came to Ash and what had happened between them, despite all the support and encouragement of her friends, she was on her own.

On Friday morning, Jess set about rearranging the shelf of hares and owls because, unlike her, their customers thought they were *adorable*, *magnificent* and *quirky*, and they were selling at least three a day. Wendy had, in deference to it being Friday – and because she knew Jess wasn't her brightest, most perky self – put the radio on, and the strains of Carrie Underwood drifted out from the storeroom.

She heard the door open, and turned to greet the new customer. It took her brain a couple of seconds to process the strawberry-blonde hair, the smart, biscuit-coloured nurse's uniform, the name badge that said 'Margaret'. Ash, of course, knew her as Peggy.

'Hello,' Jess said. It came out as a croak.

'Hey,' Peggy replied. She looked, and sounded, wary. 'You ordered a couple of mugs for me, and I had an email to say they were ready to pick up.'

'Right. Let me . . . I'll go and get them.' She gestured to the storeroom and then almost walked into Wendy, who was standing just inside, holding a box.

'OK, Jess?' She frowned.

'Fine. I'm fine. Are they the mugs?'

'I overheard. They arrived yesterday.'

'Brilliant.' She took the box. 'I'll do this.'

'Are you sure you're OK?'

'I'm great,' Jess said. 'No problemo.' She winced, knowing Wendy would see right through her, and turned around. Peggy was examining the glittery twigs by the front door.

'Here they are,' she said too loudly.

'How are you?' Peggy asked gently.

'I'm really good,' Jess said. 'Tickety-boo, in fact. Shall I wrap these?'

'Oh no, you're fine.' Peggy waved her away. 'They're just for home. John – my husband – and I love these mugs, but we had a dinner party that got a bit boisterous, and our set of six went down to four. My home aesthetic doesn't tolerate mismatched mugs.'

'That's understandable,' Jess said. Her whole body was a live wire, she was so desperate to ask Peggy about Ash. Surely, even though he hadn't come here, and had missed Mack's coffee on Sunday, he hadn't missed seeing his dad? Unless, of course, he'd listened to her and decided he didn't need to go any more. Perhaps he'd seen all three of them as obligations, and dropped the whole lot. 'These mugs are lovely,' she added blandly. 'So pretty.'

'They match our colour scheme,' Peggy said. 'When I pictured how I wanted our house to look, it was more blue than green, but now we have several feature walls that I lovingly refer to as cosy slime.' She chuckled. 'The paint was so expensive, so John said we had to at least give it a try after the effort of decorating it all, and now – with a few bright cushions and art prints – it looks pretty swanky. The slightly icky colours seem to be in vogue right now.'

'Cheerful cushions always make a difference.' Jess added an extra layer of Sellotape to the box, to make sure the bottom didn't drop out while Peggy was carrying it. The song on the radio changed to a low, melancholy tune by Fretland.

'Have you caught up with Ash recently?' Peggy almost whispered it, as if she might get in trouble for asking.

Jess's heart pounded harder. 'No,' she admitted. 'We had an argument last Thursday, and I haven't heard from him since. I've tried calling, sending messages, but—'

'Thursday?' Peggy said. 'Just over a week ago?'

'I went to his flat in Holborn, but he wasn't there.' She chewed her lip. 'His neighbour hadn't seen him either, and I know it's been so hard for him . . .'

'What has?' Peggy asked gently.

Jess nodded, expecting this. 'He told me how you know him. That his dad abandoned his family when Ash was young, but now he's in Greenwich, and he's really ill. He told me that he visits every Sunday, and that you've been looking after him.'

Peggy's smile was more of a wince. 'He's been hard on himself from the beginning. It's been such a tough situation, a difficult set of circumstances, but he still came. He was a lot stronger than he thought he was.'

Jess took a large paper bag from the shelf under the counter and opened it, sliding the box inside. 'He didn't come here last Sunday,' she said. 'And I know we'd had a fight, but he's made other friends here, too. I felt awful that what happened between us stopped him from turning up at all.' She exhaled. 'I know you can't really tell me anything, but I just – how was he, on Sunday? Was he OK?' She held her breath, watched emotions cross Peggy's face like the shadow of clouds on a time-lapse video.

'I'm so sorry,' Peggy said. 'It's not my place to say anything. But I do know he likes you, Jess. He talked about you a whole lot, and it was always good.' Her smile was soft. 'You made things bearable for him.'

'I'm glad,' Jess murmured. 'Glad I was able to help.' She turned the bag around on the counter.

Peggy took out her purse and pulled out a credit card.

'Hang on!' Wendy hurried out of the storeroom. She had a smudge of something – possibly ink – on her cheek, and Jess resisted the urge to wipe it off.

'What is it?' she asked.

'I honestly didn't mean to overhear, but this is a very small shop. Hello, Margaret.'

'Hey.' Peggy was back to wary.

'What's wrong, Wendy?' Jess asked.

'Didn't you hear what Margaret said?' Wendy's tone had softened, but she was speaking quickly.

'What do you mean?'

'I'm not wrong, am I?' Wendy said to the nurse. 'You said, *He was a lot stronger than he thought . . . You made things bearable*. Not *make*. It was all past tense.'

Jess's breath stalled. She held the card reader out, and waited while Peggy tapped her card against it, the ping of ownership filling the space.

'Ash wasn't there on Sunday, was he?' Jess said, when Peggy didn't answer Wendy. 'I told him he shouldn't feel responsible, that if he didn't want to see his dad, if it was so hard for him, then he should give himself a pass. But the way he spoke about it, the way he walked out – I never thought he'd listen to me.'

Peggy pressed her lips together, as if she was desperately trying to stop her mouth from forming words.

'Oh my God!' Jess laughed. 'So then why hasn't he been in touch? Why haven't we been able to talk through everything?' She held Peggy's receipt out, and the other woman took it, her eyes full of sympathy.

'That wasn't my first thought,' Wendy said quietly. She squeezed Jess's shoulder, but she was looking at Peggy, and Jess couldn't stop her gaze flicking between the two of them.

'What do you mean?'

Wendy sighed. 'My first thought was that Ash wasn't there on Sunday because there was no need for him to be.'

Jess frowned. 'But I . . .' she started, and then, like a heavy stone dropping onto her heart, realisation dawned: the reason why Ash had been ghosting her, had bailed on Mack, had been absent in a way that felt too big for everything they'd shared.

297

'Because his dad died,' she whispered. Her throat was thick. How had that not occurred to her before now? She stared at Wendy, then Peggy. 'Did Ash's dad die?'

Neither of them spoke. Peggy dropped her gaze to the countertop. It was all the confirmation Jess needed.

Chapter Thirty-Four

Usually, Ash felt calm in his flat. He didn't mind spending time on his own, with a book or a film or his thoughts. He wasn't the kind of person who craved company all the time, like his brother Dylan. But right now, being alone – with only the ticking of the clock above the tiny kitchen table to break the quiet – felt like a slow, solitary road to self-destruction.

He walked over to the coffee machine, saw that the jug was empty, and wondered if eleven on a Sunday morning was too early to open a beer. But he'd taken that route on Tuesday and it hadn't ended well.

Nico Lombardo was dead. The man who Ash had thought about even when he hadn't wanted to, when he was only a hazy memory of a big laugh and arms that had hugged him tightly, and a bitter feeling of being left behind. But now that laugh and those arms were gone for good, and Ash couldn't wrap his head around it. The senselessness of it, along with his anger, were bubbles inflating inside his chest, and if he didn't get them out somehow, they would keep growing until they broke him apart.

In his old life – the life of a fortnight ago – he would be on his way to Greenwich now, looking forward to chatting to Olga or Susie, anticipation building at the thought of seeing Jess. His anger had died almost as soon as he'd left her flat that Thursday, replaced by guilt at what he'd said to her; how, in the moment, he'd found the perfect, cruel words to push her away, when part of him had only wanted to bring her closer. But the phone call from Peggy the next day had changed things, and though his fingers had hovered over Jess's messages a hundred times, and he'd watched her name appear on the screen as she rang him, he hadn't known what to say.

Right now, he wasn't fit to spend time with anyone. He'd gone to work on Monday and, within an hour, his boss had come into his office, sat opposite him at his desk, and signed him off for a week, minimum. If he went to stay with his mum, he'd just make it worse for her. She wouldn't want to talk about Nico, would rather not waste any more time or emotions on him, and Ash didn't think he could sit there amongst everything that wasn't being said.

There had been paperwork and phone calls from the hospice; so much to sort out. A funeral, here in England, that Ash already knew he'd go to, even if he was the only one. He wondered how many people Nico had been in touch with in Italy, if they would have a send-off more suited to the outgoing man he'd been.

His phone buzzed on the coffee table and, closing the fridge, he went to look at the message. It was from Peggy.

I'm so sorry, Ash, but Jess knows. I wasn't careful enough with my words, and her boss guessed. Are you doing all right?

It explained why he'd had more calls from Jess over the last couple of days. They'd tailed off a few days after their argument, but now they were back, and he still hadn't answered them. How could he ask her to support him when she had thought he was doing the wrong thing visiting his dad? He sent a reply:

It's fine, honestly. How was she? I'm OK. Missing your chickpea and lemon curd sandwich right about now.

You never tried it! Jess misses you. She looked pretty cut up when she realised. You could talk to her, you know. Failing that, you can talk to me.

A smile creased his cheeks.

Your job is done, Peg. I didn't pay for the aftercare package. Seriously though, thank you for everything. And Jess deserves more than I can give her right now. Maybe in a few months. Take care.

A few months and someone else will be bringing her coffee! Don't lose the one good thing to come out of all this. Aftercare package is included. I'm not going anywhere. Px

Ash rested his head against the sofa. He couldn't get that last image out of his head, the one he'd been met with when he'd left work on that Friday lunchtime and travelled, almost blindly, to Greenwich, to the pristine front door and Peggy leading him down the familiar corridor.

Nico was still in the bed, but the monitors were silent and so was he. He looked softer, as if all the ambition and the anger that had lived inside him, tightening his muscles, had gone. More than anything, his dad had looked peaceful, and it was in that moment, when it was too late, that Ash had felt a swell of compassion for him and all the mistakes he'd made. It felt as useless as all his other emotions right now.

He got up, determined to get that beer, and there was a knock on the door. His first thought was that it was Jess, and his heart leapt, the first positive thing he'd felt in over a week.

301

He opened the door and found Mack, a newspaper under his arm, holding two mugs of coffee.

'I had to put one of these on the floor so I could knock, and you know how hard it is for me to bend. Let me in, will you please?'

Ash's jaw tightened.

'It's not a request, but you already know that.' The older man stood his ground until Ash stepped back and let him in, then he walked through the living room and put the mugs and paper on the small kitchen table, beneath the ticking clock.

'I told you I couldn't make it.' Ash's voice was rusty. He thought that the last person he'd spoken to, beyond texts and WhatsApps, had been Dylan, two mornings before.

'Because your dad died.' Mack pulled out a chair and sat down. 'I know it's hard. When you're my age you get used to losing people, but *used to* isn't the same as *easy*. What are your plans for today?'

Ash looked away.

'Right, then. Come and sit down, and we'll do the crossword together.'

'I don't have time for crosswords.'

'Because you're too busy wallowing?'

Ash glared at him.

'You can make room for a coffee and a crossword amongst all that,' Mack said, unperturbed. 'You might even find a few moments of happiness.'

'I told you—'

'And it could be that I have an interesting tale to tell,' Mack went on. 'About how someone banged on your door earlier in the week. A woman with dark hair and dark eyes, who said she was looking for you. Said her name was Jess.'

'What?'

'It was Tuesday evening.' Mack narrowed his eyes. 'I don't know where you were, but judging by the bangs in the corridor that woke me up in the early hours the following morning, I would have wagered that a pub was involved.' He flipped open the newspaper.

'Jess was *here*?' The last few days had blurred into a succession of empty hours, except that Tuesday was the one day he'd given into the urge for numbness, met some colleagues when they'd finished for the day, then carried on drinking when they'd all gone home. He'd ended up making his way to Greenwich, though fuck knows how he'd managed the route in the state he was in. He'd stood under her window like a pathetic, booze-soaked Romeo, and even imagined that she'd called out to him. But he must have made it up, and even if he hadn't, it wasn't the way he wanted to see her again: stupidly drunk and stuck in his complicated grief.

He'd had no idea that, earlier that day, she'd come to find him; that despite what he'd said to her, she cared enough to come all this way.

'Why didn't you say?' He sat down at the table.

'I would have, if you'd answered your door.' Mack glared at him, unapologetic, and Ash felt his lips twitch. Self-pity was not an acceptable state to his neighbour.

'It'd better not be a cryptic crossword,' he said. 'You know I'm hopeless at those.'

'You'll only stay hopeless if you don't try, Ash.' Mack flipped to the right page, and Ash angled his body so he could see. For the first time in days, he felt some of the tension leave his shoulders.

*

303

Once Mack had gone, he made himself baked beans on toast, something he knew would satisfy his sorely neglected stomach.

He thought about what he'd said to Jess all those weeks ago, about how it was the people who mattered at the market, not what they were selling. He'd believed that it was better for him to be by himself until he felt less untethered, but Mack's visit had shown him it didn't work like that. He needed other people to anchor him, and he needed to be honest with Jess.

He made himself a cup of tea and pulled up their messages, reading through the last few she'd sent.

> Ash, I'm so sorry. Are you doing OK? I'm here if you want to talk.

> I never should have said the things I did. I know you have so much to deal with right now, but one day I'd love the chance to apologise properly.

> Please just send me a thumbs up, so I know you're OK. This caring about people business is messing with my head. ☺ xx

He typed a reply:

> Hey, Jess. Peggy told me that you know my dad died. I haven't felt able to get in touch before now, but I owe you an explanation. You said you want to apologise, but that's what I need to do. How about the bench in the park? You say when. xx

He flung his phone aside and scrolled through the streaming services until he found one of his favourite films, hoping it would distract him. It took her less than half an hour to reply.

> Oh Ash I'm so glad to hear from you! I am so sorry about
> your dad. Yes to meeting up – I'd love that. Are you off
> work at the moment? What about Tuesday afternoon?
> It's my day off, so we could take some lunch to the park.
> xx

He rubbed his eyes, the knots tightening in his shoulders
as he replied.

> Tuesday's fine. Midday? I'll meet you in the food hall,
> then we can go together. Ax

> Perfect. And I really am sorry. I need you to know that
> now, before I see you. xx

He puffed out a breath, ran a hand through his hair. He
closed his eyes for a moment before he replied, hoping she
would look at this message in the future, and know that he
meant it.

> I know. I'm really sorry, too. For all of it. See you Tuesday.

Chapter Thirty-Five

When she saw him on Tuesday, standing against one of the pillars at the entrance to the market, his dark hair slightly too long, his navy T-shirt hugging him in all the right places and his jeans faded at the knee, Jess felt sadness and longing and relief. It hadn't been that long, but she'd missed him, and it had hurt even more knowing what he was going through.

He noticed her and raised a hand in greeting. She could see he was attempting a smile, but it wasn't quite working.

'Hello.' She stopped in front of him.

'Jess,' he said. 'How are you?'

'I'm OK.' She exhaled. 'Better than you, I imagine? I'm so sorry, Ash. I'm sorry about—'

'Hey.' He squeezed her arm. 'Let's get some food, talk somewhere that's less of a thoroughfare.'

'You're right. Japanese?'

'Great.'

They got their food and walked through the market, which was much emptier than at the weekends but still humming quietly with activity.

'Ash!' Olga held her arms out. 'You're back!'

'Just for today.' He waited while she came round her stall and hugged him, but Jess could see the stiffness in his shoulders, like he was refusing to give into her easy warmth. 'It's good to see you.'

'You too,' Olga said. 'I'm glad Jess tracked you down.'

'Oh, I didn't—'

'I know Spade goes on about market ghouls, but what would this place be, what would *we* be, without our customers? Even if you don't buy anything, just lingering here will make other people turn and look, see?'

'Sure,' Ash said.

'You were never a ghoul to me.' Olga shook her head.

'We haven't got long,' Jess said, even though it wasn't true. She pressed her hand into Ash's back and nudged him forwards. It was such a familiar movement, she'd done it playfully so many times, but now it just felt bossy. 'Sorry,' she said. 'I wasn't sure how you felt about that word.'

He looked back at her. 'What word?'

Jess chewed her lip. 'If I say it, then I'm part of the problem.'

'What? Oh – you mean ghoul?'

'Yeah.'

'It's fine, honestly,' he said, and led them out of the market.

It wasn't that long ago that they'd walked along this road in the evening sunshine, holding hands. Now it felt as if there was an invisible barrier between them, Ash gripping the paper bag with his lunch in, moving past people carelessly. Jess was glad when they reached the park, and they could walk side by side.

'How long are you off work for?' Jess asked.

'Until the end of this week. My boss is sympathetic, but he doesn't listen.' He glanced at her. 'Would you want to be away from work if you . . . if something like this had happened to you? I just want to be busy.'

'But if you're dealing with a lot, not necessarily thinking straight, then isn't it best if you're not at work? Especially considering—'

'My work is all about thinking straight,' he finished.

'And right now, you need to think about yourself and nobody else.'

'And you,' Ash said. 'I have to think about you too, after everything.'

'Everything,' Jess repeated. In the current situation, it felt like an ominous word.

When they reached the top of the hill, Jess's legs were burning. The air smelled of summer flowers and suncream, and picnic blankets were spread across the grass, people lounging or kicking balls, dogs trotting at their owners' sides in the sunshine.

'Oh,' she said, coming to a stop. There was a grey-haired couple sitting on their bench, a cooler bag between them. It reminded Jess of Ash's first visit to Felicity's house, when he'd wiggled his fingers through the hole in her National Trust cooler to defuse the tension. She watched as the man held a cloth napkin out to the woman, and she pressed it elegantly against her mouth.

Ash had stopped too, and was watching the couple intently. Then he blinked and said, 'Come on, we can sit on the grass.'

They moved a little way down the hill, but then the grey-haired man zipped up the cool bag, stood up and held his hand out, and the woman took it. Jess felt awkward as she and Ash hovered, but the woman gave them a little wave, then gestured to the bench. 'Enjoy,' she said, and the couple walked away, in the direction of the car park.

Jess exhaled. It felt like being able to sit here, on this bench that had been the site of one of their happy Sundays, was a good sign.

'After you,' Ash said. She slid onto the bench, and he sat down beside her.

308

They took out their food, the waft of soy and spices delicious and enticing. But, despite picking her favourite dishes, Jess's stomach felt heavy, and she wasn't sure she'd be able to take a single bite. She turned towards Ash, watching as he unscrewed his water bottle and took a long sip, his Adam's apple bobbing.

'I'm sorry about all the things I said, and that I told you to leave.' She rushed it out, because even though there wasn't a time limit on today, it felt more fragile than any of her meetings with Ash so far.

He shifted on the bench to face her, his knee pressing against hers. 'I'm sorry for what I said, too. It was unforgivable.'

'No.' She shook her head. 'No, I—'

'It was,' he said. 'I don't want you to be gentle with me because of my dad. This is important. Of course you have a family; it was horrible – cruel – of me to say you didn't. I lashed out, probably because what you'd said to me, about me not having to go and see my dad, was too close to everything I'd been grappling with. I felt like a fake every time I went, and the truth is . . .' He puffed out a breath. 'I didn't agree immediately. I said no to Mum for a long time, and when I finally did go, it took me three weeks – or four, I can't remember – to even go into his room. I sat in the waiting room while Peggy got me a coffee, failed to work up the courage, and then left again.'

'That's hardly surprising,' Jess said quietly.

'When I eventually went in, I thought it would be cathartic, seeing him like that. He was a really physical dad, always mending something, lifting me and Dylan up. Piggybacks, football. I hardly ever saw him sitting still, so . . .'

'But it wasn't how you thought it would be?'

'No,' he admitted. 'I was just angry and sad, and I felt as helpless as him, because I didn't think it was fair to say

309

everything I wanted to.' He shook his head. 'It's not an excuse for what I said to you, but that's the reason I said it. I agreed with you, but I was trapped: I had to go. Now he's gone, and it's worse. All those feelings are still there.'

'Ash.' She put her hand on his knee, but he flinched away.

'No,' he said. Then, more quietly, 'I can't do this, Jess.'

She went still. The breeze danced around her, rustling the leaves in the trees. 'Can't do what?'

He leaned forward, his elbows on his knees, his food forgotten on the bench beside him. 'This. Us. It wouldn't be right to subject you to all the shit I'm dealing with. It's the worst time for me to start something serious.'

'But we aren't starting,' Jess said. 'We've been meeting up for months. I know you. I'm really sorry about everything I said—'

'It's not about that.'

'What is it about, then?' She tried to keep the hurt out of her voice.

He squinted down the hill towards the trees. 'You were the only good thing about the days I came here. You and Peggy. Having something to look forward to, instead of just the dread of seeing him; it made the whole thing bearable.' He winced. 'That sounds awful. You made me happy.'

'But now your dad's dead, you don't need me any more?'

'No! Jess – that's not it.' He sat up and turned towards her. 'You know when we were shouting at each other the other night?'

She nodded. There was a sick inevitability to this scene, except this time, she wasn't the one ending the relationship prematurely.

'You accused me of not letting you in, of not being honest with you. And I do shut people out, especially when it comes

310

– came – to my dad. If we made a go of this, if we saw each other properly, I'd push you away. I'd keep telling myself that you'd understand, and that you were happy for me to share everything, but I . . . I wouldn't do it.' He looked directly at her. 'I'd be too worried about ruining it before we'd even got going.'

Jess swallowed. 'So – what? You're pre-empting it? Ending it before it has a chance to go sour?' It was exactly the sort of thing she did. She hated that she couldn't even have the moral high ground.

'I'm saying that I am not great boyfriend material right now. If we tried, then I'd fuck it up and you'd never want to speak to me again.'

'I don't get it. You're saying that, by walking away now, you're hoping to save us both some heartache, and that we might be able to pick this up again later?'

'No!' He ran his fingers through his hair. 'I mean – maybe? I don't . . .' He rubbed his forehead, and all Jess's anger leached out of her.

'I'm sorry,' she said softly. This time when she squeezed his knee, he let her.

'*I'm* sorry,' Ash said. 'I just can't give you the attention – the commitment – that you deserve. You're one of the best people I've ever met.'

Jess licked her lips, which were dry despite the three coffees she'd had earlier, waiting for the clock to tick round, far too slowly, to midday. 'So even if I tell you that I'll be here for you whatever happens, whatever you need to do, and that I want to help you through this so we can come out the other side together, you would still say no?'

He pressed his lips together and didn't answer.

'Right,' she whispered.

311

On some level, she understood it. But she couldn't ignore the voice whispering in her ear, telling her that she wasn't worth it: she wasn't good enough at this to be the one who looked after him; she wasn't Peggy, with her natural ability for caring, or Lola, with her sunny smiles and can-do attitude. She knew this about herself, but it still hurt. 'You don't think I'm strong enough to be there for you?'

His hand came on top of hers so quickly that she jumped. 'Of course you're strong enough,' he said firmly. 'But I care about you, and I don't want to push you away by being impossible to spend time with.' He let out a harsh sigh. 'We fitted, didn't we? Into this neat box.' He gestured at the park, with its dog walkers and ball games, and the proud, pale buildings kissed by the afternoon sun, the dark snake of the Thames and the winking skyscrapers beyond. 'Our one hour a week, our subtle superpowers. Kissing you—'

'We broke out of it, though.' She tried so hard not to sound as if she was pleading with him. 'We helped Felicity, we had cold pizza and breakfast together. We did more than kiss.'

He nodded. 'Then the one time I thought I could be there for you, you pushed me away.'

'But that was—'

'I'm not accusing you, Jess. I've been doing the same thing ever since we met. Not telling you about Dad, keeping it separate, like I could actually control any of it.' His voice cracked, and it broke a dam inside her, all the emotion rushing up, filling her chest and tightening her throat.

'You don't think we can get out of the box,' she said.

She felt, rather than saw him shrug. 'I don't think so, no.' He squeezed her hand and leaned gently into her, a solid wall of warmth down her left side.

The worst part of it was, everything he said made sense. Could she really comfort him through his grief when, the first time he'd come to see her spontaneously, she'd turned him away? Would she ever be confident that he wasn't keeping something from her? Their time together had been fun and it had felt safe and – in the beginning, at least – there hadn't been too many expectations. But the logic didn't match the deep ache spreading through her sternum at the thought of not seeing him again, of not getting to kiss or hold him, or drink coffees with him on a windy day on a bench in the park.

'Will we stay in touch?' she asked. 'We could still message sometimes, couldn't we?'

'Sure,' he said, then cleared his throat.

'I keep thinking of all these new subtle superpowers. The motivational quotes, they're everyone's now, but I feel like . . . the superpowers, they're just ours. I wanted to tell you, but—'

'You can always tell me,' he assured her. 'We'll build a list.'

'Keeping house plants alive,' she said.

'Never burning toast, even in an unfamiliar toaster.'

'Knowing, without a doubt, that someone will be *your* person, even though you've never spoken to them, and you've only seen them through a window, laughing and trying on hats.'

She glanced at him, and found that he was already looking at her. Her cheeks were damp but she didn't care. Ash was one of the few people she wasn't ashamed to cry in front of.

He brushed one of her tears away with his thumb. 'Being able to deliver the city's best film tour, even though you've only seen half the films, simply because you're wearing a grey trilby.'

Her laugh was watery. 'You only pulled it off because of Dave the spaniel. Otherwise it would have been a total flop. Apart from the kiss at the end.'

'Apart from the kiss,' he agreed. His smile was as broken as she felt. 'I have had an amazing time with you, Jessica Peacock. Please don't ever underestimate yourself.'

'Thank you for spending time with me, and for helping Felicity, and just . . .' She inhaled, knowing she was on the verge of losing it. 'For being you, and letting me share your youness.'

He squinted. 'Share your *youness*?'

She laughed again, this time through sobs. 'Shut up, Ash.'

His grin was so unexpected, such a strong reminder of the happy hours she'd had with him, that she almost couldn't breathe. If this had been a different time, under different circumstances, she knew they could have loved each other.

'You've changed me,' she admitted. 'For the better. I won't forget you, OK? And I'll message you my subtle superpowers, and we'll . . . still know each other, a little bit. Text friends.'

'Text friends,' he repeated, but this time his smile didn't reach his eyes, and she already knew that, even if they started out messaging each other, he'd slowly extricate himself, leave longer gaps between replies, until there was nothing but digital dust on their WhatsApp thread.

He moved to get up, and Jess felt a surge of panic. 'Will you be OK?'

'Of course,' he said. 'This is life, isn't it? I've hit a speed bump, and it'll take me a while, but I'll get over it eventually.' He sounded resolute, and she wondered if he was putting on the show for her, or for himself.

He stood up, and she went to do the same, but he leaned over and cupped her cheek, then pressed a kiss against her forehead. 'Bye, Jess.'

She inhaled, hiccuped, but couldn't hold in the sob. 'Bye Ash.'

He slid his hand through her hair, then stood up straight. 'Take care of yourself.'

She watched him turn and walk away, his head down, his long strides hurried. She waited for him to glance over his shoulder and wave at her, to change his mind and come racing back along the path, fall in the scrubby grass at her feet and pull her against him. They hadn't even hugged. She hadn't got to press her cheek against his chest one last time, or feel his arms tighten around her, and the realisation intensified the ache, made her tears fall faster, her sobs louder.

'Oh goodness!'

Jess looked up at the woman wearing a sky-blue jacket, a long, full skirt, and tried to place her through her film of tears. Then she heard yapping, and a familiar cloud of white fur was bouncing up at her, its nose snuffling against her carton of gyozas.

'Diamanté,' she said.

'Are you OK?' The woman peered down at her. 'I am so sorry about my dog. I've been taking her to behavioural training, but it's done bugger all so far, as you can see.'

Jess bubbled out a laugh. 'Can I hold her?' Her voice broke on the last word, and the woman's eyes softened.

'Of course,' she said. 'She's a yapper, but she doesn't bite.'

'Thank you.' Jess bent down and picked up the wriggling dog. She held her against her chest, and buried her head in her soft fur. After a moment, Diamanté stopped struggling.

Too late to care about embarrassment, Jess sobbed into the white fluff of the dog she and Ash had laughed about, and tried to accept that he was gone. She tried to come to terms with how horrible it felt, and that the reason she had felt everything with him, so completely – happiness and longing and desire, anger when he'd turned up unannounced, pleasure when he kissed and touched her, devastation right now – was that, despite everything, she *had* let him all the way in. She'd let herself fall in love with him.

It was a mistake she'd tried so hard to avoid in the past, and now every cell in her body was facing the repercussions.

Jessica Peacock, currently sobbing into the soft fur of the demon Diamanté dog on a bench in Greenwich Park, was in love with Ash Faulkner, and she'd realised it just as he'd said goodbye to her for the last time. As moments went, it was a pretty crap one. And yet, whereas usually such intense misery would send her running to her room, drawing the curtains and turning her phone off, right now she wanted to join in while Lola and Malik clocked up their Fitbit steps in front of the TV, eat muffins with Wendy, find Spade and ask for one of his famous headlock-hugs.

And that, she realised, as she gave the woman in the sky-blue coat a sheepish smile and handed her soggy dog back, had been Ash's gift to her. He'd made her see that she wasn't better on her own, that she could draw on the strength of the people she loved. She just wished he'd listened to his own advice.

She would always carry around a piece of him, even when the memories of their time together faded, and he was nothing more than a discarded, low-down-the-list message thread in her phone: a 'what could have been' that never was.

Jess stood up and watched Diamanté race down the hill, her owner struggling to keep up, and then slowly followed their path through the park, leaving her and Ash's bench sitting empty behind her.

Chapter Thirty-Six

It was ten days until Felicity's home sale, and Jess wanted to make sure the day went without a hitch. Their core group of marketeers were all going to be there, even though it was a Saturday: they'd got cover for their stalls, and would show potential buyers round and keep an eye on them. Roger might bring a clipboard. Kirsty was going to make a special batch of muffins. Spade said they would set up the Market Misfits in a corner of the living room for a set. If there was space, though, because—

'You're going to wear a hole in that umbrella if you keep rubbing it like that.'

Jess moved the orange polka-dot umbrella to the other end of the counter. 'It's already got a tear in it, which is why I took it off the shelf.'

'Seconds?' Wendy asked.

'I think so.'

'Mark it up then, and put it in the basket.'

Jess got the labels out from under the counter.

'When you've done that, I want you to start thinking about how the shop looks.'

'What?' She glanced at her boss, who was standing in the storeroom doorway.

'A complete autumn refresh,' she said. 'Change as much as you want. All the displays, the decor, will be down to you. How we organise the stock. Any new lines you think we should introduce. In a couple of weeks, we'll close for a day or two, once you've had a chance to plan it all out.'

'Wendy, I don't—'

'Otherwise, you're going to wear holes in all the merchandise to match the one in your heart.'

Jess scoffed. 'Come on—'

'I'm serious.' Wendy's voice was somehow firm and soft all at once. 'You need to keep busy, and I know we've got Felicity's house sale coming up, but you also have to spend a large proportion of your time here, and I want you to be occupied. She was in here yesterday, by the way.'

'Who was?'

'Felicity. With Spade.'

Jess had spent most of yesterday lying on her bed, staring at the ceiling and replaying her conversation with Ash over and over. She'd had to blow-dry her yellow yeti cushion before she went to bed, because it was soaked through with tears. She'd even considered calling her mum and dad at one point, but had talked herself out of it.

'How were they?' she asked, even though she was in constant touch with Felicity, now, and didn't need an update.

'They placed an order.' Wendy pointed at the gilt-framed mirror. 'For that.'

Jess blinked, a fresh wave of emotions washing over her. 'That . . . that is—'

'I know. She's asked me to save it for her until after the sale. Obviously, she's made some changes in her life.'

'Big changes,' Jess agreed. 'But I still didn't think she'd ever actually *buy* the mirror.'

'That's down to you.'

'Ash did more than me.' Jess may have led him there, but it had been his patience, his understanding of how to approach the situation that had encouraged Felicity to face her hoarding. 'But I'm so happy that she's confident enough to buy the mirror, and that she came up with this house sale idea, and that she's . . . you know, made friends with Spade.'

Wendy smiled. 'The most unlikely couple, and yet, somehow, perfect for each other.'

'I agree.'

'Also, Enzo's doing so much better now. His stall's flourishing, so he's sorted until Carolina feels up to working again. The Market Misfits are a hit, and Lola's raised her profile exponentially, which means all your projects are done, just as you're in need of distractions.'

'I don't need anything.'

'I beg to differ,' Wendy said gently. 'Ash doesn't strike me as the kind of person you get over easily.'

Jess's laugh was hollow. 'Thanks for that.'

'No point in sugar-coating things, is there?'

'No,' Jess admitted. 'There isn't.'

'The best movement is forward movement,' Wendy went on. 'I know it's only a small thing, but if you help me redesign the shop for autumn, then at least you'll be focused on that. It may not have worked out with Ash, but you have a whole lorry-load of people who care about you. Don't forget that, Jess.'

'Of course not,' Jess said quietly, and she knew her boss was right. It was better to focus on the positives, the things she *could* do, instead of the ones she had no control over.

'Sometimes, life is too sucky for words,' Lola said. 'I'm so fucking sorry, Jess. He's an idiot.'

319

'An idiot in hot guy's clothing,' Malik added, carrying three cups of tea into the living room. 'He sure pretended well, didn't he?'

'Did you even meet him?' Jess asked. 'Thank you for the tea.'

'Nope,' Malik said. 'But Lola's told me all about him. What a fakey McFakemeister.' He pushed his glasses up his nose. 'You don't need him, Jess.'

'Thanks, Malik.'

'And, if you want to take your mind off it, I have three thousand steps left to do. We could jiggle in front of Sunday night's *Antique's Roadshow*? Or a Bryan Adams playlist?'

'How could anyone resist such an invite?' Lola widened her eyes comically.

'You want to me to go mess about in my office?' Malik pointed at the closed door.

'That would be amazing.'

He kissed Lola on the lips, then sauntered off whistling 'Heaven', leaving Jess and Lola alone.

'However you want to deal with it,' Lola said. 'I'm here, OK? I get the feeling Ash is going to be a mountain to get over, not a molehill.'

'I'll be fine,' Jess said quietly. Why did people keep pointing that out? She was right in the middle of finding out how hard he was to forget.

Lola wafted a cushion at her, but didn't hit her because she was holding a full mug. 'I know you're acting like you didn't really care, but I know you did.'

Jess stared at the milky surface of her tea, then squeezed her eyes closed. 'I did care,' she admitted. 'I still do. But everything he said was true. It's for the best.'

'*Whose* best, though?'

'Best for both of us.' Except that, the more time that had passed since their discussion on the bench, the less it made sense. They both understood what they'd done to cause the fractures in their relationship, so didn't that mean they could have a go at fixing them?

'I don't get it,' Lola said.

'Can you help me with something else?' Jess asked, because she didn't want to go round in circles.

'Anything.'

'You know the thing with Edie and Graeme?'

'Your mum and dad?'

'Yes. The thing that I overheard?'

'Your mum lamenting the fact that you weren't close to them? That you had chosen to be by yourself almost from the moment they adopted you?'

Jess sighed. It had never made sense to her, that her mum would say that to a neighbour. It had seemed much more likely that she was telling Celine she didn't have those strong emotional ties to Jess. It had fed into what she'd always told herself.

'I know you think that everyone's just waiting to get rid of you—'

'Ash Faulkner is a case in point.'

'Don't be flippant. I think he was wrong, and I think you were, too, for not fighting for him. But that isn't what we're talking about – though I think it would help if you hadn't decided you weren't worth anything.'

'I know *you* don't want to get rid of me.'

Lola rolled her eyes. 'You're worth a lot, Jess. But you should be worth something to yourself, first, and I don't think

321

you believe you are, which is why you so readily interpreted what you heard the way you did. Have you ever spoken to Edie and Graeme about how you feel?'

'No.'

'Talk to them. Just one time, try and be honest with them. Let them in, even if it's just a smidgen.' She held her thumb and index finger up, a small space between them.

'I suppose.'

'Put a bit more welly in it.'

'I could talk to them,' she said firmly.

'But are you *going* to? There's a whole lot of distance between *could* and *will*.'

'Right. I *will* talk to them. I *100 per cent* promise.'

There was a pause, then Lola shrieked.

Jess put a hand to her chest. 'What the fuck?'

'You're *actually* listening to me about this, after all this time?'

'Maybe,' Jess said. Maybe everything that had happened with Ash was finally waking her up to what was important, and the risks you had to take to get it.

'You won't regret it, I promise.' Lola pulled her into a hug.

Jess accepted it, rolling her eyes over her friend's shoulder. But she was comforted by Lola's kindness. Between this, her sadness over Ash, and getting her to devote her self-promotion plan to helping Enzo, Jess wouldn't have been surprised if Lola had had enough of her, but there wasn't any suggestion that that was the case. And she had asked for her advice, so it would be stupid to ignore it. She thought of all the times Edie and Graeme – *her mum and dad* – had tried to get closer to her, and she'd held them coolly at arm's length. They had never given up on her, which had to mean something.

'Tell me your plans for world domination,' Jess said. 'Any record company offers for the Misfits? Any live performances planned beyond Felicity's house sale?'

'Don't you mean Felicity's party? There's going to be a band, food, themed areas. I wouldn't be surprised if Roger brought some illegal hooch along, to give out under the table.' Lola grinned, and Jess burst out laughing.

'The thought of Roger doing anything slightly frowned upon, let alone actually illegal, is too twisted, Lols.'

'I know. Spade did say something the other day about a real proper *gig, man.*' She affected the rocker's accent for a couple of beats. 'But you know how enthusiastic he gets. It might mean he's found us a good busking spot in front of the *Cutty Sark.*'

'He's got all the contacts,' Jess pointed out. 'It might actually be something.'

'It might. I'm happy, though.'

'You are?'

Lola nodded. 'I wanted a proper direction for my music: I wanted to get out in the open with it, get some feedback, and the exhilaration of playing with Spade and Braden – being this weird-ass little trio that gets people watching and clapping along, thousands of views online – it's really satisfying. Anything else will just be a cherry on top. And none of this would have happened without you.'

'No, I—'

'You introduced me to everyone. You let me invade the market, and I know it was uncomfortable for you at the beginning, but you *always* backed me up. You're the very best friend anyone could hope for.'

Jess swallowed. It was unlike Lola to be so sincere, and she wasn't sure her fragile emotions could take it. 'Well.' She cleared her throat. 'Right back at you, OK? You've put up with so much from me over the last few months – the last decade. I don't know what I'd do without you.'

'Good,' Lola said. 'That means you're never getting rid of me. Want to put Bryan Adams on and see how long it takes for Malik to notice? We'll start with "Heat of the Night", which is his siren song.'

Jess laughed and settled back into the cushions, clutching her mug of tea while Lola got her iPad. For the first time since Tuesday, she felt something close to content, Ash fading temporarily from her thoughts. She'd spend enough time thinking about him when she got home, and, since he was the one who'd walked away, it wasn't fair of him to monopolise her whole evening.

Chapter Thirty-Seven

When Jess made it to Bexleyheath on Tuesday afternoon, she couldn't help thinking that it had been a week since Ash had ended it. She had insisted they remain text buddies, but after he'd gone, she'd been too raw to even message to see if he'd got home OK, and after that it had felt too awkward. He hadn't been in touch either, which spoke volumes. She'd oscillated between angry and resigned, agreeing with what he'd done and thinking it was cowardly, and at all the points in between she found that, more than anything else, she just missed him.

Standing on her parents' doorstep, she was aware that, despite making an effort with her appearance, her lack of sleep and her seesawing thoughts had taken their toll, and her skin looked pale and slightly crepey. She felt as if she was on day six of a week-long hangover, combined with a bad dose of hay fever, though her sore eyes were from secret crying rather than the pollen count. Even Terence had taken pity on her on Saturday night, and had ordered in a feast from the Thai restaurant down the road. They'd had a Bourne marathon, Jess mortifyingly falling asleep during the third film with her head on his shoulder. She knew things were bad when he didn't even tease her about it.

'Jess!' Graeme opened the door wide, the navy gloss catching the sun and flashing a light beam into her eyes. 'So lovely to see you. Come here, eh?' He opened his arms and, after a second's hesitation, she stepped into them.

'Hey, Dad.'

He pushed back and looked down at her. 'Everything OK with the market? With your fella Enzo? Your mum and I have been keeping tabs on all Lola's TikToks, and the response has been astounding. That girl has such talent!'

'She's the best,' Jess said. 'And Enzo and Carolina are in a much better place. He seems a lot happier.'

'Don't think we didn't see your designs on full display,' her mum added, appearing in the hall holding a book, her reading glasses perched high on her head. 'Why didn't you tell us Wendy was letting you sell them in the shop?'

'It was for Enzo,' Jess said. 'That was why I came clean about them – or Lola did, actually. But it's been really good.' She smiled as she remembered how elated she'd been when Margaret – Peggy – had bought her very first print. But Peggy took her thoughts on a direct route to Ash, and her smile fell.

'We're so proud of you for taking the next step,' Edie said. 'But I hope you're not working too hard. There's clearly been a lot going on.'

'It's the same as it's always been,' she said. Her defensiveness was a reflex, and she gave herself a silent telling off. 'I *have* been busy, but also . . . I've had a – a thing. Another thing going on.' She winced at her clumsiness.

'A thing?' Graeme laughed gently. 'You'll have to be a bit more specific, Jessica.'

'Come through to the kitchen,' her mum said. 'It's much cosier in there. Tea or coffee, or a glass of wine, now we're at the four o'clock mark?'

'Wine would be great.' Jess followed them into the large kitchen, which had navy walls and a white island with stools positioned around it. This was where her parents had been sitting with Celine when she'd overheard them. She glanced at the clock on the wall. It was, of course, a sunflower, with bold yellow petals and a brown centre, glossy white hands and numbers that made it easy to read.

Edie poured out three glasses of Pinot Grigio, and gestured for Jess to sit on one of the stools, while she hopped up opposite her. Graeme sat at the end of the island, a gentle frown wrinkling his forehead.

'Tell us about your thing,' her mum said.

'My thing,' Jess repeated.

She sipped her wine, raised her glass in thanks, then stared at the countertop. It was as spotless as always, her parents existing in a space that was incredibly clean and mildly cluttered, though Jess knew that everything on the island – magazines and mugs, open post and biscuit tins – was cleared away at the end of each day. She wondered what new routines Felicity would develop, both on her own and with Spade, now she had the physical and emotional freedom to do what she wanted.

'Actually, Mum, Dad,' she said, and felt her mouth dry out. 'Before that, I—' She swallowed. 'I know I've pulled away a bit, recently.' She put her glass down. 'Not *that* recently, actually.'

Edie and Graeme exchanged a glance.

'We have noticed, love,' Graeme said. 'You've always been independent, though.'

'It was more than that. I overheard you. With Celine.'

'When was this?' Edie asked.

Jess shrugged. 'A couple of years ago.'

'*Years?*' Edie's eyes widened.

'I'm sorry, I—' What could she say? There was no other option but to plough through it. 'You were talking about me, and I heard you say, *It's hard to feel loved when you're not wanted or needed.*' Both her mum and dad opened their mouths to reply, but she had to get it out. 'Lola said you were talking about *you,* that I didn't love or need you, but I . . .' She couldn't, in the end, get the words out.

There was a heavy pause, then Edie said, 'Oh my darling. You thought I was saying I didn't love or want *you*? Jess, you are the person I love most. Of *course* you are.'

'And me,' Graeme added. 'You've thought that all this time?'

Jess could only nod, and a moment later her mum's arms were around her, her dad's too.

'It breaks my heart that you could have thought that for a minute, let alone two years,' Edie said.

'I'm sorry,' Jess managed.

'You should have talked to us,' her dad said. 'You should have confronted us, but I – I'm sorry we let it happen.'

'You didn't. I guess I interpreted it like that so I could build my walls higher.' She let out a watery laugh. 'Lola's been trying to get me to talk to you about it this whole time.'

'That girl knows what she's talking about,' Graeme said gently. 'But we do understand, Jess. You've always gone out on your own, and I suppose we just told ourselves you were living your life how *you* wanted to.'

'I am so sorry that I did anything to make you think I didn't care.' Edie sniffed loudly.

'No, Mum. It was me. It was all me, and I want – I'm going to be better.'

'It's not about being better,' her dad said. 'Just talk to us, OK? You couldn't do or say anything that would stop us loving you.'

'We love you more than *anything*,' Edie added.

Jess wrapped her arms around them and held on tightly, while the clock ticked on in the background.

'Was that your thing?' Graeme asked when they'd untangled themselves, and Edie had found a tissue to wipe her eyes.

'That wasn't it,' Jess said. 'That was something I should have said – asked you about – ages ago. And I . . . My thing was actually a guy, so it's probably unfair to call him a thing.' She laughed, and it only sounded slightly flat.

'You've met someone!' Her mum gave a final, loud sniff, then clasped her hands together. 'Oh darling, I'm so happy for you.'

'It's not gone so well,' Jess said, and wondered how she'd ever thought Edie Peacock was anything less than the best mum she could have hoped for.

'Oh.' Edie's face fell. 'This isn't some wild and wonderful romance, then?'

'More a bit *Romeo and Juliet*?' Graeme suggested.

'God.' Jess's laugh was louder this time. 'It wasn't *that* bad.'

'No, of course not.' Graeme shook his head. 'I'm not entirely up on my Shakespeare, as you know, and I fell asleep during that strange modern film.'

Edie patted the back of his hand. 'I'm sorry, Jess. It hasn't worked out?'

'No.' She swallowed, because this was the hard part. 'I'd like to tell you about it – about *him*, though, if that's OK?'

'Of course!' Her mum couldn't hide her happiness, and Jess couldn't blame her. It had been years since she'd willingly volunteered information about a boyfriend to her parents – if she ever had. Now she'd spoken to them, got the confirmation that Lola had been right all along, she was going to do better:

329

work harder at being a part of this family. Telling them would prolong Ash's presence in her life, but she didn't think that mattered. Over the last week she'd had to accept that he was going to hang around, making a nuisance of himself in her thoughts on a daily, *hourly*, basis.

'We'd love that,' Graeme said. 'And we'll help if we can.'

'Thanks Dad, Mum.' She took another sip of wine, then put her glass down. 'I met him at the market, after he chased a shoplifter who'd stolen a watch from Roger's antiques stall. One of the first things we talked about was train sets. I told him you had one in your garage.'

'Studio,' her mum and dad said in unison, because you couldn't keep a train set somewhere as lowly as a *garage*, even though that was technically what it was.

Jess laughed. 'Of course. Studio – I'm sorry. We got talking, and he asked me if I wanted to go for a coffee. He was at the market every Sunday, but only for an hour.'

'That's very specific,' Edie said. 'Did he tell you why?'

Jess let the slideshow of memories rush into place. All the figments that, put together, made up her time with Ash. As she told her parents everything – *most* things, anyway – it was as if Edie and Graeme had got hold of the ends of the thread knotting her up and pulled, loosening the tangles. By the time she'd reached the end, with the bottle of wine empty and a bowl of crisps decimated, she felt languid, softer.

'What a tragic story,' Edie said. 'I am so sorry, Jess. For you, and for him, too, and his mother. I can see why he's not thinking straight right now.'

'Not thinking straight?' Graeme asked.

'To have let Jess go,' Edie said. 'Sometimes, when people are hurting, they think they need to punish themselves:

330

to go through the hard parts on their own, because that's the ultimate test of their ability to survive. They tell their loved ones they don't want to be a burden, and go off into the emotional wilderness. It rarely ever works.'

'We weren't properly honest with each other,' Jess said. 'We didn't lie, exactly, but we pushed each other away.'

'Because you were still getting to know each other,' Edie said. 'He didn't give you a chance.'

'He said it would be best for me.'

'Part of him was thinking it would be horrible for him, and that was what he deserved. More wine?'

'Could I have tea?' Jess asked.

'I'll make a pot.' Graeme retrieved the large scarlet teapot from its cupboard. She was sure he buffed it at least once a week.

'Thanks,' she said. 'So you think I should get in touch with him? Send him a message?'

'What do *you* want to do?' her dad asked, as he poured loose Earl Grey leaves into the mesh infuser. 'If you agreed with his decision to end it, you wouldn't be telling us about it. You might never have mentioned him.'

'No.' Jess shot a guilty glance at her mum. 'I probably wouldn't have.'

'We do understand that it hasn't been easy for you,' Edie said gently. 'But I'm so glad you told us – about Celine, what you heard. We'll always support you, Jess. With anything.'

'Thanks, Mum.' Jess fiddled with her empty wine glass. 'But what if I try and get Ash back, and he isn't interested?'

'Then we'll be here.' Edie was firm. 'And we'll applaud you for trying, because it's a difficult thing, to put yourself out there when you really care about something.'

'The first time I put my trains on Instagram, I was prepared for all sorts of ridicule,' her dad said. 'But it turns out there's a whole community of like-minded people on there.'

'Who alert him to new trains and accessories whenever they become available,' Edie added wryly. 'The studio will be too full to move about in soon.'

Jess grinned. 'You'll have to show me.'

'Really?' Her dad looked stunned, and Jess's guilt crashed over her. It didn't matter how much she'd rejected them, they had always, *always* been there for her.

'After we've finished our tea,' she said. 'I know you don't want anything in there that will stain the mat.'

Graeme's smile could have powered the sun.

'And I want to see what new sunflowers you have,' she said to her mum. 'I want to – to come here more. And you can come and see the flat, if you like? Though my room is pretty small, and Terence might be eating pickled anchovies out of a jar, but—'

'Goodness!'

'But he's really nice, other than that.'

'Nice, but not Ash?' her dad said.

Jess watched him pour the perfectly brewed Earl Grey into three sunflower mugs. 'Nobody's Ash,' she said. 'Except Ash.'

'Well, then.' Edie pulled her mug towards her, and blew on her tea. 'If nobody else will do, and you're going to accept no imitations, then you know what you need to do, don't you?'

Jess copied her mum, blowing on her drink and watching the ripples spread across the surface. 'I'm going to have to convince him to give us a chance.'

332

'Exactly. And you can tell him – though I get the feeling he's discovering this for himself right about now – that it's not easy to forget Jessica Peacock, once she's in your life.'

'Not easy is the understatement of the century,' Graeme added, coming round the island to pull Jess into a hug. 'It is, frankly, downright impossible.'

'Thank you.' Jess leaned into her dad's embrace, over-whelmed by the comfort it gave her.

'We love you very much,' her mum said. 'I hope you know that.'

Jess swallowed. 'I do.' She felt as open as the sunflower clock on the wall behind her, letting in the light that Edie and Graeme were shining on her, and not, for once, trying to close up and protect herself from it. 'I love you, too.' It felt like an easy truth, and Jess wondered why it had taken her so many years to admit it.

Chapter Thirty-Eight

It's Felicity's house sale on Saturday if you're about. It wouldn't be happening without you, and I know Felicity would love to see you. I would too, of course – that goes without saying. Jess. xx

The message sat on her phone, unanswered. She'd sent it on Tuesday evening, when she'd got back to her flat after seeing her parents, her stomach full of chicken fajitas that her dad had cooked with an expertise that had surprised her. The whole visit had surprised her, and it had made her think that, if *she* could lower her walls and be more open, then perhaps Ash could, too.

But now it was Saturday, and Braden was warming up his voice in the corner of Felicity's living room, which was in a state of organised chaos that was entirely different to the piles of clutter Jess had been greeted with all those weeks ago. Early morning sunlight streamed in through the French doors, which had been cleaned and polished in preparation for today, highlighting the period features: the solid fireplace, the cornicing, the forget-me-not wallpaper below the dado rail.

There was brightly coloured bunting hanging above the front door, the beautiful white rose bush next to it was covered in delicately scented blooms, and the hallway was bright and welcoming, the black-and-white tiled floor –

a feature Jess hadn't even noticed until today – uncovered and gleaming. Felicity had suggested that Kirsty bake her muffins in the kitchen, and while Jess had been concerned about the cleanliness, and whether any of the neglected appliances even worked any more, it seemed Felicity had had the oven serviced, and the whole house smelled of chocolate and vanilla, of slowly rising batter and strong, steaming coffee.

Of the cats, only Twiggy was curled up asleep on the clutter-free sofa, unconcerned that his house was about to be invaded by strangers. Bond and Artemis were nowhere in sight.

Jess rearranged the wooden boxes, trinket dishes and brass ornaments on the display next to hers, then moved to her own table. The spacious living room had four of these mini-stalls, with more in the back garden, and even though this was about selling Felicity's unwanted possessions, she had insisted Jess had a stand of her prints, too.

There were a lot of items in this displaced, scaled-down version of the market that could make good money, as long as they had enough interest, but Roger had already agreed to help Felicity sell whatever was left over, and Jess – after Lola had planted the idea – was thinking of this more as a party, a celebration of everything Felicity had achieved. Even if nobody came, or they only made ten pounds, it was already a success.

Because of that, Jess had made an effort, wearing her black, bee-print dress, and styling her hair in tousled waves. She had done it for Felicity, and *not* because she believed Ash should be here – though of course he should be – or that she was holding onto a glimmer of hope that he might turn up, despite not replying to her message.

She picked up her latest design. It was a photo of the cherry trees in Greenwich Park, two neat rows standing guard either side of the wide walkway that was perfect for strolling along. Down the middle she'd added, in a bold pink font: *Hanging onto things for too long will hold you back – unless you're dangling over the edge of a cliff, in which case hold on tight!* She was trying to take it to heart.

'OK?' Lola stopped in front of her table, violin in hand. Her blonde hair was loose around her shoulders, her eye make-up dramatic. 'These are going to sell like hot cakes.'

'I hope so.' Jess forced a smile. 'You all prepared?'

'Yeah, just waiting for Spade to decide which of his many guitars will be in the spotlight today.' She rolled her eyes fondly. 'Sure you're doing all right?'

'Of course,' Jess said. 'But Ash should be here.'

'I know he should. Have you heard from him at all?'

'Not a peep. I know that being here, helping Felicity, wasn't easy for him, even though he hid it most of the time.' She'd made the connection a couple of days after their fight at her flat, the way Felicity's ex-husband's behaviour had mirrored Ash's dad's – leaving to travel the world while his family were discarded. It had made sense of the moment in Felicity's back garden, and so many other, tiny, things: his clenched jaw, the occasional distant looks, the way his kisses, after their Sundays here, had seemed desperate, somehow.

'I am very sorry Ash isn't here.' Jess jumped. She hadn't noticed Felicity come up behind her. 'I wouldn't have got here without him, or you. Or some other people.' She gestured at Spade, dressed in leather trousers and a Garfield T-shirt, his chosen guitar a glittering red. 'But it's still early, and you shouldn't give up hope.'

Jess nodded, her eyes darting to the doorway into the hall.

'You both need to have one of Kirsty's muffins before they

all go,' Felicity went on, holding out a plate. 'These are bacon and maple syrup, and they taste as divine as they smell.' She forced Jess and Lola to each take one, then sashayed through her living room, talking to everyone who had turned up to support her.

'She's amazing,' Lola murmured.

'The most amazing,' Jess agreed, and took a huge bite of her muffin. Maybe if she ate enough of them, she would stop feeling quite so hollow.

An hour later, and there were a few strangers milling about, browsing the items for sale, eating muffins and drinking coffee from mismatched mugs, while the Misfits played a surprisingly mellow set. Roger was standing at the large table in the bay window, in charge of Felicity's considerable collection of jewellery, and was fielding the most interest from visitors.

'The problem,' Susie said, 'is that TikTok is international. You can't really focus promotion on a particular location, so even if a hundred thousand people saw the promo about today, not many of them will be close enough to come.'

'True,' Jess said. 'But I don't think Felicity was expecting to be swamped. This is more cathartic for her than anything. And it's good for us, being here all together.'

'Let loose from the market,' Susie said with a smile. 'I'm in charge of the blanket collection, and I already know that I'm going to end up buying whatever's left. I can use them in my new Better Babies designs.'

Jess narrowed her eyes at Felicity, who was on the other side of the room, laughing at something Olga was saying. 'I wonder why she put you in charge of the soft furnishings.'

Susie gasped. 'You don't think—'

'I do,' Jess said. 'Roger's in charge of the jewellery, and I noticed a few elegant watches on that table. If there are no takers, then . . .'

'That sly old feline,' Susie said, with a mixture of annoyance and respect that nearly dragged a laugh out of Jess. She went back to her blankets, and Jess smiled as a young couple approached her table.

'Hello,' she said. 'See anything you fancy?'

The woman was blonde and smiling, and the man was handsome, with eyes that were a very particular shade of blue.

'Let's just have a look,' the woman said. 'Did you make these?'

'I did. I sell them in a shop in the market, and online too. Today is a special sale.'

'I'd quite like one of everything,' the woman said with a laugh. 'My parents live in Blackheath, and Jake and I are moving into a new flat, so we're looking for some things to decorate it with.'

'A *few* things,' the man – Jake – added. 'It's about the size of this room, not the whole house. Hester's getting a bit carried away.'

'It's more space than we had in New York.' Hester gave Jake an adoring gaze that made Jess's stomach twist with envy. 'And look at this! Have you ever seen anything more perfect?' She held up a frame, and Jess thought that the universe was really laughing at her now, because it was one of Ash's quotes – the same one Peggy had bought that day in the shop. *Flying isn't as hard as it looks, just make sure a part of you stays tethered to the ground.*

Jake laughed loudly, and a couple of people turned to look at him. 'Flying isn't as hard as it looks,' he repeated.

'You're right: this has to go up on our wall.' He took his wallet out, handed Jess a ten-pound note, then kissed Hester on the lips.

Jess busied herself wrapping the frame, and tried not to think about the very real possibility that she would never get to kiss Ash again.

When the band took a breather, Lola, Braden and Spade congregated at Jess's table, drinking coffee and orange juice, and dissecting their set. Spade saw something over Jess's shoulder, and his grin split his face.

'My dudes,' he said, as Enzo and Carolina came to join them. Enzo's wife looked just the same as Jess remembered her, except that her dark hair was cut into a bob, tucked chicly behind her ears. Another woman, slightly shorter and slimmer than Carolina, could only be her sister.

'Enzo, Carolina, hi,' Jess said. 'And you must be Sofia. It's so lovely to meet you.'

'You too.' Sofia gave them all a shy wave.

'Lovely Jess!' Carolina wrapped her in a gentle, vanilla-scented hug.

'And this is Lola,' Jess said. 'And Spade and Braden. They're the Market Misfits.'

'We can't thank you enough for what you've done,' Carolina said. 'Sofia has admitted that she prefers making jewellery to organising teenagers. Our business of two is now a business of three.'

'My hands were made for delicate work.' Sofia waggled her long, thin fingers. 'Sometimes the worst situations lead you in the right direction, eh?'

'Absolutely,' Lola said. 'I'm going to buy a necklace to celebrate. Which pieces have you enjoyed making the most?'

339

As they talked, Enzo flashed Jess a carefree smile. It was the happiest she could remember seeing him.

They called time on the sale at three o'clock, when there hadn't been any visitors through the door for half an hour.

'Not too bad,' Felicity said, surveying what was left. 'Roger and I will sell the rest of the jewellery, then I've got a home clearance man coming round to give me a price for everything else I don't want. I think he's under the impression that Mrs Felicity Chester is deceased, and he's coming to rake over her possessions.'

Susie looked aghast. 'That's horrible.'

'It's true, in a way,' Felicity said. 'The old Felicity Chester is gone, replaced by a shiny new version.'

'I love both versions,' Spade said, slinging his arm around her shoulder, his headlock-hug much more gentle than usual. 'But this one has space for my guitar collection.'

'We're going to raise a toast,' Wendy said, carrying a tray of champagne flutes into the living room.

'Jess, what are you doing over there?' Lola called.

'Nothing.' Jess had been standing in the bay window for the last half-hour, when it was clear she'd sold all the prints she was going to. She was sure that Lola, and probably every single person in that room – including all three cats, because Artemis and Bond had emerged at some point and joined Twiggy on the sofa – knew what she was doing there. She came over and took a flute.

'Cheers!' Spade said, and everyone clinked glasses.

'I want to thank you for all your generosity over these last months,' Enzo said, his eyes crinkling at the edges. 'I do not know what we would have done without you, but we are put back together now, if that is the right expression.'

'It's an excellent expression,' Roger said.

'So, Felicity, you must keep your money from today's sale. And Jess – it goes without saying that your profits are yours. I am just glad we could come, to be here with you all. We will repay your kindness.'

'Thank you,' Carolina added, holding her glass aloft. There was another round of clinks.

'I want to do one an' all,' Braden said. 'If it weren't for you lot, I'd be fucking up somewhere, getting in the shit. This is much more fun.'

'You're not old enough to drink champagne,' Wendy said.

Braden grinned at her, then took a defiant sip. 'Mind you, if I hadn't stolen that watch then none of you'd have had the joy of my creative prowess. How's that for dictionary corner, eh? My *creative prowess*.'

'That's great, dude.' Spade took his green fedora off and put it on Braden's head. 'The Misfits wouldn't be the same without you. But you need to move onto orange juice now, capiche?'

'*Dictionary corner*,' Jess whispered, her eyes straying to the window again. She didn't know how many people she'd watched walk past the house now, but none of them had had dark hair and grey eyes, and a smile that felt like her own, personal lightbulb, lighting her up from the inside.

The doorbell rang and her stomach twisted, her palms prickling with sweat. She exchanged a wide-eyed look with Lola, then leaned forward to try and see out of the narrow side window as Felicity, who had shut the front door at three, went to open it.

341

'Oh, hello,' she said. 'Come in, please.'

'Thanks.' It was a male voice, but Jess could barely hear it over her heart pounding in her ears. 'I didn't know if I'd be too late, or . . .'

Jess's shoulders slumped. It was Milo, Lola's boss at the Gipsy Moth. Lola had told her that he was a car-boot junkie, and had been thrilled at the prospect of Felicity's house sale.

'Milo,' Lola said. 'I thought you couldn't make it!'

'Problem with our keg delivery,' he said. 'Sometimes I think my staff couldn't organise a piss-up in a pub, which is pretty worrying considering they all work in one.'

As the landlord's larger-than-life personality absorbed everyone's attention, Jess slipped into the hallway and sat on the fifth stair up. It smelled of furniture polish and carpet cleaner, the white-painted banisters glistening. She wrapped her arms around her legs and watched as Twiggy stalked up the stairs to join her. He pressed his soft, warm body against her side, his purr reverberating through her hip.

It was clear, now, that Ash wasn't coming. He knew how important this was to Felicity, and to her, and Jess thought he would have been here if he could. But he needed to prioritise himself right now, and facing up to Felicity's predicament – being reminded of everything that connected them – was probably too hard on top of everything else.

She should have let go of that sliver of hope hours ago, but she did it now, and the disappointment that took its place was a heavy weight on her chest. This, along with her unanswered message, marked the full-stop to her summer with Ash, those stolen hours that had ended up meaning so much.

Still, tomorrow was Sunday, her busiest day at the market, and she was starting afresh: a shop redesign, clearing out the old, bringing in the new. As she went back into the living room, let Wendy top up her glass, slipped her arm through Susie's and asked Sofia about her children, she realised that she thought of them all as friends, now. She had other people to light her up, and she wasn't going to take them for granted any more. Friendships, like time, could be fleeting, and she was going to be better at holding onto the ones that mattered.

Chapter Thirty-Nine

For a moment, Ash thought he'd forgotten to turn his alarm clock off. He groaned, rolled over and flung an uncoordinated hand out, trying to find the offending item on his bedside table. It continued to squawk, and before he found the smooth, round button, he remembered. It was Sunday, and he had *meant* to get up this early, because today was the day he was turning over a new leaf. New horizons, new outlook.

He slid out of bed and into the shower, trying to wash away his weariness. He'd felt weary ever since his dad had gone; worse since that day with Jess in the park. But every time he had an uncharitable thought about Nico, or found himself staring at the TV screen, having watched a whole episode of *Slow Horses* without taking any of it in, or ignored messages from Dylan for longer than several hours, he was reassured that he'd done the right thing. He cared about Jess too much to subject her to all his hostility and vacant hours.

He dressed in jeans and a marl grey T-shirt, checked the time on his watch, and left the flat, jumping when Mack glared at him from across the corridor. He'd probably been waiting with a glass pressed against the wood, listening for the sound of Ash unlocking his door.

'Andrea at number twenty-one is getting my paper today,' Mack said. 'Seeing as you told me you couldn't do it.'

Ash couldn't help but smile. 'I'm sure Andrea will be more

entertaining than me, and there's somewhere else I need to be today.'

Mack's face brightened. 'Off to Greenwich, are you? Going to fix things with that woman of yours at last.'

Ash dropped his gaze to the horribly patterned carpet, his stomach twisting with guilt. 'No,' he said. 'I told you. That's over.'

'Just because your dad's gone, doesn't mean you have to give up on life, too.'

Ash looked up, his neck prickling. 'I'm not giving up on life.'

'Sure seems like it.' Mack leaned heavily against his doorframe.

Ash took a step forwards. 'Is your hip—'

'I'm having one of my better days,' Mack cut in. 'This is my thoroughly-disappointed-in-you stance. Have you lost your damn mind? That woman was miserable when she turned up here, she hadn't heard a *peep* from you, and despite that, she had more sparkle in her than everyone on our corridor put together – right now, anyway.'

'What do you mean?' Ash rubbed his forehead.

'You used to be like that,' Mack said. 'It wasn't an accident that I came to you for the paper and coffee on Sundays. *Your* company, *your* attitude. You hadn't always had it easy, but you made it your business to find the positive in everything. And then that good-for-nothing father came back into your life, reminded you of how much he'd made you suffer, and then left for good. You've let him steal your joy again, just like he did the first time he left.'

'Mack, I—'

'Get it together, son. Before it's too late.' He stepped back and, before Ash could say anything in reply, he was staring at his neighbour's closed door, the bang reverberating through his head like a warning bell.

Borough Market was, objectively, a great place to spend a few hours. Really amazing cheese, a huge vat of paella, ostrich burgers and creme brûlée doughnuts and other food options that Greenwich didn't offer, all in the shelter of the stunningly Gothic Southwark Cathedral. Ash got there as the market was still waking up, with the echo of car horns on Borough High Street, delivery lorries beeping as they reversed into tight spaces. The sun streamed in, creating pockets of light and shade, and he tried his hardest to relax.

He strolled past charcuterie and bakery stalls, pastries glistening with golden flakes, and past huge, pungent wheels of cheese, their smell overpowering the aromas of chocolate and fudge. There were no hats to try on, no antique clocks or silverware to sift through, no shimmering jewellery. No Jess. He queued for a coffee, and even the act of getting a cappuccino in a takeaway cup was thick with nostalgia. Any moment now the memories would slow down, and his brain would wake up and be interested in this new place with all its possibility.

He watched a dad and two young children standing in line for the ice-cream stall, the little girl jumping up and down, her brown ponytail bouncing. He had done a lot of FaceTiming with Dylan recently, soaking up minutes in the company of his brother and his nephews, Sadie popping her head in to say hello and ask how he was doing, the modern lines of their Auckland house in the background.

Zack and Eli always had a ridiculous story to tell their Uncle Ash, about falling off some impressive play equipment, or the hidden lake they'd found on a weekend hike, or what piece of homework their dog, Scruffit – 'like Stuff It, only more polite', Eli had said – had destroyed. It always took Ash out of himself, until they wanted to hear *his* funny stories, what he'd been up to, and he had nothing to tell them because all he'd been doing was acting like a zombie at work, drinking too much in the evenings, staring at a picture of a kite on his living-room wall.

'This is fucking ridiculous,' he said aloud.

'I beg your pardon?'

He spun on his heels, mouth open, and was met with the steely glare of a woman who, even on this balmy summer morning, was wearing a green jacket, and had a red umbrella hanging over her arm. Her hair was grey, her eyes sharp behind round glasses, and her lips were pursed in disapproval.

'I'm sorry,' Ash said. 'I didn't realise anyone was in hearing distance.'

The woman stared pointedly around her. 'We're in a market,' she said. 'One of London's busiest, on a Sunday morning. Where did you think you were? The *moon?*'

Ash almost choked on his laughter. 'Well, there is a lot of cheese . . .' He gestured to the stall behind them, but the woman just glared harder. He cleared his throat. 'As I said, I'm really sorry. I'll be more mindful in future.' He went to turn away.

'Out with it, then.'

He angled his body back towards her. 'Sorry?'

'What is . . . *flipping ridiculous*. Your coffee? The size of that wheel of Black Bomber? The fact that the young woman over there thinks she can charge eight pounds fifty for almond butter, just because she's slapped an *artisan* label on it?'

'Uh, my coffee's great,' Ash said and, as if he needed to demonstrate, he took a sip, then gave a loud, satisfied sigh. He was, quite clearly, losing his mind.

'What is it, then?' The woman folded her arms. 'I tell my grandchildren that there always has to be a reason for swearing. They're high-currency words, not to be bandied about lightly.'

'I would guess I'm older than your grandchildren,' Ash said, wondering when he'd recover the brain power to extract himself from this awkward conversation.

'They're twenty-three and twenty-seven,' she said, 'so not by much.'

'Right.' He nodded, hoping that would be the end of it, but she continued to stare at him, and he thought that maybe her question hadn't been rhetorical. 'What is . . . *flipping ridiculous*,' he admitted, 'is that I'm missing someone – a lot. She works at a different market, and I thought I could come here today and somehow banish her ghost. It was a stupid plan.'

'Is she dead, then?'

Ash turned his shocked exclamation into a cough. 'She's not dead,' he said. The thought sent an icy shiver through him. 'She's fine: alive and well. Working in her shop in Greenwich right now, I expect.'

The woman narrowed her eyes. 'Don't talk about ghosts, then. If you know where she is, why are you here and not there?'

'Because . . .' Ash floundered. He'd had enough of being interrogated by people who thought they were wiser just because they'd lived longer than him. And those unkind thoughts were the reason he had been right to walk away from Jess. But then . . . the woman's question was so simple. *Why are you here, and not there?* If he told her that it was

348

because he was too fucked-up, she'd probably hit him with her umbrella.

'Well then,' the woman said, when he didn't finish his sentence. 'You need to be purposeful.'

'I do?' He rubbed the back of his neck.

'Yes. Whether your purpose is to enjoy this market, or to go to the other market where this woman is, or to sit on a bench next to the cathedral and drink your coffee, enjoying a tiny corner of London where the birds are singing, you need to own it. Right now, you're floating around like a lost soul, swearing to yourself, stuck in between. Make a decision, then act on it.'

'Even if it's the wrong one?'

'I think you know, almost as soon as you make it, whether a decision is right or wrong. Not everyone puts stock in intuition, but I believe in it. There's a part of you that knows.' She tapped her temple.

'Right,' Ash said again, and thought that maybe she was making sense. Walking away from Jess, leaving her on that bench in the park, had been one of the hardest things he'd ever done: harder, even, than going to see his dad, lying still and silent in the hospice bed. Every step away from her had felt like he was leaving a vital part of himself behind, but he had told himself he couldn't backtrack; he couldn't give her a speech about how he couldn't be with her after all, despite their weeks together; be the cause of all her tears, watch as he broke the heart of the woman he was certain he loved – and break his own heart at the same time – then race back up the hill, make jazz hands and say, *Just kidding! I love you more than I've loved anyone, so please put up with me through the shitshow that is my life right now because I'm selfish and I don't want to spend another hour without you.*

349

No, he couldn't have done that. So he had stuck to his decision, and maybe it was the wrong one – surely if it was right, he would have started to forget about her by now, or at least stop dreaming about her – but he had made it, at least. But what had the woman said just now? That he was floating around, stuck in between. It didn't mean anything, except that this morning had been a mistake. How had he ever thought Jess, everyone and everything at Greenwich Market, could be replaced?

'Thanks.' He gave the woman a quick, perfunctory smile.

'No problem, young man.' She tapped her umbrella on the ground. 'Glad I could be of service. I somehow know when people need a snippet of advice – even if they're complete strangers. You, with your obscenities and hunched shoulders, those sad grey eyes, were a prime candidate.'

'Sort of like a sixth sense, then?' Ash said. 'Thanks again.' Now he really was going to leave. Maybe find that bench, enjoy his coffee in peace – unless, of course, the birds she was referring to were pigeons. If they were, then they could fuck off: a pigeon would nail the coffin shut on this disaster of a morning. He flashed her another quick smile and turned away.

'More like my own little superpower,' she called after him.

His breathing stuttered. Slowly, he turned back round to face her. 'What did you say?'

She shrugged, all her sternness evaporating. 'It's not earth-shattering, I know. Not like flying or being invisible, but I like to think of it as my mini superpower.'

'A . . . a mini superpower?' he repeated.

'It sounds silly, but that's how I see it. Are you OK? I know I was abrupt, but swearing really is—'

350

'No,' Ash said. 'It's fine. Honestly.' He realised he was rubbing his chest. The ache had been there, dull but unforgiving, for the last ten days. It was undoubtedly psychosomatic, because your heart didn't actually *ache* when you were heartbroken – that was reserved for serious medical emergencies like heart attacks. But now it was sharp, and it was telling him – this woman was telling him – that he'd got it wrong. He'd got it so, so wrong. 'Thank you.' He pressed his coffee into her hand.

'Oh,' she said. 'I don't want this—'

'It really is great coffee,' he called, already hurrying away. He turned to give her a smile – if she had thought he was a bit strange before, now she must think he was positively unhinged – and tripped, catching his hand on the brick wall. He kept going, hoping the woman with the umbrella would understand.

It was almost eleven o'clock: he had just over an hour to get there.

Chapter Forty

Jess knew that Felicity's party had gone on late into the night, because when she woke up on Sunday morning, there were a lot of slightly incoherent messages from Lola on her phone, proclaiming her undying love for everyone: Jess, Wendy, Roger, Spade and Braden and their Market Misfits – even her Fitbit step sessions with Malik. Jess decided she would reply later, in case her best friend hadn't put her phone on silent after finally slumping into bed.

She showered and put on a blue dress with orange fish swimming across the fabric. She wanted to get to the market before Wendy, so she could spend time in the shop while it was empty and get a sense of how best to organise it for autumn: how she could maximise its potential, make every item sing, imbue every customer who walked through the door with a cosiness they wanted to take into their own homes. The hares could have pride of place on the very bottom shelf, except for Halloween week, when she would allow them a moment in the limelight.

She tiptoed carefully through the quiet flat. They rarely bothered to close the living-room curtains, and early morning sun was streaming in through the window, dust motes dancing in the beams of light. She put bread in the toaster, got out the butter and marmalade, and scrolled through her phone. There was a message from her dad, sent last night after she had fallen, exhausted, into bed.

> Loved seeing you on Tues! Why don't you bring Lola and
> Malik round one Sunday for a barbecue? It's been ages
> since we've seen them, and I'll even open the studio
> doors. Dad. xx

Jess waited for the tight clench in her stomach, the urge to push the phone and his invitation away, but it didn't come. She spread butter and marmalade on her toast, and replied.

> Malik will go insane at your train set! Let me see if Wendy
> will let me have a precious Sunday off, and I'll check dates
> with L and M. It was really lovely to see you too. xx

When she'd finished her breakfast, she padded quietly down the stairs and out into the pale, early morning sunshine. She walked along roads with only the lightest traffic, the pavements dusty, pigeons cooing while they pecked for morsels in the cracks. The world was waking up slowly, but Jess felt more awake than she had done in days.

She had decided, after Ash's no-show yesterday, that she had to try again. She didn't know whether to start with a gentle trickle of messages he couldn't ignore, or go all out with a return visit to his flat, but she wasn't giving up on him. He was one man in a city of millions, and the sensible part of her brain said she should move on, that their meeting on the bench had been the final act. Usually, by now, she would have consigned him to history.

But yesterday evening, surrounded by her friends, and people she considered her family, she had realised that if she tried and failed to win Ash back, they would look after her. She had good people around her, and she wanted him to be one of them: she wanted him to have those people around him too.

She waited at the lights for a taxi to pass, a slumped figure in the back seat on an early trip to the station, or on the way back from an epic night out. The greasy spoons were open already, the salty scent of bacon wafting into the air, the metal screech of rising shutters accompanying her as she crossed the road.

She entered the market down the side alley, where she'd watched Ash holding onto Braden all those weeks ago. There was activity at some of the food stalls, hotplates turned on and coffee machines fired up, ready for hungry workers on the way home from night shifts, desperate for a latte and a sausage sandwich.

Jess smiled and waved at the people she recognised, and wondered if, in a few months, she would know more names; if, now that she was more open to it, her market family would continue to grow.

She walked into the main space and Roger called over to her. 'Wonderful day yesterday.'

'It was lovely,' she called back. 'I know Felicity appreciated us being there.'

'I wouldn't have missed it: a chance to spend time with everyone away from here. I think you and I left earlier than most.' He chuckled.

'We're going to be perkier than some of the others, that's for sure. See you later!' She waved goodbye, then walked along the side of the market, burrowing in her handbag for the keys to No Vase Like Home. Lit by the early morning sun, the shop looked fresh and sparkling – as if everything was covered in fairy dust. Her prints were colourful and enticing, and she'd noticed Wendy moving the candles the other day to give her more room.

Now Enzo was safe, Wendy had told Jess she could be a proper supplier, that she'd pay for batches of her prints upfront, and she would expect new designs on a regular basis. Jess had readily accepted, because it gave her the best of both worlds: getting to work in a place she loved, but being creative in her own right, seeing people pick up and fall in love with her designs. She wondered if she should branch out: create a range called *Subtle Superpowers*, take the miraculous mini-skills she and Ash had come up with – that she was still coming up with – and make prints of those, too.

She bent down and picked up a hare. This one was on its hind legs, and looked ready to start a fight.

'*Are* you a witch?' she asked, gazing into its stony eyes.

'I might have drunk too much yesterday, but that's a bit harsh.'

Jess spun round to find Wendy grinning from the doorway, the purple smudges under her eyes enhanced by her pallor. 'Sorry!' she squeaked.

Wendy waved her away. 'You're entitled to the moral high ground, because you left Felicity's at a sensible time. But I will need at least three of Kirsty's muffins today – if she's alive – and coffees every half-hour.'

'I can manage that.' Jess grinned. 'Breakfast muffin?'

'I could *murder* a breakfast muffin.' Wendy turned on the storeroom light and the radio. 'And I'm sorry, about yesterday.'

Jess stopped in the doorway. 'What did you do?'

'No, I mean that Ash didn't show. I had thought . . .' She sighed. 'I really thought he'd come.'

Jess swallowed. 'Me too. Let me go and get those muffins.'

'And a smoothie,' Wendy called after her. 'The greenest, healthiest-looking one. I'll pay you back!'

The morning was busy, the warm sunshine and gentle breeze perfect for enjoying all of Greenwich's delights, and Jess didn't have a whole lot of time to think about hares or shop redesigns or anything else, especially with Wendy's constant grumbling and her need to take frequent breaks away from the shop floor so she could sit down.

She'd left her propped up behind the counter, and was burrowing among the storeroom shelves for a sea-salt candle that a customer had asked for, when all the clocks struck midday. It was such a familiar sound that she barely noticed it any more, but the gentle chimes reminded her it was their time. It *had been* their time.

'Jess, come out here,' Wendy called.

'Just a sec,' she shouted back. 'I'm elbow-deep in the candle box.'

'Jessica Peacock,' Wendy said, and Jess jumped, then turned to find her boss in the doorway.

'What is it?' she asked. 'Are you feeling sick? Need another break?'

Wendy shook her head. 'I'll find the candle. You get out there.'

'Why?'

'Because I say so.'

'You are a proper grump when you're hungover,' Jess said, and slipped past her boss, laughing at her consternated expression and then, stepping into the sun-bright shop, came to a stumbling stop.

The woman waiting for her candle was next to the counter, but there was someone else standing just inside the doorway. Jeans and dusty Vans, a grey T-shirt, his hair falling over his forehead. He was holding two coffee cups in a cardboard carrier.

356

'Hey,' he said. His smile was tentative. 'Sorry I'm late.'

A shocked laugh slipped out of her. 'You're not late. Though I don't . . . I hadn't planned on . . . I didn't know that you—'

'Off you trot,' Wendy said, waggling the sea-salt candle.

Jess mouthed 'thank you', then she walked over, took hold of Ash's T-shirt, turned him round and manoeuvred him out of the doorway. He stuttered out a laugh, and let himself be pushed.

Her mind was a blur. She thought about the park, the riverside, the heath – all the places they'd been together, somewhere that would be quieter. But her heart was beating in her throat, and she couldn't wait, so she stopped them almost immediately, in front of the large picture window of No Vase Like Home, the sparkly twigs visible through the glass, and turned to face him.

'Have you thought of a subtle superpower that was too good to message me?' She didn't know how else to start this; what to say to him that wasn't an overblown declaration of her feelings, which might well send him running back to Holborn.

'Not me,' Ash said. He was gripping the coffee carrier with both hands, and he looked tired, with his Sunday stubble and cracked lips. To her he'd never looked more beautiful. 'I met someone this morning. A woman who told me her mini superpower was knowing when strangers needed advice.'

Jess's mouth fell open. 'Seriously?'

'Seriously.' Ash nodded. 'Those were her exact words – *a mini superpower*. At first I was pissed off with her for even talking to me – for telling me off for swearing – but then she said that, and I realised.'

'What did you realise?' Jess croaked out. She was finding it difficult to breathe. A couple barged past them and she pulled Ash closer, tucking them against the front of the shop.

357

He held his hand out between them, his palm facing up. He had a graze there, and it looked recent. 'I realised that I have been a monumental idiot, and that I have got this all so wrong: the whole "deciding to go through this on my own" thing. I am not cut out for martyrdom, as much as I felt like I shouldn't ask for anyone's help. For *your* help.'

Jess slid her hand on top of his. His skin was warm, and his fingers curved gently around her wrist. 'I could have told you that,' she said. 'When we met last time, I told you I agreed with you that this wouldn't work because of timing or circumstance or . . . whatever it was. But I realised, almost as soon as you left, that I *didn't* agree, but—'

'You respected my wishes,' Ash said. 'Even though I was being obstinate.'

'The *most* obstinate. But you were hurting, too. I knew that.'

He nodded, his Adam's apple bobbing. 'I was. But I-I've realised another thing, too, since then. That there is always going to be bad timing and difficult circumstances. Life doesn't let you press pause so you can get to know a person without the real world getting in the way.'

'If it did, then you wouldn't be getting to know them properly, would you?' Jess was warming to his theme, because it felt like all the conversations she'd been having in her own head over the last fortnight. 'There is no relationship utopia. There's only messy, everyday life, with all its ups and downs, its hurts and high points, and if you get to navigate it . . .' She stopped.

'Jess?' He squeezed her hand, his gaze warm and concerned.

She swallowed, tried to even out her voice. 'If you get to navigate it with people who you care about, and who care about you, then that's so much better than doing it alone.'

'Exactly. So.' He let out a long, shuddering breath. 'I came here to apologise for what I said, and the way I behaved: for upsetting you so much, and for not replying to your message about Felicity's house sale.'

'That's OK.'

He squeezed her hand again. 'It's not. None of what I did was OK. And I also wanted to say that – well, to ask – if you might be prepared to forgive me? To take me on, with all my mess and my dark bits, my stubbornness, and also, if you'd let me take you on, too? Because I am here for all of you. I think that I might *love* all of you, and I don't want to do these hours on Sunday, or any day, without you.'

Jess swayed, her shoulder pressing against the window. 'You love me?'

'I do.' Ash dropped his head. 'I just said that I *might* love you, but that isn't right. It isn't strong enough. Jessica Peacock, I am in love with you, and I'm sorry I walked away, and that I didn't tell you about my dad, and for all the hundreds of things—'

'I love you too,' she rushed. She took the coffee carrier and put it on the floor against the wall, then closed the gap between them. 'Let's stop being sorry about things that have already happened, and be happy about this, instead.' She pressed her hands on either side of his face, his stubble prickling her palms, and felt his arms come around her waist. She leaned up and in, her lips inches from his. 'About the fact that we're stupidly in love with each other, and we're actually going to *let* ourselves be, too.'

'I'm down with celebrating being stupidly in love,' he said. 'But is now the right time—?' She kissed the words out of his mouth, running her hands up into his hair, while he tightened his hold on her, bringing their bodies flush. They kissed to the soundtrack of the market at lunchtime, shouts and laughter and the melodious notes of a wooden wind chime on one of the stalls.

Eventually, she pulled back to look at him, his grey eyes shining and his cheeks flushed, his lips pink from where they'd been reminding each other how well they fitted together.

'Do you know what?' she said, lacing her fingers through his.

'What?' His voice was deep and rumbly and perfect, threaded through with the wonder that she was feeling like an earthquake.

'I think for us, Ash – for you and me – all the time is the right time. It just took us a while to realise it.'

'I'd agree with that,' he murmured, and kissed her again.

Wendy came out of the shop ten minutes later, staring at them with a mix of feigned irritation and barely disguised glee.

'You're scaring the customers away,' she said. 'Nobody is going to come into the shop while you're re-enacting a Richard Curtis finale on the doorstep.'

They pulled apart, but Ash kept his arms around her waist.

'Sorry, Wendy,' he said, not sounding sorry at all.

'Ash is great at film re-enactments.' Jess grinned. 'Hasn't he told you?'

Ash coughed out a laugh.

'I'm very glad to have you back,' Wendy said. 'But just to manage my expectations, are you planning on kissing out here for the rest of the day, and taking up all my best colleague's time?'

'I don't know,' Ash said, turning to Jess. 'What do you think?'

'I think you could help me in the shop for a bit, then, when you get bored, spend some time wandering around the market, catching up with everyone, and then we could go to mine when I finish at four thirty?'

'I can see that working so well,' Wendy said dryly, but she stood back to let them both into the shop ahead of her. Jess retrieved the coffee carrier from the floor. 'I'm not paying you though, Ash.'

'I wouldn't dream of it,' Ash said.

Wendy straightened an hourglass on a shelf and narrowed her eyes. 'I'm going to keep a close eye on you, and you're not allowed to be in here alone together. Any coffee runs – that's down to one of you.'

'Understood,' Jess said.

'Yes, boss.' Ash squeezed Jess's hand. 'Shall I go and get us some lunch?'

'Wonderful idea,' Wendy said. 'Something carb- and fat-laden for me, please.'

He gave her a quick salute, kissed Jess on the cheek and left.

When he'd gone, she gazed out at the market, the stalls full of brightly coloured, enticing objects: hats and bracelets and art prints and trinkets that you didn't even know existed until you turned up here, and then, after a few minutes with a stallholder, a slick demonstration given or impassioned story woven, you realised you couldn't live without.

'He couldn't give up your hour, then?' Wendy said lightly.

'Apparently not.' Jess turned to her boss. 'Maybe there were still some of Olga's hats he hadn't tried on.'

Wendy laughed. 'I think he's picked his favourite thing in this market, and it isn't one of Olga's hats.' She tapped the counter and strode into the storeroom. The radio filled the space with an upbeat pop song.

Jess stayed by the window, looking out at the stalls and the customers, waiting for Ash to come back with their lunch. She was counting down the minutes to four thirty, when they could escape together and go back to her flat, start making up for all the time they'd lost. It wasn't just one, happy hour she had to look forward to with him: she had him for good, and she wasn't going to take a single second for granted.

Epilogue

What about someone who remembers the name of everyone they ever met?

Nobody can do that. That's genuine superpower territory, nothing subtle about it.

A person that can stop a toddler screaming just by smiling at them?

That's a good one, but is it actually possible?

Just watched it happen, right now, on the boat.

But how do you know that person does it every time? Hang on – you're still on the boat?

There was a delay at Canary Wharf. Five more minutes to Greenwich, then I'll run, promise. I love you. x

I love you too. See you soon. xxxx

'Felicity, where do you want the sausage rolls?' Jess put her phone back in her pocket and picked up the plate of crispy savouries that she'd moved off the cooling rack before messaging Ash. The gleaming, sunshine-yellow crockery Felicity had bought complemented her redesigned cream and duck-egg-blue kitchen. The Russian dolls even had their own shelf, where they were displayed properly, next to one of Spade's framed tour posters from the Eighties.

'Just out here, on the occasional table.' She appeared in the doorway, in jeans and a turquoise blouse, her hair elegantly styled. She'd softened since the clutter had gone from her life and Spade had come into it, and now the property close to the park was every bit as stunning as Jess had imagined it to be before she'd set foot inside it last summer.

'I've got the sound system set up,' Spade announced, 'and the playlist good to go.'

'Is it some of your old tracks?' Roger asked, sipping from a glass of lemonade. 'No set from the Market Misfits?'

'I might have sneaked a couple on there.' Spade flashed him a wink. 'The Misfits are having a day off. We've got gigs three nights next week, and Friday in the theatre, so we need to rest our instruments.'

'I need to look after my throat.' Braden reached for a sausage roll, then paused when Felicity gave him a cool stare. He shoved his hand back into his sleeve.

'That's only because you talk so much. *All* the time.' Lola rolled her eyes and Braden shook his head, mock-disappointed. 'It's OK, I love you really.' She grinned, and the teenager returned it.

The success of the Misfits had spread beyond the online world, and the three of them were enjoying low-key but well-attended gigs, supporting acts in indie venues throughout south London. Jess often got calls from her best friend, breathless with the wonder that people knew her name, paid to watch her and her friends play, sought her out via social media to tell her how much they loved her. She was living her best life – chaotic, busy, full of new experiences – and the Misfits still performed regularly at the market, never forgetting where they'd started.

Right now, Lola was on the sofa, sandwiched between Malik and Terence, who had found a jar of chargrilled artichokes from somewhere, and was working his way through them with a spoon. Jess wondered if she should have left him at home, but it had felt sad not to invite him today, especially as it was their last day as roommates.

A gust of flower-scented breeze blew in from the open French doors, and Artemis raised his head, perturbed at the interruption, then went back to his snooze.

'Hello, it's me! I've brought cupcakes!' Susie stepped into the hall.

'And I have courgette cake,' Olga added, following her in. 'Less sugar and carb. Healthy veg.'

'Less joy,' Braden said in his loudest possible whisper.

'Now now,' Roger tutted, but the corners of his mouth lifted up under his moustache.

Jess glanced at her watch. Wendy was due here in twenty minutes, for the big birthday party that they'd secretly planned – Jess had started the ball rolling – and they needed her to be last, because otherwise the surprise would be ruined.

'The cake's here!' Felicity called, and Jess hurried out into the hall to greet Kirsty, who was carrying a huge cardboard box, with Enzo, Carolina and Sofia behind her.

'Kirsty's here too,' Kirsty said with a wry smile. 'But I appreciate the cake is more important. Red velvet muffin with vanilla twirls, and – of course – the pièce de résistance.'

'Out in the kitchen,' Felicity said, leading the way. 'And I'm terribly sorry, Kirsty, of course you're more important than the cake.'

'Am I, though?' Kirsty laughed, then added, 'Don't worry, Felicity,' when the other woman's cheeks went red. 'Here we go.'

She put the cake on the counter and everyone crowded in. Jess could smell Spade's spicy aftershave, and Olga was breathing in her ear.

'This is so lovely, isn't it?' Peggy said to her husband John, a quiet man with pale skin and dark hair, who occasionally came out with the most wicked jokes Jess had ever heard. 'I love your yellow crockery, Felicity.'

'Thank you, dear,' Felicity said.

Jess and Ash had bumped into Peggy and John at the Trafalgar Tavern one Saturday night, and over the course of the evening – as they'd all got to know each other beyond the stark setting of Cherry Blossom Lodge – they'd discovered that Peggy and John lived on the next road over from Felicity. When Jess had told the older woman, she'd made it her business to knock on Peggy's door and invite her for tea. Now the house was restored to all its glory, Felicity's new favourite hobby was inviting people round for tea – and showing off the original pieces of Carolina and Sofia jewellery she'd bought.

With Carolina's arthritis being managed, and Sofia working on pieces alongside her sister, Enzo was busier than ever running their stall, and had even asked Jess for advice on how to set up an Etsy shop. Over the last few months he'd paid her and Wendy back the money they'd given him – even though both of them had put up a united protest – and Carolina and Sofia had made them both, and Lola, Spade and Braden, unique pieces as thank-you gifts. Jess only took off her kite-shaped pendant in the shower. It was her favourite item of jewellery.

'Ready for this?' Kirsty lifted the lid off the cake box, and there were coos and aaaahs and applause, and Jess felt suddenly sick.

'Oh my God,' she said. '*Seriously?*'

'They're made out of icing,' Kirsty announced. 'I worked really hard to capture all their expressions. It's my most intricate creation ever.'

'The *hares?*' Jess couldn't keep the horror out of her voice. 'You didn't think there were enough of them in the shop – and Wendy keeps ordering more like she's fully possessed, by the way – you had to *recreate them* for her birthday cake?'

Kirsty's eyes widened in alarm. 'She loves them though, right?'

'She really does.' Felicity sounded amused. 'But I don't think Jess shares that sentiment.'

'They're secretly witches,' Jess blurted out. 'I'm sure of it. And this – this is them, getting inside your head. They want to spread, take over the world, and—'

'Who wants to take over the world? Hey, guys. Enzo, Carolina. How are you?'

'We are very well, Ash, thank you.'

Jess pushed through her friends and flung herself at him, and he wrapped his arms around her waist, pressed his lips against her neck. 'You're here,' she said.

'Of course I'm here,' he laughed. He was slightly breathless, as if he'd had to run from the jetty. 'You knew I was coming, we messaged on the boat and – oh fuck. Are they the *hares?*'

'What do you two have against the hares?' Susie asked. 'I think they're sweet.'

'Right, out of the kitchen, all of you!' Felicity clapped. 'We have ten minutes until Wendy gets here, and I have some bits to finish. Go, find drinks in the living room.'

'What can I do?' Jess asked.

'Take your man into the garden for a few minutes,' Felicity said. 'You've been here since the crack of dawn.'

'But I—'

'Come on, Jess.' Ash took her hand and dragged her out into the garden, where the water feature was burbling happily and a long-tailed tit peeped noisily from the laburnum tree. He wrapped his arms around her and kissed her. 'I missed you.'

'I missed you, too. You're staying tonight though, right?'

'Yeah, the flat's packed up, ready for the movers tomorrow, so I haven't got anything to do until the morning.'

Jess bounced up and down. 'And my room's packed, apart from the bed and the yeti cushions.'

'Oh, of course.' Ash gazed down at her. 'We need a final night in your room, to say goodbye to it properly.'

'Then, our own place,' Jess whispered, and still, she couldn't quite believe it. Almost a year together, and being with Ash had never felt like wasted time, because with each new dawn and sunset, kiss and dinner and movie on the sofa, even with each new fight, she fell more in love with him. She had proved she was strong enough to help him through the messed-up grief of losing his dad, and he had shown her how good it was to be loved completely, to be taken care of and stood up for, without being scared that it would all disappear.

And now they were moving in together, into a ground-floor flat fifteen minutes' walk from the market, that had more space than Jess had ever expected to get, but needed a whole lot of work before it could be considered even remotely homely. She couldn't wait to get started, and knew her discount at No Vase Like Home would help when they were ready for the finishing touches, along with the extra money she'd saved from being one of Wendy's most valued suppliers. Her new line of Subtle Superpower art prints was proving particularly popular, and she signed each one with the moniker *Jess&Ash Designs*, seeing as he came up with at least half of them.

Ash, too, was excited about the move, sending her endless links for paint colours, and photos of ambitious layouts that involved knocking down interior walls and were probably against the flat's leasehold terms. He was still working for the bank, but had two interviews closer to Greenwich. The role at the museum service, overseeing company practices and managing staff wellbeing, looked particularly promising, and Jess wondered if – hopefully *when* he was successful – he would resurrect the grey trilby and run film and ghost tours as a side hustle.

'I thought, after the party, we could go to our bench,' he said now.

'In the park?' They had revisited it more times than she could count since getting back together, so she no longer thought of it as the place where she'd lost Ash. Instead, they found a little bit more of each other every time they went – and they often bumped into Diamanté the demon dog, too.

He nodded. 'If you'd like to?'

'Want me all to yourself, do you?' she teased.

'Always. But we have to celebrate Wendy's birthday first. Obviously. I mean, that's why we're here.' He laughed, glancing away from her to the back of Felicity's garden.

'Hey.' Jess touched his chin, forcing him to look at her again. 'You OK?'

Ash hesitated, his grey eyes widening. 'Of course! Why would you ask that? I'm fine. Great.'

Jess laughed. 'OK, now you're being really weird. What's going on?'

He squeezed her waist. 'Can a guy not have an hour with his girlfriend, just before they move into a new place together, one of them potentially starts a new job and everything gets crazy? I just want . . .' He huffed. 'I want to have this time with you, OK?'

'OK.' Jess smiled at him, her insides dancing like butterflies waiting to get at a buddleia. The Sunday before, they'd gone for dinner at her mum and dad's house, and Ash and Graeme had disappeared into his studio for ages. She wouldn't have thought much of it, except that when they'd emerged, Ash had smelled of the expensive whisky Graeme kept for special occasions, and her dad's eyes had been red around the edges. It was why Jess had worn her favourite dress today, postbox red with white hearts printed on it and a low-cut neckline, a floaty skirt that fell just below the knee. Not just to celebrate Wendy's birthday, but because of what might come after.

And, if it didn't, that was OK too, because she had planned her own elaborate, romantic setup that, even if Ash got there first, she would still put into motion. It involved the Queen's House and a very friendly security guard, and being allowed to stay for an hour after the other visitors had gone home for the night (as long as they promised not to do anything that would upset the memory of the much revered Henrietta Maria). But, as she kissed her boyfriend in Felicity's back garden, and the party started inside before Wendy had even arrived, one of House of Cards' old songs thumping through the speakers, Jess thought Ash's plan might be the better one: more traditionally romantic.

She kissed him harder, squeezed him tighter, then pulled

back and smiled up at him. 'I thought of another subtle superpower.'

'Oh?' He raised an eyebrow. 'I think I've already won today: the guy on the boat who smiled at the toddler and got her to stop crying.'

'He could have been her uncle.'

'I don't think he was.'

'Perhaps he was secretly Ronald McDonald.'

'Ronald McDonald is creepy as fuck. He'd have made her cry harder.'

'Not if he wasn't in his costume, but she might have recognised him anyway, and—'

'You're getting a bit far-fetched now, Jess,' Ash said affectionately. 'What've you got?'

She stretched up and kissed his chin. 'What if someone had a subtle superpower that meant they could absolutely, one 100 per cent sense when a person was going to propose to their soul mate?'

Ash went completely still. Jess grinned, but he recovered quickly. 'Who does that help?' he asked. 'What does that do, other than spoil a surprise?'

'I don't know,' she admitted. 'I just thought – it's a bit like that woman you met at Borough Market, who said she could sense when complete strangers needed a nugget of advice. A gut feeling.' She shrugged. 'But perhaps it isn't one at all.'

'Certainly not a great one,' he agreed. 'Not as good as the toddler whisperer.' He caught her hand as she turned away from him, and pulled her against him, so her back was pressed to his front.

'No, the toddler whisperer definitely wins,' she said. 'Even if the guy *did* dress up as Santa Claus at the Christmas party she went to the year before, and she recognised him despite him not having the beard.'

'Totally ridiculous,' he murmured against her neck. Then she felt him take a deep breath, and he said, 'If someone *did* have that superpower, where they could sense a person was going to propose, what do you think they'd do with it?' There was no mistaking his anxiety, and Jess smiled to herself before turning round in his arms.

'I think,' she said, meeting his gaze, feeling the deep flutter inside her that had only strengthened with time, the certainty that being with him made her more alive than anything else, 'that mostly, they would just be quiet about it, hold on to that subtle superpower knowledge, and watch the whole thing play out.'

'You're sure that's what they'd do?' He searched her face.

'Oh, definitely. They wouldn't want to spoil anything.'

'Right. And if they were . . . if they didn't just *know* about the imminent proposal, but were in the position to have a say in the outcome, what do you think their answer would be?'

Jess opened her mouth to speak, and found that her throat was clogged up. She swallowed, took a second to listen to the trickle of the water feature and her friends laughing and talking through the open French doors, the bird singing in the tree. She felt the strength of Ash's arms around her, holding her tightly.

'Jess?' he prompted quietly. 'What do you think she would say?'

Jess smiled up at him, the warning prickle of tears in the corners of her eyes. 'I think she'd be sensible enough to say yes. What do you think?'

'I think saying yes would be the best superpower of all,' Ash told her. 'But I guess we'll have to wait another few hours to find out for sure.' He pulled her close and kissed her in a way that showed Jess he wasn't unsure about anything, and that, no matter how much time passed before he finally got to ask her the question, they both already knew the answer.

Acknowledgements

As with every book I write, these words would be sitting on my laptop, unread and gathering digital dust without the support, enthusiasm and hard work of so many people. Thank you to all these wonderful people for contributing in some way to *The Happy Hour*.

Kate Bradley my fantastic editor, who had huge faith in me and this book, and whose edit notes and insightful suggestions have made it at least 80 per cent better than it was to start with. I love working with her and am so lucky to have her as my editor.

Alice Lutyens, my utterly brilliant agent. This is our first proper book together (although she has already done so much to support me and progress my career) and I couldn't be working with a better, more enthusiastic or lovelier agent. I am excited about all our future books too! Thanks, also, to her colleagues at Curtis Brown, including Olivia Bignold and rights agent Emma Jamison.

The whole HarperFiction team works tirelessly on my books, from the sales teams to marketing and PR. Thank you especially to Lynne Drew, Susanna Peden and Meg Le Huquet, and to Penelope Isaac and Kati Nicholl for the copyedits and proofreading that made such a huge difference in the final stages.

Have you all seen the cover? I am still not over it. Every time, I say *this is my favourite cover* but this one?! I could not thank designer Emily Langford and illustrator Camila Gray more for taking my book, and a few lines about what my characters look like, and turning those into such a stunning design. These honestly are Jess and Ash made real, and I am so grateful that my story gets such a beautiful jacket.

Thank you so much to Kirsty Connor for bidding to have a character named in my next book, with proceeds going to the brilliant Good Books campaign and Young Lives Vs Cancer. I really hope you like your namesake in this book, her role in the market and her edible creations.

There are so many writing friends who have encouraged me with this book – when it was just a germ of an idea several years ago, right up to it being a fully-fledged story, with chapters and everything. The biggest, warmest and most appreciative hugs to Kirsty Greenwood, Sheila Crighton, Pernille Hughes, Isabelle Broom, Katy Marsh, Cathy Bramley, Katy Colins, Sam Holland, Jane Casey and Sarra Manning. Thank you also to a castle in Scotland and Pearl the dog, who were a big part of the editing process this time round. Thank you also to Lee, Kate and Tim, and Kate G.

David always gets one of the biggest thank yous, because he is with me through all of it, the bouncy bits and the hard bits, and he supports me – seemingly without effort – the entire time. But he gets an extra special thank you for *The Happy Hour*, because he let me pillage his life story, ask him endless questions about the ins and outs of adoption and what it felt like, and let me use some of that as the basis for Jess's history. I hope I have done the truth of it justice, even if I've made some of Jess's outcomes rosier than David's were. He surprises me every day with how strong, kind and generous he is, and I am so lucky to have him.

The Happy Hour would probably not exist without Mum and Dad, who took me on endless weekend trips to Greenwich Park and the market, down to the Cutty Sark (before it was entombed in glass) and for coffee in the lovely Greenwich Waterstones when I was growing up. This book is partly a tribute to all those *happy hours* (ha) I had, and even though I have taken the market and replaced all the real people, stalls and shops with fictional ones, I hope it gives a sense of what a special place it is. I could not have asked for better, more supportive and warm parents, so I have to give a huge thank you to Mum and Dad, not just for Sunday trips to the park but for forty-two (!) years of being the absolute best.

Lovely readers! None of this would matter without you. I really hope you enjoy this one, that you love Jess and Ash and everyone in the market, and don't mind *too* much that it isn't set in Cornwall. I am so grateful for your enthusiasm for my books and characters, for sending me emails and messages, sharing photos and thoughts on social media, for selecting my stories from shops, libraries and websites. I try to write characters that people will take to their hearts – I always take them to mine, perhaps a little too much – and I really hope this is the same for you and the people living within these pages. I really hope you spend a few, happy hours with *The Happy Hour*.

EXCLUSIVE ADDITIONAL CONTENT
Includes Cressida McLaughlin's top ten romantic tropes
and details of how to get involved in *Fern's Picks*

Dear lovely readers,

This month get ready to be swept away by a gorgeous, uplifting romance from Cressida McLaughlin.
The Happy Hour is the perfect feel-good escape; you'll be rooting for Jess and Ash from the first page.

After their very own meet-cute in Greenwich Market one Sunday, Jess and Ash start meeting at the same place, on the same day, for just an hour each week. For that hour every Sunday, they are completely happy. But how well do they really know each other? And is one hour a week enough time to build a relationship?

With a charming location, and characters you can't help but fall for, you will be captivated by *The Happy Hour*. I can't wait to hear what you think.

With love

Fenny x

Fern
Britton
Picks

Exclusively for
TESCO

Look out for more books, coming soon!

For more information on the book club,
exclusive author content and
reading group questions, visit Fern's website
www.fern-britton.com/ferns-picks

We'd love you to join in the conversation,
so don't forget to share your thoughts using
#FernsPicks

Ten Romantic Tropes

(that we can't get enough of!)

By Cressida McLaughlin

The meet-cute

The first time the heroine and hero meet each other is one of the most important scenes in a romance, and how it happens can dictate how their relationship is going to go. Is it funny, romantic or awkward? Do they hate each other on site? Do hearts appear in their eyes? In *The Happy Hour*, Jess and Ash meet when they both chase a pickpocket through Greenwich Market. It's not the easiest or most relaxed meeting, but it brings them together and gives them a reason to talk to each other. Without that thief disrupting their Sunday, who knows what would have happened? Here are some other romance tropes that I'm a huge fan of.

Enemies to Lovers

This is one of my favourites. Sparks fly between the hero and heroine from the very beginning, a romance between them seems utterly impossible, and the sexual tension is off the charts. Soon, though, they come to realise that there is a very fine line between love and hate. Charlie and Daniel in *The Cornish Cream Tea Bus* started out as enemies, and I loved writing the chemistry between them.

Grumpy and Sunshine

A specific version of opposites attract, this is where the sunny disposition of the heroine threatens to dismantle the carefully cultivated grump of the hero. It can be reversed, so the heroine is having none of the hero's joyful attitude to life, but there's something completely irresistible about a brooding, taciturn hero. In *The Cornish Cream Tea Christmas*, Hannah is full of the joyous potential of her trip to Cornwall, and Noah is having none of it. Will she be able to break through his barriers?

Fake dating

I can't resist a fake dating romance. Why must these two people pretend to be together? Will this foolhardy plan lead to them developing romantic feelings for each other? I love this kind of setup, and the confident way the characters go into it. It often leads to hilarity and misunderstandings – the possibilities for romcom fun are endless. In *The House of Birds and Butterflies*, Abby agrees to accompany Jack to a fancy London event, and gets a lot more than she bargained for.

Second-chance romance

Second-chance romances often tug at the heartstrings because they come with missed chances and endless pining. A gulf has formed between the heroine and hero that has to be breached after years of distance, and it's never an easy road back to each other. I loved writing a second-chance romance in *From Cornwall with Love*, exploring the memories and shared history Maisie and Colm had together.

There's only one bed!

This often goes hand in hand with fake dating, where the hero and heroine end up in a situation where there is only one bed/a tiny cabin for them to share, or a remote ranch where they have to hide away from whoever is after them. The tension, the tantalising closeness . . . it's the perfect situation for feelings that have been bubbling under the surface to spill over. In *The Staycation*, Jake is trapped in his hotel room because of an injury, and it is Hester's job to entertain him. But all those hours together, creating a romantic holiday atmosphere, makes things a lot more complicated.

Friends to Lovers

I love this trope too! Especially if one half of the friendship has been pining, and their 'best friend' is oblivious to their secret adoration. Maybe the sparks don't fly as much as in enemies to lovers, but there is something so satisfying about two people who care about each other realising that their feelings go deeper, plus there's always the worry about whether embarking on a romance will ruin their friendship – is it worth taking that chance? Ollie and Max in *The Cornish Cream Tea Bookshop* are friends from the very beginning, and over one twinkly, event-filled Christmas, that friendship edges towards something more.

Forbidden romance

Are their families at loggerheads, like poor old Romeo and Juliet? Is the hero her boss, or significantly older than her, or her brother's best friend? There is so much sizzling delight in a plot that involves lots of sneaking around, whispered conversations, trying to act entirely disinterested around each other in public. And there's always the ticking time bomb of discovery and its repercussions hanging over the whole thing. Delilah and Sam in *The Cornish Cream Tea Summer* come from very different worlds, and with such high expectations on Sam and his career, his romance with Lila might not be the wisest decision either of them have ever made.

Secret identity

I love books where one of the protagonists is hiding their identity. They could be a bestselling romance author who writes under a pseudonym, or a world-famous celebrity trying to escape the limelight, or the owner of a stately home and not, as it turns out, the gardener. Sometimes their opposite number is ignorant of their fame or status for only a couple of chapters, sometimes it's for most of the book. I love that it puts them on an equal footing to begin with, and then brings a whole load of challenges when the truth comes out. In *Christmas Carols and a Cornish Cream Tea*, Finn's charm leads Meredith to distraction, but there's something he isn't telling her about who he is or why he's in Cornwall.

Holiday romance

When you're on holiday all bets are off. You can be more indulgent, bolder and braver, because you've left your real life behind for a while. Romances bloom that otherwise might not, but what happens when you're bumped back to reality? I love being swept away to other places when I read, and I love the challenge of the heroine and hero trying to make their love last once they've left the sun-soaked beaches or vibrant city lights behind. Thea meets Ben under these circumstances in *The Cornish Cream Tea Holiday*, and she is swept up by all the possibilities. Can she keep her holiday going longer than she intended?

You can find all of these irresistible tropes in Cressida's other fabulous novels …

Find out more at: www.cressidamclaughlin.com

Questions for your Book Club

Warning: contains spoilers

- The majority of the book takes place in the vibrant atmosphere of Greenwich Market. Did you enjoy the setting? Have you ever been to Greenwich Market?

- The prologue to *The Happy Hour* hints at where the story is heading, before we even see Jess and Ash meet. Did it alter your reading experience?

- Jess and Ash's chance meeting, or 'meet-cute', sets the entire story in motion. How do you think their lives would have been different if even one of them hadn't chased down the pickpocket on that first day?

- What was the most significant, pivotal moment in Jess and Ash's relationship, in your opinion?

- How do you think the main characters change over the course of the book? Do Jess and Ash change as a result of meeting one another?

- *The Happy Hour* is a fun, feel-good and romantic novel, but the characters face some tough situations within it. Do you think it is important for romance novels to have serious moments too? Why?

- Which romantic tropes did you spot in the novel? Discuss which was your favourite and how it supported the story.

- Would you recommend this book to a friend? What three words would you use to describe it?

An exclusive extract from Fern's new novel

The Good Servant

March 1932

Marion Crawford was not able to sleep on the train, or to eat the carefully packed sandwiches her mother had insisted on giving her. Anxiety, and a sudden bout of homesickness, prohibited both.

What on earth was she doing? Leaving Scotland, leaving everything she knew? And all on the whim of the Duchess of York, who had decided that her two girls needed a governess exactly like Miss Crawford.

Marion couldn't quite remember how or when she had agreed to the sudden change. Before she knew it, it was all arranged. The Duchess of York was hardly a woman you said no to.

Once her mother came round to the idea, she was in a state of high excitement and condemnation. 'Why would they want *you*?' she had asked, 'A girl from a good, working class family? What do you know about how these people live?' She had stared at Marion, almost in reverence. 'Working for the royal family... They must have seen something in you. My daughter.'

On arrival at King's Cross, Marion took the underground to Paddington. She found the right platform for the Windsor train and, as she had a little time to wait, ordered a cup of tea, a scone and a magazine from the station café.

She tried to imagine what her mother and stepfather were doing right now. They'd have eaten their tea and have the wireless on, tuned to news most likely. Her mother would have her mending basket by her side, telling her husband all about Marion's send off. She imagined her mother rambling on as the fire in the grate hissed and burned.

The train was rather full, but Marion found a seat and settled down to flick through her magazine. Her mind couldn't settle. Through the dusk she watched the alien landscape and houses spool out beside her. Dear God, what was she doing here, so far away from family and home? What was she walking into?

When the conductor walked through the carriage announcing that Windsor would be the next stop, she began to breathe deeply and calmly, as she had been taught to do before her exams. She took from her bag, for the umpteenth time, the letter from her new employers. The instructions were clear: she was to leave the station and look for a uniformed driver with a dark car.

She gazed out of the window as the train began to slow. She took a deep breath, stood up and collected her case and coat. *Come on, Marion. It's only for a few months. You can do this.*

Available now!

Our next book club title

The call of Greece is getting stronger …

Hydra, the picturesque Greek island, is a paradise for most, yet for sisters **Ella** and **Georgia**, it is a place where their darkest secrets dwell. And now the time has come for them to confront their past as they return to Greece to scatter their mother's ashes.

Ella is haunted by a love song that was written for her by the man who broke her heart years earlier, and longs to find peace so she can move on with her life.

Georgia pretends everything in her life is perfect, but she is plagued with guilt. If what she's kept hidden for decades was revealed, their family would never be the same again.

The island is urging the sisters to confront the truth, but can they build a future on the ruins of their past?

Get swept away by the breathtaking, escapist third novel from Emma Cowell, perfect for fans of Carol Kirkwood and Karen Swan.